OUT OF LOVE

Noëlle Sickels

LA SIRENA PRESS

ALSO BY NOËLLE SICKELS

Walking West

The Shopkeeper's Wife

The Medium

OUT OF LOVE

Noëlle Sickels

ISBN 10: 0615859364
ISBN 13: 9780615859361

Printed in the United States of America
First printing, 2014

Cover photo by Annie Carmona
Author photo by Annie Carmona and John Millo

La Sirena Press
Los Angeles, CA

lasirenapress@gmail.com

To Ruby,

walking talking love

PROLOGUE

Summer 1965

JANINE SPLASHES COLD water on her face and dries off with a rough brown paper towel. She pulls the elastic off her tight ponytail and shakes her long hair loose, working her fingers through it as she hurries down the hall. Taking a Certs from a roll in her pocket, she slips it into her mouth and sucks it against the roof of her mouth. She steps out into the humid night where Dan is waiting in his mother's aquamarine Chevy, Cousin Brucie on the AM radio. The Temptations, the Kinks, the Supremes.

When she opens the car door and slides across the seat towards Dan, he gives her an elated, relieved smile, as if it's been weeks and not just one day since he saw her last. He turns down the music.

"Hey, you," he says, and kisses her. With her tongue, she pushes the half-melted Certs from her mouth into his. He smiles again.

She turns the radio volume back up as Dan pulls out of the nursing home parking lot onto Grand Avenue. She lays her head against his shoulder. Except for a half-hour break, she's been on her feet for eight hours. She nudges her shoes off and wiggles her toes, and the achy tiredness in her legs and feet begins to fade. The human sorrows she's witnessed during her shift drop out of her mind — the woman with black bedsores down to the bone, the man who cried while she fed him his supper, all the forgotten people who never have visitors and the visitors who never talk but only watch television in the lounge with their mother or father frail and oblivious in a wheelchair beside them.

Dan works days as a lifeguard at Graydon Pool, and evenings as a Good Humor man, and Janine is a nurse's aide on the 3:00 to 11:00 shift. Dan is still in his Good Humor white shirt and starched white pants. She's wearing white, too, a short-sleeved no-iron dress with big patch pockets handy for keeping wrapped sterile swabs, and bobby pins, and packets of Sweet'N Low for the patients who like it. The car windows are rolled down, and a breeze brushes her face, but they are sitting so close, Janine can smell caramel and chocolate on Dan's shirt. That sweetness and his Aqua Velva mingle with the antiseptic odors clinging to her dress.

They drive to Jones Road, a dark street with only a few houses widely separated by big yards. Dan parks in the usual spot. It is their place, as private as a locked room.

Dan, a year ahead of Janine, will be off to college in September, but she's trying not to think about that. They've been dating two years. They've made promises. She wears his heavy class ring on a short gold chain around her neck.

For now, they have the summer. Janine sleeps through the early part of each thick, hot day, and in every deep, lazy night, she is in Dan's arms, with Dan's mouth on hers, Dan's hands enchanting her. She loves his touch. She loves his reactions to her touch. They are joyous together, and she's sure their joy is unique, their own discovery and creation. It can almost seem, in the heavy-bodied Chevy on Jones Road, that this slow season will never end, that the skies will never grow gray and cold again, that she and Dan will never have to part.

Dan shuts off the engine and turns towards her. Nothing is as important and real as this moment and place, not their families or friends, not school or teachers or priests, and certainly not the wide-open, faraway future. She begins, slowly, to unbutton her dress. He watches, holds back from reaching out. They have time.

<hr>

Fall 1965

JANINE DOESN'T KNOW what has awakened her so suddenly. Groggy, she sits up. Sunlight edges the drawn window shade. She takes a nap almost every afternoon now. A powerful drowsiness often overwhelms her within an hour of lunch. Sleep is an escape, too. Two hours of oblivion. She dreams at night, but not in the afternoons.

Though the shade is down, the window is open. She can hear raised voices coming from out front, her father's and Dan's, but their words are indistinct.

Her heart thudding, Janine gets up, but before she reaches the bedroom door, it opens. Her mother blocks the doorway.

"Don't go down there," she says.

"Janine! Janine!" Dan's voice is right below her window now.

She rushes across the room and pulls up the shade. He's in the back yard looking up at her. Her father rounds the corner of the house.

"She doesn't want to see you!" he shouts at Dan.

"I don't believe you!" Dan shouts back.

"I'm calling the police," Janine's mother says behind her. She pushes Janine aside and leans out the window.

"I'm calling the police," she yells down to Dan.

She shuts the window and pulls the shade down again. She leaves the room without looking at her daughter.

Janine bends back the edge of the shade and peeks out. The yard is empty. Neither Dan nor her father is anywhere in sight. Everything gets very quiet.

"Time marches on," her mother has told her.

Nothing lasts forever, she means. Neither the good nor the bad. Don't look back, she means.

Janine knows that if she stays upstairs long enough, when she goes down later, her parents won't mention Dan's unexpected visit. They don't talk to her much these days anyway. They'd only be repeating themselves. They've all said as much as they can.

1

Summer 1984

ON THE DAY the phone call came, Janine was helping her mother clean out the garage to make room for her father's new boat, a used Boston Whaler.

Half the two-car garage had been a crowded catch-all for years. A small area in front was kept clear for winter storage of the mower and lawn furniture, and summer storage of bags of rock salt and snow shovels, but the rest of the space was crammed with stacks of cardboard boxes.

"It's a boat, for Chrissakes," Rose had muttered when they'd dragged the first two boxes out onto the driveway. "What's it need to be inside for?"

But it was not up for debate. Al was a quiet, undemanding man, but when he did stake out something for himself, he was unmovable. He had his own shelf in the bathroom medicine cabinet, and no one would ever consider taking an aspirin from "his" bottle or using "his" toothpaste because the family tube was empty. The basement workshop was his inviolate, tidy domain, Rose's clutter confined to the corner where the washer and dryer sat. His tools were immaculate, well-oiled and well-honed. Of course his boat couldn't be left in the driveway exposed to the rain and snow and baking sun of the northern New Jersey seasons.

"Mom? Mom? Can I keep this?"

Janine looked up from surveying an array of cast iron pans, mismatched dinner dishes, and various odds and ends of bric-a-brac spread

1

out on the grass to see her six-year-old son emerge from the garage holding aloft a metal canteen clad in a canvas carrier with a woven strap. His twin brother was close on his heels, and close to tears.

"I opened the box," Tim complained as both boys reached her. "Larry was afraid of spiders."

"You're scared of thunder!" Larry countered.

"All right, enough. You can have the canteen, Larry. And, Tim, you can choose something else to keep."

"I'll help you look," Larry encouraged his brother.

The canteen slung over one skinny shoulder, it was easy for Larry to be magnanimous. But he was usually quick to forget conflicts anyway, and always happy to take part in someone else's pleasure. He took after his father in that. Clark had worn his heart on his sleeve. You always knew where you stood with him. His love had been like a river flowing steadily beneath Janine's daily life, percolating up into her joys, buoying her over the rough spots. It was a little over two years now since Clark's death, and there were still moments when she couldn't believe he was gone.

"We can open *all* the boxes," Larry continued.

"Yeah! And I can pick *anything* I want!"

"Whoa, I don't want you guys unpacking any more. Gram and I will call you when we find good boxes."

Rose emerged from the back door with a tray on which sat four glasses, a pitcher of lemonade, and a plate of homemade pignoli cookies. Her flowered house dress fluttered around her plump knees in the June breeze. She'd tied a red bandana over her short, salt-and-pepper hair to keep off the dust in the garage. She looked like someone's cleaning lady. Janine went over to lift the heavy pitcher off the tray. When Rose had settled the tray on a small wrought iron table in the shade of the apple tree, the twins each grabbed a cookie. Rose started pouring lemonade into glasses.

"I want mine in my canteen," Larry said.

"Better wash it out first. That thing's as old as the hills," Rose said.

"What hills?" Tim asked, looking around the flat, grassy yard edged with flower beds and a small vegetable patch where Rose grew tomatoes and peppers.

"Any hills," Rose replied. "Hills are just old, that's all."

Janine followed Tim's scan of the yard. Except for the sycamore tree her father had had to take down because it was rotted with fungus, the yard looked as it had every summer of her life, neat, green, and sunny, as ideal as a picture in a first-grade primer. Her gaze came around to Rose, who was mopping the back of her neck with a large white handkerchief.

"Ma, I think we should knock off and start again early tomorrow."

They'd been working since dawn, when the air had been moist and cool against their bare arms. Janine enjoyed rising with the first light. It was her habit at home in Cape May Point, where the early morning mists carried the smell of the sea. But now, at 11:00, the day's heat had blossomed, and the humidity was rising.

Inside the house, the telephone began ringing.

"Message machine is on," Rose said.

"It might be my neighbor," Janine said. "He's keeping an eye on things for me."

She sprinted to the house, hoping that if it were her neighbor, his news wouldn't be too irksome.

⸻

"Is this the Pettorini residence in Teaneck? 528 Terhune Street?" a man asked after Janine had said hello.

"Yes, but if this is a sales call, I'm not—"

"We're trying to locate a Janine Pettorini."

"Who is this?"

"I beg your pardon. My name is Hector Wilson. I'm an attorney-at-law in New York City. We have come into possession of a document that may be of interest to Janine Pettorini."

"That's me. But my name is Linden now."

There was a pause, and Janine heard the shuffle of papers.

"The document, Mrs. Linden, relates to the legal matter we handled for you in 1966. You met with Mr. Greenspan. He's since retired."

Janine didn't remember the name, but she remembered the year. She flashed on a fat man seated at a wide desk in a room lined with bookcases. On the other side of the desk, she and her mother were sitting in identical leather chairs, but Rose sat erect, as if poised for battle, while Janine slumped, wanting to disappear. Whom did Rose think was left to battle? Janine had capitulated months before then.

"What kind of document?" she said to Hector Wilson, a tremor in her voice.

The lawyer cleared his throat.

"It relates, as you may have surmised, to your son."

Janine had fainted only once in her life, when she was 12, during a noon Mass in a crowded church in August. People often fainted in that church in summer. The ushers set up folding chairs in the shade of the open doorways in readiness for the people who fainted. Janine didn't remember the actual faint, but she remembered what she'd felt right before, and now she experienced that same foundering — a rush of heat to her face, dizziness, the surge of a black shadow between herself and her surroundings. But this time she didn't collapse. Her head cleared. Nevertheless, she felt physically disturbed, as if something deep inside her, some square peg that had been partially wedged into some round hole for a long, long time had shifted, turned, and come loose.

"I can't say more at present," Wilson was going on. "We'll need you to come in, bring identification."

Rose appeared in the doorway. She gave Janine a quizzical look.

"All right," Janine said into the phone. "I can probably be there tomorrow. What's the address?"

She fumbled in the drawer of the telephone table and found a pad of paper, two pencils with broken leads, and a ball point pen. She scribbled down what Wilson was saying about subway stops and parking lots.

"Didn't sound like that was about your house," Rose said when Janine had hung up and was standing staring at the slip of paper.

"No."

"What, then?"

"A lawyer in New York. He's got a document for me."

Rose pulled the bandanna off her head and squeezed it into a ball.

"A document?"

"I'm going into the City tomorrow to get it."

"Can't they mail it?"

"Ma, it was the adoption lawyer."

Frowning, Rose jammed the balled-up bandanna into the pocket of her dress and looked up briefly at the ceiling, as if some noise had attracted her attention. Then she directed her frown at Janine.

"Do you really think it's a good idea to—"

"I'm keeping the appointment. End of discussion."

———⊷⊶———

THE SECRETARY GOT up from her desk and walked away down a short hallway. The woman was wearing a tailored navy blue suit whose large shoulder pads made her appear formidable. A paisley scarf in neon colors did nothing to soften the look. Janine suddenly felt her own outfit to be somehow inappropriate. She'd worn a full cotton skirt printed with yellow flowers and a scoop-necked Mexican blouse with white on white embroidery down the front, and she'd pulled her hair back with a silver clasp. She was definitely out-of-step with the current styles of big hair and gaudy jewelry. With her olive skin and dark hair, she looked difficult-to-pinpoint "ethnic." She wondered if she matched what the secretary expected a woman who'd given away her baby to look like.

Janine sat down on the Danish modern couch in the waiting area and forced herself to stop such musings. It was ridiculous to think the secretary was passing judgment. Janine had done nothing shameful, in any case. Most people would say she'd acted nobly and unselfishly,

5

certainly sensibly, when she'd placed her son for adoption. It hadn't been what she'd wanted, but she had kept her word. She hadn't changed her mind at the last minute, or sought, in all this time, to interfere with her child's life. She had given him all she could at 17: a chance with someone else, someone better. Why, then, could an assessing glance from a power-dressed secretary so unsettle her? Because, she decided, the woman knew her secret. She didn't know *her*, but she knew her secret. And Janine had to admit that she herself found there was, despite everything, shame in it.

A man in a seersucker suit came out to the waiting area followed by the secretary, who returned to her desk without looking at Janine. Mr. Wilson introduced himself and shook Janine's hand, then led her to his office which, like the waiting area, was furnished in Danish modern. Janine wondered if it were the same room she'd been in on that rainy spring afternoon in 1966.

After she'd shown Mr. Wilson her driver's license and an electric bill with the Pettorinis' address, he took a sealed envelope from a file folder on his desk.

"Your son left you a letter," he said. "We don't know what it contains. I'm going to step out so you can read it in private."

"He was here? How did he find you? Did you tell him I was coming today?"

Mr. Wilson wore a pained expression, which looked more like impatience than sympathy.

"I think, first, Mrs. Linden, you ought to read your letter. Then we can delve into the practical implications, and I'll be happy to answer what questions I can."

He left the office, closing the door gently behind him. Janine sat down and stared for a moment at the envelope. It was imprinted in the corner with the address of the law firm. He must have written the letter here in the office. Had he come expecting to get information on how to contact her directly? Might he have meant to show up one day on her doorstep? Or on her parents' doorstep? Was he as brave as all that? Or as foolhardy? He was young, she reminded herself. She knew what it was to be young and impulsive.

The envelope contained one sheet of plain paper, hand-written in dark blue ink from a fountain pen. Provided by Mr. Wilson? By the prim secretary? If the pen belonged to the boy, what did that say about him? Clark used to use a fountain pen to grade essays. He said it helped him think.

The letter was dated May 25, 1984, a month ago. It began *Dear,* but the word had been crossed out. Below that, *To Whom It May Concern* had been written, but it, too, had been crossed out. The boy had finally launched into the letter with no salutation at all.

Sorry about the dumb beginning. I didn't know I was going to have to write to you. I figured I'd come here and get your name and address and then go see you or call you. I didn't have a plan of what to say to you or anything. But all they'll tell me is that they have "some means" that they might be able to find you and that if they do, they'll let me know, but only if you say it's okay. But I'm putting this all backwards. I should've started by saying I've been wondering about you and about my real father and how we might be alike or not, and other things, too. The lawyer said keep it brief and not put in any identifying information, so I guess I'll stop now. I hope you get this soon and will say yes to meeting me. Because I really need to.

From, Hunt (The lawyer made me promise not to put my last name, and I don't want to do anything that might make it that he wouldn't look for you as hard.)

Janine's hand was shaking when she replaced the letter in the envelope. Yes, she decided, it sounded as if he were brave. And foolhardy. And young. She was desperately afraid of meeting him. Afraid of disappointing him. Afraid of learning that he'd had a hard or unhappy life. Afraid of his resentment, anger, or blame, all of which were very plausible reactions. But she'd have to meet him. She owed him that, didn't she?

Every year on her son's birthday, and many other times, too, she had thought of him and wondered where and how he was. The wondering was a rusty knife twisting in her heart. So maybe she owed it to herself, too, to meet him. Maybe, then, the rusty knife could be pulled out.

There was a rap on the door, and Mr. Wilson poked his head in.

"I'm finished," Janine said.

He went to his desk and sat down. Leaning back in his big chair, he looked at her expectantly.

"Is his name really Hunt?" Janine smiled feebly. "It seems so...so dramatic. Under the circumstances."

"Yes, it is."

"He wrote that he has questions. I guess that's understandable."

"I would imagine. But you're under no obligation."

"Obligation?"

"Nothing is legally required of you."

"It's a bit of a shock. I never thought..."

"It's happening more often these days. Adoptees seeking their natural mothers. Fathers, too, sometimes, though fathers are usually harder to locate. Unless the mother has some clue."

"I don't know where the father... We didn't see each other after..."

"I'm not inquiring, Mrs. Linden. We're getting ahead of ourselves anyway."

"What's next, then? Do you give me his address and phone number, or do I authorize you to give him mine?"

The lawyer put up his hand as if he were a traffic cop in a busy intersection.

"Let's not be precipitous."

"Precipitous? This letter's been sitting here for weeks!"

"We acted with due deliberation, I assure you. Our files showed only your maiden name and your address at the time of the relinquishment, which was your parents' home. We left four phone messages there without result. I was about to inform Hunt that we'd had no success in finding you, but my paralegal suggested we try once more. She's a bit of a sentimentalist."

"You left messages? When?"

The lawyer opened the folder that had held Hunt's letter and consulted a sheet of paper.

"Let's see...May 28, June 4 and 11, and last week, on June 18."

Today was Thursday, June 28. Wilson's office had been trying to reach her for a solid month, and her parents had said nothing to her. Were they hoping the lawyer would give up and go away? And if he had, would they have ever told her? She was 35 years old, a painter who actually managed to sell from time to time, a widow with two children and her own business as a framer, and they were still trying to manage her life.

"These situations are fraught with pitfalls," Mr. Wilson was going on. "I advise, as a next step, that you answer the letter. Nothing extreme or emotional. No promises. Just tell him a little about yourself. But not anything that would enable him to find you. Ask him about himself. School, hobbies, things like that. Establish a correspondence. Our office can forward the letters back and forth. Once Hunt gives us an address."

"But he said he wants to meet me."

"That can happen, in due course, if you find you're still willing."

Apparently, Wilson was not a sentimentalist.

"I'm sorry, Mr. Wilson, but I can't make him wait. There was something in his letter, something between the lines…"

"Well, young people can be melodramatic. Or, if he *is* troubled in some way, all the more reason to proceed with caution."

"Do you know something you're not telling me?"

"I'm just speaking in hypotheticals. It's a lawyer's disease."

"I can't ask him to wait any longer."

"Mrs. Linden, your generosity of spirit does you credit. But these things are tricky. Quite often, reunions don't work out in the long run. The parent who gave up her child can't fit him into her present life or doesn't want to, and the child feels rejected or deserted. Or, conversely, he may turn away from you. It's better to go slowly."

"I want his information, and I want him to have mine," Janine insisted. "Now."

The lawyer sighed. Janine realized that he was honestly trying to protect both her and Hunt. She also realized that part of her insistence on barreling ahead was a belated defiance of her parents, who had bullied her during the pregnancy to get her to agree to adoption and who had kept the lawyer's messages from her. A small voice was telling her not to be ruled by such feelings, but she stifled it.

"Hunt called here a week after leaving the letter, but not since," Mr. Wilson explained. "And the number he provided us isn't a personal line. My secretary says that whoever answers merely says a message will be posted. We'll try reaching him again, but if I were you, I wouldn't get my hopes up."

"You're not me," Janine said, standing up. "I'd like the number, please."

"Mrs. Linden," he replied, oozing reasonableness, "there's no need to get upset. I strongly advise that you—"

"Mr. Wilson, I'm sure your advice is well-meant and valid, as far as it goes. But this isn't simply a legal matter. It's a...a thing of the heart. If that makes me sound like a ranting, illogical female, so be it. I need that number."

Mr. Wilson inflated his chest and glowered at Janine.

"We will make every appropriate effort to reach your son, Mrs. Linden. When and if he assures us, in writing, that he has no objection to your being given access to his contact information, we will call you. That's the best I can do."

Janine felt like grabbing the lawyer by his punctilious lapels and shaking him. She wanted to dump out all the filing cabinets and ransack every drawer in every desk in the entire office suite until she found Hunt's number. Not that such wild actions would be likely to get her what she wanted. Oh, but wouldn't she make a lovely mess?

"Well, it's not the best I can do," she said tersely.

Her implied threat was a shapeless blob even to her own ears. Mr. Wilson appeared unperturbed. Janine turned and left.

———

JANINE HAD TAKEN public transportation because she hadn't wanted the hassle of Manhattan traffic. But now, crossing the George Washington

Bridge ensconced in the frigid air of a New Jersey Transit bus, she longed for the freedom of her car. Then she could be speeding off anywhere instead of heading towards the two people she least wanted to see at the moment.

"Be careful," Rose had warned her as she was leaving the house.

"Careful?" she'd replied. "What do you think is going to happen, for heaven's sake?"

And what had happened? Janine thought as the bus reached the Jersey side of the Hudson. A lot and not a lot. Almost too much to bear, and yet not nearly enough. I've heard from my son, she thought, tightening her grip on her purse, where she'd tucked Hunt's letter into a zippered pocket. It was more than she'd ever expected, but it raised more questions than it answered. And despite her parting words to Wilson, she didn't know how she'd find answers. Or if she ought to try.

Had it been left to her parents, she wouldn't have the option. Hunt's letter would have been returned to him or filed away in some dusty box labeled "old cases." She wouldn't know it had ever existed. Hunt would be left with even more unanswered questions than she. Worse, he might decide that he'd gotten an answer, which was that she had turned her back on him. Again.

She flirted with the idea of getting off the bus and catching another one back into the City to walk its crowded, anonymous streets until dark. But when the bus reached her stop on Cedar Lane, she disembarked and set off on the long walk down Catalpa Avenue. As she trudged along, the sun's heat simultaneously bearing down on her head and floating up in waves from the black macadam did nothing to improve her disposition.

Turning left on to Terhune Street, she heard her boys squealing with delight. They were at the curb in front of her parents' house helping their grandfather wash his new boat, and they were almost as wet as the soapy hull.

"Mom!" yelled Tim, waving a dripping sponge over his head. Larry popped his head around the stern of the boat and waved, too.

Garden hose in hand, Al smiled hello at Janine. He was a vigorously handsome man, with wavy, snow-white hair. People liked seeing him smile, and he knew it.

"How'd it go?" he asked.

"Grandpa, we're ready to rinse!" Larry said, coming up beside them. Janine drew the letter out of her purse.

"Where's Ma?" she asked her father.

He raised his eyebrows at the sharp tone of her voice, but she knew he wouldn't question her. He mostly stayed out of interactions between his wife and daughter, as if they were both members of some mysterious tribe whose customs he could never hope to understand.

"Out back," he replied, pointing, as if she didn't know the way. Maybe he just wanted to discourage her from engaging him further.

———

ROSE, SURROUNDED BY half-empty cardboard boxes, had her back to Janine. She was pawing through a large plastic bin, shaking out old table-cloths, then re-folding them and adding them to a stack on the ground.

Janine recalled packing up Clark's belongings six months after he died. She'd spent hours going through his desk and dresser, his side of the closet, the shelves in the garden shed. She carefully put away items the boys might want in the future — Clark's watch and battered wallet, his first editions of Hemingway and Woolf and D. H. Lawrence, the notes from the anthology he was working on at the time of his death, his mitt and cap from the Teacher's Union softball team, and his own father's pipe, still smelling of apples and burnt tobacco after decades of disuse. She kept out the old shirt of his she liked for sleeping in summer, and his favorite sweater. Then in one final, frantic hour, she'd boxed up everything else and driven with it to Goodwill.

The donation center was closed when she arrived. She'd broken into tears, hauling the boxes out of the trunk and the back seat and piling them haphazardly in front of the building. She had to struggle not to look at them as she drove away. River's rising, keep your wits dry, her mother was known to say. She had a storehouse of such sayings. What was that other one? It's all blood under the bridge.

"I'm back," Janine said.

Rose straightened up, a white tablecloth bunched in her arms.

"This one's long," she said. "Help me fold it."

Tucking Hunt's letter in the waistband of her skirt, Janine took one end of the rectangular cloth, and together, they folded it into a neat packet. Rose plopped it on top of her pile.

"Come on inside," she said. "I've got iced tea." She started towards the back door.

"Ma!"

Rose turned around.

"Why in the hell didn't you call that lawyer back?"

Rose looked abashed.

"You knew, didn't you? You knew what it was probably about."

Janine saw Rose's hand begin to reach for her, so she stepped back out of touching range.

"He called for *me* — for *me*, not you — and you didn't tell me!"

Janine was holding her voice down so that the boys wouldn't hear, but her anger was nearly choking her.

"You have so much on your plate, honey, I didn't want you to have to—"

"What am I, made out of glass?" Janine was louder now. "Do you think I'm some kind of basket case who can't handle her own life?"

"No, of course not." Rose wiped her hand across her sweaty brow. "But just look how upset you are. Maybe I wasn't so wrong, was I? It's not healthy to stir up—"

Janine shoved Hunt's letter at her. Slowly, Rose opened it and read it. When she raised her head, her eyes were brightly alert, like a hawk's.

"What's it mean?" she said hoarsely.

"Just what it says."

Rose re-folded the letter and handed it back.

13

"You have your own sons to think of, Janine," she said sternly. "They need you now more than ever. How will you explain that boy to them?" She pointed to the letter. "Tim and Larry should come first. That's what Clark would have wanted."

"Clark would have backed me up 100%, no matter what. And 'that boy' is my own son, too."

"Not really, Janine," Rose said, her voice gentler. "Not in the same way. He has a mother, and it's not you."

This should have made Janine angrier, but instead, it deflated her. It was her deepest guilt voiced. She wasn't Hunt's mother in any important sense, except for basic biology. If they ever met, surely he'd see that, too, no matter what romantic notions he might be harboring, no matter how welcoming she was. His bones and muscles and organs had formed inside her, her body had fed and sheltered him for nine months, but all the rest of his growing and shaping, physical and psychological, had happened without her. Someone else had stayed up with him at night when he was sick. Someone else had read his report cards, pulled his splinters, cooked his meals, taught him to drive, guided his values. She had forfeited any claim to his good regard on the day she signed the relinquishment paper.

"I have to answer his letter somehow, Ma. In whatever limited way I am his mother, I have to try."

Rose's face, soft with concern a moment ago, tightened. She was not accustomed to defeat.

"But you can't expect—" she began.

"Boat's done!" Larry shouted, running down the driveway, Tim running beside him, Al walking a few yards behind.

"Grandpa says we can pour Coke on it the first time it goes in the lake," Tim announced. "Instead of champagne. That's what they do for battleships."

"Hungry, Al?" Rose asked. "I've got chicken salad and fresh tomatoes for lunch."

"I'm hungry!" exclaimed Larry.

14

"Can we have grilled cheese?" Tim said.

"We've got chicken salad," Rose repeated.

"That's too slippery," Larry replied. "We like grilled cheese better."

"Go inside and wash up, boys," Janine said.

Larry threw her a beseeching look, but then he scooted after Tim.

"And put on dry clothes before you sit on my chairs," Rose added, following them.

Al turned to go in, too, but Janine planted herself squarely in front of him.

"And what did you think about covering up the messages about my baby?"

"They never said it was—"

"Because they could only say it to me. You know: me, your grown-up daughter? The one who can make decisions for herself now, thank you very much?"

He stood glumly silent. She gave him the letter. He read it and re-read it. Shaking his head, he gave it back to her.

"She thought it was best, Janine," he said softly, looking down at the ground. "We both did."

Janine studied his downcast face. Was he referring only to hiding the messages from the lawyer, or did he mean to include persuading her to put her baby up for adoption 18 years ago? Could it fairly be called persuasion? At the time, she'd felt like a dry leaf being swept on a raging flood into a storm sewer. No, nothing so poetic as a leaf — a crumpled, empty cigarette packet maybe, or a sticky, discarded candy wrapper. Except that she hadn't been empty. But she couldn't ask her father for clarification. She was too perilously close to tears. And there seemed way too much to cry over to give in to the catch in her throat, the knot in her chest.

"I do know you're able to make up your own mind," Al went on, looking into her face. "But you'll always be my little girl. I can't help that."

She nodded. It was all she could manage. Then she went to rescue the boys from the excessive mayonnaise of her mother's chicken salad.

2

ON SATURDAY, JANINE was inspecting packages of pork cutlets in the supermarket when she heard a woman call her name.

"Janine? Omigod. Janine, is it really you?"

Turning around, she found herself face to face with Lee Brady.

Lee had been one year ahead of Janine in high school, but they'd been on the girls' volleyball team together, and when Lee was a senior and Janine was a junior, they were in French III together, followed by lunch.

Lee had had a boyish, muscular body as a teen, but now her hips and bosom were well-padded with flesh. Her face was rounder. But she was still unmistakably Lee. The merry eyes were the same, the old scar on her chin from someone's wildly swung field hockey stick, the thick, curly hair, wrangled now into a Farrah Fawcett look.

"Yes, it's really me," Janine said with a genuine smile.

Lee engulfed her in a long hug while the twins stared, as intent and curious as wildlife biologists sneaking up on big game.

"How long are you here for? Are you back for good? We have *got* to catch up. What about lunch? Do you need a sitter? I've got a gem. I can call her for you, or, wait, I'll write down her number..."

Lee rummaged in her purse, but after a few seconds, she gave up.

"Of course, I don't have a pen. Or paper. Some things never change, do they?"

Janine laughed. She'd had to supply Lee with either pen or pencil or paper so often in French class, she got in the habit of bringing extras.

The laughter was refreshing. It lifted Janine temporarily out of her worry about Hunt's letter and her confused anger with her mother. Lee used to have that effect in the past, too, jollying her out of fussing over exams and term papers and deadlines.

"The Holy Roman Empire? Quadratic equations?" she'd exclaim. "Who gives a fig leaf? What I want to know is what you're wearing to the CYO semi-formal. Now there's some information worth its weight in spit."

Lee had been off to college by the time Janine knew she was pregnant. They hadn't kept in touch. Janine hadn't stayed in touch with anyone from high school. The pregnancy had divided Janine's life. The lives she'd lived on both sides of the divide were, in her mind, just that, two separate lives, not a continuous flow of time through one life. She knew, rationally, that the fruits of one had their roots in the other, that she hadn't died at 17 and begun afresh at 18, but at the time, it felt like it.

Janine had thought she had no interest in the distant past nor in what that past had become without her, but the person she'd been at 17 was still alive inside her somewhere, and the visit to Wilson's office yesterday had stirred that phantom girl. That girl wanted to remember and to know. Hunt's letter had perforated the hard dividing line between Janine-before and Janine-after. And here, by remarkable chance, was someone else from the other side, ebullient, affectionate, speak-before-you-think Lee.

"Lunch would be wonderful," Janine said. "And I don't need a sitter. I'm at my parents' for a few days."

"Lucky you! My mother will only take my kids one at a time, and I have to pack them a lunch and a change of clothes, like they're setting off for the Amazon or something."

Lee turned her gaze to the boys, who were rocking the shopping cart back and forth, having lost interest in the adults now that they were simply talking and not making a dramatic tableau that forced other shoppers to detour around them. Janine grasped the handle of the cart to stop their game.

"That's Larry," she told Lee. "And this is Tim."

"Any more at home? I've got four myself. Not quite sure how *that* happened!"

"These two are enough for me."

"Well, you've still got time. Not that I'm recommending it..."

"Let me give you the number at my parents' house," Janine said, pulling a small notepad out of her purse.

"Is your husband with you? It might be fun to get the families together."

"No," Janine said, wishing the topic hadn't come up in such a public place.

It was always hard to tell someone about Clark and then to have to witness their confusion about what they ought to say. She often felt a kind of guilt for having discomfited the person, and, sometimes, depending on the person and how they responded, another, stranger kind of guilt, as if she were confessing to a terrible carelessness or ineptitude by admitting she'd "lost" her husband so young.

"My dad's dead," Tim piped up. No longer distracted by playing with the cart, he'd caught both the word husband and the hesitation in his mother's voice.

Surprise and disbelief flashed across Lee's face. The stock confusion was there, too, but more fleeting than in most people.

"Oh, Janine, I'm so sorry. Truly. How awful for you. When did it happen?"

"Two years ago, April."

Tim slipped his hand into Janine's and leaned his body against her thigh. She was feeling stronger than she had in months, but she could still be swept into eddies of grief by the smallest, most unexpected things — the scent of a hedge in bloom, Clark's brand of coffee on a supermarket shelf, a sentimental television story. Now, Tim's tenderness coupled with Lee's forthright sympathy brought tears to her eyes. I won't cry here, she told herself. Disengaging from Tim, she pulled a tissue out of her pocket and blew her nose.

"Foodtown!" Lee said. "What a place for a conversation like this! Or maybe it's our version of the old village well. Anyway, we'll talk more another time. I want to hear all about him. Why he was such a great guy. He *was* a great guy, am I right?"

Janine smiled. "Yes, he was a great guy."

Lee gave Janine another hug, less enthusiastic than her earlier one, but just as long.

"You, boy," Lee called to Larry, who was working his way down the freezer aisle opening and closing the glass doors. "You can come back now. We're done."

Larry scrutinized Lee for an instant, then trotted back to rejoin his mother and brother, more, Janine thought, because of the novelty of a command from a stranger than because he was at all through with his survey of the frozen foods.

⁂

LEE CALLED THE next day to invite Janine and her boys to the YMCA pool at Spring Lake Park. Janine was more than happy to accept. Things were tense at the Pettorinis'. Conversations among the adults were being kept carefully neutral. The boys provided useful, legitimate distractions, as did the practicalities of preparing meals, completing the garage re-arrangement, and getting the house and yard ready for the big Fourth of July party.

Janine didn't want to hear what either of her parents was thinking or feeling about the situation, though she knew they were as shaken as she, just in different ways. The past, like a comatose patient, was waking up and groping for life. It would have been difficult enough to talk about if Janine and her parents were on the same page. As it was, she didn't want a fight. She wasn't ready for that.

At the pool, Lee's oldest, thirteen-year-old Lulu, corralled Janine's boys and her three brothers and set off for the shallow end. Janine and Lee spent a peaceful hour stretched out on lounge chairs in the shade of a large umbrella while Lulu patiently supervised the five boys. She and a girlfriend sat perched on the edge of the pool, their legs dangling in the cold water, both of them wearing foam headphones plugged into the same Walkman cassette player.

Lee had rattled on for a while, catching Janine up on high school girlfriends she still heard from and reviewing gossip about others, chronicling how she'd met her husband, Red, and how they'd moved around for a while, then settled back in Teaneck after their second child, Sam, was born. She didn't ask for details about Clark, for which Janine was grateful. She seemed satisfied to hear only about the little house in Cape May Point, Janine's picture-framing business run out of a studio in her backyard, and Janine's efforts to create her own art through painting.

"The only art we have up at home are finger paintings," Lee said, lowering her chair to its fully reclined position. "And a paint-by-the-numbers landscape my sister-in-law did. She even signed it! Can you imagine? Red was too soft-hearted not to hang it."

She pulled her chair out of the umbrella's shade, lay down on her back and put her hat over her face to shield it from the sun.

"An artist!" she said from under the hat. "I don't remember you being arty in high school. But you always were a deep one. The sphinx, we used to call you. Did you know that?"

Janine hadn't known. It stung. It wasn't an insult, but it stung. I don't want to be a sphinx, she thought. Not any more.

"I met a ghost this week," she said suddenly.

Lee took the hat off her face and propped herself up on one elbow. "What?"

The whole story about Hunt spilled out of Janine like beans out of a ripped bag. She hadn't planned on telling, but Lee was so friendly and familiar, and Janine had been bottled up for days thinking about the letter. She'd been alone with the larger story for most of her life. Only her parents and Clark knew it. The unvarnished facts of the story, that is. No one knew the gnarled thicket of emotions that had grown within her as inexorably as Hunt had, and that, shrunken and dried but still thorny, continued to occupy a corner of her heart. She could have described the thicket to Dan. But Dan had been gone longer than Hunt and just as thoroughly.

Until Clark, Dan was the only man Janine had loved without reservation, without doubts, without caution. Clark had actually been a bit jealous of him.

"First love," Janine had told Clark. "It's in a special category all its own."

"But he let you down."

"He didn't really have a chance to do anything else."

"He could've gone after you. He could've made his own chance. That's what I would have done."

"We were teenagers, Clark."

"So it wasn't really love. Not true love."

She'd put her arms around him and laid her face against his chest. She wanted to be holding him when she answered, and she didn't want to see his puzzled, slightly wounded face.

"Yes, darling. It was true love. And this, now, with you, this is true love, too."

He was silent for a moment.

"*Last* love, then," he whispered. "I'll be your last love. Okay?"

Clark *had* been her last true love. Dan at 16 and 17, then Clark from 25 on. In between, there had been passion, both short-lived and longer-lived, and enough love to generate plenty of giddy bliss and tormented tears. But nothing solid and sure. Nothing true.

At the end of Janine's recital about Hunt, Lee let out a long, low whistle.

"Knock me down and pick me up and knock me down again. Girl, you have blown my mind."

Janine had felt a kind of elation as she was telling her tale, but now she was self-conscious and a little regretful. Lee was going to be full of questions, and Janine was not full of answers.

"What are you going to do?" Lee said.

21

"I don't know. I was thinking of maybe going to Shadyside."

"Shadyside?"

"Shadyside Home for Unwed Mothers."

"Whoever came up with that sure had a warped sense of humor!"

"It was an old mansion, and Shadyside was its original name. Lots of big trees around it. Anyway, I thought they might have records about Hunt's family, and that there might be something to point to where the family is now."

Janine was pleasantly surprised to find that saying it out loud made the idea feel more possible and sensible than when it'd been merely a vague notion swimming around in her mind.

"But won't Shadyside be as cagy as the lawyer?"

"I can't think of anything else to do."

"Maybe Hunt will call the lawyers. Maybe he's been out-of-town."

"I'm worried he might think I refused to see him. He only called Wilson once to ask if I'd gotten the letter and that was a week after he'd left it. For all he knows, I ripped it up and threw it away."

Lulu came over to get towels for her youngest brothers, Howie and Max, who were standing shivering at the edge of the pool.

"They wanna go to the playground," she told Lee, who nodded permission.

Lulu glanced back and forth between the two women with some curiosity. Janine remembered being a keen observer of adults herself at 13 and even before then. But she'd been an only child, Rose having had an emergency hysterectomy at 30. Janine had needed to watch the adults in order to steer through the shoals of their relationships. They were the constants of her world, more fascinating than her playmates and cousins, all temporary company. Lulu was one of four children. They outnumbered the adults. Maybe it was being the oldest and the only girl that set her apart and alone. Or maybe sphinxes were just born that way.

"Shoo!" Lee said as the girl lingered, digging through the food bag. Lulu scowled at her mother, grabbed a large bag of potato chips and the towels and left.

"To be honest," Janine continued. "I'm not that keen on going to Shadyside. Its halls aren't exactly ringing with happy memories."

"God, it's times like this I miss smoking. Shouldn't we both have cigarettes dangling out of our fingers for this conversation?"

Janine looked away. Lulu had taken up her post. Tim and Larry were still cavorting in the shallow end.

"I didn't mean to be flip," Lee said. "I get like that when I'm about to step on somebody's toes."

"What do you mean?"

"You said the kid mentioned Dan in his letter. You think he wants to ask you about him?"

"I guess so."

"Are you gonna tell him? Dan, I mean. Are you gonna tell him his son is looking for him?"

Janine picked up her tote bag. She dug out a tube of sunscreen.

"I think I'd better dose the boys again," she said. "They burn easily."

"Look," Lee said, "forget I asked about Dan. None of my god-damned business."

"No, Lee, it's fine," Janine protested. "You don't know what a relief it is to talk about this with someone halfway sane."

"Halfway sane: that's me to a tee!"

Janine smiled.

"It's just that it's too soon to think of Dan. I've got to make my own peace with Hunt first — if I ever meet him. Besides, I have no idea where Dan is."

"If you *did* know where to find him, would you still wait?"

Janine gazed out over the swimming pool, filled with splashing, shriek-ing children. A lifeguard blew his whistle and told a boy to stop dunking his sister. Janine recalled coming out of the changing house at Dan's pool and holding back from looking up at his lifeguard stand, postponing the delicious moment when she'd see him, lean and brown in his red trunks and red sun visor, his nose comically slathered with white zinc oxide. Just remembering it now, she could almost smell it, a summer odor, the scent of new desire.

23

"Yes, I would still want to wait," she finally said.

"Even if Hunt didn't want to?"

"Even then."

"Okay. Well, whenever you're ready, you just let me know."

Janine looked at her questioningly.

"You noticed Lulu's braces?" Lee said. "Dan Gannon is her orthodontist."

"You're kidding!"

"Nope. And consider this: what if Hunt's got more information than just that lawyer's name? What if he's given up on you, but he knows something that's led him to Dan? It wouldn't hurt to ask him."

Janine felt a surge of excitement that was immediately muddied by an apprehension close to alarm. It must have shown on her face.

"Or maybe it would hurt," Lee said quickly, "but he's not like the maternity home, am I right? I figure you gotta have some good memories of him along with the tough ones."

Lee stood up and began unpacking sandwiches from the food bag.

"For what it's worth," she added, "he seems like a perfectly nice man. Lulu likes him, and Lulu hardly likes anybody."

3

DAN GANNON PULLED into his wife's driveway, turned off the Volvo's engine, and sat taking his ritual three deep breaths before going inside. He thought of it as his wife's driveway even though he was paying enough support, not to mention the mortgage, that the driveway must be at least half his. He and Robin had been separated for over a year, and funds had been flowing steadily in her direction from his bank account every month like a lusty mountain spring.

He didn't begrudge Robin the money, for their daughters' sakes. The girls were still young, Vanessa five, and Sally four, and his payments allowed Robin to stay home with them. The break-up had been hard enough on the girls without their having to adjust, in addition, to a working mother and full-time day care. Maybe down the road. But not yet.

Dan wasn't taking deep breaths to ease the reminder of financial obligations that the house evoked. Nor were the breaths to gird himself for a nasty encounter with Robin. They had never had shouting matches. Their relationship had declined by degrees, until she had finally buckled under the weight of quiet desperation, which is what she called it during one galling evening of wretched truth-telling. She didn't love him any more. She accused him of never having *truly* loved her. She wanted out.

And that's what the breaths were for. Because even after the lengthy time apart and the establishment of a reasonably successful system of co-parenting, there arose, every time they were together, a moment when Dan felt like a failure. Sometimes it was something Robin said. She was a master of understated, well-aimed criticism. Sometimes it was merely a look that crossed her face. Sometimes, though this was rare, it was something one of the kids said or did that tore at Dan's heart and made him feel that it was all, all his fault, that he'd let them all down, and himself, too. Why couldn't he have held it together, this creaking, leaky boat that he and Robin had set out in with moderate if not high hopes and that they'd populated with two innocent, trusting children who couldn't swim?

He knew the moment would come. All he could do was go in there in a calm frame of mind and hope the zing this time wouldn't be too sharp, that when he left, he could rid himself of the sense of failure as handily as he'd pick burrs off his hiking socks.

No-fault divorce. That's what the lawyers called it. What they meant was that neither Dan nor Robin was making grievous accusations like adultery or extreme cruelty. They simply had to live apart for 18 months, and then one of them could serve the other with papers. He'd been served last week. Robin had filed against him on the exact date they reached 18 months. A few more months and they'd be divorced. A complaint of divorce, the papers were labeled. Complaint, fault, no fault — no matter how politely it was termed, it could still feel like a shameful miasma to Dan, especially when Robin zinged him.

Actually, today he thought he knew where the zing might come from. Today it might be his clothing. After dropping the girls at pre-school, as he did every Monday, he was going to give a lecture at the dental school at Fairleigh Dickinson, so he was wearing a suit. It was well-tailored of beautiful, cream-colored fabric, discreetly expensive, and Robin didn't like it. He'd bought it while they were still together, and she once remarked that it seemed like a bachelor's suit — too inviting to the touch for a husband, too easily stained for a father of young children. She'd said that when he wore that suit, she felt that he was not theirs.

Dan knocked loudly on the front door to announce himself, then he unlocked it and went in. There was a burnt smell in the dining room, visible smoke when he entered the kitchen. Robin was lifting two blackened slices out of the toaster. In one smooth, balletic motion, she dropped them in the trash, pushed the window open wider, and turned to face Dan. He could still appreciate how gracefully she moved.

"Well, there's another rule shot to hell," she said.

"Rule?"

"Someone turned the knob to the darkest setting, and it wasn't me."

"Well, it wasn't me," he said, keeping his voice light. "Good morning, by the way."

"Do you let them make their own toast?"

So it wasn't going to be his suit after all.

"Yes..."

Sighing and shaking her head, she turned to put two new pieces of bread into the toaster.

"Hey, I've seen you let them push the buttons on the blender and set the oven timer and start the dishwasher."

She looked at him with a tight smile.

"Under supervision," she said.

"C'mon, Robin, it's only toast."

He knew it wasn't the right thing to say. Robin believed that little things mattered, and that rules mattered. She believed that's what glued the big things together. Robin always had about her an air of purposeful attention, as if living life were like driving a manual transmission car. Could he have softened her if he'd tried more? Don't worry, he wanted to say now. The girls are fine. They're going to be fine. There's a limit to what we can control. In the end, children go their own ways. We'll probably be left stupefied.

But he didn't say any of it. Instead, he went to the bottom of the back stairs that led from the kitchen to the second floor and called the girls' names. There was a sound of running feet overhead. The clatter stopped abruptly at the top of the steps.

"Mommy," came Vanessa's outraged voice from above, "Sally's wearing jellies. Teacher said no jellies."

"I want to!" Sally insisted.

"You can't!" Vanessa countered loudly.

"Forget about it!" Dan shouted up the stairs. He'd only raised his voice to be heard. There was no ire in it.

A momentary lull followed, each child probably assuming that the other was the one who should forget her point. Then they started down the narrow spiral staircase, walking slowly and in single file as Robin had taught them. They must have sped up at the end, though, because Vanessa burst into the kitchen as if she'd been shot from a rubber band, Sally only one step behind.

"Mommy," the older girl wailed. "Teacher said—"

"All right, Vanessa," Robin interrupted. "Sally, you know jellies aren't good for climbing. They don't grip."

"I don't want to climb today."

"You might want to climb when you get to school."

"I can climb in jellies. It's easy to climb in jellies."

"No, it's not," Vanessa objected.

"Girls, please," Robin said. "Vanessa, take the snack bags and wait on the porch for Daddy. Sally, go put on sneakers. Right now."

Robin's tone was brittle enough that both children moved immediately to obey, Sally stomping noisily back upstairs. Vanessa's compliance was more gracious; she was reserving any show of triumph for later.

"Oh, I just remembered," Robin said to Dan. "Let me give you the girls' field trip permission slips."

She went to the living room, and Dan followed. While she was shuffling through a pile of mail on the coffee table, he called up the front staircase.

"Sally! Hurry up! I don't want to be late."

The little girl came, but she wasn't hurrying. Head lowered, feet dragging, she walked down the steps with an exaggerated air of dejection.

"Let's go!" Dan urged.

Sally took the final three steps in one leap, shining a grin of accomplishment at her parents. But as she ran toward the front door, she tripped over the untied laces of her sneakers and fell full out on the floor. She let out a bellow which, Dan knew, covered both the pain in her banged knees and the injustice of having had to change her shoes.

Vanessa flung open the front door and ran in, deftly jumping over her prone sister.

Racing to the stairs, she called excitedly back over her shoulder, "It's show-&-tell day! I almost forgot! Sal, it's show-&-tell day!"

Whimpering, Sally got to her feet and slowly headed upstairs again.

"I give up," Dan said. "I'm going to pull the car out of the driveway."

After five minutes, Robin and the girls emerged onto the porch. Sally and Vanessa ran to the car. Robin waved to their unseeing backs. Dan knew he wasn't included in the farewell, but he waved back at her anyway.

"I brought a seashell for show-&-tell," Vanessa said, as Dan was buckling her into her car seat.

"I brought my jellies," Sally said smugly.

Vanessa and Sally inhabited each event, however small, as crucial and complete in and of itself, letting the larger realms of days, weeks, and months take care of themselves. They could be sunny companions one moment and mortal enemies the next, or the other way round, without the slightest hesitation, as if they lived at perpetual noon, casting no shadows, neither ahead nor back.

Dan pulled away from the curb. A few blocks outside their neighborhood, the girls began to sing.

Little red caboose

Chug, chug, chug

As Dan glanced over his shoulder to make a left turn, he saw their arms mimicking the rotation of the wheels of a train engine.

Smokestack on its back, back, back, back

Comin' round the track, track, track, track

Little red caboose behind the train

Toot! toot!

They started again, their voices quickening and growing louder with each line. Sally, who couldn't get all the words in fast enough, was substituting garbled shrieks in some places.

"Girls, girls!" Dan shouted.

In the sudden quiet, he could hear them panting.

"What if the train were going up a hill?" he suggested.

"You can't go fast up a hill," Vanessa said seriously. "Let's do it slow, Sally."

Dan glanced back and saw them get their arms in position. Like a record on slow speed, they drawled the words, and mercifully, they were singing more softly, too.

The relative quiet in the car and the familiarity of the route allowed Dan's mind to wander. He thought of Robin on the porch, or, now, in the kitchen perhaps, having a peaceful second cup of coffee. He wondered if she were lonely. He was. Their marriage hadn't been all bad. Much of it, in fact, had been good, especially in the beginning. However sure he was that he didn't want that former life back, there were losses to mourn.

He wasn't planning on doing anything about his loneliness just yet. He might not be ready to condemn relationships wholesale, but he was definitely not in the market for romance.

"The train's at the top of the hill!" Vanessa told Sally. "Now we have to go down the other side."

"Really fast!" Sally said.

Fortunately, the little red caboose's noisy descent coincided with the arrival at school, so Dan had to endure only half of the rollicking song.

"Good morning, Vanessa. Good morning, Sally," the teacher said as they skipped through the gate ahead of Dan.

Vanessa returned the teacher's greeting, but Sally did not. Instead, she ran off to the jungle gym where two of her best friends were perched. Dan knew Robin would have required Sally to come back and say good morning, but he didn't feel like making a big deal of it. The teacher seemed unfazed. He'd never seen her flustered, not by fights or tears or blood or damaged property, certainly not by a lack of good manners.

"Good morning, Miss Stewart. Beautiful day, isn't it?" Dan said as he wrote the girls' names on the sign-in sheet.

She looked into the sky, which was studded with massive white cloud florets and so blue it made your heart billow.

"Yes, it is."

Dan felt dissatisfied with her response. He'd made the remark merely to compensate for Sally's lapse, but once said, he'd become strangely invested in it. He wanted Miss Stewart to take a deep breath and sigh, to clasp her hands over her perky, twenty-something breasts and nod in conspiratorial appreciation of the sky, the balmy day, and his sensitivity at taking note of them. Though Miss Stewart was pretty enough, Dan's wish didn't arise from an attraction to her. He only wanted, for one moment, to be more than just another nondescript father. He wanted, in the eyes of this young, unattached woman, to be seen as a man who might, under different circumstances, merit her interest.

Miss Stewart's gaze didn't linger on the sky. And it didn't turn Dan's way. Her attention was on two little boys running towards her with earnest determination.

"Teacher, Richie's throwing sand," one of them called.

"Let's go talk to him," Miss Stewart said.

She walked off, the boys charging ahead of her. After a few feet, she turned and gave Dan a mild, neutral wave. He nodded at her, feeling abandoned. Don't be an ass, he told himself. But he couldn't shake his sense of disappointment. It stayed with him for the first few minutes in the car, finally dropping away when he pulled onto River Road and turned on the radio.

The cheerful beat of an oldies station filled the car and restored Dan's spirits. After all, it *was* a beautiful day, whether or not Miss Stewart was up to taking in the full measure of it, or of him, for that matter.

Dan turned his thoughts to the lecture he was to give on the esthetics of a smile. It was his favorite topic, since it inserted into the science of orthodontics some of the considerations of art. The same golden proportion that Leonardo da Vinci had used in painting could be applied to dentition. Teeth were most pleasing to look at when their widths were related to one another in the golden proportion, that is, when the proportion of smaller to greater was the same as the proportion of the greater to the whole. He'd write the proportion on the blackboard, 0.618 to 1. A mathematical description of harmony.

A smile, he'd tell the dental students as he clicked through his 22 slides of smiles, can express not only joy, but also exhilaration, embarrassment, enchantment, pride, and even hatred. A number of factors went into the overall appearance of a smile: the contours and positioning of teeth, the light-reflecting properties of enamel, and the three dark spaces. He'd emphasize the role of the dark spaces because, in his opinion, too many dentists and orthodontists gave it too little thought.

When a person smiled with parted lips, the buccal corridor yielded two dark spaces, between the teeth in the upper jaw and the cheeks. Another dark space was formed by the edges of the front teeth and the lower lip, the incisal silhouette. The character and harmony of these dark spaces were key to an attractive smile. Dan was intrigued by the idea that the goodness or rightness of something had as much to do with absence as with presence, or, more precisely, that it was the interplay between a void and its neighboring illuminated surfaces that determined how the whole was evaluated.

Dan reviewed the smiles he'd encountered that morning. The grins of his daughters: mad glee. Miss Stewart's weak offering: politeness. Robin? Hers had been close-lipped, ambiguous. She'd hoarded her dark spaces.

As Dan entered the faculty parking lot at the dental school, the radio began playing Andy Williams' version of "Moon River." Dan pulled into his assigned parking spot and kept the motor idling to listen to the whole song. Years might pass between times he heard it. It was always accidental, like today. And it always had the same effect on him, which was to fill him with a palpable ache that was part nostalgia, part sadness, part pleasure.

It had been "their song," his and Janine Pettorini's, during his junior and senior years in high school. He couldn't remember how it had come to be their song — it certainly hadn't been a popular hit among teens, and there was nothing about the movie "Breakfast At Tiffany's" that had special meaning for them — but he remembered slow dancing to it with her, at a dance in a dimly lit gymnasium, in his mother's basement rumpus room, at a friend's party. Wherever they were when they heard it, they'd get up and dance. Once, when they were walking along the crowded boardwalk at Point Pleasant, they caught the strains of "Moon River" coming out of a bar down a side street, and they'd stopped and danced right there on the boardwalk, oblivious to the stares and occasional snickers of passers-by, the damp night air smelling of ocean, Janine's hair smelling of almonds.

The song ended, and a commercial for mattresses blared into the car. Dan turned off the radio and the engine and got out of the car, going to the trunk for his slide carousel. He slammed down the trunk lid and cut across the grass to the classroom building. If he hurried, he'd just make it on time.

He pushed away the mood of the song. One brief dip into those emotions was enough. Passion, he'd decided long ago, was a dangerous thing. He'd learned that while he was still a boy. Janine had made him forget it for a dizzying while, but in the end, they'd both paid for it. They didn't go off to see the world together, like the song promised and they'd promised each other. Despite what his father had told him about leprechauns when he was little, no one ever gets to the end of the rainbow.

4

DAN PICKED UP the girls from pre-school at 12:00. They spent the afternoon running errands, finishing up with a swim in the pool at Dan's apartment complex and a late supper of take-out fried chicken.

Vanessa and Sally spent every Monday overnight and every other weekend with Dan. In the first months, he'd packed the schedule with outings — movies and pizza and ice cream, the zoo in Van Saun park, the Natural History Museum in New York — but the girls got cranky if the drives were too long, and he was often bored and vaguely disappointed that they weren't all having more fun, like the laughing families in television ads.

Finally, one Saturday when he was pulling on the girls' snow boots for a trip to Bear Mountain, Vanessa had declared with a pout that she wanted to make her own snowman in her own back yard. Dan felt a pang — the villainous moment of guilt — because he didn't have a back yard to offer, but in the next instant, he'd impulsively suggested they build a whole row of snowmen in the strip of snow between the front of his building and the sidewalk. They had done just that, and though the snowmen were small and lumpy, after an hour and a half, there were six of them standing in a sassy line. Afterwards, Dan and the girls had gone inside and made hot chocolate, and the rest of the weekend had been whiled away over coloring books, Candyland, and snowman repairs. Dan felt he'd actually had a relaxing three days, including some time to himself while the girls were playing with their Rainbow Brite dolls or watching Captain Kangaroo. Plus, the kids had seemed happier than he'd seen them in months. After that, he didn't feel compelled to entertain the girls when they were with him. There were still special activities from time to time, but mostly they just did "real life."

"Daddy," one of them would say on a Friday evening or a Monday morning, "are we going someplace, or are we doing real life?"

"Real life," was the answer more often than not, and "oh, goody," was the usual reaction.

It seemed, in "real life," that he was always wiping something — a child's nose or chin, a sticky countertop, dollops of toothpaste on the bathroom floor, feathery black mold inside Tupperware containers. But, gradually, such chores and the unstructured, organic hours with his daughters helped Dan feel he was still important in their lives, that he could learn, was learning, how to function alone as a parent, how to be a father without being a husband. He couldn't totally banish the fear that despite his best efforts he'd ultimately be left on the edges of his daughters' lives, but he was determined to keep that fear from bruising his relationships with them. He wouldn't let his fear lead him to withdraw from them, nor would he let it lead him to demand proof of their love or interest.

After Dan gave the girls their bath and put them to bed, reading the requisite two storybooks and one begged-for extra, he checked his service and got the message that a bracket had popped off one of Lulu Davidson's upper teeth, and something sharp was irritating the inside of her cheek. He called Lee Davidson and told her she could bring Lulu in the next morning. In the meantime, she could wedge cotton balls or a folded scrap of clean cloth beside her gums to keep the irritant away from the inside of her cheek.

In the morning, after delivering the girls to school, Dan drove straight to his office so he'd arrive there a half-hour before Lee and Lulu Davidson. His office was the converted first floor of a large, gracious Victorian house, and he enjoyed spending time there alone. Everything had its place and was in it. There were no unexpected toys underfoot, no uncleaned corners or surfaces. Nor, at this hour, any need for cheery greetings to his assistant, Miriam, and his office clerk, Valerie.

He went in through the back entrance, which opened into a small workroom where Miriam mixed the compound for making the molds of patients' bites that she'd later cast in plaster. Neat rows of these casts sat on long shelves lining the walls. Dan thought of it as his "before" gallery, these bright white models of badly fitting teeth. He liked to show them frequently to his patients, in the beginning to demonstrate the need for braces, and later, to stifle complaints of sore mouths and lack of progress. Using the casts and calipers, he could show patients that changes were, indeed, slowly occurring.

"See?" he'd say. "This tooth doesn't overlap that one as much as it used to. And the space here has closed up a bit more since last month."

Getting braces on a patient was no great feat of persuasion. Most of his patients, after all, were still under the thumbs of their parents. And in the rare case of very crooked teeth, vanity was on Dan's side as well.

Retainers were the real challenge. By then, his patients were older teenagers. Exultant at having their mouths free of uncomfortable, unsightly metal wires and rubber bands, they loved their beautiful, liberated smiles, and, with the stubborn certainty of youth, they were convinced perfection would last indefinitely with no particular main-tenance efforts on their part. What's more, all through the years that their teeth had been slowly straightening, their parents' influence on their behavior had been eroding in the same inexorable, almost invis-ible manner. A centimeter or two could make all the difference, Dan thought, whether the measurement was physical or metaphorical.

Parents complained that their sons and daughters refused to wear their retainers or "forgot" them, lost them in school cafeterias and locker rooms, didn't clean them properly. They wanted Dan to read the kids the riot act, to convince them or scare them or command them. But the kids were beyond convincing, scaring, and commanding. If they wore their retainers, it was on their own schedule, for their own reasons. And most of them, Dan knew, wouldn't wear them as they should, every night for a couple of years. How could someone, at 16 or 17 or 18, be expected to know the need for restraint?

Nevertheless, Dan did remind them. He tried to instruct them. It was part of his job, part of what the parents paid for. But he held out no great hopes for compliance. The regressions in the corrected teeth would not be gross, at any rate — a slight shift in the bite, a little more vulnerability to decay. Despite his daily struggle to harness and align natural forces inclined to their own peculiar paths, Dan did not really believe in the possibility of perfection.

Dan continued on through the large examining room, with its three dental chairs facing a picture window that gave out onto an English garden, past the waiting room and Valerie's reception cubicle papered with Polaroids of smiling, brace-free adolescents, to his own large office. Robin had furnished the office, and though it was handsome and comfortable, Dan always felt it looked more like a lawyer's office than an orthodontist's, all dark woods and leather upholstery.

"What, exactly, would make it an orthodontist's office?" Robin had asked querulously. "Big white chairs in the shape of teeth?"

Dan had not protested further. On the day the office was done, Robin gave him a solid silver toothbrush as a paperweight. She meant it as both a concession and a joke, and he acted amused, but something about it annoyed him, and he had put the thing in a bottom drawer of his desk and never taken it out again.

Really, he thought for the umpteenth time as he flicked on his desk lamp, I have got to get this place re-done.

Robin thought he had no standards of beauty, that he was like the proverbial lout who knew what he liked and was content to leave it at that. But it wasn't true. Dan did have standards, or one standard, anyway, and that was irregularity. There must be some flaw, however minor, or some small surprise in an object or a scene or a room for Dan to consider it beautiful, for him to feel satisfied by its beauty. He felt the same about people. Robin's smooth, conventional prettiness, for example, would be so much less appealing if she didn't have that tiny gap between her two front upper teeth.

The gap was how they met. She'd come to him to have it closed. She was a hand model then, and she wanted to move into print ads for cosmetics. Dan talked her out of braces, which would have made a permanent change, and into a false sliver that could be inserted and removed at will to give the appearance of a perfect smile. He had touted the speed of the remedy, the ease of it, the economy. But all the time, he'd wanted simply to save that gap and the fortunate way it revised her precise good looks and saved her face from being bland. After they were married, Robin stopped using the prosthesis, except in the annual photo for their family Christmas card.

Dan opened the wooden blinds. The office brightened with sunshine. Outside the windows, a row of deep pink hollyhocks nodded on their tall stems. He saw a car pulling up out front. Taking his white coat from the bent wood coat rack, he put it on, buttoning it up on his way to unlock the front door.

Lulu stood alone on the stoop.

"My mom went to get gas," she said, pointing to the car, which was already nearing the stop sign at the corner.

"Well, we won't be long at all, Lulu. Come on in."

The repair was quickly accomplished, and Dan engaged Lulu in small talk until they heard the chime that signaled that the front door had opened. He walked with Lulu to the waiting room to say hello to her mother and to explain what had gone wrong with the braces. Lee was standing by Valerie's desk. Another woman was sitting in the far corner of the waiting room. She stood up when Dan got to the desk.

"Hello, Dan," she said.

"Dan, you remember Janine Pettorini, right?" Lee said hurriedly. "Well, of course you do. We're going to do some shopping, and when I told her you were Lulu's orthodontist, well, of course, she wanted to come in and... I haven't seen her myself in years, absolutely years. We ran into each other by chance in Foodtown."

Janine had moved forward during Lee's spiel. Dan hadn't taken his gaze off her from the first moment she spoke. His chest was a confusion of sensations. It was "Moon River" amplified. She looked so much the same. A little heavier, but by no more than five or six pounds;

softer across the belly. She was wearing a belted sun dress. Her bare arms looked more muscular than he remembered them. Her hair was shoulder-length. It used to reach halfway down her back. Her face was as beautiful as ever, maybe more so, because now it fit her better than it had in high school. Then, her beauty had been almost too strong. It had seemed, sometimes, not to be part of her, but some splendid cloak too heavy for her young shoulders. And there were the startling eyes, one brown, the other half brown and half blue, eyes that wouldn't let you look away until they permitted it.

"Janine," he said, aware that both Lee and Lulu were watching him. She gave him a small, careful smile.

"I'm here visiting my parents."

"Your parents. How are they?"

"Oh, same as ever. Older."

"Aren't we all?" Lee put in. "Janine's got twins. Twin boys."

"Really? I've got two girls. Four and five."

"Mom," Lulu whined. "I told Mary Ellen you'd drop me at Bergen Mall at 10:00. She's gonna be waiting."

"These kids," Lee said to Janine and Dan, cocking her head toward Lulu, "they've got busier schedules than God. And to hear them tell it, just as important."

"Mom!"

"Oops, now I've embarrassed her."

"We should go, anyway, Lee," Janine said. "I'm sure Dan's busy, too."

Lee looked like she wanted to argue. Instead, she headed for the door.

"Good-bye, Dr. Gannon," Lulu said. "And thanks."

Janine smiled at Dan again, an apology it seemed, and turned to follow Lulu out.

"Say hi to your folks for me," Dan said when she reached the door.

Lee was out on the stoop. He saw her give Janine a little poke on the arm.

"They're having their annual Fourth of July barbecue tomorrow," Janine said. "You'd be welcome to come by. And your family, too, of course."

"My wife and I are separated," Dan said. "And I don't have my kids on Wednesdays."

"Oh."

It appeared she was going to say more, but she didn't.

"But I'd like to come anyway. If you're sure it's okay on such short notice."

"She asked you, didn't she?" Lee called over Janine's head. "Case closed."

Janine raised her eyebrows at Dan, in the same spirit in which Lulu had exclaimed "Mom!" after Lee's comment about God.

"Case closed," Janine said and stepped out into the sunshine, pulling the door shut behind her.

Dan stood in place for a moment in the silence. Then he moved across the room and peered out one of the small glass panels in the front door. Lee's car was angled slightly away from the curb, waiting for a break in traffic. Dan saw a figure in the passenger seat and another in the back seat. He assumed Janine was in front. The car windows were lightly tinted and it was a good 30 yards from his door to the curb, so he couldn't tell for sure. As the car started to move away, the passenger in front shifted in her seat. Was it to turn her head in his direction? She probably wouldn't be able to make out his face in the little glass panel.

He thought he felt a force leap at him from the car. It was like the jolt he used to experience all those years ago in high school when he and Janine passed in the halls during the change of classes and their glances met briefly, or at Graydon Pool when he'd catch her exit from the changing house, he seated, hot and bored, on the tall wooden lifeguard stand and she, pausing long enough to let him look at her, to let him appreciate and want her. That pause told him not only that she knew he was looking, but that she wanted him to know she knew. They never spoke of those moments in the halls of the high school or at the pool. It

40

would have diminished their power. Despite their youth, somehow they both knew that. Or, maybe, in some unremembered way, Janine had taught him that, as she'd taught him so much else.

He turned away from the door. Of course Janine hadn't been looking. Why would she? They hadn't seen each other since the September after his senior year. There'd been some calls and letters subsequently, but that had stopped abruptly in January. Over a year later, he heard from a friend she'd left town, the friend didn't know where. It had been like a death. Worse than a death. Because, he used to think in the early years, Janine might still be standing somewhere bathed in sunshine, waiting for him to spot her.

5

THROUGHOUT THE REST of the day and into the evening, Dan went back and forth in his mind whether or not to go to the Pettorini barbecue. What would it be like to be in that house again? To pass more than a few words with Janine? To meet her husband?

By morning, he still hadn't decided. He got up at dawn and drove to the Palisades. It was one of the things he liked best about living in Alpine, the closeness to the Hudson River and the steep woods and sheer rock cliffs that ran along it on the Jersey side. He kept a pair of hiking boots in the trunk of his car so that he could go there whenever the fancy struck him. Often he hiked the Long Path, high above the river, but today he wanted to be close to the water, so he drove to the Englewood Boat Basin and set out along the Shore Trail towards Greenbrook Falls. There was a light mist hovering low over the river, the oak and maple woods were shady, and the morning air was cool and fresh.

As a boy, Dan had played in the woods along the Hackensack River in Teaneck. It wasn't a pretty river, except in the general way any natural body of water is, and the woods weren't thick or deep. The river's surface was black and oily, and on hot days, a sewer odor drifted from the muck at its edges. But Dan had loved the area for its relative isolation. There he could escape the hubbub of his crowded home and his mother's constant assignment of chores and errands, which had increased many-fold after his father's death when Dan was 11.

Sometimes Dan would take his younger brother, Brian, with him, and they'd fish for killies with improvised poles of sticks and string and bits of baloney for bait. But more often, he went alone, and then he'd lie on his back watching the sunlight through the trees or sit staring out at the slow-moving river, occasionally dropping in a leaf or twig to follow its lazy, spiraling journey away from him toward the drag of the seaward current.

Dan had daydreamed a lot in those days. He remembered his mother harping on him to get his head out of the clouds. But he couldn't recall what he had dreamed about in those stolen, idle hours. Were dreams so perishable, as liable to wither as unwatered houseplants? Or did neglected dreams skulk away only to return later in new garb, like resistant bacteria? For surely some dreams were as much an infection as an inspiration. Some dreams people were better off without.

The woods along the Hackensack were gone in most places now, reduced to scattered stands of trees among houses. During Dan's teen years, however, there was a swath where you could get out of sight of people and houses, even though you still might spot back door lights here and there through the brush and hear dogs barking or trash can lids being banged shut. He'd taken a few girls there in ninth and tenth grades. The girls had wanted to make picnics, or they had wanted to locate a cool breeze off the water on a hot summer night. They'd always needed excuses. None of them dared appear as baldly calculating as he, who wanted only to be in a place where he could stretch out beside them and reach inside their clothing without their resisting.

Then, the summer after tenth grade, he'd met Janine. As their relationship progressed, she became as frankly determined as Dan to find private places, and if none were available, she was not above manufacturing a facsimile, like the time she took off her bathing suit top and let him stroke her breasts under a towel on a populated beach; or when she was pressing so close against him in a corner of the gym at the Sadie Hawkins dance that a chaperone came over and suggested strongly that it was time for a Coke; or the night in the playground when they'd had sex on a swing, her skirt bunched around her slender hips, her head thrown back, her throat white in the moonlight. Who would notice back door lights or banging can lids with a girl like Janine in his arms? Who would think to dream of anything else?

Dan reached a small beach and walked to the Hudson's edge. A pair of mallards dabbling in the shallows flapped their wings wildly, lifted awkwardly, and flew away upriver. Squatting, Dan scrabbled among stones, selecting several smooth, flat ones. He stood up and flung them one by one out over the river, ridiculously pleased at how they skipped across the surface three, four, five times before sinking.

"WELL, I SUPPOSE you'd better come in."

It was almost a greeting. When Rose answered the door, Dan had said her name and then his, lifting his voice nearly to the pitch of a question on "Gannon," but instead of bolstering her recognition of him, as he'd intended, it sounded as if he were unsure of his own identity.

He hadn't seen the woman in 18 years. She'd shrunk in height and gained in girth since then, and he'd grown up. He was a successful professional and a family man. Not as much success there, admittedly, but his girls were great, and he could take some credit for that. Yet Rose Pettorini still intimidated him. He felt again like a boy in high school, cowed by her confident authority, by her ability to block him from Janine, which she'd wielded like a linebacker once she'd made up her mind he was no good for her daughter.

"You're early," she announced as he stepped inside, sounding none too pleased.

Robin had always been flustered by early arrivals when they entertained at home, but Mrs. Pettorini didn't strike Dan as the fusspot hostess type. He recalled one raucous barbecue at the Pettorinis' when a bunch of the men got drunk and a couple of them fell into a rose bush and Mr. Pettorini burned the burgers until they were hard. Dan and Janine had had to make a run to the store for more meat. He remembered Mrs. Pettorini laughing a lot that day and letting the little kids eat as many toasted marshmallows as they wanted. She didn't even get angry when one of them threw up on the kitchen floor. So her comment about Dan's early arrival must be a protest against his being there at all.

"I'm sorry," he began, "Janine was a little vague about the time..."

"Never mind. We'll put you to work."

"Sure, whatever I can—"

"Janine's peeling potatoes. You can help there."

After pointing toward the kitchen, she headed upstairs, sparing him the lie of how nice it was to see her again. Sparing, perhaps, both of them. After all, the last time they'd seen each other, she'd threatened to call the police.

Dan paused in the doorway of the kitchen. Janine was at the sink, her back to him. Strains of "La Boheme" were booming up from the open door to the basement. Dan remembered that Al Pettorini loved opera. Whenever Dan came to see Janine on a Sunday afternoon, the house rang with opera from the radio in his basement workshop. Al liked it at full volume.

Janine was wearing shorts and a tank top. Her legs were still good. It had been the first thing he'd ever noticed about her. He'd been drowsing at a table in the town library, where he often went to do his homework. Lifting his head from the open book he'd been using as a pillow, he spotted a pair of beautiful legs moving slowly down a row of books across from his table. The rest of the girl's body and her head were blocked from view by the shelves. When she finally turned the corner and came into view, he wasn't disappointed.

The opera reached its finale. Mimi was dead. In the ensuing quiet, he heard the rhythmic, slippery scrape of a peeler against a potato.

"Still the Sunday soundtrack," he said to Janine's back.

She started a little, then turned around, a potato in one hand and a peeler in the other. The soundtrack of doomed love, he thought.

"I've been assigned to k.p.," he told her.

"Assigned?"

45

"By your mother. Seems I'm too early."

"Oh, never mind that. There's not much left to do."

Five unpeeled potatoes waited on the counter.

"Got another peeler?" he asked.

"Maybe in here." She knocked a drawer with her knee.

His hand was only inches from her bare leg when he opened the drawer. As he bent to dig around in its jumbled contents, he could smell cocoa butter lotion on her skin. She still used cocoa butter lotion. He found a peeler and straightened up. Janine had been paring the potatoes over the sink, letting the peels drop into it. She moved over to share the space with him. He picked up a potato and stood staring at the side of her face.

"You were never in the Army, were you?" she said.

"No. Why?"

"Because you'd never get away with doing k.p. like that in the Army."

"I guess not," he said, embarrassed, and began peeling his potato.

They worked in silence a few minutes. Through the open window above the sink, they could hear occasional shouts from Janine's twins, who were in the back yard running through a sprinkler.

"So, you're an orthodontist."

"As you saw." He rinsed off his peeled potato. "That was one hell of a surprise."

"Yeah, I remember you always used to talk about becoming a forest ranger. Tramping through the woods, coming home to a little cabin with a wood fire burning..."

"That's not the surprise I meant."

"I'm taking a lemonade break," she said, dropping chunks of cut potato into a pot of cold water. "Want some?"

She dried her hands on a dish towel and went to the refrigerator.

"Yeah, thanks."

Dan cut up his potato and added it to the pot, then turned to watch Janine fill two tall glasses with ice and pour lemonade from a pitcher.

She carried the glasses to the sink and handed him one, but when he lifted it to drink, she put her hand on his wrist to stop him.

"Wait."

She broke a few leaves off a green sprig sitting in a jar of water on the windowsill and dropped two into his glass and two into her own.

"Mint," she explained. "My special touch."

Her special touch. In the fleeting moment of her hand on his wrist, he had felt a surge of longing that was not mere lust, nor pure sentimentality, nor poignant sense memory but a heady confusion of all three, plus something more, something undefinable, something his body understood but his mind couldn't tell the meaning of.

"To be precise," she continued, apparently unaware of his discomfiture or ignoring it, "my husband's trick. It's how his mother made lemonade, and he taught me, and now...I've shown you."

In the pause near the end of her little story, her voice had changed, quieted and slowed in the smallest way.

"Is he here? Your husband?"

Janine shook her head.

"He died two years ago."

"Gosh, I'm sorry, I didn't know."

"Of course you didn't," she said, her eyebrows knit together in a small frown.

"Was he sick? If you don't mind my asking."

"Heart attack. Very sudden." She snapped her fingers.

"Guess you never know what's coming around the next corner."

"No."

"Like us standing in this kitchen," he dared to say.

She stirred the ice cubes in her glass with the tip of her pinky.

"Yeah, I guess that would count," she said.

Dan took a swallow of lemonade.

"I like it," he said, pointing to the mint sprigs.

Janine peered out the window, though she didn't seem to be focusing on anything in particular.

"So, I'm an orthodontist. What do you do?"

"Hmm?" She turned to him. "Oh, I'm a framer. And I paint. Pictures, not houses."

"Really? I'll bet that's—"

"Listen, Dan, it wasn't as accidental as Lee made out, my coming to your office."

"I didn't think so."

She shot him an assessing look. He held his gaze steady, even though he wanted to avert his eyes, wanted, for one mad instant, to do an about-face and leave. What was she searching for? He definitely felt scrutinized. His stomach clutched up, like it did when he stood on the brink of a sheer cliff and looked down.

"Lolly-gagging!" Rose said loudly as she entered the kitchen. "You two were always lolly-gaggers. What about my potatoes? People count on potato salad on the Fourth of July."

"We're almost done, Ma," Janine said, putting down her lemonade and taking up her peeler again.

Dan put down his glass, too, but Rose waved him away from the sink.

"You can dice the onions," she said, indicating a cutting board and knife next to a bowl of onions on the table. Dan obediently sat down.

"If your eyes tear up," Rose instructed, "stick your head in the freezer, and it'll go away. Or hold a piece of white bread in your mouth while you're cutting. Bread box is over there."

"I'm okay."

"Suit yourself."

Dan took an onion from the bowl and started pushing off its dry brown skin. Would he and Janine be able to find a quiet corner this afternoon to finish their conversation? Or would she retreat from the brink he was positive they'd been on? He'd try to lead her back if the opportunity arose. Or he'd propose another meeting. Coffee somewhere. A walk along the Hudson.

He sliced the onion in half. His eyes began to burn. And it's only going to get worse, he thought. It'll only get stronger. But he was damned if he was going to put his head in the freezer.

ROSE SENT DAN into the back yard while she and Janine finished up in the kitchen. Al was out there starting the coals and setting up lawn chairs. He didn't give Dan any warmer welcome than Rose had, but he was more polite. He seemed, more than anything else, embarrassed at meeting Dan again. He introduced him to Janine's sons, who were wrapped in towels and sitting at the picnic table playing checkers. They turned their identical faces up just long enough to say hello. Then Al gave Dan a beer, and they chatted about Al's boat, Dan's practice, the Yankees, and the summer Olympics, due to start in Los Angeles in a few weeks. Dan did most of the talking.

When Al excused himself to go inside and check on the meat marinade, Dan wandered to the far end of the yard and stood surveying the back of the house, so eerily exactly as it had been all those years ago. What the hell was he doing here? In the kitchen, Janine had hinted at a purpose behind her invitation, but he wasn't at all convinced she was going to follow through. They'd been interrupted by her mother, yes, but there'd been a reluctance in Janine, and a tension, and even without the interruption, she might not have gone on. Did he really want to hang around all afternoon on tenterhooks, waiting for her to speak again, all the while under the vaguely disapproving regard of the Pettorinis? But now he was stuck. There was no graceful way to leave until more guests had arrived, until he'd had something to eat. And the meat wasn't even on the grill yet.

As far as underlying purposes went, what was *his* purpose in being here? Did he have one? He'd come on impulse, half-cocked, rank with memory. He'd come because he couldn't not come. Because encountering Janine yesterday had sparked something inside him that he thought was long dead, if he ever thought of it at all. Which he would have honestly said he never did. But when he saw her, he realized she'd always been alive to him, that, in fact, he'd sub-consciously measured every woman since against her, measured every romantic relationship against theirs. So, he supposed, his purpose today was to face that head-on and to see if it was something he ought to root out and dispose of, or, if it was, instead, some kind of inconvenient but necessary truth that he would just have to keep carrying.

Guests began arriving, walking down the driveway or emerging from the kitchen door. Al was outside again, dispensing beers and hearty greetings, shaking men's hands, kissing women's cheeks and taking from them pies and plates of brownies and Rice Krispie treats. Janine and Rose went back and forth from the house, bringing out large bowls covered with plastic wrap and setting them on a long table under the apple tree. Janine had changed into a white skirt and a plaid sleeveless blouse.

Dan moved closer to the action. Al offered him another beer, but Dan hadn't half finished the first one yet. Al left him to introduce himself to people. More small talk ensued: the Yankees again, the weather, the bounteous spread of food. The guests were all in the same age group as Rose and Al. It looked as if Janine hadn't kept up with anyone from high school. That was oddly gratifying to Dan. It hadn't been only him she'd closed out. It shouldn't matter after all this time, but it did.

Lee and her husband, Red, and their brood arrived after the hamburgers and steaks and chicken were sizzling on the grill. Except for Lulu, who plunked herself down on the grass at a far corner of the yard to read a book, the children — Lee's other three and Janine's boys — instantly organized a game of tag that sent them in wild circuits around the house and yard, using a corner of the garage as home base.

Janine was circulating with a tray of melon cubes wrapped in thin slices of prosciutto. She came to Dan, who was standing off to the side of the crowd watching the kids race around. He speared a piece of melon with a toothpick.

"Such simple things make them happy," she said, also watching the boys play. "A lawn sprinkler. A game of tag. Ice cream."

"Scavenger hunts?"

She gave him a probing look.

"I do remember," she said. "If that's what you're asking."

Janine had loved scavenger hunts as a child, and she'd once told Dan that. For her seventeenth birthday, he'd surprised her with an elaborate hunt, posting rhymed clues at all their favorite haunts around town, starting in her own mailbox and ending up in the locker room at the YWCA — he wouldn't reveal how he'd gotten in there — where she found a huge bouquet of daffodils, her favorite flower, and a birthday cake from Gratzel's Bakery on a bench in the last row of lockers.

"I'd better get back to work," she said.

She lifted the tray to him, and he speared another melon chunk. She didn't say anything more, but she aimed a smile at him that was both encouraging and apologetic and that said, I'll be with you when I can. At least it *could* mean that. It was enough to extend his patience.

After she left, he looked around for someone to talk to. Lee was engaged in a lively conversation with Rose, Red standing beside them appearing supremely disinterested. He caught Dan's eye and gravitated to him. Each of them knew who the other was, but they hadn't been introduced, so they exchanged names and shook hands.

"So," Red began, "Lee said you and her and Janine went to high school together."

"Yes."

"Old home week then."

"I guess so."

"Funny, all of you bumping into each other again at sort of the same time. Or Janine, anyway. Of course, Lee's been seeing you all along at Lulu's appointments."

"A lovely girl, Lulu."

"We like her."

Red grinned at his own feeble jest and took a swig of beer.

"The first-born is always special, no matter how many more you have later on," he continued.

"Yes, I think you're right."

"So, you got more kids?"

"More?"

"More than just one. We got four," Red made a sweeping gesture that included the three red-headed boys racing around with Janine's twins. "So far." Again, his foolish grin. "But our Lulu, she stands out. I guess you could say she broke us in."

"Breaking in is a good way to put it."

"Yeah, each one gets easier. Or maybe we just get lazy."

"I think it's more that after the first, you relax. I remember with my first, Vanessa, everything was so new and so amazing, and sometimes confusing and scary, too. With my second daughter, it was all smoother."

"Vanessa?" Red said. "I thought your first was a boy."

Dan was flabbergasted. Obviously, Lee had told her husband about Janine's teenage pregnancy. Had she neglected to also tell him that Dan had never met his son, that he was his first-born in statistical fact only, not in direct experience?

"That's not something I usually—"

"Sorry, sorry," Red quickly interrupted. "It's just such an incredible story, I guess I let curiosity get the better of me."

"A pretty ordinary story, really."

"Well, maybe the first part. High school sweethearts and all that. But to have the kid come looking for you — that must be a trip and a half. I don't know what I'd do if something like that happened to me."

Dan's heart lurched. He stared at Red's pale, freckled face with its inquiring expression and felt, suddenly, like punching it.

"I have no idea what you're talking about," he said coldly. "And even if I did, I certainly wouldn't discuss it with you."

"Oh, God, you didn't... Jeez... Again, man, I'm sorry. I just—"

"And furthermore, you do *not* have my permission to discuss this with anyone else. Not anyone. Am I clear?"

"Yeah, sure. Chill. No harm done."

Abruptly, Dan walked away from Red. If he'd stayed a moment longer, he actually might have hit him, as uncharacteristic as that would be. He scanned the party guests for Janine and spotted her standing at the grill with a platter of buns onto which her father was placing cooked burgers.

"I've got to get going," he said to her when he reached them. "Walk me to my car?"

"But you haven't eaten."

"Thanks for stopping by, Dan," Al said. "Nice seeing you." He took the platter from Janine and carried it off to the table, where it was descended upon by all the children.

"Walk me to my car," Dan repeated. He knew his voice was harsh. He didn't care.

They set off together down the driveway. When they reached the sidewalk, out of sight and earshot of the party, Dan stopped. Barely realizing what he was doing, he put both his hands on Janine's upper arms.

"What's going on?" he said.

"What do you mean?"

"Why did you invite me here? Why did you come to my office?"

"It was just a—"

"Janine, don't lie to me. Please." He let go of her. "Red said our son is looking for me."

"Goddamnit, Lee never could keep her mouth shut! I guess she married someone with the same disease."

"Is it true?"

She was holding her hands at waist level, her thumbs tucked against her palms with the fingers wrapped protectively around them. It was a gesture Dan remembered well. It said, help me, I don't know what to do. Seeing it, he felt the urge to comfort her. But he didn't know what the comfort would be for. And he was too angry to offer it with no questions asked.

"Oh, Dan, this isn't how I wanted you to tell you."

"What, third in line? Oh, no, wait, it's probably fifth in line. I assume you've already told your folks."

"Yes, but—"

"Look, it's a little late for regrets. Just tell me."

Janine took a deep breath.

"I got a call the other day from the law firm that handled the adoption. They had a letter for me. From...Hunt. That's his name."

"What did it say?"

"That he wanted to meet me."

Dan looked up, over the top of her head. He couldn't bear to see her disquieted face, her tucked-away thumbs. He bent his head farther back to stretch out the lump thickening his throat. Above him, the sky was a hot blue. Tree branches with dark green leaves screened part of his view of it. It all appeared simultaneously real and unreal, like a hard edge painting. It was apart from him, alien. No, he was apart from it, apart from everything around him. He looked back at Janine.

"And me?" he said.

She seemed puzzled by his question.

"And me?" he repeated.

"He mentioned you. He said he had questions."

"Have you met him?"

"No. The lawyer said I have to wait until he gets in touch with them again. They haven't heard from him in weeks. I thought maybe I'd go to Shadyside and ask for information there. And then I wondered if maybe Hunt had tried to find you, if maybe you knew something."

"Don't you think if that had happened, I'd have found some way to contact you?"

She looked miserable. He fought against a rise of pity.

"Let me ask you this, Janine: if you *had* met him, would you have let me know? When, if ever, were you planning on telling me any of this?"

"I don't know, Dan. God forgive me, I really don't know. I was confused, scared. I was just putting one foot in front of the other."

Confused and scared. The very words he'd said to Red only minutes ago. Only minutes? It felt like years.

"Dan, I was wrong. This was a horrible way for you to find out. I thought it was a shock getting a phone call out of the blue, but this is worse, and it's totally my fault."

That was his cue to say it was all right, to take her hands in his and unfold her fingers. His anger was draining away, but he didn't feel all right, and he wouldn't tell her he was.

"I've got to go," he said.

She put her hand on his wrist, as she had before adding mint to his lemonade. That seemed like years ago, too.

"Would you help me find him?"

Her arresting brown and blue eyes were filling with tears. He saw that she was working hard to hold them back.

"I came here today to find *you*, Janine."

"Will you help?"

"Why don't you just do what the lawyer says and wait? You don't need help for that. If Hunt turns up on his own, you won't need me at all."

"If he does, I'll call you. I promise."

"It'd be nice if that had been your attitude from the start."

He took his car keys out of his pocket and headed for his car, which was parked directly in front of the house.

"Dan?"

"Being left out once was hard enough, Janine. Being left out twice is too much."

He opened the car door.

"Left out? Left out of what?" Her tone was withering.

"Everything," he said angrily, feeling suddenly like the powerless, frustrated 18-year-old he'd been.

"Left out of going into hiding for six months? Or lying on a hospital bed in pain, totally alone, with nurses treating me like a bedpan they have to empty? Left out of watching my baby being carried down a hallway and out of my life forever? Which part do you feel deprived of, Dan?"

He felt accused and lashed, and even though he knew that his pain was no match for what she'd endured, it was still pain. He couldn't take hers on, too.

"I didn't know about all that. How could I? Your parents kept me off the approved list to call or visit, remember? But I wrote you at Shadyside. More than once. And you didn't answer."

"They read our letters," she said bitterly. "They blacked things out. Sometimes, if they didn't like what was written, they'd tear a letter up right in front of you."

Dan clenched the keys in his hand until they dug into his palm.

"That's awful," he said, "but it's not my fault."

"It's not mine, either."

They stood staring at each other over the roof of the car, Dan at the open door on the driver's side, Janine on the curb. He felt as if he were sinking into a sucking bog of sulfurous black mud.

"I'm sorry, Janine, I just can't help."

"You mean you *won't*."

"Have it your way. I won't."

He got into his car and pulled away. He saw in his rear view mirror that she remained standing on the sidewalk watching him go.

6

DAN TURNED LEFT at the end of the Pettorinis' block, drove four blocks, and pulled over. He needed to calm down. Hadn't there been a stop sign one block back? He didn't remember having stopped or even slowed.

He was parked on a tree-lined street of wood frame and brick houses fronted by small green lawns. Large flowering bushes hugged the houses — lilacs, yellow forsythia, blue and pink hydrangeas. A few homes had American flags hanging from their porches. It was a comfortable neighborhood of older homes, not luxurious by any means, but well-cared for, with a reassuring air of solidity and permanence. Dan's boyhood neighborhood was more modest than this one, but it had that same reassuring air, as if nothing bad or ugly could happen there. Of course, that was a myth. Children might trust in it, but adults knew better. Older children sometimes came to know better, too, usually by hitting up against some hard or disillusioning fact of life.

Cancer and other feared diseases happened in those healthy houses. A boy on Dan's street had had polio. Arguments happened, too, and disappointments. Sometimes they spilled out into the neighborhood by way of raised voices and open windows, or slammed front doors and the squeal of angrily departing cars. It was rare, but it did happen. Men lost jobs or went on strike so long it amounted to the same thing. One year, Dan's father had been on strike for five months. He got a night job driving a delivery truck, and days he did odd jobs, anything he could find. The union gave them a turkey at Thanksgiving.

Yes, you wouldn't think of it to look at these quiet, tidy houses on a bright day in July, but things could happen to the people inside them, no matter how good or kind or trusting they were. Accidents happened, like the one that took Dan's father. Surprises happened. When you least expected it, when you were feeling carefree, with a girl who loved you and whom you loved back, and summer jobs that didn't keep you cooped up inside, a phone call came. Janine was pregnant. They had made a baby.

That's how she had said it. "I think we made a baby." As sweet and scared and trying to sound confident as those girls who'd said, "Let's make a picnic." Then she'd gone off and finished making their baby on her own. Dan did a quick mental calculation. Hunt, now, would be just the age Dan had been when he fathered him.

And another unexpected phone call had brought it all back. Dan was amazed at how vivid his memories were, at how readily they were returning. The tears. The terror. The rage and frustration when the Pettorinis and his mother teamed up to keep him and Janine apart. They didn't want to hear the apologies that burned inside him. They didn't consider his and Janine's getting married a desirable or even a sensible solution. They all said such a marriage was doomed to fail, and with all of them against it, maybe it was.

Two boys on bicycles rode past Dan's car. They both looked back over their shoulders at him. He realized that a solitary man sitting in a parked car on a residential street could raise nasty suspicions. When he was a boy, the same situation would have evoked only curiosity or perhaps an offer of assistance. The neat houses and the friendly neighborhood might appear just as they had 20 or 30 years ago, but the myth of safety had taken some battering since then. Dan decided he'd better shove off. His mind had stopped churning, and he thought he could pay better attention to the road now. He started the ignition.

"Damn," he said, hitting the steering wheel with the flat of his hand.

He'd just recalled that he'd promised to visit his mother today. The assisted living facility was 20 miles from his apartment, but it was only three miles from the Pettorinis' neighborhood, so he'd called his mother this morning to let her know he'd be by later. As much as he wanted to be alone right now, maybe head back to the Palisades for a more challenging hike than he'd done that morning, he didn't have the heart to cancel on her. Hell, she might take his mind off things. He'd stop at Tabatchnick's and get a couple of deli sandwiches and containers of cole slaw and macaroni salad, some half-sour pickles. She loved that kind of food. Besides, he was suddenly very hungry.

———✺———

"THEY PUT RUSSIAN dressing on my roast beef?" Betty Gannon asked, lifting one corner of rye bread.

"Of course, Mom."

"Good."

Dan slid the container of cole slaw towards her across the small table in her tiny kitchenette. She took most of her meals in the community dining room, but when he visited, she preferred to eat take-out food in her apartment. Deli, Chinese, lasagna, roast chicken. He was glad to bring it. It was a painless way of pleasing her.

"Did you bring Russian dressing?" she said.

She lost the thread of conversation more often these days, forgot what had just been said, what had already been asked and answered. It was best not to point it out to her.

"It's already on the sandwich, Mom."

"Good."

While she was slathering cole slaw on to her sandwich, he opened the large bottle of Dr. Pepper and poured some into each of their glasses. She'd had him take out the heavy cut-glass tumblers that his father used to drink his Jim Beam in. With her arthritis, it was hard for her to lift them even when they were empty, but using them was her way of making the little meal special. When Vanessa and Sally came, she delighted them with the old Flintstone jelly jar glasses, the decals worn almost invisible in spots.

"Dr. Pepper," she grunted. "Hoffman's cream soda is better."

"Hoffman's has been out of business for years, Mom."

"I know that. I got a *few* marbles left. All's I'm saying is nothing beats Hoffman's."

"Well, I've got to agree with you there."

Robin used to claim that Dan and his mother were like an old married couple, and he sometimes saw the truth of that when they were alone together. As the oldest boy in a family of six children, Dan had become the man of the house at 11. After his father's death, his mother had gone to work as a maid for a plastic surgeon in a huge stone Tudor house on Winthrop Road. They let her have the baby with her until his older sister, Eileen, picked him up after school each day. Eileen and Dan's other sister, May, made dinner for everyone at 6:00 every evening, but Dan always waited until 8:00 to eat a warmed-up meal with his mother. He'd fill her in on all the small doings of the family's day, leaving out any spats or tantrums, and she might have an anecdote about the doctor's spoiled Pekingese dogs chasing the mailman or the Dugan bread man, or a passing remark on some local item in the newspaper, but mostly they ate in silence, she weary and he shy, both of them worried.

The silence today allowed Dan's mind to drift to Janine and the incredible news about Hunt, and to all the old pain and bewilderment. Once the adoption decision was definite, his mother had never again brought up the pregnancy, and Dan had followed her lead. The child had become a ghost even before it was born.

But by 18, Dan had had long experience with living with a ghost. After his father's funeral, his mother didn't mention her husband again, and she quickly trained her children not to mention him either. The wedding photo in the living room — Betty Gannon in a veiled cloche hat and a simple cloth coat with an orchid corsage pinned to the lapel, and Conor Gannon in his World War II Navy uniform — disappeared. Dan had looked for it one day two weeks after the funeral. He'd pulled out every drawer in the house, and dug into the back of every closet. He'd even peered under his mother's bed and pawed through the shelf of diapers in the linen cabinet. He finally concluded she must have thrown it away, frame and all.

Eileen had found the photo three years ago, when she'd been packing up the house before their mother moved to assisted living.

"Where the hell was it?" he'd asked.

"Inside an empty Cheerios box in the pantry. The box felt heavy when I picked it up, so I looked inside, and there it was."

"Does she want to take it with her?"

"Good lord, I'm not going to ask her that."

"Well, give it to me, then. I'll keep it."

He'd taken it home and shown it to Robin. She'd set it on his dresser, but after a week, he'd put it in a drawer under a pile of tee shirts. It was in the same place now, in his new apartment. He knew how to live with ghosts. He didn't know how to live with a man in a picture staring out at him with eyes shaped like his, with a mouth configured in the same boggled smile.

"The girl baked a cherry pie," Dan's mother said to him when he was rinsing their sandwich plates and glasses in the sink. "When I told her you were coming."

"That was nice of her."

"The girl" was Emma, an aide who came every day for a couple of hours to tidy the apartment, help his mother bathe and dress, run errands.

"She used a store-bought crust."

"It was still nice of her."

"You used to like my pies."

"Best thing about Sunday supper. Your pies."

"Hers is in the cabinet, top shelf."

Dan took down the pie. The crust was golden brown, quite decent-looking, with red juice oozing out of four slits in the top. But the top was a flat circle of dough, not the high-crested, billowing pastry lid with the promise of mounds of sweet fruit beneath it that his mother had always produced. He was glad. He didn't want her to feel that she'd been surpassed.

"Want some coffee with it?" he said, setting out clean plates and dessert forks.

"That'll help," his mother said, frowning at the pie.

Emma had set up the coffee-maker for morning, so all Dan had to do was push a button. He began slicing the pie.

"Just a small one for me, Danny."

He put a thin slice of pie on her plate and cut a thicker wedge for himself. He got out coffee cups and stood by the coffee-maker waiting for the pot to finish filling.

"You'll never guess who I saw today," he said, not quite sure if it was a good subject to bring up, but feeling as if he might burst if he didn't say it out loud to someone, especially to someone who'd know what it meant.

"Robin?"

"No, not Robin."

Dan's mother wasn't a particular friend of Robin's, but she didn't approve of divorce. She'd stopped trying to talk Dan into "working it out," by which she really meant *sticking* it out, but she still held out hope that by some miracle he and Robin would reconcile.

"Robin sent me a card for Mother's Day. She always sends me cards."

"I saw Janine Pettorini today, Mom. Except she's Janine Linden now."

"Janine Linden? Who's that?"

"Janine Pettorini. *My* Janine."

His mother stared at him, as if still trying to place the woman he'd named. Or maybe she was simply registering the shock of that personal pronoun, my. He'd shocked himself a little by using it.

"Where?" she finally said.

"At her parents' house. She came to my office yesterday and invited me to their July 4th barbecue."

"She came to your office?"

"She's friends with a parent of one of my patients."

Betty looked past him at the coffee-maker, which had finished.

"All I got is evaporated milk," she said. "The regular milk keeps going sour. The girl says I don't use it up fast enough."

"Evaporated's fine."

Dan prepared the cups of coffee and brought them to the table. He ate a mouthful of pie and nodded appreciatively, but without excessive enthusiasm. As a hostess, Betty would want him to like the pie. As a cook and a mother, she'd want him to like hers better.

"Who's this Linden person then?"

"It's Janine's married name."

"So she's married."

"Widowed. With twin boys a bit older than Nessie."

"A widow," Betty said, making it sound faintly criminal.

"It was so strange being over there, Mom. It looked the same, and yet it wasn't the same."

Betty broke off a piece of crust with her bent fingers and put it in her mouth. She chewed it thoughtfully.

"What does she want?" she said ominously.

"Why does she have to want something? We were catching up, that's all."

Dan regretted having started the conversation. It had been a relief of sorts to tell his mother where he'd been, and a bit of a bad-boy thrill to needle her with the information, but those effects hadn't been worth the prickly path they were heading down now. He shoveled the last two bites of pie into his mouth and began clearing the table.

"Sorry to eat and run, Mom, but I promised the girls I'd take them to the fireworks tonight, and I have to stop home first."

"Does she know you're separated?"

"I did mention it, yes."

His back was to her as he put things away.

"It's a trap, Danny. She's trying to trap you."

He turned around.

"Don't be ridiculous. She's not like that."

"How do you know? You don't know her."

"I *used* to know her. Very well. That's more than you can say, Mom."

Betty got up slowly, leaning on the table with one hand and wincing with pain as she straightened her knees. Ordinarily, Dan would have stepped in to help her, but he didn't move. She shuffled across the floor to him and laid a gnarled hand on his cheek.

"I know her *kind,* son," she whispered. "And so do you."

She turned and exited the kitchen, heading slowly for her bedroom. Dan waited until she'd closed the bedroom door behind her, and then he left. He didn't take the leftover pie, though he knew she'd want him to.

⸺◦◦◦⸺

IT HAD HAPPENED on a Saturday in June, 1959. Dan was home alone, his siblings scattered on various Saturday pursuits, his mother down the street somewhere visiting neighbors, his father putting in screens for old Mrs. Sproul up at the top of the hill.

Dan's Little League coach had just dropped off his new uniform. As soon as the coach left, Dan put on the uniform and went into his sisters' room to look at himself in the full-length mirror. The shirt, emblazoned with TEANECK in an arc of block letters, and the knickers, with a stripe down the sides, were baggy on his skinny frame, but Dan figured that would just give him room to move. He adjusted the black gaiters over his white socks, tucked his cap down tightly, and practiced a throwing gesture and a catcher's squat. He struck a batter's stance with an imaginary bat and tried out a couple of swings — what he thought a homer should look like, and a bunt. He would have been mortified if Eileen or May had come in and caught him posturing in front of the mirror, but he did wish someone were home to see him in the glory of the bright new uniform. He decided to go to Mrs. Sproul's to show his father.

Dan was halfway to Mrs. Sproul's house when he spotted his mother up on Mrs. Dawson's porch. Betty Gannon had one-year-old Mickey propped on one hip, and she was pounding on the front door with her free hand, which was balled into a fist.

Puzzled, Dan stopped. His mother didn't know Mrs. Dawson, except in a nodding kind of way. They certainly weren't friends, exchanging recipes and watching each other's kids and sitting with cigarettes and beer in one another's yards on hot summer evenings like the other women in the neighborhood did, and Dan had never known his mother to go to Mrs. Dawson's house, except once to deliver Girl Scout cookies when May had the mumps and couldn't make the deliveries herself and the money was due in.

Mrs. Dawson didn't have any kids, which was maybe one reason she wasn't part of Dan's mother's circle. She didn't have a husband, either. He'd been killed in the War, his father had told him. Mrs. Dawson wore high heels and hats, which the other women only wore for church on Sundays, and she took the bus every day to a secretary job in Manhattan.

"Claudine, open up!"

Dan's mother was shouting now, as well as pounding on the door. Mickey began to cry.

"Claudine! I'm not leaving."

Across the street, Mrs. Abrams, drying her hands on a dish towel, came out onto her porch. She descended two steps, as if she meant to go over to Mrs. Dawson's, but when she spotted Dan, she made an imperative motion with her hand, encouraging him to go to his mother. He'd begun to wonder, on his own, if he should, and Mrs. Abrams' urging decided him.

"Mom!" he called as he vaulted up Mrs. Dawson's brick steps to her walkway.

His mother stopped thumping the door and turned around. Mickey had revved up his crying and was furiously kicking his fat legs, but she wasn't doing anything to soothe him. Suddenly, a woman screamed in Mrs. Dawson's back yard. Dan's mother rushed off the porch and around the corner of the house, Dan close on her heels. When they reached the back yard, she stopped so abruptly, Dan collided into her.

"Conor," he heard her say, and it sounded as if someone were choking her. "Conor!"

His father lay sprawled on his back on the flagstone patio. He was bare-chested. His shirt was clutched in one outstretched hand. He had his pants on, but his belt wasn't buckled. He was barefoot. Dan recalled these confusing details of his father's appearance later that night, but right then all he saw was that his father was lying very, very still and that a thin line of blood was running from one corner of his mouth.

"Is he all right?" came an anguished voice above them.

Mrs. Dawson was leaning out a second story window. A small roof extended out from the window, sloping steeply downward. Dan looked away quickly. The woman was wearing only a slip. Even in that one instant, and even in the midst of panic, Dan had noticed large, dark nipples pressing against the sheer, silky fabric as she strained forward.

"You've killed him!" Betty Gannon shouted up at the woman in the window. Then she knelt by her husband and touched his shoulder with the tip of one finger, as if she feared his skin might burn her. She let go of Mickey, who crawled to a patch of grass and sat there whimpering.

"I'll call an ambulance," Mrs. Dawson said, withdrawing from the window.

Mrs. Abrams appeared and picked up Mickey. Her five-year-old, David, was with her. She tugged gently on Dan's arm.

"Come on," she said, "we'd better go to your house."

"Mom?" Dan said fearfully.

She looked up at him, but it was a blank look, as if she didn't know who he was or where she was or why they were there. That blankness in his mother's face was almost as frightening as his father's immobility. She didn't say anything, and after a moment, she turned again to his father. This time she flattened her hand firmly against his broad, bare chest.

"Come on," Mrs. Abrams repeated, and Dan obeyed. "It'll be all right," she told him as they were walking away.

But despite being nauseated by fear and desperate for hope, Dan knew it wasn't going to be all right.

They heard the ambulance siren just as they reached Dan's house. His siblings were home, and they came tumbling outside to see what was going on. Mrs. Abrams explained that their father had fallen off Mrs. Dawson's roof and that he was being taken to the hospital. Little Gloria started to cry, and May and Brian looked like they were on the verge, so Eileen sternly ordered them to get their rosaries and go into their parents' room to pray. Mrs. Abrams stayed until their mother came home two hours later, and she sat with the family while Betty told her children that their father was dead of a broken neck.

"He landed wrong," she said.

She said that again and again in the next few days, to neighbors and relatives, to the funeral home man and the priest. She said it to Eileen and Dan the night after the funeral, but with a new elaboration.

"He stepped out of line," she said, "and he landed wrong. You start out wrong, you end up wrong."

"You mean his feet weren't steady on the roof?" Eileen asked.

"Wasn't nothing steady about him."

Dan thought his mother was mistaken. He remembered steadiness as one of his father's main characteristics. A steady worker, a steady church-goer, a steady householder, always keeping the grass cut and the pipes repaired and the oil changed in the car, and a steady bowler in the men's league at Feibel's, a reliable if not a spectacular scorer. You could call him a steady neighbor, too, like how he did chores for old Mrs. Sproul and didn't charge her anything, and how he helped Mrs. Kelly carry her crippled son up the stairs in his wheelchair when her husband wasn't around to do it.

"It was just an accident," Eileen said, her voice quavering. "It wasn't his fault. It was a just a horrible accident."

Betty rolled her head as if to get a kink out of her neck. She didn't answer her daughter. Eileen got up from the kitchen table, where the three of them had been having tea and cinnamon toast.

"I'm going to bed," she said.

A minute after she'd gone, Dan got up. He still had half a piece of toast left, but he didn't want to stay in his mother's company any longer. There was something in her mood that made him wary.

"Give my shoulders a squeeze before you go, Danny. They're awful tight."

He stood behind her chair and worked rhythmically at loosening the tense muscles of her shoulders and neck, as he'd done many times before.

"Mom," he said carefully, "why did you say Mrs. Dawson killed Da?"

"Did I say that?" she answered just as carefully.

It was the first either of them had spoken of the terrible and strange scene at Mrs. Dawson's house. Dan had been trying hard to forget the alarming sight of his half-clothed father on the ground and the blood at his mouth, an image that had been asserting itself every night when he closed his eyes to sleep. He'd taken to singing as a way to push away the feelings of grief and dread the image evoked. Just about anything worked — Take Me Out to the Ball Game, I've Been Workin' on the Railroad, The Ants Go Marching — as long as he sang aloud, though he had to sing softly so as not to wake his brothers. When his feelings overcame him in the daytime, he found that it helped to run until he developed a stitch in his side. He didn't know what he'd do when he was back in school. Maybe, by then, his father being dead wouldn't hurt as much.

"You said it right after...right after we found him. You said it to her."

Betty sat up straighter, and Dan stopped his massage, but she didn't turn around to face him, and he stayed where he was behind her.

"Maybe I said it because it was true, Danny."

"You mean she pushed him?"

It was the only conclusion he'd been able to reach when he'd tried on his own to make out what his mother might have meant, but it didn't feel believable.

"I mean she *pulled* him. She pulled him in, and he went with a smile on his face and a spring in his step, not caring a thing about any of us here at home waitin' for him. Only caring that he didn't get caught."

"He did too care, Mom. He *did*. Everybody said so. The priest and everybody."

"People always say nice things at funerals, Dan."

"He loved us, Mom. I know he did."

Finally, she turned around. She took one of his hands in hers.

"He loved you children, I won't take that away from him. And he probably thought he loved me, too. Well enough, anyway. But there was a wildness in him all the same, and in the end, he let it rule him."

"It was only an accident, like Eileen said," Dan insisted.

His mother let go of his hand.

"It was an accident, Danny. But it wasn't only an accident."

He had to sing all three songs twice that night before he could relax enough to go to sleep.

7

STANDING ON THE sidewalk watching Dan's car depart, Janine heard a burst of raucous, male laughter from the backyard. A result, no doubt, of her uncle Bud telling one of his corny, slightly off-color jokes, the kind that aroused in the wives no more significant protest than a shake of the head or a cluck of the tongue. But coming when it did, just as Dan's car was disappearing around the corner, it felt personal to Janine, a gathering into one loud, derisive explosion all the disregard and condemnation that had surrounded her pregnancy with Hunt and all the silent lies, doubts, and pretense that had surrounded its memory in the years since.

Unlike the parents of some of the other girls in the maternity home, Janine's parents hadn't thrown her out or castigated her in any way. The mother of one of her roommates had chased the girl through the house with a carving knife when she learned of her daughter's pregnancy. Another roommate's father had called her a slut and slammed her against a wall. When Janine told her parents she was pregnant, in the kitchen on a muggy August night, her mother had gasped, clutched the front of her blouse, and immediately started crying. Dazed, her father had sat down shakily, looking as if he, too, might begin to cry, something Janine had never seen him do.

"We'll get through this," her mother had said, grabbing a dish towel and wiping her face. "We'll find a way through."

Al had nodded agreement. Janine held his gaze for a few agonized seconds, until he lowered his head and stared at the floor. She heard him make a strange, gulping sound, more like an injured animal than a man. It was, for Janine, the deepest moment of shame in the whole experience, even though, later, the social workers at the Home and the medical personnel at the hospital all drummed shame into her with deft and varied weapons.

"You have nothing to give a child."

"You should be grateful that decent, loving people want the baby."

"Your mistake is causing problems for a lot of people. Do the right thing now."

"It would be selfish of you to keep the baby and cheat it of a good life."

It was always "the" baby. No one ever said "your" baby. Janine wasn't able to have even that small recognition of motherhood. And no one ever asked her what *she* wanted. No one ever tried to help her figure out ways she might keep her baby. She was led to believe that giving him up was the only option.

Another burst of laughter from the barbecue guests reached Janine. She turned away from the empty street, but she couldn't bring herself to rejoin the jocular crowd in the backyard. Instead, she sat down on the porch steps. As she folded her skirt under her, she remembered sitting on these steps with Dan on the night before she told her parents she was pregnant.

It had been hot and sticky. Not a breeze stirred. She was wearing a large shirt long enough to cover the unbuttoned waistband of her Bermuda shorts. Her hair was pushed back from her sweaty forehead by a madras headband. She and Dan were making plans. In hindsight, it was almost laughable how naive they'd been, both in the course they were laying out for themselves and in their belief that they'd get to decide what was going to happen.

"After Labor Day," Dan was saying, "I'll get a real job."

"Lifeguard is a real job. Driving the Good Humor truck, too."

"Not in the winter, goose."

"I'll get a job, too."

"No."

"They're gonna kick me out of school anyway, so I may as well make some money."

"It's not right. I'll take care of you. Besides, did you ever see any-body pregnant working in a store or an office or anywhere?"

She hadn't.

"I was thinking of the post office," Dan went on. "That'd be a good steady thing. But I might have to take a test."

"Oh, you'll pass," Janine said loyally. "You'll probably do so good, you'll get a promotion right off the bat."

He put his arm around her and pulled her against him.

"I love you, you know that?" he said.

"I guess I do," she teased.

"You guess?"

"I love you, too."

"You'd better, Mrs. Goose."

He lifted her hand to his mouth and kissed her palm. Pleasure rip-pled through her.

"You know that makes me feel hot," she said.

He grinned and kissed her palm again, this time flicking his tongue between her fingers.

It was such a reliable, engulfing thing, her appetite for him. She trusted it, the rightness and inevitability of it, and she trusted him because she knew he was as captive to it as she. Sex wasn't the source of their unedited expo-sure of their inner selves to each other, but it was the underpinning. They were afraid about the pregnancy and afraid of telling their parents, but they weren't afraid of being on their own together. It was the future they had both expected, just sooner. They were already partners, a unit distinct from everyone else. Inseparable and invincible, they would have said that night on the steps, if they'd thought they needed to find words for it.

"I bought two African violets today," she said, slipping her hand out of his. "For our windowsill..."

They hoped to live in the small apartment above the Gannons' garage. The most recent tenant had vacated two weeks ago, but Mrs. Gannon hadn't advertised the place because she wanted Dan to re-paint it first and put new linoleum in the bathroom. Janine had made a deposit on a double bed at a thrift store. They'd have to borrow from her father to buy a mattress. She imagined them lying cozily together each night talking over the past day, previewing the next day. She imagined them making love. They'd never made love in a bed before.

"Did you ask your mom yet?" she said.

"I was waiting until you told your folks."

"Why?"

He shrugged.

"It just seems like the right order."

But Mrs. Gannon never did agree to letting them have the apartment. And it wasn't because Dan had asked at the wrong time or in the wrong way. To Betty Gannon, it was Janine who was wrong. Janine, and the bastard baby, and the whole crazy, unsupportable notion of marriage. The Pettorinis would have to deal with their daughter in some way that didn't include her son. They hadn't raised Janine to be respectable, and now they'd have to reap the whirlwind. Dan was supposed to go to college that fall. He had a promising future. Time for a wife and babies later, when he could afford it. A suitable wife, too, not a low-class girl who slept around. Mrs. Gannon would contribute to the doctor bills, though Lord knew she could ill afford it. She recognized her duty. But let her son squander his life because Janine Pettorini couldn't keep her legs together? Not by a long shot.

It turned out that the Pettorinis agreed with Mrs. Gannon — not her opinion of Janine, of course, but her reaction to the young people's wish to marry. As a minor, Janine needed her parents' permission, and they steadfastly refused. It was not a good start for a marriage, Rose insisted. It wouldn't last. It couldn't last. And then where would Janine be? No decent man would ever be interested in her with a fatherless child in tow. And what kind of way was that for a child to grow up? Always looked down upon and whispered about, called names on the playground. And Janine would suffer the same ostracizing. She'd never live it down. Nor would the family. Besides, she was too young to be a mother. She was pregnant, but she wasn't a mother.

The Pettorinis and Mrs. Gannon didn't like each other. In defending her own child, each mother denigrated the other child. But they were united in their opposition to marriage, and they cooperated in keeping Dan and Janine apart. Phone calls were prevented or cut short. Dan no longer had use of his mother's car.

Circumstances, too, conspired to make meetings more difficult. Janine stopped going out with girlfriends. She dropped out of school. In one last, desperate attempt to buck the parents, Dan had refused to leave for college, but faced with fewer and fewer contacts with Janine and more and more decisions being made without his input, he started second semester, leaving town right after Christmas.

These steps were our last real meeting place, Janine thought, standing up, the last pure occupation of our private world before all the outsiders came crashing in. And we didn't know it.

She couldn't remember how they'd parted that night. In the usual way, she supposed, with kisses and lingering hand-holding, entranced with longing. Dan probably wished her luck with her parents. He probably told her to call him right afterwards. They hadn't known on that hot, firefly-speckled night that they'd never again manage a solid grip on hope.

Still reluctant to face the barbecue crowd, Janine went in the front door and headed to her old bedroom, which was now Rose's sewing room. As she started along the upstairs hall, she heard Lee's voice behind her on the stairs.

"Oh, you're all right," she was saying over the whimpers of a child. "Mrs. Pettorini says there's band-aids in the bathroom. Maybe Superman band-aids, she said."

Janine swung around to find Lee ascending the stairs carrying her youngest son, Max, who had a scraped, bloody elbow.

"Janine," she said, surprised. "I thought you and Dan went for a walk. That's what I told your mother. She was looking for you."

"I walked him to his car," Janine said, trying to tamp down the fury bubbling up in her.

"He left?"

"Yes."

"Did you get to—?"

"No."

"I don't want any stingy stuff, Mommy," Max spoke up. "Just the band-aid."

"We have to wash the scrape first. You know that," Lee replied, looking up and down the hallway.

Janine pointed to the left. Lee carried Max to the bathroom. Janine heard the sound of running water and a squeal of protest from the child. In a few moments, he emerged with two flesh-colored band-aids on his clean elbow. He ran down the hall, shooting a glance at Janine as he passed.

"No Supermans," he informed her. "Only Donald Duck." For which he was, apparently, too sophisticated. He scampered down the stairs.

"What happened with Dan?" Lee said in a conspiratorial voice, coming up to Janine.

"You happened."

"Huh?"

"Red told Dan about Hunt before I had a chance to say anything. He was pretty steamed about finding out like that."

"Oh, no."

"You just had to let Red in on the juicy gossip, didn't you? Couldn't you at least have warned him to keep his big mouth shut?"

"Hey, hold on!"

"Do you have any idea how *hard* it was to finally talk about this?"

"No, I don't," Lee answered testily. "But if there were *rules* about it, you should have said so. I'm sorry Red blabbed — that was a huge, stupid mistake — but that's all it was, a mistake."

"Yeah, well, I guess my stupid mistake was confiding in you in the first place."

"If you feel like that, I guess it was."

Lee made an abrupt about-face and took the stairs at a rapid pace. At the bottom she stood a moment with her hand on the bannister.

"Listen," she said penitently, "you have every right to be mad. I get that. But I honestly didn't think it would be a problem to tell Red. Or anyone, really. Except Dan, of course — you can bet Red's gonna hear about that. But I thought that you were done with secrets. Sick and tired and done. And I thought you were brave, too, to let it all out. Really brave."

Janine made no reply, though it was obvious from Lee's face that she was hoping for absolution. Crestfallen, Lee left.

Janine went to the sewing room. She peered out the window at the back yard below. She saw Lee beckoning to her children. She saw Lulu close her book and get up. With their children bobbling around them, Lee and Red spoke to Rose, presumably thanking her and saying good-bye. The rest of the guests were scattered around the yard eating, drinking, talking. The desserts hadn't been touched yet. The party would go on for a while. Janine scanned the yard until she located Tim and Larry swinging together in the hammock. Then she walked away from the window and lay down on the roll-away cot that had been brought in for her stay.

She stared at the ceiling. The same hairline crack meandered across it that had been there when she was a kid. How many different things that crack had been to Janine over the years. The yellow brick road of Oz, a fragment of map from Treasure Island, Moon River. She remembered lying on her bed in the early weeks of pregnancy, transparent with nausea, her breasts softly aching, resting her hands on her still flat belly and imagining the trusty crack to be the path of her life. Where on the line am I? she had wondered. There, where it made a sharp veer to the right? Or there, where it was intersected by another crack that petered out to nothing after a couple of inches? Now, stretched out on the hard cot, Janine considered the crack as the trail Hunt had followed to find her. She figured it hadn't been a straight, easy route. And he was still on it. They both were. But were they moving towards each other or apart?

Sighing, she rolled on to her side. Her anger with Lee clung like a leech, yet it was the weakest of her emotions. Her feelings about Dan were more intense and more tangled. She did regret the shock she'd unwittingly exposed him to, but she also resented his insistence on his own hurt. *I am suffering*, she should have shouted. Not in a bid for mercy or forgiveness or even understanding, but as a declaration of self. A declaration, at last, of a throbbing, unvarying part of herself that she'd hidden from the world for 18 years. She'd told Clark her secret, and hints of the continuing pain of it had emerged in her paintings, almost against her will, but otherwise, it had remained submerged. Even her closest friends had no idea.

I gave away my baby. What admission could be more horrible than that? Once that was out in the light, to one person or to multitudes, what had Janine to fear? People would take her or leave her. As she was. As she truly was. Lee was right. She was sick and tired and done with secrecy. If she was going to march into offices and demand information, if she was going to poke into old wounds — hers, Dan's, her parents' — if she was, ultimately, going to face Hunt, she had to get over keeping secrets. She had to learn to live with open truths. And so would everyone around her. Very tentatively, like the first split of a seed casing, Janine felt the push of a tendril of faith that people, indeed, could do that, that *she* could do that.

She yearned for Clark, for his warm shoulder and his capacity to listen. She'd never taken advantage of that capacity with regard to her secret, beyond the initial, basic telling of it. She hadn't revealed the details she'd just spit out at Dan in the street. Clark hadn't known, either, about her annual ritual, on Hunt's birthday, of a cupcake buried in the garden and a silent prayer that he was well and well-cared for. He hadn't known about the times, in parks or while passing school-yards, when she'd wonder if she and her son might walk by each other unawares. He didn't know about the nights during her pregnancy with the twins when she'd lain awake worrying that she would be afraid to love them.

Janine had gone through all that alone. Since Clark's death, she'd gone through lots of other things alone. The ratcheting up of her framing business. Her recent application to show her paintings in a New York gallery. Being a single parent at events designed for two parents. Ordinary tasks, too, that used to be Clark's and that the boys were still too young to take on: dragging the full trash cans to the curb on Wednesdays, mowing the lawn, putting up the window screens in spring and taking them out in fall.

And all those years ago, she'd done other things alone. She'd carried a baby to term. She'd given birth. She hadn't made a fuss when they took her baby away. She hadn't contradicted everyone's assurances that she'd be able to move on with her life as if nothing had happened. Now, alone, she'd find Hunt. Or do her damnedest trying. She would have liked Dan's help with strategies and footwork and morale, but it wasn't crucial.

Janine knew about aloneness. She'd learned the hard way, as a pregnant teen, as a secret-keeper, as a widow. She'd taken steps beyond all three of those roles, and she meant to keep on striding. She might have to *act* alone, but she wasn't going to *be* alone with her history any longer.

8

"I'VE NEVER HAD a request like that before," said the reference librarian, a broad-shouldered woman who looked as if she ought to be driving a truck or working in a field.

Suddenly, Janine felt like a trespasser. The bright idea she'd awoken with — to begin her search for Hunt at the town library — didn't seem so bright after all. Old messages were kicking in.

"There are wonderful, deserving people waiting for the baby. You're carrying it for them."

"The baby will be better off without you."

"You're going to meet someone and get married. You'll have other babies. You won't even remember this one."

The town library was unlikely to yield anything other than general information, so Janine was tempted to cancel her inquiry and leave.

"I'm trying to locate someone," she'd said when she came in, "and I don't know what references might be appropriate. It's...he's my son. I gave him up for adoption 18 years ago. All I know is when and where he was born, and his first name."

And the librarian had said, "I've never had a request like that before." And nothing else.

Resisting the urge to walk away and looking directly into the librarian's eyes, Janine straightened her spine, a confidence-building trick her father had taught her as a young girl. Faced with this attitude of intransigent expectation, the woman uttered a sound halfway between a sigh and a throat-clearing. It seemed, to Janine, the equivalent of rolling up one's sleeves for a dirty task.

"Are you in a rush? Is there a deadline of some kind?"

"No."

"If you come back tomorrow or the day after, I'll try to have some resources for you to consult. Although, without a full name, most public records will be useless to you."

"There isn't any way to get started today?" Janine said. "I've got to be here for an hour anyway. My boys are at the puppet show in the Children's Room."

"Well..." the librarian said, "I suppose I could look up the statutes on adoption records. To see if what you want is allowed."

"Thank you, I'd appreciate that."

"They're on microfiche. I'll have to go to the basement to get them."

The librarian stood up and came out from behind her desk.

"Is there anything I can do in the meantime?" Janine asked.

She thought she detected a flicker of pity in the woman's eyes. Or perhaps librarians had a code, like the Hippocratic oath of doctors, and it had finally been activated.

"Why don't you take a seat in the Reference Room and write down everything you can remember? It's surprising what the mind hides from itself sometimes. You may have clues you don't know you have."

Janine went to the Reference Room, sat down at a table, and took a pen and her sketchbook out of her shoulder bag. She looked around the room with a wave of nostalgia. She'd spent many hours writing school reports in that room, encyclopedia volumes stacked in front of her, sunlight pouring in the tall arched mullioned windows on the rear wall, or rain or melting snow running down their panes.

Turning to her task, she printed HUNT in block letters at the top of a blank page, followed by his birth date and the name of the hospital. She didn't know the doctor's name. The girls at the Home were followed by a number of physicians and were attended at delivery by whomever was at hand. Next, she wrote her name and birth date, and Dan's. She wrote Shadyside Home, Trenton. Then she hesitated.

Should she record everything she remembered about the place? The physical lay-out, the other girls, the staff, the routines of chores and school work, the rare outings, the medical check-ups? She knew if she got started recalling even the most mundane details, the floodgates of memory would open. Personalities would come back to her. Incidents. Things she might not be glad to resurrect.

Just jotting down Trenton Memorial Medical Center had reminded her of how someone from the night shift at the maternity home had driven her to the hospital when she was in labor and dropped her off at the emergency entrance, instructing her to tell whomever she met inside that she was from Shadyside and that they'd know where to send her. She remembered, too, the hours and hours alone, except for nurses coming in to check her pulse and blood pressure and interns to conduct painful internal exams, no one explaining anything. One nurse had scolded her for making too much noise. How would raking up such harsh scraps provide clues to finding Hunt? Finally, she decided to write about the first week of his life. Maybe there'd be something there.

The policy at Shadyside had been that if a girl didn't want to see her baby, she didn't have to. All the mothers were heavily sedated for the birth itself, and babies were kept in a nursery on a different floor of the hospital, so a girl could easily avoid meeting her child. Some of them never even knew if they'd had a boy or a girl. But if a mother did want to see her baby, the procedure was that after their three days in the hospital, she and the baby would return to the maternity home and spend five more days together. They were housed in a separate area of the Home, with its own outside entrance and locked doors between it and the main part of the building. The pregnant residents were never to be exposed to babies, nor to their friends' stories about labor and birth.

Most of the staff advised girls against seeing their babies even once. A few, including Janine's social worker, were neutral. Rose hadn't wanted her to do it.

"The baby's not going to be yours," she said. "It'll be too hard on you."

It was the one thing Janine had insisted on. All through her pregnancy, she'd talked to her baby. She'd told him she loved him and that his father had loved her. She told him he was going to have a good life. Everyone kept promising her that. She wanted to see this little companion in the flesh. She wanted to count the fingers and toes, like they said new moms always did. She wanted to look for Dan or herself in the little face. She wanted to play his mother for eight days. She wanted to say good-bye in person.

The social worker came to the hospital with papers for Janine to sign on the day after the birth. But by then, Janine had held the baby and given him a bottle. She'd begun to realize what a huge thing giving him up was going to be.

"You know it's the right decision," the woman told her. "The baby will have a loving, stable family who can give him everything."

"I know. But can't I sign later?"

The woman looked irritated.

"Every day you delay costs your parents money, you know. We have a family waiting for him. You're making them anxious."

Let them be anxious, Janine thought. I'm supposed to worry about them? And I'll pay my parents back.

"You made the right decision," the social worker repeated. "For everyone."

"I'm going to sign. I am. But not today."

The social worker had made a big show of putting the papers back in her leather case and getting up and pushing her chair aside and putting on her coat, as if it was all such a lot of hard, unappreciated work.

The baby was perfect. He not only had all his digits, he also had beautiful brown eyes, a shock of silky, black hair, and, Janine was convinced, Dan's thick eyebrows. She named him Daniel. She could be entertained for hours just watching him sleep, but she liked it when he cried, too, because then she got to soothe him.

She couldn't believe how much she loved him. Love poured out of her like something tangible, blanketing the baby, linking her to him.

He still seemed part of her body, his physical need for her was so total. He fractured her sleep; he demanded to be fed, cleaned, carried, and caressed. It occurred to her that all mothers, not just kangaroos, should be equipped with pouches. But then, she'd thought, she'd miss the intoxicating smell of his ponderous, round head dozing on her shoulder.

There was a middle-aged woman who worked in the section of Shadyside where the new mothers and their babies stayed. She carried in the girls' meals, brought their infants to them, stocked the supply cabinet, changed the linens, things like that. She was friendly to all the girls, complimented them on their beautiful babies, always wished them a cheerful good morning and a warm good night. The staff called her Hildegard, but she told the girls to call her Hildy.

When Hildy brought Janine her breakfast tray on her second day in the nursery wing with Daniel, Janine asked her to unlock the little telephone room.

"Who is it you want to call?" Hildy said. Telephone use was highly restricted at Shadyside.

"My social worker."

"She'll be by tomorrow or the next day, won't she?"

"I have to talk to her today, Hildy."

Hildy put down the tray. Janine opened the little box of Frosted Flakes and the half-pint carton of milk. Hildy never left a girl until she saw that she'd begun to eat.

"You see, Hildy," Janine said, trying to sound much more together than she felt, "she needs to come get Daniel today."

"Haven't you got three more days with him?"

"Technically," Janine said, keeping up her pose. "But I've had five days already, and I've decided I'm ready to go home now."

Hildy shook her head. It wasn't a critical, condescending shake like the social worker's when Janine had postponed signing the papers. It was a shake full of concern and compassion.

"I think that's a bad idea."

Janine was too surprised to be offended.

"Why?"

"You're gonna want these days later on. You're gonna be glad you had 'em, tears and all."

"You really think so, Hildy?"

"You asked for this time, didn't you? You weren't one of those girls afraid to see their baby, or too beat down to ask for it. You asked for it, and you should have it. *All* of it."

Because it was the first advice Janine had gotten that included *her* needs, and because she trusted Hildy's warmth and sincerity, Janine didn't go home early. She took all her days with Daniel. And when the morning came that she handed him to the social worker and watched her carry him down the hall, the tail of his blue receiving blanket flapping at the woman's waist, Janine knew it wouldn't have been any easier if she'd done it a few days early. Hildy was there to hold her while she cried. Hildy helped her pack her few things into a shopping bag. She was dry-eyed when she walked out to the car where Rose and Al were waiting for her. She'd had her days.

All these years later, she still had those days. It was one of the things she'd tell her boy about when she found him. His name was in print somewhere. *He* was somewhere. He'd always been somewhere. Which is why, despite all the assurances she'd been given to the contrary, Janine had never been able to forget him.

9

A HALF-HOUR LATER, the librarian came into the Reference Room carrying three books and a couple of sheets of paper. She led Janine to her desk out in the main room, where they could talk without disturbing other patrons.

"I thought you might want to check these out," the librarian said, patting the small stack of books.

Janine picked them up and read their titles. Two were personal accounts by adoptees of their lives, and the third was a scholarly work on the history of adoption and contemporary issues in adoption. Scanning the flap copy on the adoptee stories, Janine saw that one of them had searched for and reunited with her birthmother.

"Birthmother," Janine said.

She'd spoken under her breath, to herself, but the librarian, whose ears were attuned to low voices, heard her.

"That's the proper term, it seems," she said. "One word, like grand-mother. Adoptive parents don't like the terms 'natural' mother or 'real' mother because the implication is that they're not 'real' parents, and the mothers who've given up their children don't like 'biological' mother because it implies they're no more than mechanical baby producers. Interesting, isn't it?"

"Yes," Janine said, though she was agreeing only to forestall further discussion.

She could understand how the librarian, having, probably, a mind pre-disposed to delight in the discovery of facts, would find the battle of ter-minology interesting. Janine couldn't consider it as coolly. She hadn't ever consciously put a name to herself. Thinking about it now, she supposed that if someone asked her, she'd say she'd been an unwed mother. But "birthmother" possessed so much more gravity. It had a ring of dignity.

"I didn't read the full statute, of course," the librarian was saying, looking at a photocopied paper. "But for your purposes, I think the relevant section is this one about records."

She handed Janine the paper.

"People who are adopted have two birth certificates," she went on. "The original, on which the birthmother's name and sometimes the birthfather's name appear, and an amended one, on which the adoptive parents' names appear instead. But the records are sealed. You have a right to a copy of the original certificate only, which wouldn't tell you anything you don't already know, and your son would have access only to his amended certificate. Other documents, such as the petition to adopt and the final order of adoption are also sealed."

"In other words, they don't want us to find each other."

"In essence, yes," the librarian replied in a faint I-told-you-so tone. "You can petition the court to open the files, but in the quick search I did, it seems that rarely succeeds. Even if the court says yes, it's never for full access, only non-identifying information."

The librarian looked past Janine as a group of children noisily entered the main room from the Children's Room. She put her finger to her lips and loudly shushed them.

"I guess the puppet show is over," Janine said.

"It looks to be. We like to foster library use early, but it does make for a bit of chaos now and again."

"Well, my boys will be waiting for me. Thank you for all your help, Ms....?"

"*Miss* Standish."

"Thank you, Miss Standish."

"Another item before you go," the librarian said, holding out a piece of paper with a handwritten address on it. "There's a support group that might interest you: CUB, Concerned United Birthparents."

"Oh, I don't think a support group is really—"

"This is the address of their national headquarters. They can tell you the nearest branch."

Janine accepted the paper, folded it in fourths, and slid it into the back pocket of her jeans, but she had no intention of looking into the organization. A month after Clark's death, she'd enrolled the boys in a 12-week support group for children who'd had a parent die, but she'd declined attending a widows' group. She wasn't a group person.

"CUB has tackled another interesting terminology question," Miss Standish said informatively. "Surrender."

"Surrender?"

"The CUB founders decided that instead of saying they gave up their babies or placed them, they'd say they surrendered them. They felt that surrender fit their experience, that they'd been in a battle and lost."

The librarian lifted her eyebrows. Janine couldn't tell if she was expressing her undiminished disapproval of parents searching for their relinquished children, or her professional appreciation of facts, any facts.

Surrender. The term fit Janine's memory of the experience, too. But she didn't make a reply. She sensed that Miss Standish wasn't interested in her personal testament.

—⁂—

Janine stopped at Rocklin's stationery store on the way home, and while the boys browsed the Pez dispensers, she evaluated notebooks for use as a search journal. She settled on a 3-ring binder, then dallied over the size. She wanted something small enough to be portable but capacious enough that she wouldn't end up having to get another one later on. She decided on a standard one-and-a-half-inch size, such as a student might use. The fat, three-inch-wide binders were too daunting. She couldn't imagine digging up enough information to fill a large binder, and to look at it half-full would be disheartening.

"We're ready, Mom," Tim said. "I picked Mickey Mouse. And I want lemon Pez."

"I want cherry," Larry said. "And I got a jack-o-lantern and a rooster."

"Only one, Larry," Janine said, walking to the cashier's counter.

"But I can't pick."

"Want me to pick?" Tim offered eagerly.

"No."

"Only one, Larry," Tim warned.

Janine smiled in amusement. Tim's disinterested tone had exactly reproduced the one she'd used. But, of course, in reality, he wasn't disinterested at all. Janine knew that Larry's small dilemma was of absorbing interest to his brother, one, because he enjoyed seeing the usually cocksure Larry squirm a little, and two, because the outcome intrigued him in and of itself, like waiting to see which movie had won Best Picture.

"The pumpkin!" Larry decided.

"But it's not Halloween," Tim protested.

"That's why," Larry replied, with a grin that implied he knew something Tim didn't.

Janine saw that the subtlety wasn't lost on Tim, who placed his Pez dispenser and candy on the counter with a frown. Once again, Larry had come up smelling of roses. Janine wondered if Hunt were in any way like either of the twins, impulsive and resilient like Larry, faithful and dogged like Tim. How much did genes influence personality and preferences? Larry and Tim had in common a curiosity about the world and a propensity to forgive each other easily. Was Hunt like that, too? He'd certainly shown curiosity in seeking her out. If he found her, would he forgive her?

"This one's on sale," the clerk said, picking up Larry's dispenser. "On account it's not Halloween."

Now it was Tim's turn to sport a knowing grin, but Janine could see he wasn't very confident about it. She said a silent thank you in her head

88

when Larry didn't make any comment, and in the next moment, the boys were busy loading their dispensers, all displays of one-upmanship having evaporated like water on a hot griddle.

When they got home, Rose was weeding the vegetable garden and Al was off playing golf. The boys showed their grandmother the new candy dispensers, then went into the house to watch their one allotted hour of cartoons.

Janine got a hole punch from the kitchen junk drawer and took her binder and papers and books to her room. She inserted five tab dividers into the binder, but she was able to think of only three labels: Resources, Questions, Memories. She punched holes in the margin of the photocopy of the adoption statute and put it in the Resources section. She used Rose's fabric scissors to cut down the drawing paper on which she'd written the account of her few days with Daniel, first looking out the window to make sure her mother was still in the garden. Rose didn't like her fabric scissors used on paper. Then Janine punched holes along the edge of the paper and put it into the Memories section. She wrote down the titles and authors and Dewey decimal numbers of the three books she'd checked out and added that list to Resources. She loaded the binder with lined and unlined paper. Then she hitched her hands in her back pockets and regarded the binder as if it were a painting-in-progress she were studying to determine what was needed next.

Pessimism was creeping in. How was she ever going to accomplish this? Despite Miss Standish's begrudged jump start, Janine didn't know where to begin. Or, rather, the beginnings available to her seemed doomed to futility: writing up more memories, sending away for Daniel's original birth certificate, hounding the lawyer. All they promised were dead ends and heartache. There was Shadyside, but she didn't really expect anyone there to be helpful, either because they wouldn't want to or because they wouldn't know anything. If she could only get her hands on one thread, one solid lead. And if she could catch a lucky break. Luck, she felt, was going to play a big part. It had been pure chance that Wilson made his final call to the Pettorini house during her stay there and that she'd been the one to answer the phone.

She picked up the book by the adoptee who'd reunited with her birthmother and read the flap more closely than she had at the library. Her heart sank when she saw that the author had searched for her mother for ten years before finding her. Ten years! Did she have that kind of stamina? That kind of drive? Why, really, was she doing this at all? If Hunt hadn't come looking for her, would she be on this quest now? Maybe, she thought suddenly, that's where I ought to begin: with my own motivations and expectations.

She put her mother's sewing machine on the floor, sat down at the little table, and opened the binder to one of the unlabeled sections. WHY, she wrote at the top of a lined page. She turned to the next page and wrote POSSIBLE OUTCOMES. Then she flipped back to the WHY page. She knew from conversations with Clark about his creative writing classes that brainstorming could be a fruitful technique for plotting, or for fleshing out vague ideas or inventing characters. She'd adapt it to her situation. As Clark used to have his students do, Janine would list as many things as she could think of in each of her categories, trying not to censor herself and not stopping to critique her jottings. Write until you're dry, Clark used to instruct his students. And then write one more thing.

The first thing Janine wrote under WHY was *Because Hunt came looking for me.*

Because he didn't answer Wilson's phone messages.

Because I want to know he's all right.

I've always wanted to know if he was all right.

Deep down, I always hoped we'd meet again.

She was scribbling rapidly now, barely aware she'd dropped the becauses. She'd begun, quietly, to cry.

"One more thing," she said, wiping her eyes.

Because I want him to know he came from love. I want him to know he was wanted. It wasn't for lack of love, it was for lack of everything else.

She turned to the POSSIBLE OUTCOMES page and oriented her mind to the new topic.

I won't find him was her first entry.

I'll find him and I won't like him.

He won't like me.

He'll hate me.

We'll become friends, and he'll be a big brother to Tim and Larry.

He'll want to meet Dan, and Dan will say no.

Dan will say yes.

Hunt and I will meet only once and then he'll disappear again.

Hunt will tell me he has good parents and a good life.

He'll tell me he's had an unhappy life.

Sighing, Janine looked up from the list and out the open window. From her seated position, all she could see were deep green treetops. She turned back to the paper. One more. Her heart pounding, she wrote, *I will find him but he'll be dead.*

"What are you so busy at?"

Rose's voice from the doorway made Janine jump. She closed the binder and stood up.

"I called you from downstairs but you didn't answer, so I came up to see if you'd fallen asleep. The boys want to go to the wading pool at the park. That okay?"

"Not by themselves."

"It's half a block, Janine, and they've got recreation aides to supervise. You used to be down there every day on your own."

"As young as Tim and Larry?"

Rose shrugged.

Janine tossed the binder on the cot and bent to retrieve the sewing machine.

"You can leave that on the floor if you need the table," Rose said, glancing curiously at the binder. "And I can take the boys to the park if you're busy."

"That's all right. I'm done for now."

"Writing letters?"

"No."

"Sketching?"

"No."

Rose shrugged again.

"Sorry, Ma. I don't mean to be mysterious."

"And I don't need to know all your business."

"In a way, this 'business' concerns you, too." Janine paused. "I've started my search for Hunt."

If Rose was surprised, she didn't show it.

"But you don't even know his last name."

"Yes, well, that's a problem."

"And he may not want to be found."

"*He* came looking for *me*, Ma."

"*And* he thought better of it and stayed away. You have no right, Janine, to barge into that boy's life. Into his parents' lives. To stir up the past."

"No right? How can you say that?"

Though Janine had thought the same thing herself in the library, hearing it from someone else — hearing it from her own mother — was infuriating.

"It's all over and done with, Janine. You forgot it once, and you can forget it again."

"No, Ma, I *didn't* forget. Did you?"

Rose glared angrily at her, but Janine saw that there was something else mixed in with the anger, something that diluted it, something that muddled it.

"I put it out of my mind. I had to."

"Why? So our cousins and neighbors wouldn't look down their noses at you? So they wouldn't be able to point and gossip? *There goes Rose Pettorini whose daughter got herself in trouble. Rose's only child, too, what a shame. We all thought they were such a nice family — it goes to show that appearances can be deceiving.*"

Janine was horrified at her own cruelty, not only in what she was saying but in how she was saying it, in a disrespectful, mocking tone.

She noticed a tiny tic at one corner of Rose's mouth, but besides that, her mother hadn't flinched.

"Appearances are important," Rose said quietly and firmly. "And it was *your* reputation that we cared about most."

Janine felt stymied. Her mother was not retreating an inch.

"It was the only way," Rose said.

"Was it, Ma? And you have no regrets?"

"There's things it's better not to talk about, Janine."

Janine sat down heavily on the cot.

"So, what should I tell the boys?" Rose said.

"Tell the boys?"

For one unglued instant, Janine thought her mother was asking how much they were to be told about Hunt.

"The park," Rose said flatly, either unaware of the possible double meaning of her question or, more likely, refusing to acknowledge there could be more than one interpretation.

"I'll take them," Janine said wearily.

"I'll tell them to put on their suits, then."

"Wait."

Rose stayed obediently in the doorway.

"All those years ago, I did what you and Pop and everyone else said was the right thing, the best thing, the 'only' thing. And in all the time since, I've handled it your way. I've kept quiet. I didn't rock anyone's boat."

Rose nodded warily.

"Now I've got to do what *I* think is best. I'm going to search, and I am truly sorry if that upsets you, but you're not going to stop me. Not this time."

Janine could see the rapid-fire working of Rose's mind in her eyes as she digested her daughter's speech.

"Is that it?" she said at last.

"That's it."

Janine watched Rose walk down the hall, not expecting her to turn around and come back, but half-wishing she would.

10

WHILE TIM AND Larry were getting their swimsuits, Janine went to the phone and dialed Lee's number.

"Hello?"

"Hi, it's Janine."

"Oh... Hi. Hold on a sec."

Lee must have laid the phone against her chest or cupped her hand over the mouthpiece, because Janine next heard a muffled "no, you can't take that outside" and "because I said so" before Lee's voice came to her loud and clear with "Sorry, just had to nip something in the bud."

"Is this a bad time?"

"Oh, no. Just the usual state of near–mutiny."

"Look, Lee, about what I said to you yesterday..."

"Stop right there. I deserved it. I'm so, so sorry that I blabbed to Red. I know it created an awful situation for both Dan and you."

"I was still off base jumping on you like that."

"You were upset. I was a handy target. Plus, a culprit."

"Well, I want to apologize anyway."

"Thanks. I appreciate the sentiment. I truly do."

The twins appeared, towels draped around their necks. Larry also had his canteen slung over his shoulder.

"We're ready!" they announced.

"Ready for what?" Lee said, having overheard them.

"The wading pool at Terhune Park."

"How about I pop over there with Max and Howie? The neighbors took Sam down the shore overnight, and Max and Howie are practically nauseous with envy. They need an outing, however humble."

"Sure. Great," Janine said, relieved at Lee's easy resumption of good relations.

A half-hour later, Lee and her two youngest arrived at the park. The boys dug four water pistols out of Lee's voluminous tote bag, kicked off their flip-flops, and ran into the pool, splashing to the center to join Tim and Larry where the water was deepest, reaching just above their knees.

"Ugh! Hot," Lee said, flopping down on the bench beside Janine. "I may have to go wading myself."

Janine chuckled.

"Don't laugh. The other night after the kids were asleep, I stripped down and stretched out in their little inflatable pool in the back yard, and I'll tell you, afterwards I slept like a log."

"Clark used to take the boys outside right before bed on hot nights and run the garden hose over them. They would screech and hop around, but they loved it, and it did help them sleep. They called it hosing off."

Lee rummaged in her bag and drew out a Japanese paper fan, which she unfolded and began waving in front of her face and neck.

"You really are hot, aren't you?"

It was 82 degrees, but the humidity was low, so it wasn't oppressive. There was a steady, light breeze, and they were sitting under the shade of a large tree.

Lee looked sideways at Janine.

"I have a confession," she said. "Well, more a news bulletin, I guess, though in our family, it hardly even rates as a side bar. More dog bites man than man bites dog."

"What do you mean?"

"I'm pregnant."

"Really? Congratulations!" Janine put her hand affectionately on Lee's arm. "It is congratulations, isn't it?"

"Yeah, it is, though it wasn't in the plans. But Red's pleased as punch. That man is crazy about babies. I'll be able to feel a lot more cheery about it once fall comes and the heat's over with and I'm not hanging over the toilet every morning."

A child's scream drew the women's attention to the pool. It had come from a little girl who was being squirted from all sides by both Janine's boys and Lee's boys, who had her surrounded. There were a couple of large gaps in the boys' loose circle where the girl could have made an escape, but instead she was standing still and screaming. It wasn't clear whether she truly felt trapped or if she were only play-acting damsel in distress. Janine suspected it was a bit of both. Nevertheless, she called out sharply to Tim and Larry. Tim turned his head in her direction, but he didn't lower his pistol. Larry completely ignored her.

Just as Janine was about to call again, Lee raised two fingers to her mouth and let out a piercing whistle. Without looking at their mother at all, Max and Howie immediately stopped squirting the girl and turned their aims on each other instead. Faced with this inexplicable desertion, Tim and Larry stopped squirting the girl, too.

"That's a pretty neat trick," Janine said to Lee.

"Survival tactic."

The girl in the pool seemed bewildered by her sudden rescue. She remained for a moment watching Max and Howie's duel, then waded out of the water, where an older boy tossed her a towel.

The park was emptying out, children taking off on bicycles or on foot, in the company of friends or baby-sitters. The recreation aides were putting away the balls and board games and arts and crafts materials. One of them shut off the pool sprinklers and turned a valve that opened the drain. Max, Howie, Tim, and Larry took off for the swings.

"I have another confession," Lee said abruptly. "And this one really is."

Janine was surprised at the seriousness in Lee's voice and face.

"At the barbecue, in the house, when you asked me didn't I realize how hard it was for you to talk about your secret, I said that I didn't know anything about that. But that wasn't true."

"How so?"

"You weren't the only girl in high school having sex."

"Well, of course not," Janine said, a bit peeved. "The only difference between me and the other girls was that I got caught."

"I sort of got caught, too."

"Sort of?"

"I was dating this guy... Maybe you remember him: Manny Napolitano on the football team?"

"I didn't know you dated him. The whole cheerleading squad was after him."

"Yeah, and I think most of them got him, too. Or vice versa."

Janine grinned in spite of herself. High school. What a hotbed of longings and insecurities and melodrama. She'd been insulated from much of it by her relationship with Dan, but she still heard about the crushes and broken hearts and romantic strategizing of others.

"Anyway," Lee continued, "I dated Manny for a little while. I mean a matter of weeks. I knew that he could get just about any girl he wanted. To make a long story short, I let him do the deed, thinking that would tie him to me forever."

Lee gave a snort.

"What a little dunce I was," she said.

"What happened?"

"Manny moved on to greener pastures, and I cried myself to sleep for a few nights. But I'd always known in the back of my mind it couldn't last with him, so I got philosophical pretty fast, or as philosophical as you can get at 16. And then I missed my period."

"You got pregnant?" Janine said, amazed. How had Lee not told her this sooner?

"No, as it turned out, I wasn't pregnant, which is why I didn't mention this when you told me about Hunt. It seemed like such a trivial story next to yours."

"So why are you telling me now?"

"After our set-to at the barbecue, I started remembering. It came back to me how scared I'd been when my period was late. I was always very regular, never more than a day off. I don't know, maybe it was the stress of Manny breaking up with me, but my period was two weeks late, and I was terrified every minute of those two weeks. And totally alone with my worry. I didn't dare tell anyone."

Lee stopped speaking and stared off into space. Her eyes seemed focused on some distant scene. Perhaps, Janine thought, she's seeing that frightened 16-year-old lying awake at night wondering what she was going to do, how she would ever tell her parents, making promises to God if He would only make it not so. Then Lee gave her head a little shake and looked again at Janine.

"It's not the same, I know. Not the same at all," she said. "But I wanted you to know that I *do* understand, at least a little. I had a taste of it."

Janine didn't know what to say, so she just nodded.

"There's more," Lee said, her voice breaking.

"What?"

"This is the first I've ever told anyone about this. Even Red doesn't know. He thinks I was a virgin when we got together! So I know about secrets, too. Secrets that get kept so long you can't imagine ever telling them, because you think if you did, the sun might not come up the next day or something."

Lee dug a tissue out of her tote bag and blew her nose. She flashed Janine a weak smile.

"Hormones," she said. "Can't live with 'em, can't live without 'em."

She stood up and once again gave her piercing whistle. Max leapt off his swing in the middle of its upward arc, and Howie scraped his feet on the ground to execute a sudden stop.

"It's time I went home and scrounged up some sort of dinner," Lee said to Janine.

The women gathered their things and went to the boys, who were waiting next to the swings excitedly comparing the powers of He-Man and Skeletor. They all walked together to Lee's car, where Lee and Janine hugged each other farewell.

"If the sun *doesn't* come up tomorrow, you know who to call," Lee joked.

As Janine and her boys walked slowly home to her parents' house, she thought about Lee's secret. It wouldn't have marked her life as deeply as Janine's had hers, but it was, nevertheless, an important truth about herself that she'd intentionally kept hidden. And because of that, there was no one anywhere who knew Lee in the fullness of her being.

Janine wondered about the support group the librarian had mentioned. Is that what it was about — release for secret-keepers? Compatible listeners — listeners who'd gone through the same thing — would know firsthand the intricacies behind the bare facts of your story, all the subtleties and echoes and corollaries so hard to put into words. You could be known in a way you hadn't been known before. And doing the listening would be healing, too, because in understanding someone else's story, you'd understand your own better. Variations on a theme. A chorus. A veritable chorus where, before, there'd been one solitary voice not knowing the right key for her song, convinced that singing was not allowed.

Janine was glad Lee had confided in her. She was glad for both of them.

11

ON THE FOLLOWING day, Janine was scheduled to take slides of ten of her paintings to Belle Martine, a gallery manager in the East Village. The gallery was run by a collective of artists. Each member paid modest dues to cover rent and staffing, and allowed the collective to keep fifty percent of any sales. Janine had applied two months ago with three slides, which had passed muster with a committee of painters, the first hurdle to admission to the collective. The final decision fell to Belle Martine, who evaluated work not only on artistic merit but also on marketability.

Getting into the collective would be a big step. Showing in New York was a feather in any artist's cap. So far, Janine had been represented by galleries in Cape May and Atlantic City, and had participated in a few group shows in Philadelphia. If she got into the collective, she could keep one piece in the gallery at all times, rotating it out occasionally, and at some point, she'd be part of a month-long three-person show in which she could hang a dozen or more paintings.

Janine had spent a lot of time at home selecting the ten slides, but with all that had happened between the meeting with the lawyer eight days ago and the first tottering steps of her search for Hunt yesterday, she'd barely given the important appointment with Belle Martine a second thought.

Now she was standing outside Big Apple Artists Collective, on Second Avenue at Tenth, and she was feeling jittery. And alone. No one was waiting for her over a cup of coffee in the bakery around the corner, as Clark would have done. In less than an hour from now, she'd exit the gallery either exultant or dejected, and there'd be no one watching for her, impatient to hear the results. This was the kind of situation in which she used to miss Clark keenly, and she still did wish he were here to share it, but in recent months, it was the aloneness itself that bothered her, not just the separation from him specifically. She missed having a partner. She had friends, she enjoyed the boys, and she derived deep satisfaction from both her framing jobs and painting — from the labors themselves and from the solitariness of executing them — but she missed having a partner.

Janine had had a great-aunt whose husband was killed in World War I. As a child, Janine thought the dashing soldier in the big photo on the piano was the old lady's son. Even after the mistaken impression had been rectified, Janine could not imagine the smooth-faced young man with the rakishly angled cap putting his arms around her skinny, wrinkled great-aunt and spinning her across the dance floor of a hotel ballroom, as her grandmother had said he'd done. When Janine pictured the scene, she saw the young woman break away from the soldier and go out of the room, and she saw him freeze like a mannequin, arms lifted in empty embrace. Now, in the same way, she had walked away from Clark, and he had remained behind, unchanging. He would not grow old beside her, nor anywhere else. Death had forced her to exit the metaphorical ballroom in which she and Clark had been dancing. She would be leaving him the rest of her life.

Janine opened the door to the gallery and went in. As she'd seen through the plate glass front, it was a large square room packed with art. Once inside, she was astounded by the variety. The walls were crowded with pictures: oils and watercolors, abstracts, landscapes, still lifes, portraits, etchings, prints, collages, photographs. A scattering of tables held ceramics and small sculptures in bronze, stone, wood. A few mobiles dangled from the ceiling.

At a narrow table in the back of the room sat a middle-aged woman with a mane of platinum hair piled carelessly atop her head and fastened with a large clip in the shape of a bird. She stood up and came forward with her right hand extended.

"Belle," she said warmly, shaking Janine's hand. "And you're Janine?"

"Yes. Hello."

Belle's face was free of make-up except for shiny red lipstick, which she'd applied beyond the natural line of her lips. She was wearing a long, full black skirt and a bright green blouse with sequins on it. Janine felt positively pallid in comparison. She'd worn white silk trousers and a tailored brown and white checked shirt. Oh stop, she told herself. It's the paintings she's here to judge.

"I've got a projector in the back," Belle said. "If you'll just bring your transparencies..."

Janine followed her into an adjoining room whose white walls were lined with paintings. The display here was more orderly than the riot of works in the outer room, and a quick scan of the paintings told Janine that they were the products of only two artists.

"This is where we hang our monthly shows," Belle said, continuing briskly through the room.

She unlocked a door, and she and Janine entered what must have been meant to be a storeroom but which had been outfitted as an office. A slide projector sat on a small desk beside a stack of file folders. A few paintings and folded-up folding chairs leaned against the walls. A tall black file cabinet occupied one corner. Janine handed Belle her little box of slides, and Belle inserted them into the projector and showed them one by one against a blank area of white wall. At the end, she cycled back to the third painting.

"This is my favorite," she said.

It was a bright acrylic of a spring flower garden — lavender irises, white and orange lilies, yellow daffodils. At the left-hand edge, two pale blue butterflies were dancing in that close, twirling way butterflies have. There was no sky visible, only the various greens of leaves and grasses, and the browns and purples of turned earth, with here and there fat, pale shoots struggling up through it. The lower third of the painting was given up to the dirt. As in a science textbook cutaway, Janine had depicted roots and stones and burrowing creatures — worms, ants, centipedes, and a menacing, big-headed Jerusalem cricket. As far as Janine was concerned, this underground scene was the picture's reason for being.

"You do that a lot, don't you?" Belle said.

"What?" Janine replied, genuinely interested in the woman's opinion.

Her nervousness had ebbed as her paintings were flashed on the wall. She was proud of them. The work was solid, whether it got her into the collective or not.

"Exposed and hidden. Parallel worlds, parallel activities conducted in ignorance of one another, yet related nevertheless. The inside and outside of things. Makes for a nice, spicy tension."

Belle clicked to a slide of an oil painting of a tide pool. A child's rusting pail was wedged between two barnacle-encrusted rocks. Janine had rendered the peeling paint on its side so that you could just make out a frieze of wild-eyed carousel animals. Floating beside the pail was a band-aid with a smear of old, brown blood on it. At the pail's other side sat a fleshy anemone, its sticky tentacles flailing. A plump orange starfish hunched around a rock.

"There's menace in this one," Belle said. "The sea creatures look both pathetic and dangerous. It's the band-aid, I think, that gives the effect. And the pail — well, the pail is just sad."

"You're right," Janine said. "I am interested in the outside and inside of things, and in juxtaposing seemingly unconnected things."

Belle looked at her with open curiosity. "Only things? Never people?"

"I include people sometimes — like the one with the child sleeping on the riverbank next to the beached canoe — but most of my subjects come from the natural world."

"Yes, the child," Belle said, clicking to that slide. "You've caught how vulnerable people are in sleep. And something more. Trust. The sleeper trusts the person who's gazing at her as she sleeps, yet one wonders if she should. And the canoe as a vagina — brilliant."

Janine laughed. "Vagina?"

"Of course," Belle said confidently. "An elastic, labial, silver vagina."

"I didn't intend... It's a canoe. Sort of an impressionistic, out-of-focus canoe. Not a vagina."

Belle started taking the slides out of the machine and returning them to their little box.

"That's what Georgia O'Keefe said about her flowers."

She handed the box to Janine.

"Not that I'm equating your work with hers."

Janine wasn't sure what to say next. Should she continue the discussion? Did Belle enjoy spirited debate with artists? Was the woman playing gadfly, or did she mean what she said? *And am I in or not?*

Ignoring Janine's confused silence, Belle went to the filing cabinet and took out a stapled set of papers.

"We'll need a short bio," she said, leading the way back into the main gallery. "And a list of places you've shown, any important collections that contain your work, plus—"

"You mean I've been accepted?"

"Well, of course," Belle said, handing Janine the papers she'd taken from the filing cabinet. "This explains all our policies, plus there's a contract for you to review and sign. You're out-of-town, right? You can return everything by mail, ship whatever painting you want shown. Be sure to price it. Call me if you have questions."

Belle sat down at the table where she'd been when Janine entered the gallery. She smiled broadly at Janine.

"Congratulations," she said. "And welcome to the Big Apple Collective."

"Thank you."

As Janine left, she schooled herself not to skip or jump. But as soon as she was out-of-sight of the gallery's plate glass front, she let out a whoop of triumph. She was single-mindedly, delightfully happy.

∞

ALL THE REST of Friday, Janine remained on cloud nine. But on Saturday morning, the first thing she spied upon opening her eyes were the spines of the three library books stacked on her mother's sewing table.

Janine came to her parents' a few days before the Fourth of July every year and usually left on July 5, but her appointment at the gallery yesterday had held her and the boys over. Staring at the books, she decided to stay through the weekend so that she could at least skim them for ideas.

As it turned out, she had a good chunk of Saturday afternoon to herself. Rose had gone to her sister's to help her hem and hang new curtains, and Al had taken Tim and Larry to play miniature golf. Janine took the books and her search journal to the chaise lounge on the screened back porch. She'd meant to rifle through the books quickly, but she kept getting sucked into reading whole sections in full, seduced by an anecdote or interested by a suggestion.

By the time her father and the boys were back, she had identified two tasks she could do right away. The first one was to register with the International Soundex Reunion Registry. If Hunt registered, too, and his information matched hers, Soundex would notify them both and tell them how to reach each other. Janine didn't know if Hunt would know about Soundex, but the service was confidential, it was national, and it was free, so she decided it was worth the gamble. After dinner, she and the boys walked to the mailbox five blocks away and mailed her registration.

On Sunday morning, while Rose and Al were at church and the boys were busy building an elaborate Lego structure, Janine tackled the other, thornier task: generating a list of questions for her mother and father, and generating the gumption to ask them.

Rose and Al probably didn't possess any large knowledge about Hunt's adoption, but their memories might be harboring facts. If Janine asked the right things, or even if she just managed to get her parents talking about that time, maybe she could jar such facts loose. She told herself, too, that it would be good practice to interview them before attempting to interview official people. Practice in teasing information out of reluctant or forgetful respondents, practice in thinking on her feet in order to follow slim or unlikely conversational leads, and practice in keeping her cool in the face of frustration or disappointment. With all this in mind, she took her search notebook into the living room that evening after the boys were in bed.

"Do you mind if we turn off the t-v?" she began. "I'd like to talk to you both."

"It's your father's favorite show," Rose said.

They were set up in their usual positions, Al in his La-Z-Boy, Rose beside him in her easy chair. Two glasses of beer sat on coasters on a small table between the chairs.

"It's all right, Rose. I guess Janine would wait if she could."

"Well, I could wait, but then it'll be late," Janine said, beginning already to lose her nerve.

Rose got up and turned off the television, with an expression more appropriate to disconnecting someone's life support system than to ter-minating an episode of *Murder She Wrote*. She returned to her seat next to Al, and they both looked expectantly at Janine, hopeful, she thought, that this wouldn't take too long and they might catch the second half of the show.

Janine sat down on the couch and opened her notebook on her lap. She was holding a fine point Koh-I-Noor drawing pencil.

"Very formal," Al said.

"Just to help me keep track, Pop."

"Keep track of what?" Rose asked.

"So I'm sure to get in all my questions, and so, later, I don't forget what you said."

"Questions?" Rose said, bristling.

Janine sighed. Would she ever get past her mother's defenses? Sitting there, scooted to the forward edge of her comfortable, television-viewing chair, Rose seemed on high alert and impregnable. And her father's casual slouch in his chair was deceptive. He could prove just as impregnable. The difference was he'd do it more passively, with shrugs and evasions instead of refusals and objections. Janine knew it wasn't too late to turn back. Her parents would not only go along with a return to the years-long silence on the topic of her illegitimate child, they'd welcome it. But she wasn't going to turn back. She was going to face them. And she was going to make them face *it*, it being the deed they'd all been party to so long ago.

"Yes, questions. I need both of you to help me remember anything that might lead to finding out Hunt's last name and where he lives."

"We don't know that," her father said gruffly. "We're not supposed to know that."

Not supposed to? Janine wanted to shout. But that would get her nowhere. It would get her worse than nowhere. It would bolt shut a gate before she'd even put her hand on the latch.

"I've been trying, myself, to remember all I can from when I was at Shadyside," Janine proceeded, ignoring her father's statements. "I made a list of questions for you two to help me fill the gaps. If you don't know the answers, that's okay. But it would mean a lot to me if you'd try to remember."

"What are you going to do if you find out where he is?" Rose said.

"Write to him, I guess. Let him know he can talk to me if he wants."

"If it wasn't for that nosy lawyer, you wouldn't even be doing this."

"Probably not. It's always felt like forbidden fruit. I didn't think I deserved ever to see him again."

A pained expression passed over Rose's face.

"Well, I guess we can't stop you," Al said.

Janine stared hard at him. She knew there was resentment in her expression, but she didn't try to hide it.

"No, Pop, you can't. But you can make it harder. Or you can make it easier."

Al shifted around in his chair and emitted an exhalation that was more grumble than sigh.

"All right, shoot. What's your first question?"

Janine smoothed her hand over her page of questions.

"What do you know about the people who adopted my baby?"

"Nothing," Al replied.

Rose shot a quick glance at him, then looked back at Janine.

"They said the husband was a professional man," she offered.

"What profession?"

"I don't know."

Janine wrote *adoptive father may be white collar* in her notebook.

"Do you have copies of the relinquishment paper I signed?" she said. "Or a copy of the baby's birth certificate?"

"We never got a birth certificate, did we?" Rose said, addressing Al.

"Of course we didn't. Why would they give us a birth certificate?"

"Well, Pop," Janine said, "according to law, they should've given one to me. But from the research I've done, I found out most girls in my situation didn't get one."

"Okay, if you say so," he said. "But we don't have it."

"What about the relinquishment paper?"

Rose rearranged herself in her chair.

"I burned it," she said, lifting her chin like a scrappy terrier.

"What?"

"It would only be a reminder, Janine, and you needed to forget. Even if the people changed their minds about adopting, that baby wasn't coming to you. They'd just find him someone else."

"I can't believe this," Janine said, despair wrestling with anger inside her.

"It wouldn't be any help, anyway," Rose said quickly. "It was only your consent for the agency to be his guardian. So it was legal for them to find him a home. There wasn't anything about the people who were going to adopt him."

"How can you be so positive?" Janine asked irritably.

She almost didn't care how her mother answered. She was going to finish interviewing her parents mainly to save face. She no longer held any hope that they knew anything useful.

"Because when I read that paper — and it was a mean-spirited paper, Janine. It didn't have to be so mean—"

"Now, Rose," Al said, "don't get yourself worked up. It was just lawyers' mumbo-jumbo."

"When I read that paper," Rose continued, "and I saw there was nothing there, I asked them."

"Asked them what?"

"I asked them about the people. That's when they said it was a professional man. But what I really wanted to make sure was that the family was Catholic. And they promised me that they were."

Janine forced herself to write *Catholic* in her notebook. A professional man. A Catholic family. Not much, but two more facts than she'd had at the outset.

"What I remember about Shadyside," Al said meditatively, "is that time I came and took you out to lunch with a couple of your friends from there. As a treat."

It had been a Saturday afternoon. They'd gone to a diner, and they'd had to sit at the counter because one of the girls was so big, she couldn't squeeze into a booth. Al had been embarrassed by the small scene of the girl trying to wedge herself between the padded bench and the table while Janine and the other friend loudly made both serious and silly suggestions and all three giggled uncontrollably.

It was her father's embarrassment that Janine recalled most vividly — the way he'd stood beside the booth looking like he wished the earth would swallow him up, and later at the counter, how he'd mostly stared at his plate or watched the short order cook, as if the three pregnant girls had no connection to him. She knew that his intentions had been noble, but she was bitterly disappointed at how obviously he regretted acting on them. Not wanting to be a wet blanket on her friends' fun, she'd hidden her anger at him then. But now, here he was talking about the outing as if he were sharing a fond reminiscence.

"It *was* a treat, Pop," she said, "but you wouldn't have done it if Shadyside had been here in Teaneck, would you?"

Her father lowered the foot rest of his chair and sat up straighter, as if preparing to rebut her, but he said nothing.

"Don't be ungrateful, Janine," Rose said sharply. "How many of those other girls' fathers did something nice like that?"

"And you," Janine said, turning on her mother, "you never came at all until the baby was born and that 'mean' paper had to be signed."

To Janine's amazement, Rose's eyes were filling with tears. Instead of softening her to her mother, they goaded her to strike out again.

"I was your child," she said. "You should have taken care of me. But you sent me away to strangers, and when I came home, you pretended none of it had ever happened."

"You show some respect," her father admonished her. "Did you forget the letters your mother sent, the packages of cookies and magazines? She called you every Sunday."

"To ask if I'd gone to Mass."

Rose stood up and walked towards the archway leading to the entry hallway and the staircase to the bedrooms.

"What, now you're leaving?" Janine said angrily.

Rose turned.

"The hardest thing I ever did in my life was taking you to that place," she said. "I just couldn't go see you there."

"Rose," Al said tenderly.

"I'm not leaving," Rose said to Janine. "I'm going to get something."

While Rose was gone, Janine and her father didn't speak. She stared out the window at the black, leafy trees, silhouetted by the street lamp. The windows were open. There were moths flattened against the screens, yearning to get inside to the lights. Al got up from his chair and busied himself stacking up newspapers and magazines on the coffee table. The task enabled him to keep his back to Janine. Then he picked up the glasses of beer, which had lost their foamy heads, and took them into the kitchen. He and Rose returned at the same time. Janine wondered if he'd waited in the kitchen until he heard her mother's steps on the stairs.

Rose had a large manila envelope in her hand. She held it out to Janine.

"It's the hospital record. It's all I have."

Her stomach sinking, Janine took the envelope. It was unmarked, fastened closed with a small metal clasp.

Al had sat down in his chair again, but Rose remained standing in front of the couch. Janine looked up at her and suddenly felt like a small child waiting for her mother to take her hand before she stepped into a busy intersection.

"Open it," Rose said.

Janine undid the clasp and pulled out a single piece of paper with the letterhead Trenton Memorial Medical Center. The information was scant — Janine's name and age; the time of birth; the attending doctor's name; the baby's Apgar scores, length, and weight, and notations of standard procedures he'd received, like silver nitrate eyedrops. Some of it was typed, some hand-written. But Janine's gaze skated past all that to the bottom of the page. There, side by side in slightly smudged black ink, were her thumbprint and a tiny baby footprint.

"Oh, my God," she said, touching the footprint with her finger.

She looked up at her mother.

"Oh, my God, Ma. He's real."

It was the most apt way to express the confused enormity of what she was feeling, though she was aware it sounded odd.

"I know," Rose said softly. "I know."

And with that simple recognition, Janine felt the heat lessen under the long-simmering grudge she'd held against her mother. She thought about Rose's claim that taking her to Shadyside had been the hardest action of her life, and she thought about Tim and Larry and how it would tear her in two to have to send them out of reach of her touch and her comfort when they might desperately need her, and how she'd do it anyway if she believed it was for their good.

Al got out of his chair and came over to Rose. He escorted her back to her chair like an usher. Then, surprisingly, he sat on the couch next to Janine.

"More questions?" he said gently.

"Just a couple," Janine said, discombobulated.

Referring to her list, she asked for more details on the adoptive parents: what state they were from, how long they'd been married, if they had other children. Rose and Al said they'd never had any of that information. Nevertheless, the back-and-forth served to quell the strife between Janine and her parents. She asked them if, not counting the recent calls from the lawyer, they'd been contacted by either Shadyside or the law firm any time over the years. They said they hadn't.

"Why would they contact us?" Al said, but there was none of the rancor in his voice that there had been when he'd asked why they would have been given a birth certificate.

"To update the records?" Janine guessed.

"They never asked us for anything for the records except a health history of our family. And that was right at the beginning, not later on."

"And we told them to put in there about the baptism," Rose said, "but that was at the beginning, too. Before you even left the hospital."

"Baptism? What baptism?"

"You know your mother," Al said. "She wasn't taking any chances."

"You want something done right, you do it for yourself," Rose said. "Haven't I always said so?"

"Yes, Rose, you have."

"What are you two talking about?"

"The baby," Rose said, as if Janine were a simpleton. "We got the baby baptized."

"But how did you—?"

"There's always priests hanging around hospitals," Rose said, "so I just grabbed one, and he did it."

"But who are the godparents?"

"Nobody," Al said.

"Nobody?"

"The priest said they like to have at least one godparent," Al explained, "but church law just says if possible. There doesn't *have* to be one."

"He said," Rose continued, "that if the baby went to a Catholic family, they could name godparents then. They couldn't be added to the baptism record because they weren't *there*, but they could do what godparents are supposed to do — help the parents raise the child in the Church. And we told him we were definitely expecting the baby to go Catholic. So he obliged."

"Why didn't you tell me?"

Her parents looked at each other apprehensively.

"After everything," Al said, "we thought maybe you'd say no, and we didn't want a fight."

"I guess I might've said no," Janine admitted. "But I wish I'd been there."

"We were there," Al said. "It wasn't a regular baptism, with a white gown and a party afterwards, but the baby wasn't alone. The priest wrote us down as witnesses."

"Wait a minute," Janine said excitedly. "I wonder if that priest ever sent the baptismal certificate to the adoptive parents. If it was in Shadyside's records that the baby had been baptized, don't you think the parents would have wanted the certificate?"

"We didn't get a certificate," Rose said. "We just told the Home."

"But there had to have been a certificate. What was the name and address of the church?"

"Oh, honey," Rose said, "we don't know that. The priest did the baptism in the hospital chapel with holy water from his Extreme Unction bag. I don't know what church he was from."

"What was his name?"

Both her parents shook their heads.

"It was a name could go two ways, I remember that," Rose said.

"Two ways?"

"Like it could be a first name or a last name. Like Father James or Father Charles or something like that."

Janine turned to a clean sheet in her notebook. She wrote *ask for baptism information,* and above it in block letters she wrote SHADYSIDE. It was time, she thought, to prepare for that visit. She'd call there tomorrow and make an appointment.

It was an unreasonable feeling, she knew, but she had the sense that time was running out for her and Hunt. It had something to do with that tiny footprint, buried for years in her parents' attic. She had a mad, fleeting thought that now that it had, literally, come to light, it would vanish — evaporate off the paper like disappearing ink — and that Hunt, too, would vanish, would slip back into the unknown life he'd occupied so long without her or into a new life, equally unknown to her and perhaps forever inaccessible.

12

"BUT DR. GANNON, I just *have* to have my braces off before Labor Day."

"Labor Day?" Dan said, amused at Addie Blair's vehemence. "You need a good six months past Labor Day."

"What if you, like, took them off for a few days and then put them back on again?"

"That would be very expensive, Addie."

"But you don't understand. I have to totally not be wearing braces on September first."

"What's so important about September first?"

"Actually, August 27th to September 8th. That'll cover the week before, and our trip, too."

"You want your braces off to go on vacation?"

"*Honeymoon*, Dr. Gannon. My *honeymoon*. I'm, like, getting *married* on September first."

Addie flashed a broad, metallic grin. Dan was astounded. The girl had just graduated from high school a few weeks ago.

"You're getting married?" he said, aware of how fuddy-duddy he must sound.

Addie nodded excitedly.

"And I can't have all this grody junk showing in my wedding pictures." She pointed to her braces. She had uppers and lowers.

"What do your parents think?"

It was somewhat unprofessional to ask such a personal question, but Addie seemed perfectly comfortable with the topic. From time to time, patients spontaneously confided in Dan — a college acceptance, a tough teacher, a team win or loss. Addie's news was in a far more serious category than any of that, but, Dan mused, maybe, incredibly, to her it wasn't.

"I didn't ask them yet, but for sure it'll be okay with them if I get my braces off. Besides, Bobby totally thinks I should, and he's more—" She interrupted herself with a laugh. "Oh, did you mean, like, what do they think about me and Bobby getting married?"

"Yes, if you don't mind my asking."

"At first, they said we're too young, but of course we can't, like, wait or anything because of the baby, so now they're totally fine with it. My mom's taking me shopping for a dress tomorrow, and they're going to help me and Bobby get an apartment and, like, help with the rent and all so we can still go to college. Except now Bobby will have to transfer to Rutgers 'cause it's cheaper and that's where I got in, but I was thinking I'll take only one or two classes, not go full-time, ya know?, so I can take the baby to the park and stuff."

As Addie's babble washed over him, Dan couldn't help but think about how different things had been for Janine. When she was Addie's age, teenage pregnancy was generally taken as proof of a girl's promiscuity, or, at the very least, her immorality. No one seemed to consider that it could have happened because she'd been naive and unlucky, or because she and the boy were in love and seeped through with the pleasure of sex, or any combination of those. In 1966, when Hunt was born, an unwed mother was, by definition, a delinquent, or as close as she could get to one without being locked up. And, essentially, those girls *were* locked up, sent to maternity homes, as Janine had been, or shipped off to relatives so that their swollen bellies couldn't be stared at and commented upon by people they knew, their infants, too, efficiently whisked away from censorious scrutiny.

"So? Dr. Gannon?"

With a start, Dan realized Addie had stopped talking and was waiting for him to reply to something.

"Sorry. What did you say?"

"I *said* can you take off my braces in August?"

"Technically, it can be done."

"Excellent!"

Addie practically bounced in the chair. Dan wouldn't have been surprised if she'd clapped her hands, as his daughters did when they got what they wanted. What a child this girl still was.

"However," he continued, "I need your parents' permission first."

"I *told* you, it'll be *fine*. Leastways, I know my *mom* will say it's okay."

"That may be, but I want to hear it directly from her."

Pouting, Addie slid out of the chair.

"All right," she said, mustering a rude tone that made the concession sound anything but. Perhaps she considered that as a soon-to-be married woman, she was owed more deference.

She flounced out of the room. Dan followed her in order to put her chart on Valerie's desk out front. When Addie entered the waiting room, a young man stood up to meet her. Before they turned to leave, Dan caught a glimpse of his face, acned and bespectacled, long bangs brushing the upper rim of his eyeglasses. He thought the boy looked subdued and worried, but maybe he was reading too much into the boy's bad posture and the way his glasses magnified his eyes. Dan hoped, however, that Bobby was at least a little worried. Worry might indicate a sense of responsibility and sobriety and a more balanced vision of the future than Addie's focus on wedding photos and idyllic walks in the park with a fantasy baby whom she probably pictured as perennially pretty, clean, and quiet.

"Roy Schecter's mother called," Valerie told Dan. "He's got strep throat, so they had to cancel."

"Then that's it for today."

He turned to go, then turned back.

"Did you know Addie Blair's getting married?" he asked Valerie.

"Yeah, she told me when she came in."

"I can't imagine that girl with a baby."

117

"Oh, they'll manage somehow. Lots of people do."

"And lots of people don't."

Valerie began clearing her desk, glancing at papers and putting them in various drawers.

"Well," she said distractedly, "the Blairs won't let them starve."

"I didn't mean just the money."

"No, I know. God bless and good luck is all I can say."

She turned the lock in the top drawer, switched off her electric typewriter and put the dust cover over it.

"I'm coming in a little late Tuesday, Doctor — you remember? — so I pulled the files for your first few appointments and put them on your desk."

"Thanks, Val. See you Tuesday."

An appeal to God and luck. We did better than that for Hunt, Dan thought as he took off his lab coat and hung it on the bent wood coat rack in his office. We did the best we could at the time. Still, he hoped God and luck had followed his and Janine's baby boy, wherever he'd ended up.

⸙

WHEN DAN GOT home, he felt restless, so he went for a swim in the apartment pool. He usually avoided the pool on Saturdays because it could get crowded. Today, however, there were only two women and one man lounging poolside, and in the water, three pre-adolescent boys noisily playing keep-away with a beach ball, and a mother and toddler dabbling at the shallow end.

Keeping to one side of the pool to avoid the cavorting boys, Dan swam laps, enjoying the stretch in his arms and legs and across his back. He was a good swimmer, economical and precise in his movements. Robin had said she first knew she loved him while she was watching him swim in the ocean. She'd walked along the shore, paralleling his course beyond the breakers, keeping her gaze fixed on him.

"You're so graceful and strong out there," she'd said, "and so at ease. I thought that if you wanted to, you could go on forever."

It had been an extravagantly romantic thing for her to have said. It was too early in their relationship for him to know how rare such remarks would be. But then, that was part of what had attracted him to Robin: her reserve, the absence of extravagant emotions and gestures and utterances.

After Janine, Dan had tried to stay away from passionate women. He fancied he could peg them right off, could read it in their eyes. Or, rather, he'd notice in himself a feeling as if he were falling into their eyes, a feeling that he didn't care what else happened around him or to him as long as they would not look away. He trained himself to be the one to look away.

One of the delights of Robin had been that he could bring her sometimes into her own wildness, that he could revel in her there when he liked, but that she would never compel him to it. Of course, eventually there became less of that between them. It was only natural, he told himself. It was the way of marriage. He'd been satisfied with their sex life and all the rest of their life together, too. But, it turned out, she hadn't been. Her complaint was not that their relationship was tame — she was all right with that — but that much of the time he wasn't really there, that she didn't feel she had a real hold of him, that she couldn't get to him. He was still not sure exactly what she meant or what, precisely, she'd wanted that he hadn't delivered, but he knew there'd always been a distance between them. A benign one, he would have said, one that suited them both.

After a rigorous fifteen minutes, Dan hoisted himself out of the water and sat on the rim of the pool in the declining afternoon sun, his feet dangling in the water.

The toddler at the shallow end was repeatedly hurling himself off the edge of the pool into the water. His mother would catch him and instantly lift him up to the surface and then out of the pool. They were both laughing. The child leapt again and again. His faith in his mother was absolute. He never doubted she would be there every time.

It was July 7th. Dan had heard nothing from Janine since the 4th, but he hadn't expected to. The conversation with Addie had led him to think about Janine, but now he realized she'd been at the back of his mind all along, hovering like a hummingbird, darting out of sight whenever his thoughts made the slightest move to draw closer.

He still felt she'd behaved unfairly towards him, but he saw that he'd been unfair, too. Indulging his wounded pride or sense of entitlement or whatever it had been was hardly better treatment of her than his mother's harsh insinuations and snap opinions. Janine had made an error of judgment, that's all. She'd apologized, and she'd asked for his help, and he'd abandoned her.

He hadn't been able to help her all those years ago, not as fully as he'd wanted, certainly not nearly as fully as she'd needed, but he would help her now. They would do this together — find their son, make him understand. Turn back time in a way. They'd ended, he and Janine, but they had never really finished. At least, he'd never felt finished. He'd known that the moment he saw her in his waiting room.

Dan sat up, grabbed his towel, and went inside to call Janine. Please, he entreated the universe, let her still be in town.

⤜∞⤛

ON MONDAY MORNING, seated in a booth at the Teaneck Diner and already on his second cup of coffee, Dan was fidgety. He'd arrived early for his appointment with Janine and bought a newspaper to pass the time, but he hadn't been able to stick with any article to its end. He kept looking up at the door. Now, he interrupted an item about this year's Miss America, Vanessa Williams, the first black woman to wear the crown, and a threat by Penthouse magazine to publish old nude photos of her. He began reading an editorial speculating on Geraldine Ferraro's chances of being chosen by Walter Mondale as his running mate.

"Good morning."

Dan put down the paper to find Janine standing beside the booth.

120

"Good morning," he said as she slid onto the banquette opposite him.

"So, you're one of *those*. Nose in the newspaper at breakfast."

Dan felt himself blush. When was the last time that had happened?

"No, not really. Well, maybe sometimes, I guess."

He folded the paper sloppily and put it on the seat beside him. The waitress came over with a pot of coffee. Janine turned over her cup to be filled, but Dan covered his half-empty cup with his hand. They ordered eggs and French toast and melon.

"So, you said on the phone that you're heading back to Cape May Point today?"

"We always come for a few days around the barbecue," she answered. "We're actually overdue to leave."

"An annual visit."

"For several days at Christmas, too, and a few other weekends. The boys don't have grandparents on their father's side. My folks used to come to us once in a while, but they've gotten to where they don't like making the trip. My father tends to get sleepy behind the wheel."

"All those trips, and you never thought to look me up?"

Janine stared at him a moment. What was that in her face? Surprise? Embarrassment? Annoyance?

"Why would I?"

"Of course. Why would you?"

He took a sip of coffee, cold now. What the hell was he doing? This wasn't what he'd intended. He'd meant to be a knight in armor, and he was coming across as a slimy lounge lizard, or, worse, a crybaby.

The waitress arrived with their food. Janine became very busy with salt and pepper and butter and syrup.

"I had this girl in my office Saturday," he said. "She's barely 18, she's pregnant, and she's about to get married."

"Good for her."

"I'm not trying to offend you, Janine."

She put down the syrup pitcher.

"What *are* you trying to do, Dan?"

"I'm trying to make amends."

"For Wednesday?"

"For that. And for...well, for all of it."

Janine rested her hands in her lap and looked at him with a softer expression.

"I don't blame you for anything, Dan. I really don't."

God, how he wanted to touch her. Lay his hand against her cheek, tuck a strand of hair behind her ear, cup her shoulder. Anything.

"I want to help, Janine. I want to help you find him."

She brought her hands up onto the table. She grasped her napkin in one hand and played with the handle of her cup with the other.

"I don't know..."

"You asked me to."

"I know, but it's already so... My feelings are...well, they're all over the map. With you... I don't know, it could get even more tangled." She leaned forward. "But I promise I'll keep you informed. I won't make that mistake again."

Was this it, then? If she truly didn't want his help, should he bow out? If he were acting purely to help her, then that's exactly what he should do. But he found he didn't want to. He couldn't turn his back on this now and let her do all the work. He believed her when she said she'd keep him informed. If she found Hunt, he knew she'd tell him. He'd be able to meet him, if the boy would allow it. But he wouldn't have earned it. Besides, he realized with a small shiver, he didn't want to turn his back on Janine yet either.

"Have you got any idea how to start?" he said, taking a neutral tack.

"Actually, I have started," she said, relaxing.

She told him about her visit to the library, her search journal, the Soundex registry, and her conversation with her parents. She described the process of trying to get an appointment at Shadyside, which had required a bit of detective work all its own. Though the building was still standing — renovated and modernized inside while retaining the charm of its Gilded Age exterior, Janine had been assured on the phone — it was no longer a maternity home. The agency that had taken over Shadyside was called A Future For Families. It provided counseling, classes, and other support services to pregnant teenagers and teen-aged parents. The old records from the maternity home were in storage somewhere else. Janine had had to wait for an appointment in order for her file to be located and recovered.

"And," she said at the end of her story, "my appointment is with a social worker in the agency's main office in Newark. So I'm to be spared having to go back to Shadyside. Or I'm being cheated out of it. I haven't quite decided which."

The waitress came and laid the check face down on the table. Janine picked up her purse.

"Let me go with you to the appointment," Dan said.

"Dan, I told you—"

"If turns out to be a problem in any way, I swear I'll stay out of the rest of it."

She sat immobilized, her wallet extracted half-way out of her purse. He could tell she was wavering.

"I want to do this, Janine. I never saw him, I never heard him cry, I never felt him in my body like you did, but he's my son, too. Let me go with you."

She deliberated a moment longer.

"All right. I'll call you with the address. It's ten a.m., July 16. Exactly a week from today."

"A Monday, then?"

"Are Mondays bad for you?"

He'd have to arrange for Robin to keep the girls. He suspected she'd make a big deal out of it, play the martyr. But maybe not. He'd never asked her to change their set-up before.

"Nothing I can't re-schedule," he said.

Janine turned over the check to read it.

"This is on me." Dan reached for the check.

Janine placed several bills on the table. "Oh, no. We're keeping this on a strictly Dutch treat basis."

"Come on, it's just breakfast."

She gave him a look he hadn't seen in 18 years. It was stern but affectionate. It said *don't mess with this, I mean it.* He hadn't liked it when they were teenagers, but he'd abided by it. She hadn't used it often. Now, it actually pleased him to see it. He didn't care whether or not she'd ever used it on other men. She was using it on him now, and she was relying on him to know what she meant by it. It showed that she remembered the unspoken language of their past and that she was confident that he did, too. He drew his wallet out of his back pocket.

"Dutch treat it is."

They walked out to the parking lot together. The sun reflecting off the parked cars was an assault. Dan looked up at the cloudless, bleached-out sky.

"I guess my girls and I will be spending the afternoon in the pool."

"Sounds like a good plan."

Janine stopped beside a Honda wagon. She fished keys out of her purse.

"What time are you leaving?" Dan asked impulsively.

"Not too late, I hope."

"I pick up my kids at twelve. Why don't you and your boys come over for a swim before you leave?"

"Thanks, but I'd like to get on the road."

"Just a quick dip. It'll cool everybody off for the ride."

"My car's air-conditioned," she said, giving him a mock scowl.

It wasn't an outright no. He decided it was safe to push a little more. He wanted some time with her, however brief, that had at least the potential for ease and ordinariness. And what could be easier and more ordinary than playing with kids in a pool on a hot day?

"We won't talk about one serious thing," he said.

She was sizing him up, as she had before agreeing to let him accompany her to her appointment with the social worker. This was something he didn't recall about her, this cautiousness. Did he, in particular, evoke the reaction? He didn't think so. It had the air of habituation about it, the air of instinct. She was protecting herself, she who'd been so free and impetuous that she'd almost vibrated with it sometimes. He'd admired that quality even while he feared for her because of it. He'd decided early on in their relationship that he'd be her protector, though he'd had no real sense, then, of what that might ever mean. But he hadn't protected her, had he?

"Honestly," he said, drawing an X over his heart with his finger.

"Okay," she said. "Where do you live?"

———— ✇ ————

DAN DIDN'T BOOK appointments on Mondays. He had his daughters all afternoon, and the morning hours between taking them to pre-school and picking them up afterwards usually sped by. He reserved Monday mornings for errands, journal-reading, paperwork, and other activities, like the lecture he'd given at the dental school. Besides, since most of his patients were in high school or junior high, their preferred appointment times were in the late afternoon or on Saturday morning.

After leaving the diner, Dan went directly to Robin's house. He figured the more notice he gave her about next Monday the better, and he felt that dealing about it in person and without the girls around was a wise approach.

Rather than use his key, he rang the doorbell and waited for her to answer. He didn't want to alarm her by simply walking in. Since they'd split, he'd never once arrived when he wasn't expected.

When she didn't answer, he rang again and then decided to go around back. The garage door was open and Robin's car was inside, so she must be home. He called her name to give her warning, and before he got to the end of the walkway, she rounded the corner of the house and met him.

"Dan," she said in alarm. "Is anything wrong? Are the girls all right?"

"Everything's fine. I just wanted to talk to you about something. I was nearby and thought I'd drop in instead of calling."

Robin eyed him suspiciously. She was dressed in baggy overalls and a thin t-shirt, and she had on gardening gloves. Her short hair was pulled back into a stubby pony-tail from which curls had escaped on all sides. There was a smudge of dirt on her chin. At one time, Dan would have found all this charming.

"You're sure nothing's wrong? Your mother's okay?"

"Same as ever."

"I was just repotting some plants," she said, turning.

He followed her to the back yard, where she had a work table set up with variously sized clay pots and bags of potting soil, fertilizer, and vermiculite.

"So, what's up?" she said, carefully tapping a pot of variegated ivy to release a ball of roots and dirt.

"I need a favor."

She suspended her actions and stood holding the ivy above its new pot.

"Something's come up, and I can't take the girls next Monday. I was wondering if you could keep them."

"Something's come up?"

"An appointment."

"Well," she said, continuing with the re-potting, "that's enlightening."

"Do you really need to know the details?" Dan said. "I wouldn't ask if it weren't important."

"Why did you make an appointment on one of your days?"

"It was the only time available."

Robin was packing soil around the ivy with more vigor than Dan thought was called for.

"As it happens, I have an appointment, too, next Monday."

"For what?"

She smiled at him. It wasn't a friendly smile.

"Do you really need to know the details?" she said with exaggerated sweetness.

"Look, if you can't keep the kids, just say so, and I'll get a baby-sitter," he said, sounding peevish in spite of his best efforts not to.

"For the whole day?"

"I'll handle it."

She picked up another pot, this one with a pink begonia in it, and banged it on the table to loosen the soil around the plant roots, again with more vigor than Dan thought was required.

"Never mind," she said. "I'll keep them."

"What about your appointment?"

"It's just for a haircut. I can change it. Or I'll take them with me. Vanessa's looking a little shaggy. She can get a trim, too."

The shaggy remark was aimed at him. Haircuts were one of Dan's responsibilities. Robin had created a list when they were working out custody — haircuts, dental and pediatrician appointments, new shoes, school fund-raiser work, library books, ballet class, and so on — and divided up the chores between them. She'd taken on the bulk of them, in recognition of the fact that he had a job and she didn't. Nevertheless, it seemed to Dan that she felt put upon to some extent, so he tried to be scrupulous about the things on the list assigned to him. He conjured up a picture of Vanessa as she'd looked this morning. He had fastened her bangs with a barrette to keep them out of her eyes, though Vanessa wasn't complaining. Was that considered shaggy?

"Thanks," he said. "I won't make a habit of this."

"I should hope not. The girls will be disappointed. To say nothing of confused."

"Confused?"

"Vanessa knows the names of the days of the week, but she doesn't really understand what a week is, and Sally's completely lost in time. All they're going to know is that Daddy was supposed to show up and he didn't."

"God damn it, Robin, get off my case! I'll explain it to them, whether you believe they can understand or not. And I'd appreciate it if you'd reassure them and explain it to them again if they're confused that day. They're not going to think I'm a deadbeat unless you *make* them think it."

Robin took off her gardening gloves and threw them on the table.

"How dare you suggest I'd do anything to hurt my girls?"

"I could say the same, Robin. And you know it."

He watched her face as she struggled to suppress her anger. He also worked on cooling down. It was pointless to let anger rule him. They were getting divorced, but because of the children they'd always be partners. It was a strange kind of partnership — sometimes friendly, sometimes adversarial, not romantic but not purely business either. It was the "until death do us part" piece of marriage reconfigured. They were yoked together and they always would be, even when the kids had grown up, even if they each found new spouses.

"Is that all?" Robin said in a controlled voice.

"That's it. Thanks again for being flexible."

"Don't mention it."

"No, really, I appreciate it."

"I said, don't mention it."

She pulled on her gloves again and stooped to pick up a large pot of coleus that was sitting on the ground. Dan saw that it must be heavy, but he resisted the urge to lift it for her. He was sure she wouldn't let him. He left the yard without saying anything more.

13

THE FOUR CHILDREN stood on the cement skirt of the pool staring at one another. Vanessa and Sally wore inflated swimmies on their upper arms, and Tim and Larry were sporting water goggles. Dan and Janine were a few yards away, opening lounge chairs.

"They look like two alien races checking each other out," Dan whispered to Janine.

"We don't have a lot of time," Janine called to her sons. "If you guys are going to swim, you'd better get to it."

Tim shuffled closer to the steps leading into the shallow end of the pool. Larry marched past him and jumped in.

"You splashed us!" Vanessa squealed.

"Yeah!" Sally shouted, brushing water droplets off her legs.

"If you don't want to get wet, stay away from the pool," Dan said.

He was ridiculously anxious for his daughters to be gracious hostesses. Not only were they not doing that, they were being thorough *girls*, whining about being splashed, holding back from entering the water. Normally, they raced to the pool, and he had to admonish them to wait for him before going to the deep end. Neither girl was a strong swimmer yet, but the swimmies made them so buoyant, they had no fear of water over their heads.

"I don't know what's up," Dan said to Janine. "They're usually regular fish."

"Boys," Janine said.

"Boys?"

"Starts early, doesn't it?"

"What should we do?"

"Nothing."

Janine spread a beach towel on a lounge chair and lifted her loose, smock-like dress over her head. She was wearing a strapless, one-piece red bathing suit. The fabric in front was shirred, enhancing the curve of her breasts and the mild swell of her belly, and in the back, a center seam separated her round, high buttocks in a particularly flattering way. The skin of her back was smooth except for a mole on her left shoulder blade. Dan had forgotten that mole. Now he recalled that she had another one, on the inside of her left thigh. He tried to catch a glimpse of it when she reclined on the lounge chair, but he couldn't. She put on a pair of dark sunglasses and looked at him.

"Starts early and keeps on," she said.

He knew then she'd noticed him ogling her. He couldn't see her eyes to tell if she were annoyed or not, so he was relieved when she flashed him a quick smile.

Dan turned his attention to the children. Tim had joined Larry in the waist-high water at the bottom of the steps. The two of them were flailing around in the midst of some combative game, raising lots of splashes. Vanessa and Sally were standing on the top step, ankle-deep in the water, well within the splash zone, but they weren't squealing any more. Finally, Vanessa descended the steps and doggy-paddled majestically away from the busy game to the side wall, where she grabbed hold of the rim of the pool and hung on, watching the ruckus from a distance. Sally sat down on the step she'd been standing on and turned her back to the boys to shield her face from splashes.

"Janine," Dan said.

"Hmm?"

"Remember that swimming pool game where you ride on someone's shoulders and try to knock down somebody else riding on someone's shoulders?"

"Chicken."

"What?"

"It's called Chicken."

"Oh, yeah. Want to play?"

She took off her sunglasses and stared incredulously at him.

"You want me to get on your shoulders?"

"No, no. We'd each take a kid. Inject some fun into this stand-off," he said, pointing to the children.

"You're on."

The children were a bit leery when the game was explained to them, but they were excited by the prospect of their parents getting into the water, so they agreed to give it a try. Janine took Larry onto her shoulders, and Dan took Vanessa. After a couple of timid passes at each other, Larry and Vanessa entered the fray in earnest, reaching and lunging, shouting at their "mounts" to turn this way and that, to back up or charge ahead. On the sidelines, Tim and Sally were vociferous cheerleaders. Finally, Vanessa, avoiding a shove from Larry, leaned so far back that she caused Dan to lose his balance, and they fell over into the water. When Dan surfaced, he was pleased to see Vanessa bobbing beside him wearing a grin.

"We won! We won!" Larry was exclaiming.

Janine dropped backwards, toppling him into the water. He came up grinning, too.

The two children paddled side-by-side to the steps, engaging in good-natured banter the whole way.

"Beat you!" Larry said.

"It was my Dad's fault."

"Yeah, and my Mom fell on purpose."

"That was funny!"

"Yeah!"

"Now Tim and Sally get a turn," Janine said.

"How about boys against girls this time?" Dan proposed.

Tim was dubious about getting on Dan's shoulders, but his hesitation didn't last long. Sally, however, balked at teaming up with Janine.

"I want my turn with my Daddy," she said.

"Next time," Dan said. "I promise."

"Go on, Sal," Vanessa said. "Girls against boys!"

Janine held out her hand to the little girl. Slowly, Sally walked to the edge of the pool. Janine, standing in the water, turned her back so that Sally could climb on.

The contest lasted a bit longer this time. The adults maneuvered cooperatively so that Sally could stay seated long enough to relax and enjoy herself. Once, Dan pretended to stumble and almost fall. He was rewarded by a look of amazed delight on Sally's face.

"Go, Sally!" Vanessa cheered.

"Get them, Tim!" Larry shouted. "Knock them over!"

After a few more advances and retreats, Dan pretended to stumble again, but this time Janine seized the opportunity to close in. Holding on to Sally's ankles, she chanced leaning forward to extend the girl's reach. Sally managed a solid push against Tim's chest, and with Dan balanced on only one foot, the boys' team went down. But Sally's push had destabilized Janine's precarious stance, and a second later, the girls' team went down, too.

"The girls won!" Sally said when she'd gained the steps.

"It was a tie!" Larry declared. He gave Tim a high five after he'd climbed out of the pool.

Panting, Dan looked over at Janine. She was watching the children and smiling broadly. Her wet face and shoulders and back gleamed in the sun, making her skin look like it was a source of light. Her hair was slicked back, sleek and dark, and her strong profile was that of a classical Greek statue. Or what one of those statues might look like if it brightened with life. She turned her head and caught his eye. Her smile lessened ever so slightly. But it didn't disappear. He moved closer to her so that he could speak without the children hearing.

"You look beautiful," he said, "like some kind of fabulous mermaid."

"You need to get out more."

He smiled. "You're right. I do."

"Re-match!" Larry called, and the other three children echoed him.

"No, boys," Janine said. "It's time to dry off and get ready to go."

"I've got food inside," Dan said to her.

"We were going to grab a late lunch on the road."

"We're hungry now!" said Larry.

"It's no trouble," Dan said.

"All right," Janine agreed. "But can we eat out here?"

Dan went into his apartment and returned with a large insulated bag slung over his shoulder. He had a package of Oreos in one hand and Sally's Care Bears lunchbox in the other. The insulated bag was loaded with drinks and plastic containers of watermelon slices, orange wedges, carrot sticks, and peanut butter and jelly sandwiches with the crusts cut off. In the lunchbox were two club sandwiches. He'd gone to three different places to get the best ingredients: roast turkey and bacon from one store, good rye bread from another, and fresh lettuce and Jersey tomatoes from a farm stand in Demarest.

The four children, wrapped in towels, were seated around a glass-topped table happily chattering to one another. Janine was standing behind Vanessa braiding her hair.

Dan handed Janine the lunchbox.

"That's for us," he said.

While he opened the containers of kids' food and set them on the table, Janine carried the lunchbox to the lounge chairs. After passing out juice boxes, Dan took two bottles of Perrier out of the insulated bag and joined her.

"This looks great," Janine said, unwrapping her sandwich.

Dan nodded and bit into his sandwich. They ate in silence for a few minutes. The children were far enough away that their steady conversation was unintelligible. Their voices made an almost musical backdrop.

"Do you think Vanessa's hair is shaggy?" Dan asked after a swig of sparkling water.

"Do you mean the braid? I just did that for fun. You don't get to do stuff like that with boys."

"But would you call her hair shaggy?"

"It's hard to tell when it's wet. Anyway, shaggy can be a style."

Janine set her empty bottle down on the ground beside her chair.

"That was an odd question," she said.

"I'm in charge of haircuts."

"In charge?" Janine said, teasing him. "For the town?"

"No," he replied with a smile. "Just for Vanessa and Sally."

"Well, if you're in charge, then I guess it's your call what's shaggy and what's not." She paused. "Or is it more involved than that?"

"A little."

"Uh-oh. Are we going to talk about your divorce now?"

Dan balled up the paper his sandwich had been wrapped in.

"Definitely not."

"Daddy!" Vanessa called, running to him. "Can we have the Oreos now?"

Dan gave her the package.

"Tim, Larry," Janine said, standing up. "You can eat your cookies in the car."

"Time to hit the road?" Dan said, trying not to sound disappointed.

"Time to hit the road." She handed him a slip of paper from her bag. "The address of A Future for Families. But, really, you don't have to come."

"I told you, I want to."

She nagged her boys to get a move on, then turned back to Dan.

"Actually," she said, "I'm glad you're coming. Gives me courage."

"I'm sure you've got plenty of that. But I'm glad you're glad." He stood up. "And on that goof-ball note..."

Janine smiled. "It did sound kind of goofy. But it was nice all the same."

The children surrounded them then, bumping up against them but basically paying attention only to one another, engrossed in a series of knock-knock jokes whose punch lines were totally invented, illogical, and not at all funny. They still evoked gales of laughter.

Dan, Sally, and Vanessa walked their guests to the parking lot, but the girls, barefoot, complained about the hot pavement, plus Sally insisted she had to pee "real bad." Dan hoisted them up awkwardly, one straddling each hip, and headed for the apartment. The girls called out good-byes over his shoulders.

Dan didn't like walking off while Janine was still there, helping the boys change into dry clothing in the back seat. It was an incomplete close to the day. But it had been, all things considered, a good day. He might even say an important day. A day imbued with a future. A very limited future, but a future nonetheless.

———❧———

DAN VISITED HIS mother once a week, and he took the girls to see her once a month, always on a Monday evening. This was one of those Mondays.

Robin didn't wholly approve of the girls going to the retirement home, for fear they'd see things that might upset them, but she had no defensible grounds for objection. Betty Gannon lived in a section of the home where the people were not seriously ill or incapacitated. Not all the residents wore their old age gracefully, but the girls were unlikely to be faced with any truly disturbing sights. Their biggest shock so far had been the grizzled, sunken lips of an unshaven man who wasn't wearing his dentures.

There was a routine to the girls' visits. First, they'd all go to Betty's apartment and sit and talk a while. Dan would drink a cup of tea into which his mother invariably put too much sugar. Betty would let the girls water the houseplants lining her tiny terrace. They'd finish up in the dining hall, where Betty would order them all vanilla ice cream topped with Hershey's chocolate syrup and Cool Whip.

The girls' presence in the dining hall was usually a minor event. Inevitably, several of Betty's friends and acquaintances would stop by the table to say hello and remark on what pretty, well-behaved grand-children she had, and to ask the girls how old they were and if they

135

were enjoying their ice cream. The girls always looked out for one old gentleman who possessed the marvelous ability of producing quarters from behind their ears.

"Come in, come in," Betty said, opening the door of her apartment.

The girls entered sedately. Though Dan had never coached them, they somehow knew that at Granny's place, it wasn't done to run or shout or touch the Hummel figurines arranged in groups of two and three on every available surface. Maybe Robin had instilled this decorum in them. He wasn't above accepting the credit for it from both his mother and her friends.

"We brought you pictures, Granny," Vanessa said, holding out a crayon drawing of flowers and a rainbow.

"Me, too," said Sally. Her drawing was an oval with two dots inside it and five lines sprouting from it. "It's a dog."

"Let's put them on my refrigerator," Betty said.

The girls followed her into the kitchen, where she taped up their drawings and turned the heat on under the kettle. Dan stayed in the doorway. The small room would have been too cramped if he'd gone in, too.

"I've got Earl Grey today, Danny," his mother said. "Mrs. Litman moved to Extended Care, and her daughter gave me some things from her cupboards."

"Old Mother Hubbard had a cupboard," Sally said.

"So did old Mrs. Litman," Betty replied.

Betty made Dan's tea and they all returned to the living room and sat down. There were only two upholstered chairs, so the girls sat cross-legged on the floor.

"So now, what's your news?" Betty said to her grandchildren. The query was as standard a part of the visit as the tea and the ice cream.

"We learned a new song at school," Vanessa said.

"Make New Friends," Sally added.

"Sing it for me."

The girls looked at each other, Sally waiting for her sister's nod so they'd start together. She was a beat behind anyway, but she caught up by the end of the first line. It was a simple song about how new friends were silver, but old friends were gold. Surprising everyone, Betty joined in on the last lines.

"A circle is round, it has no end," she sang in a high, quavering voice. "That's how long I want to be your friend."

"How'd you know that?" Dan asked.

"Oh, kids were singing that when you were little. Maybe even when I was little."

Sally frowned, presumably trying to puzzle out how her grandmother could ever have been little.

"We made some new friends today," Vanessa said. "Boys."

"Boys, eh?" Betty said. "Were they silver?"

"No," Vanessa replied seriously. "They were just boys."

"Where'd you meet them?"

"At Daddy's pool," Sally said. "And their mom, too."

"Oh?" Betty said, shifting her gaze to Dan.

"Moms can't be friends," Vanessa told her sister authoritatively.

"Moms can be friends with dads," Sally asserted.

"Sally's right," Betty said, still looking at Dan. "Moms can be friends with dads."

"Before this goes any further, Mom, it was Janine and her boys."

"We played Chicken," Vanessa said. "And the girls won!"

"Girls often do," Betty remarked.

If they'd been alone, Dan would have found some acceptable way to tell his mother to cut the crap. If they'd been alone, the crap would be much worse, too. But he didn't want to show his irritation in front of his daughters.

"Bring Granny her sweater, Nessie," Dan said. "I think it's time we went and had our sundaes."

Vanessa retrieved her grandmother's sweater from the back of a chair in the kitchen and tenderly draped it around her shoulders.

"Thank you, dear. Why don't you and Sally go ahead and ring for the elevator? We'll catch up in a minute."

"I'm pushing the button first," Sally said.

"I'm pushing second," Vanessa affirmed, as if someone else might be waiting to claim that privilege.

They walked out of the apartment hand-in-hand. Betty put out her hand for Dan to help her rise. When she was standing, she linked her arm in his. Her progress out of the apartment was slower than usual, but not so much so that he could safely accuse her of deliberate dawdling. Her energy and physical strength did vary from day to day.

"So now you're seeing Janine?" she asked as she locked her door. "What does Robin think of that?"

"I'm *not* seeing Janine. It was just a swim with the kids. And even if I were seeing her, it would be none of Robin's business."

Betty took his arm again, and they made their way slowly down the hall towards the elevator.

"The girls don't seem to suspect, at least."

"Suspect? There's nothing to suspect, Mom. And I don't want to hear any more about it."

His mother stopped walking and gave him an evaluative look.

"Be honest with me, Danny."

Dan wondered what being honest meant at this moment. Should he tell her about the search for Hunt? About breakfast in the Teaneck Diner and how eerily familiar it had felt to sit across the table from Janine? Did he dare mention the alluring red bathing suit and the gleam of afternoon sunlight on Janine's wet shoulders? No, honesty certainly didn't require those kinds of details. But he felt suddenly that he didn't want to hide his connection to Janine from his mother, nor minimize it, that if he did, it would demean the task he and Janine were setting out on and insult the memory of their past love.

"Janine is trying to find our son," he said, "and I'm going to help her in whatever way I can."

Betty gripped his arm tightly, and her face was full of alarm.

"No, Danny."

"Yes, Mom. We can talk about it more another time. So you'll know what's going on. Not so you can talk me out of it. Because you can't."

It was mildly thrilling to have it set out so simply. He felt calm and clear. He was actually grateful to his mother for forcing the issue. The agitation that had begun last Tuesday when Janine appeared in his waiting room had finally ebbed.

"The elevator's here," Vanessa called.

Patting his mother's hand where it rested on his forearm, Dan urged her forward and picked up the pace. She kept up just fine.

14

THROUGHOUT THE FOLLOWING week, whenever Dan was at loose ends, he'd begin to wonder what the interview with the social worker was going to be like, which soon led to his becoming anxious about it. He was still sure he wanted to go, but away from the resistant wall of his mother's dismay, he felt his confidence in his potential usefulness slipping. It was much easier to act and feel self-assured when he was taking a stance in opposition to Betty's disapproval than it was when he was alone with his thoughts.

To minimize these uncomfortable times, Dan filled his week with distractions. He began writing up a case study for the American Journal of Orthodontics that wasn't due for four months. He reorganized his storage bin in the apartment garage. He took the girls to a nail salon for their first-ever manicures. He worked with Valerie on a new filing system she'd been wanting to institute. He volunteered for a work crew at the pre-school and spent most of Sunday sanding and painting tables and benches.

At last, Monday came around again, and Dan found himself in the lobby of a vaguely Soviet style office tower in downtown Newark waiting for Janine. As at the diner, he'd arrived early. He was just about to step outside and look for a newspaper vendor when Janine came in through the revolving door.

"I'm not late, am I? I got a little lost."

"You're right on time. In fact," he said, checking his watch, "there's ten minutes to spare."

"Good. I wanted to coach you a bit before we go upstairs. Based on the reading I've been doing."

"Okay."

"The most important thing is that we shouldn't say we're searching for Hunt or that we have any intention of contacting him."

"Why not?"

"The sealed records laws bar us from getting identifying information, but what constitutes identifying information isn't spelled out. Obviously, names and addresses, but beyond that, it's up to the individual social worker or judge or records clerk or whoever. If our appointment is with someone who's against adoptees reuniting with their birthparents and she thinks that's what we're up to, she could completely shut down on us."

"God, I hope I don't put my foot in it."

"Just follow my lead." Janine pulled a paper out of her purse and read it. "Suite 608."

As the elevator glided to a stop on the sixth floor, Janine placed her hand lightly on Dan's sleeve.

"I'm no expert, Dan. I could put my foot in it, too."

The elevator doors parted open. They stepped out into a bright reception area decorated with the kind of grand landscape photographs that might be found on a Sierra Club calendar. Dan wondered if they were in the right place. What did mountains and waterfalls and fields of wildflowers have to do with babies and young families?

When Janine told the receptionist her name, the woman made a call, and a minute later, a tall woman wearing a pants suit and a pussybow blouse came out and introduced herself as Mrs. Marcos. She led them to her office, which was done all in beige except for two small still life watercolors. She beckoned them to sit down.

"Well," she said, after they were settled, "we do get the occasional inquiry from a Shadyside alumna, but I don't believe we've ever had a father come in before. And our agency subsumed Shadyside ten years ago."

Dan wondered how Janine felt about being called an alumna. It seemed a ludicrous designation. And he, the rare bird — was that going to be an advantage or a liability?

"How have you been, Mrs. Linden?" Mrs. Marcos asked, apparently not expecting them to respond to her opening comment. "You've married, obviously. Any children?"

"Twin boys. Six years old."

"Splendid. And your husband? What does he do?"

"He was an English teacher. He died two years ago."

Mrs. Marcos was taken aback. "Oh my, I am sorry to hear that. So young to be widowed..."

"Yes, it was very unexpected."

Dan marveled at Janine's composure. He was sure it was taking an effort.

"I hope you don't mind my questions," Mrs. Marcos continued. "Even though we don't run a Home any longer, we do still work with young women facing the challenges of unplanned pregnancies, and it can be instructive for us to hear how someone's life has turned out."

"I understand."

"Although girls today tend to keep their babies. Back when you were at Shadyside, 80 percent of babies from single mothers were placed, nationwide. Now it's down to four percent."

Janine nodded, as if she'd come just for this information. Dan faked an interested expression.

"And do you work?" Mrs. Marcos asked Janine.

"I have a picture framing business that I run out of my home. And I'm a painter, though that's not a reliable source of income."

"An artist!"

Dan couldn't tell if the woman was impressed or just at a loss for words. Was she thinking *an artist, how interesting*, or was she thinking *an artist, no wonder you were pregnant at 17*?

"Our director is an avid photographer," she said. "Perhaps you noticed his work in the reception area?"

Janine smiled and nodded.

"Those are fine landscape photos," Dan said. "They make you feel like you're there."

"Yes, well, I prefer hotels," Mrs. Marcos said with a sniff.

Dan shifted in his seat. Was Janine going to let this woman go on forever?

"I was sent your records, Mrs. Linden," Mrs. Marcos said, as if reading Dan's mind. She tapped a dark brown folder on her desk. Dan was able to make out the bold face type on the file tab: Pettorini, J. (Kate).

"I guess this could have been handled by mail," Janine said, "but I wanted to come in. Actually, I thought I'd be going to Shadyside."

"They told you, didn't they, that it's a counseling and education center now?"

"Yes."

"We want to be helpful, of course," Mrs. Marcos began in a tone that convinced Dan she was leading up to being just the opposite, "but we labor under certain restrictions, as I'm sure you know and would respect."

"We're very grateful you agreed to see us. I knew so little, all those years ago, about the family who adopted my baby, and I do wonder, sometimes, what his life is like, if he's all right."

Mrs. Marcos opened the folder and scanned its contents, picking up and putting down several sheets of paper. Dan saw that a couple were official forms, while others were typescripts, possibly chart notes. The social worker put all the papers back into the folder. Dan had a wild urge to grab it and run for the door. Weren't there exit stairs right next to the elevator? Would Janine be quick-witted enough and bold enough to jump up and follow him? Of course she would. Mrs. Marcos laid her right hand flat on top of the closed folder. Was she really a mind-reader? If so, they were sunk.

"There's nothing here, Mrs. Linden, dating past the finalization of the adoption. We sometimes hear, in later years, from adoptive parents, but it's not usual. And it didn't happen in this case."

"Could you tell me when that was, the finalization?"

"You'd have to petition the court for that information."

"Which court?"

Mrs. Marcos folded her hands together. They were still resting on Janine's folder.

"I couldn't say."

"I've heard that sometimes babies spent time in foster homes before going to their adoptive families."

"That did happen, but usually for no more than two or three months. It's why relinquishment papers were worded to give guardianship to Shadyside, who then later gave it to the new parents."

Dan wondered where Janine was going with this line of questioning. If she got enough information to locate the adoption decree, how likely was it that a judge would release a copy to her? And would foster parents remember the names of a couple who'd adopted a baby who'd been in their care for only two or three months 18 years ago? Long shots, at best. Plus, the social worker was getting stiffer with each exchange.

"Oh, it's no matter," Janine said, sounding sprightly. "What I really wanted to find out was what kind of family he went to. You said you don't have current information, but can you tell me if the people who adopted him had other children at the time, if they lived in an urban or rural or suburban area, what kind of work the father did, if the mother worked or stayed at home...things like that?"

Mrs. Marcos stared at Janine, who smiled at her. The woman glanced briefly at Dan and turned back to Janine.

"And why, Mrs. Linden, do you want to know these things?"

The jig is up, Dan thought.

"Since having my boys," Janine said, not missing a beat, "I've learned what a big job being a parent is. It's something you don't really appreciate until you do it yourself. And losing my husband... That reminded me how unpredictable life can be. And then I started thinking about what life might have brought my son, and I wanted to know that he was all right, that things had worked out..."

"As I said, I have no information along those lines."

Janine smiled again, a sad, almost defeated smile.

"But you do know how things started out for him, don't you?" Dan asked. "What his situation was at the beginning?"

He hoped Janine wouldn't find fault with him for jumping in. He didn't dare try to catch her eye.

"And you, Dr. Gannon. What is your interest in all this?"

"Curiosity. Concern. Helping Janine put her mind at rest."

"Not compelling reasons," Mrs. Marcos said, and Dan knew his reply had been a mistake. "Not as compelling as protecting the baby."

"Baby?" Dan said. "He's 18!"

Mrs. Marcos ignored him and focused on Janine.

"I'm afraid, Mrs. Linden, that I can't answer your questions. We are not permitted to provide any information that might lead to identifying where an adoptee might be. Not that you are attempting to discover that."

"No, no, we're not," Janine murmured.

"Because you wouldn't want to disrupt someone's life, would you?"

"No."

Dan hated watching Janine wilt under Mrs. Marcos's intransigence. It flashed on him how cowed she must have been as a teenager standing alone against the likes of Mrs. Marcos and maybe worse, and how unsure she must have been of her right to ask or know anything specific about the future of the baby she was leaving behind.

"There is one thing you can tell us," Dan said brusquely.

The social worker turned to him with mild surprise on her face, as if she'd forgotten he was there.

"Did he go to a Catholic family? His grandparents had him baptized, and they want to know if he went to a Catholic family. No identifying information there."

"Yes, Dr. Gannon," Mrs. Marcos said, sounding resentful. "He went to a Catholic family."

"He was baptized Daniel," Janine said.

"Oh, they hardly ever kept their names," Mrs. Marcos said.

Dan felt as if he'd been punched in the chest. When Janine told him about the baptism, he had stupidly not thought to ask what she'd named the baby. He was profoundly moved to learn she'd given him his name. It didn't matter if the name had been erased later. It didn't matter that Hunt probably didn't know it. He'd heard it. Janine had whispered it into his little ears for a few days. For the first time, Dan felt a visceral connection to this child he had never seen.

Mrs. Marcos pushed her chair back from her desk.

"I have a meeting in a short while that I need to prepare for. If there's nothing else?"

Janine stood up, so Dan did, too.

"I'd like it recorded in the file that we came today," Janine said, reviving. "I want it recorded that we showed an interest."

"If you wish."

"And I'd like to add a Waiver of Confidentiality."

Mrs. Marcos smiled, the smile of a cat who's cornered a mouse.

"So you *are* searching."

"No, I'm not," Janine insisted, with just the right tone, Dan thought admiringly, to convey that she was insulted by the woman's accusation but that she was above making an issue of it. "But if my son ever contacts you looking for me, I want to make it easier for him by untying your hands."

Mrs. Marcos's back was up, but she couldn't repeat her accusation. Janine had spoken too carefully.

"The rules are for your protection, too, Mrs. Linden."

"No one ever asked me if I wanted to be protected. And just to be clear: I don't."

Mrs. Marcos nodded, an expression of condescending pity on her face. Dan's reading was that she pitied Janine not for what she'd suffered as a mother giving up her baby, nor as woman encountering obstacles while trying to find out if that baby had grown up healthy and happy. Mrs. Marcos's pity, Dan surmised, arose because she thought Janine was misguided or perhaps even a trouble-maker and that she was headed for a fall.

"The receptionist can give you a waiver form."

"Thank you." Janine headed for the door. She stopped with her hand on the knob.

"Is the relinquishment paper in there?" she asked, pointing to the folder on the desk.

"Yes."

"May I have a copy?"

Mrs. Marcos opened a drawer and put the folder inside.

"I don't think so," she said, with manufactured regret.

"Excuse me," Dan said, "but are relinquishment papers considered sealed records? Legally, I mean. Because we wouldn't dream of asking you to do anything illegal."

"It's only my signature, isn't it?" Janine said. "It could identify me, but not anyone else."

"Our agency considers the entire file sealed."

"Can you cite the law that specifically forbids Janine's access to the relinquishment paper?" Dan said, keeping his voice reasonable yet firm. "So we can decide how to move forward with this request."

Mrs. Marcos looked confused.

"If you need to check with your supervisor or look something up, we don't mind waiting," he added.

Mrs. Marcos opened the drawer and took out Janine's folder.

"I'll make a copy," she said. "If you'll wait outside."

IN THE ELEVATOR on the way down, Janine opened the folded document Mrs. Marcos had given her. Dan watched her read it. Her face flushed red.

"My mother was right," she said. "This thing is horrible."

She passed it to Dan. He stood in the building's lobby and read it, waves of shock, anger, and impotence passing over him.

This certifies that I, Janine Annette Pettorini, am the mother of a child born in Trenton, NJ on March 16, 1966, and that this child is indigent, destitute and homeless. Feeling that the welfare of said child will be promoted by placing him in a good home, I do hereby voluntarily and unconditionally transfer him to the care of Shadyside Home, with the understanding that the agent of said organization will provide him with a home in the United States until he shall reach the age of 21 years, unless prevented from doing so by some physical or mental disease, by the gross misconduct of the child or by his leaving the place provided for him without the knowledge or consent of Shadyside Home, and I pledge myself not to interfere with the custody or management of said child in any way, or encourage or allow anyone else to do so, and I hereby expressly authorize and empower Shadyside Home to consent to the adoption of said child without notice to me, as if I personally gave such consent at the time of such adoption and do hereby myself consent to said adoption. I hereby attest that the within transfer of said child is my free act and deed.

"Christ, this is like something out of Charles Dickens," Dan said. "What do they mean the baby was destitute and homeless?"

"I don't remember anyone explaining the fine points. I guess there had to be some kind of reason given for surrendering him. Legal mumbo-jumbo, like my father said."

"Did you read it when you signed?"

"Yes, I did," Janine said miserably, "but I didn't remember that until reading it just now. Until now, all I remembered from that day is how I felt after I signed, which was totally worthless."

Two tears were rolling down her cheeks. Dan thought he might start to cry, too. He wanted to enfold her in his arms and tell her to forget, but something in her posture warned him that doing so would be more harm than help. Instead, he put a hand on her elbow and guided her to a secluded corner of the lobby, beside a tall potted plant.

"You know," she said, "as awful as it is to see in print, he really was destitute and homeless. I had nothing to give him."

"That's not true. You had yourself to give. Only you weren't allowed to. Free act, my ass."

Her eyes were filled with gratitude.

"Do you think it's like a contract?" she asked. "Do you think that it's still binding now that Hunt's grown up?"

"I don't know." Dan scanned the document again. "It seems like it's mainly meant to cover his guardianship until he was adopted and to make it so that they didn't have to get you to sign something else once they found him a family."

"What about the part about not interfering and not letting anyone else interfere?"

"You'd have to ask a lawyer about that."

He returned the paper to her. She folded it and put it into her purse.

"I'm not consulting a lawyer," she said vehemently. "I don't care what this paper means now. As far as I'm concerned, Hunt's the only one with the authority to tell me not to interfere."

"Atta girl. So, what's our next move?"

"Dan, if there's a chance we could get into some kind of legal trouble, maybe you shouldn't—"

"Hell, I don't care about that."

"Are you sure?"

"Janine, please don't make me keep having to say I want to do this."

"All right." She sighed. "But I don't know what's next."

"I suggest grabbing a coffee and danish somewhere and doing some strategizing. Two heads are better than one, like they sing on Sesame Street."

"Do you have the time?"

"My whole day is clear."

They found a greasy spoon luncheonette four blocks from the office building. There were only three tables and a counter with six stools, but there were no other customers, so they chose a table, and Janine spread out her search notebook.

"Mrs. Marcos didn't add much to the mix," she said, turning to the questions section.

"She did confirm he was adopted by Catholics."

"I already knew that."

"No. You knew he'd been baptized."

"You're right. But how does that help?"

"Well, it's a corroborated fact now. We don't have many of those."

The waitress arrived with their coffees and pastries. Janine picked up the little cream pitcher, then put it down without pouring any cream into her coffee.

"Dan, how many Catholic churches do you think there are in Trenton?"

"I don't know. You could probably find out from the Yellow Pages."

"Do you think it's safe to assume that the priest my mother cornered in the hospital was from a local parish?"

"Makes sense."

He took a bite of danish. Greasy spoon the place might be, but the danish was a perfect blend of sticky sugar, butter-sodden dough, and mildly bitter cheese.

"Wait a minute," he said with his mouth full. "You mean we canvas the churches and try to find the priest?"

"Exactly. And we hope he registered the baptism in the church records and that, later, a copy got sent to the adoptive parents."

"*If* Shadyside told the parents the baby had been baptized, and *if* they had the priest's address to pass on to them. Didn't you say your mother didn't know his name?"

"She doesn't remember it, but she did know it then, and she must have given it to Shadyside. Damn, I wish I hadn't alienated Mrs. Marcos. I'll never be able to go back and ask more questions."

"It wasn't you, Janine, it was her. She wasn't going to crack, no matter what."

"I guess."

"You know, as far as corroborated facts go, I've been thinking about the name Hunt. I had a patient once whose first name was Price. His mother told me it was her maiden name and that it's common in the South for boys to be given their mother's maiden name as a first name. She was from Georgia."

"So you think Hunt could be the adoptive mother's maiden name?"

"It's possible. I don't know where that supposition might lead us, but—"

"Not to Georgia, I hope."

"Not today, anyway. Today we're going to Trenton."

WHILE DAN ORDERED sandwiches to go, Janine used the luncheonette's pay phone to call her parents and let them know she'd be longer than she'd expected.

They left Janine's car in the parking garage and took Dan's, and within a half-hour of having made the decision, they were on the New Jersey Turnpike heading south, the radio tuned to a pop station. Dan thought that even without the music, he would have felt comfortable with the silence between them. This was Janine. He'd never been closer to anyone than he had been to her. It didn't matter that they'd both experienced significant life events in the years they'd been apart. He had the sense that he could say anything to her, or even better, that there was much he didn't need to say outright, and that she would understand him because she knew the real Dan underneath all the roles he'd assumed since high school.

When the opening bars of Prince's "When Doves Cry" began, Janine switched the radio off.

"Do you mind?" she asked.

"Not at all."

"I've been trying to think of how to approach the churches. What do you think of saying we're doing genealogical research?"

151

"I like it. We could be brother and sister. Putting together a family tree."

"Brother and sister?" she asked, amused.

"No?"

"I think the less fiction we put out the better. We don't want to trip ourselves up."

"How about husband and wife, then?" Dan said cautiously. "It's closer to the truth."

In his peripheral vision, he saw her staring at the side of his face. He kept his gaze trained on the road. She turned away to look out the side window.

"The truth," she said quietly. "Now there's a murky topic."

"Not really. Not for me."

Janine made her seat back recline.

"Tell me about this clear truth, Dan. Something un-murky would do nicely right about now."

He glanced at her. Her eyes were closed. Her long lashes striped her cheekbones with tiny shadows.

"We loved each other, Janine. In a pure, total kind of way that's maybe only possible when you're young and innocent. That doesn't go away. It gets covered up, it gets pushed aside, it gets almost forgotten. We pat it on the head and tell it to be good and be quiet, and it does do that, but it doesn't go away."

He shot her another quick glance. She hadn't moved. She hadn't opened her eyes.

"A pretty story. You're telling yourself a story."

"It's how I feel. I'm not saying anything has to be done about it. It's just how I feel."

She adjusted her seat belt and turned onto her side so that her back was towards him.

"I'm going to take a nap."

"Okay if I turn the radio back on?"

"Sure."

Springsteen's rollicking refrain from "Born in the U. S. A." filled the car. Not exactly a lullaby. Dan switched to a classical station. Chopin. Better.

"I remember how you used sleep in the car on long drives with your head leaning against my shoulder," he said softly.

"That was before seat belts and bucket seats."

"Yeah, I guess teenage romance isn't the same any more. Automotively speaking."

The piano notes moved toward a crescendo. Dan lowered the volume. He thought he detected a change in Janine's breathing, the slow measure of sleep, so he was surprised when she spoke.

"Dan?"

"Yes?"

"Your story..."

"What about it?"

"I feel something like it, too."

He felt an intense, joyful peace settle over him. He turned off the radio and drove the rest of the way with only the sounds of his tires against the road and the occasional swoosh of a passing car or truck. Janine didn't stir until they were at the exit toll booth, when she sat up and looked around at the nearly featureless landscape with an expression he couldn't read.

15

THERE WERE NEARLY a dozen Catholic churches in Trenton, as well as several parishes in suburban towns near enough that a priest might have made visits to the Trenton hospital. Dan and Janine slated the suburban churches for future investigation if their inquiries in the city didn't yield anything. By late afternoon, they'd gone to five churches, with a break before the fifth one to buy sodas in a bodega and eat their sandwiches in the parked car.

They dropped the genealogical ruse after Blessed Sacrament, when a nun who was helping out in the rectory office told them that as a matter of diocese policy, sacramental registers more recent than 1900 were never made available to genealogical researchers. Nevertheless, she did consent to look in the Baptismal Register, and she informed them that there was no record of a baptism performed during the third week of March, 1966.

The pastor at Our Lady of Mt. Carmel was out, and no one else was authorized to handle the sacramental records. At Saint Columba's, Dan and Janine posed as an aunt and uncle applying for a copy of their nephew's baptismal certificate so that he could get married, but the priest told them they'd need their nephew's written permission for a copy. He also looked at his church's register and was able to inform them that, in any case, only one baby had been baptized during the week in question, and it had been a girl. At Saint Lucy's, Dan and Janine were still the aunt and uncle, but this time they asked only that the register be checked so that their nephew would know which church to write to.

Their story was that his parents were deceased, and no one in the family could remember the name or affiliation of the nice priest in the hospital who'd baptized him.

"Priests are supposed to baptize only members of their parish," the church secretary had remarked. "You see, the priest must have a moral certitude that the child will be raised Catholic, and that's more difficult with someone unknown to him. Might it have been an emergency baptism?"

"As a matter of fact, it was," Dan quickly lied. "The poor little guy was born with a hole in his heart. The doctors discovered it when he was two days old, and they had to operate right away."

"In that case," the woman said, "the baptism would have been registered in the parish of the parents."

"Our nephew checked there, with no luck," Janine said. "That's why we thought we'd inquire at the Trenton churches."

"No need to trot all over town," the woman said. "If the priest didn't report the baptism to the parents' parish, he would have reported it to the parish in which the hospital was located. In the case of Trenton Memorial, that would be St. Bartholomew's."

Now Dan and Janine were getting out of Dan's car, parked in front of St. Bartholomew's rectory. It was a squat, sturdy house of dark red brick with a slate roof. The church next door was of the same brick, and though not a magisterial building, it was substantial and dignified, fronted by a curved, columned portico and graced by a tall square bell tower on the south side.

Janine stood beside the car and stared at the rectory's facade.

"Maybe we shouldn't be doing this," she said.

"Doing what?"

"Tracking him down. Disrupting, like the social worker said."

"Forget her, Janine. All we're doing is gathering information. Nothing more."

"For now."

"We haven't disrupted Hunt's life. You could say he disrupted ours. But I don't think that's the way to think of it on either side."

155

"All right." Janine started down the flagstone walk. "But no more pretenses. We play it straight this time."

"Even though we risk getting tossed out on our ears?"

"Even though."

A heavy metal knocker was mounted in the middle of the wooden front door. As if to underline his commitment to the new honesty policy, Dan lifted the knocker and gave three hard raps. The door was opened by a middle-aged woman wearing an apron.

"We came to inquire about a baptismal record," Dan said.

The woman stepped aside to let them in. They entered a dimly lit entry hall. The planks of the polished floor gleamed darkly, and the walls were painted a soft yellow. A statue of the Infant of Prague wearing real cloth vestments stood on a side table, and on the wall above there was an oil painting of the church and a photo of Pope John Paul II.

"You'll need to see Father O'Hanlon," the woman said. "You can wait in there."

She pointed to an open doorway and went to fetch the priest. Janine and Dan entered a small room, which was set up as a library, with tall bookshelves covering two walls, three comfortable chairs, each paired with a floor lamp, and a bank of leaded windows looking on to the church next door.

It was a welcoming space, but neither of them sat down. They both knew that most likely, somewhere in this staid, old-fashioned house, neatly printed in some leather bound book, lay Hunt's last name and the address of his parents at the time of his adoption. It was unsettling to be so close to these vital facts and at the same time so far away.

Dan had misgivings about the strategic wisdom of Janine's decision to tell the truth, but he wasn't going to argue against it. He sensed that she was beyond strategy, had abandoned it, that her desire to be straight now came from something deeper and more important than strategy. She needed to do it this way. She needed to succeed or fail in just this way and no other. He would not oppose that, not even with gentle advice. He believed that was how he could best help her now.

A short man with a tight, round belly bustled into the room. He was dressed in black slacks and a black short-sleeved shirt with a white clerical collar. He had a full head of snow-white hair, a close-clipped white beard, and a ruddy complexion, his nose being redder than the rest of his face. Dan suspected the priest might enjoy a stiff drink or two of an evening, yet he couldn't shake the impression that the man was more Santa Claus than souse.

"Father O'Hanlon," the priest said, motioning them to sit down and taking one of the easy chairs himself. "How may I help you?"

"I'm Janine Linden, Father, and this is Dan Gannon."

The priest leaned forward to shake first Dan's hand and then Janine's.

"Mrs. Weaver said you were interested in a baptismal record?"

Janine gave a concise account of their situation — the youthful pregnancy, her mother's corralling of the priest in the hospital, the adoption, the boy's recent attempt to contact her, their hopes of discovering his whereabouts.

Dan watched the priest's face while Janine talked. Father O'Hanlon's expression never wavered. It was consistently attentive and interested. Not sympathetic exactly, but not judgmental. Except that he did seem to be evaluating Janine on some level. Trying to see into her soul, perhaps. Dan supposed the man had long experience in listening to tragic stories. Theirs was probably easier to hear than many others. No one in their story was dead, no one was going to burn in Hell. Did the Catholic Church still believe in Hell? Even if it did, Dan couldn't imagine this Santa Claus ever trying to frighten a sinner with the threat of eternal flames. Anyway, if Dan recalled his catechism correctly, the worst part of Hell was supposed to be that you never got to see the face of God.

"I can look in our Register," the priest said when Janine had finished. "And I'm happy to let you know if the baby's baptism was recorded here or not, but beyond that, my hands are tied. By church statute, we can issue certificates only to the person who was baptized, or if he's a minor, to his parents. The adoptive parents, in this case."

"I understand, Father."

"Your mother is sure the baptism occurred? Because the church recommends that baptism not take place until after an adoption decree has been completed and an amended birth certificate has been issued by the state. Additionally, in the case of an unwed mother, the priest would want assurances that she was no longer..."

"Living in sin?" Janine finished, bitterness creeping into her voice.

"Living in a morally unhealthy situation."

Dan said, "We weren't together by then, if that's what you mean."

"Your mother would have needed supporting documentation, too," Father O'Hanlon continued, "so that the priest would know that the parents' names and the date and place of birth were accurate."

"She had the hospital record," Janine said.

"That would do."

"My mother is a very persuasive woman, Father. If anyone could get a priest to act against recommendations, it would be her."

"Well, God bless her, I say. Just between us, years ago it was common for babies in Catholic orphanages or homes for unwed mothers to be baptized before adoption. The nuns just scooped them up and took them to be baptized. Nuns are often very persuasive women, too."

"I wasn't in a Catholic home. There wasn't an opening when I needed it."

"There are very few homes these days compared to the 50's and 60's," Father O'Hanlon said, "but there aren't waiting lists to get in any more."

The priest excused himself and went to get the Baptismal Register.

"What do you think?" Janine asked Dan.

"That bit about the nuns... I think he's on our side."

Father O'Hanlon returned with a large ledger. His thumb was stuck inside it, holding a place. Embossed on its spine in gilt were the numbers "1960 - 1969." The priest took his seat and lay the half-closed book on his lap, his thumb still inside it.

"When I was a young priest, I worked for a while with Catholic Charities," he said. "They were the largest adoption agency in the country back then. One of my duties was to accompany young women to court or to lawyers' offices to sign the papers giving up their babies. We had no doubt, any of us, that it was absolutely the right thing for everyone concerned. The workers at the homes for unwed mothers counted it a failure if a girl kept her baby. Not many did."

"I had doubts," Janine said quietly.

"Oh, I'm sure you did," Father O'Hanlon said. "I meant none of us adults doubted the rightness of what we were doing, of what we were convincing the girls to do."

Dan said, "You sound as if you have doubts now."

The priest was lost in reverie for a moment.

"Not doubts exactly," he said. "But even at the time, whenever I witnessed a girl signing those papers, I was struck by the solemnity and magnitude of what was happening. It didn't matter if the girl was crying or stone-faced, repentant or brazen, if she'd been cajoled into signing or if it had been her idea. I was always struck by the solemnity and the magnitude, and by the deep, deep sadness of it."

"Did you tell the girls that?" Janine asked.

"No, I didn't. I used to tell them I'd pray for them and for their babies. And I did."

There was an awkward silence.

"Did you find something, Father?" Dan said, pointing to the book.

"Yes, I did."

He opened the book to the place he'd been keeping with his thumb, but he tilted it so that Dan and Janine couldn't see the surface of the page.

"I remember this priest," Father O'Hanlon said, reviewing the entry. "Everyone in the diocese knew him. He was a colorful character with a big voice and an even bigger heart. If anyone would baptize a baby under questionable circumstances, it would have been Father George."

"So my mother was right?"

"Your mother was right. Your son was baptized Daniel Pettorini by Father George on March 18, 1966, witnesses Alfonse and Rose Pettorini, mother Janine Annette Pettorini, father ignotus."

"Ignotus?" Dan said.

"Unknown."

"But that's not true," Janine exclaimed. Turning to Dan, she added, "I told them to put your name down. At the hospital and at Shadyside."

"It was your parents," Dan said caustically. "They didn't want me on record."

"Don't assume that, son," Father O'Hanlon said. "Without a sworn, witnessed declaration from you, even Father George would have been reluctant to enter your name on anything official."

"No one ever asked me to swear to anything."

"Unfortunately, in those days, the father was often listed as unknown even if he did declare paternity, and not just by the Church. It made the adoption process easier if only one parent's consent was required."

Ignotus. Pretty close to ignoble. That's about how Dan was feeling. Ignoble. Inferior. Contemptible. How did he and Janine ever suppose they had any chance of making a life for themselves and their baby when the whole world, it turned out, had been arrayed against them?

"Is there anything else you can tell us, Father?" Janine said.

The priest sighed and looked down at the floor.

"Anything," Janine repeated.

"Was a baptismal certificate issued?" Dan said.

The priest looked at the book again.

"Yes. There's a notation that an adoption took place and that the information from the original record is never to be released. The certificate we sent would have had only the child's new legal name and the names of the adopting parents and the priest's name. The date of baptism stays the same, of course. You only get baptized once."

"Do you have the address where the certificate was sent?" Dan dared to ask.

"I can't tell you that. It's not a court record, so it's not sealed by law, but the diocese has policies..."

There was apology in the priest's voice and sorrow in his eyes. Dan was convinced they could get something out of him if they just cleared an avenue for him.

"But the address is 18 years old," Dan pressed.

The priest didn't respond except to lift his eyebrows.

"Is there a way to tell if the family is still there?" Janine said.

She'd caught Dan's lead. Indirect questions were the way to go. The priest wouldn't give them outright information that he shouldn't, and asking him to would squelch any chance of gaining peripheral facts. He was willing to collude with them to some extent, but they had to enlist him carefully.

"Each parish keeps its own sacramental records," Father O'Hanlon explained. "But if other sacraments are administered to a person, such as confirmation or marriage or holy orders, notice of that must be sent to the parish that holds the original baptismal record, in addition to being recorded in the parish where the sacrament was given. Your baptismal record is meant to be the primary record of your status in the Church, no matter how far afield you roam."

"So if our son had been confirmed, his parish would have notified you?" Janine asked.

"Correct."

"And did they?"

"We have a notation that he received the sacrament of confirmation."

"At the same parish where the baptismal certificate was sent?"

"Yes."

"Which means," Dan said, "that the family was in the same parish, if not at the same address, at least until he was 12 or 13."

"Thirteen," the priest said.

Dan knew the priest wouldn't let the cat out of the bag, but was this a signal that he was willing to let them peek inside, to get a glimpse of a paw or a whisker?

"Father, we think we may know the adoptive mother's maiden name," Janine said. "Do you have that information?"

"Yes, I do."

"If we tell you the name, can you say whether we're right?"

The priest shook his head. "I don't think I should."

161

"Father," Dan said quickly. "If we say the name and it's right, what if you just stay silent? Don't say yes or no. Don't even blink. Can you do that?"

The priest looked supremely uneasy.

"What's the name?" he finally said.

"Hunt," Janine answered.

The priest remained as still as a statue.

"Thank you, Father," Janine said, standing up. "We won't keep you any longer."

The men stood, too, and Dan and Janine bowed their heads while Father O'Hanlon gave them his blessing. Then he walked them out.

"Everything is in God's hands," he intoned as he opened the front door for them. "Whatever happens, He will be there."

———∞———

DAN WOULD HAVE liked a few moments to collect his thoughts before driving off, but Father O'Hanlon remained in his doorway, determined, it seemed, to see them off. So Dan started the car, giving the priest a wave as he pulled away. But he turned at the first corner and drove only a few blocks before parking the car again.

"How are you?" he said to Janine.

"My head's spinning a bit. How about you?"

"About the same."

They stared out the windshield a few moments.

"That parish could be anywhere," Janine said, discouraged.

"Maybe with the maiden name, we could search marriage records," Dan suggested. "Check New Jersey, and maybe New York and Pennsylvania. Say, for the five years before Hunt's birth."

"Five years?"

"I figure they must have tried for a while to have their own kids before they adopted."

"I don't know," Janine said dubiously. "We don't have her first name, we don't have the man's name. It sounds like a wild goose chase."

"Isn't that our specialty?"

Dan put his hand on the key in the ignition. Janine reached towards his hand, but she stopped short of touching him. He didn't turn the key.

"You really have the whole day clear?" she said.

"Yup. What's left of it."

She folded her hands together in her lap like a schoolgirl. Dan saw her tuck her thumbs into her palms.

"I'd like to go to Shadyside," she said.

"Really?"

"Not inside. That's probably all changed anyway. I just want to see it from the outside."

"Why?"

"I sketched it the other day. I remembered more than I thought I would, but I couldn't remember all of it."

"You want to check the accuracy of a sketch? Come on, Janine. I don't buy that."

"Never mind then. It was a stupid idea."

He gripped the steering wheel tightly, feeling dismal. He felt so safe with her. Did she not feel safe with him?

"I'm the stupid one. I shouldn't pry."

"No, Dan. I'm not trying to hide anything. Honestly. I don't know why I want to see the place. It was the scene of so much pain for me, but it was a refuge, too. There was a freedom there I didn't have at home, where I had to stay inside so the neighbors wouldn't see my belly, where none of my friends could come over because I was supposedly in Florida taking care of a sick aunt. At Shadyside, I was just one of the girls, not some kind of freak."

"You don't think it'll be upsetting to see the place?"

"It might be." She took a deep breath. "That's why I wanted to go there with you."

He started the car.

"Where is it?" he said.

16

SHADYSIDE WAS IN a dilapidated neighborhood of rambling old houses that must have been grand a century ago. Rows of mailboxes nailed to wide porches were evidence that the houses weren't single-family dwellings any longer. Occasional gaps where, presumably, houses had been torn down were occupied by small businesses — a grocery, a laundromat, a liquor store, a variety store with dusty window displays of school supplies, economy size bottles of soda, plastic toys, hair products, and rolls of gift wrap. One house was boarded up, its roof charred and partially caved in. It looked like it had been shuttered for quite a while. The area was saved from total dreariness by the huge trees lining the sidewalks and looming up out of back yards.

"Was it like this when you were here?" Dan asked as he and Janine walked towards Shadyside from their parking space three blocks away.

"No, but it was definitely past its heyday. A lot of the homes had been converted into apartments or duplexes. There were little stores moving in. But it never felt dangerous. Not that I went out much."

"So they did let you out?"

"Three afternoons a week. We had to tell them where we were going, and we had to be back by dinner. Mostly, we went to the corner store for potato chips and other forbidden treats, or once in a while downtown to a movie. After we'd dutifully donned our fake wedding bands."

Janine stopped in front of a large, three-story house of chiseled gray stone surrounded by a wrought iron fence. It had a pillared front porch and a smaller side porch on the right. The windows on the ground floor had been fitted with security bars. There was an auxiliary wing on the left side of the house, added, perhaps, early in the house's history to accommodate a newly wed couple or an aging grandmother. Janine said it'd been the nursery in her time. It had since been shrouded in aluminum siding.

A bright red and yellow sign on the patch of lawn in front identified the place as A FUTURE FOR FAMILIES, INC. Italicized letters below repeated the name in Spanish: *UN FUTURO DE LAS FAMILIAS.*

"I remember the day I arrived," Janine said. "It looked so big and spooky. The spiked fence. Closed curtains at every window. It was like a house in a horror movie. I remember my mother opening the car door for me, and my father reaching in his hand to help me out. My legs felt like lead."

"Because you didn't want to go."

"I did and I didn't. I was afraid. I didn't know what it would be like. But I was relieved, too. Here, I wouldn't have to worry about people I knew judging me. I wouldn't have to sit at the dinner table and watch my parents pretend not to be disappointed in me."

She walked a bit past the house so that she could see the side of it.

"That was my room up there," she said, pointing to a small dormer window protruding from the third floor mansard roof.

Dan peered up at the window. Its sash, like all the trim on the house, had been painted canary yellow. To coordinate with the sign, he supposed, and perhaps to convey a sense of optimism and cheerfulness. But to him, it struck a discordant note. Despite the building's weathered age and the unfortunate aluminum siding on the old nursery wing, the house had a certain crumbled grace, like a beautiful old woman. The slashes of yellow turned the quaint architectural elements into parodies of themselves.

"Did you have roommates?"

"Three. There were 20 girls in all. But sometimes there'd be more. Girls were happy to sleep on couches or on cots in the hall just to get in."

"I don't suppose you've kept in touch with anyone."

Janine looked at him in disbelief.

"Kept in touch?" she scoffed. "We didn't even know each other's names or where we were from. We were only allowed to use first names, and they were all made up. I was Kate."

Dan remembered the Kate in parentheses on the folder holding Janine's records at the Newark office of A Future for Families.

"Nobody told?"

"There was one girl who was a bit of a rebel — she actually saw her boyfriend on the sly once. She told us her real name was Sylvia and that she was from Kansas City. The rest of us...well, basically, we were obedient, 'good' girls used to following rules, plus we were trying to show we were trustworthy and redeemable. Even Sylvia didn't tell us her last name, and she didn't insist on being called Sylvia. She used the name they gave her. Gladys, I think it was. Or Gloria. Something like that."

"Strange."

"Not really, if you think about it. The whole idea of this place was that we had screwed up but that it was just a temporary problem. We were going to go back into our lives, we were going to be set back on the right path, and we needed secrecy and privacy to do that."

She looked away from the house and across the street, where a group of six Black girls about nine or ten years old were playing jump rope with a length of clothesline. Two were turning the rope, and one was jumping. The others waited in line, their bodies as taut as sprinters on their marks for a race. They were all chanting a rhyme, and Dan and Janine could hear the words clearly.

Miss Lucy had a baby, she named him Tiny Tim,
put him in the bathtub to teach him how to swim.
He drank all the water, ate all the soap,
died last night with a bubble in his throat.

As the rhyme moved into its second half, girls ducked in under the swinging rope one by one and joined the original jumper until there were four of them jumping in unison.

In came the doctor, in came the nurse,
in came the lady with the alligator purse.

"Do you think the lady with the alligator purse was a social worker?" Dan said to Janine.

He was watching the girls, but Janine had returned her gaze to the house.

"They told us it would be like it never happened," she said dreamily. "They believed it, too. But they weren't the ones giving up their babies. They had theories, but we had the babies, real flesh and blood babies."

Dan looked at Janine's meditative expression and flashed on the births of his daughters. He remembered sitting with Robin through the long hours of labor, rubbing her back, supporting her when she wanted to walk, wiping her face and throat with a cool cloth. Time slowed almost to stopping. Time became a huge misshapen burden he was required to drag ceaselessly through a muddy, rough-hewn tunnel with no end in sight. But when the baby arrived — Vanessa sliding out of Robin like some fantastic sea creature stretching, and Sally, a Caesarean baby, scooped from the uterus still a curled ball of crouching limbs — time had sprung forward anew, and Dan had nearly levitated out of his chair.

With Vanessa, he'd been unprepared for the intensity of his feelings. But it hadn't been any less intense with Sally. In an instant, the mind-numbing fatigue and worry of the preceding hours had evaporated, replaced by joy and awe. An even deeper emotion took hold as he held the swaddled newborn, who'd stopped crying and was looking around her as if to say *well, let me see where I've ended up.* A distinct new being had entered the room, entered the world. Everyone there knew it. Anyone could feel the force of it. Even, probably, a scared, confused teenaged girl.

"If we walk around the block," Janine was saying, "we can get a view of the back of the house and the yard."

The back yard was small, and much of the space was taken up by a climbing structure and a slide and swing set. There were two large shade trees, each with a bench under it, and a small plot of red, white, and pink geraniums.

"There wasn't any play equipment when I was here," Janine remarked. "We didn't need it."

"You stayed three months, right? It must have seemed like a long time."

"That was about average, though some girls came later in their pregnancy. One girl booked in only six weeks before her due date. Her family couldn't afford to send her sooner, so she'd been living like a prisoner in her house. If someone came over, she had to stay in her room and not move around or make any sounds. When they went anywhere in the car, her mother made her lie down on the floor in the back seat until they were out of the neighborhood."

"You didn't feel like a prisoner here?"

"Sometimes I did. Other times I felt like a patient, or a sorority girl. Or a sleepwalker."

She was staring at the back door of the old house, her face lively with emotion. Dan suspected scraps of memory were gliding through her mind like eels.

"That door opens to the kitchen," she said. "My job was helping prepare lunch — cutting up vegetables, making Jell-o."

"What did you do the rest of the time?"

"Most of us were still in high school, so we had school work to do. A few girls worked as mother's helpers in doctor's homes, to pay their bill at Shadyside. And there were classes in sewing, cooking, home nursing, grooming, how to be a hostess."

"You're kidding."

"They were priming us to become good wives and homemakers."

"What about baby care?"

"Oh, no, nothing about that. Not a word about labor or delivery or postpartum, either. And the girls who'd had their babies were kept apart from the rest of us, so we didn't even get anything through the grapevine. Even in the hospital, no one told me what was happening, if it was normal for it to hurt so much. Pairs of interns would come in and do vaginal exams, but they never said anything except to tell each other numbers. Dilation and effacement, though I didn't know that then. After I started pushing, they put a hard rubber mask over my face, and everything went black."

Everything went black. So Janine hadn't met her baby as Dan had met his daughters, as astounding new presences.

Abruptly, Janine turned and began walking quickly back in the direction they'd come. Dan hurried to catch up.

"Are you all right?"

"I thought I could do this," she said, struggling to keep her voice steady. "I thought that I wanted to do this... But it's... It's sucking me down. Oh, Dan, it's sucking me down."

She stopped walking and covered her face with her hands. They had rounded the corner and were again on the street that the house fronted. It loomed ahead like a dark iceberg, its yellow trim garish and incongruous. Hesitantly, Dan put one arm around Janine's shoulders. She leaned into him for a few minutes. Then she stepped away and looked into his eyes.

"Most of the girls were dumped by the fathers of their babies. The guys didn't want any part of them once they got pregnant, or they refused to believe it was their baby. One boy got five of his friends to spread the lie that they'd all slept with the girl."

Dan waited. She was leading up to something.

"A few good things happened for me in that house, and some hard, hard things, but I never had to feel like you'd thrown me away. That helped. I held on to that. I stopped writing to you and I cut you out and you went on without me, and all that hurt, but I knew you would've stood by me if you could have. It's important to me that you know that."

"You gave him my name," Dan said, and his voice felt husky in his throat.

She nodded.

"Let's go up one more block and circle around to the car from there," he said. He didn't want her to have to pass by the house again.

As they walked, each of them hewed to the edge of the sidewalk so that there was a wide space between them. This careful positioning heightened Dan's awareness of his own body and of hers. The very air between them seemed to form an elastic, palpable shape, like the invisible, pushing life between the opposing poles of two magnets.

In the car, Janine spread a map open on her lap and navigated the way out of Trenton. They were thrown off twice by one-way streets, but eventually they saw signs for the Turnpike, and Janine folded up the map and put it in the glove compartment. Dan was relieved that the traffic on the highway was moving at a steady pace, and he quickly revved the car up to 65 and held it there. He felt as if they were fleeing a pursuer.

They rode for half an hour without speaking. There was nothing outside the car windows worthy of comment, and small talk would have been a sham. Dan felt no pressure to get things said. The search would probably necessitate their meeting at least two or three times more. He had no solid reason to assume their connection would continue longer than that, yet he was infused with a sense of bounty and leisure. She was next to him now, which was something of a small miracle. He wouldn't be greedy. He was content in this moment, and he felt more alive than he had in years.

"There was a rec room," Janine said.

He started, surprised to have the silence broken.

"A rec room? Like with ping-pong and a jukebox?"

She laughed, a free, loose sound. He realized it was the laugh he remembered and that it was the first he'd heard it since meeting her again.

"Hardly. There were some books, and card tables with jigsaw puzzles. A radio. A t-v that was on all day, soap operas mostly. As if we weren't all living soap operas."

"Did you spend much time there?"

"No. It wasn't very inviting."

"I guess with three roommates, you didn't get much privacy."

"You learned to be private by closing in. Most of the girls were good about seeing when somebody wanted to be left alone."

Dan knew Janine would have appreciated that. She'd always had an inward-looking streak in her personality. In high school, people often thought of her as stuck up or cold until they got to know her. She rarely opened the cloistered garden of her inner self. She'd let him in, but then, later, she'd barred the door. She'd built a room he'd never been allowed to enter, the room in which she'd finished her pregnancy and had her baby and given him away. Had anyone ever seen the inside of that room?

"Remember that pink make-up case one of your sisters gave me?" Janine said. "She was going to throw it out because the lock was broken."

"I think so. Kind of a square box with a handle?"

"That's what I took with me to the Home to carry my things."

"For a three-month stay?"

"We each got only one dresser drawer and part of a closet. They had a room in the basement filled with donated maternity clothes. We called it the belly store. You took what you needed to use while you were there, and then you left the clothes behind for the next girls. I left that pink case, too. I didn't want it any more after that."

The sun, fiery red in a pale cloudless sky, was setting on Dan's left. He moved the visor to the side window, but the sun was too low on the horizon for the visor to do any good, so he moved it back.

"That girl, Sylvia," Janine said cautiously. "She really wanted to keep her baby. Most of us did, but none of us knew where to start. We weren't fit for any decent-paying jobs, and nobody explained about welfare. We thought welfare was for poor people, and we weren't poor. But Sylvia fought. She argued with the social worker, she argued with the doctors, she argued with her parents. We heard she was so much trouble in the hospital, they gave her tranquilizers. She swore she would never give up her baby."

"What happened?"

"Her father threatened to have her locked up in a psychiatric hospital if she didn't sign the relinquishment paper, and he had a doctor ready to commit her, so she finally caved in. I was in the nursery when they came for her baby. She was screaming. I almost thought maybe she should go to that psych hospital. They had to pull the baby out of her arms. I was determined that I wouldn't let that be the last memory Daniel had of me, as fighting and hysterical. If babies that little can remember."

"I think they can, on some level."

"I saw her the next day, when she was leaving. She was like a zombie. I gave her a hug, and she just stood there like a piece of wood. And she said — it still gives me chills to think of it — she said, 'they don't call it giving up for nothing.'"

Dan sighed deeply. He didn't know how to respond to the terrible story. This Sylvia sounded like an extreme case, but maybe it was just in her behavior, not in her desires and her desolation. Just because Janine, or other girls, hadn't pushed back against the forces shepherding them toward giving up their babies didn't mean it wasn't just as painful for them. It was obvious that some of Janine's emotions were still raw, all these years later.

"Janine?"

"Yes?"

"Did you tell your husband about the baby?"

"Of course."

Dan was embarrassed to feel a twinge of jealousy.

"What did he say?"

"He was very sympathetic. He said it must have been a very difficult thing."

She shifted in her seat, angling her body towards him.

"You didn't tell your wife?"

Dan thought of Robin, her vacant prettiness, like the idealized face of a doll. It wasn't a face that invited confidences. He'd never considered telling her about Janine and the baby because he assumed she wouldn't want to know. It had happened before her time. It didn't touch them. What was the use of stirring up trouble? Robin liked things neat. Had he given that too much weight? He'd thought he was protecting her and their life together. Wasn't that what he was supposed to do?

They were behind a big tractor-trailer. The truck was moving at a good clip, above the speed limit. Nevertheless, Dan accelerated and pulled out to pass it. Janine gripped the armrest. He cut back into their lane after the truck was several car lengths behind them.

"I never told anyone," he finally said.

Janine picked up her purse from the floor and dug around in it, coming up with a roll of Lifesavers. She peeled back the paper and put a candy in her mouth.

"Want one?" she asked, holding out the roll.

"No, thanks."

She put the candy away and dropped her purse on the floor again.

"Clark came along after I'd had a turning point. Maybe I wouldn't have told him anything if I'd met him before that. And I didn't tell anyone else, not even my closest friends. Not at the time, and not later."

"A turning point?"

Janine reached for the radio knob.

"That's another story for another day," she said.

"Another day," Dan repeated, but he wasn't sure she'd heard him over the static and garbled voices as she fiddled with the dial to tune in a station.

―❧―

THAT NIGHT, DAN sat on the small balcony of his second-floor apartment with a glass of Irish whiskey. The apartment was dark behind him. Below, there was a globe lamp on a post illuminating the walkway to the pool, but it was several yards to the south and was screened by the leafy branches of a large alder. All he could make out in the muted light were the black shapes of clipped bushes along the walkway. Across the courtyard sat the rectangle of another building, its facade freckled with lit windows. He appreciated the lack of visual details. It enhanced his sense of being insulated and hidden, ignored even. The day had been so eventful. Now he wanted to sit and think. Not in order to plan or evaluate, but just to gather in all the impressions of the day and take quiet possession of them.

He reviewed the big things that he'd said to Janine and that she'd said to him, and he thought about the trivial, commonplace things that had happened, like eating their sandwiches in the car, getting slightly lost while driving around to the churches, riding the elevator at the uncertain beginning of the day. Somehow it felt all of a piece, their revelations of the heart and the simple accumulation of hours in each other's company. What was it Janine had said? It was important to her that he know she hadn't felt he'd thrown her away? That was important to him, too. But, really, he thought, taking a swallow of whiskey, all of it was important, the momentous and the small. They had had a day together, and being with her had been as natural and as strong as it had always been. Janine had had to deal with some painful memories, and if he could have spared her that, he would have, but at least he'd been beside her. And she'd let him comfort her.

Dan went inside to refresh his drink. Relishing the darkness, he walked slowly across the living room, and once in the kitchen, he switched on only the small light over the stove so that he could locate where on the counter he'd left the bottle of Bushmills. He added a splash of whiskey to his glass and opened the freezer to get a couple of ice cubes. When he shut the door, he stood for a moment looking at the snapshots of his daughters stuck there with magnets.

When Robin was pregnant with Vanessa, he'd told her the child would be a girl.

"You've got a 50-50 chance of being right," she'd said, laughing.

"I'm serious. It's a girl."

"Why are you so sure?"

"I had a dream," he replied, though it wasn't true.

"Oh, pooh, I don't believe you. You're not that kind of dreamer. Besides, dreams don't mean anything. Not anything about the future, anyway."

174

They hadn't discussed it further. He'd participated in choosing two names, although he simply agreed to the first boy's name Robin suggested, while they went back and forth among a number of girls' names for weeks before settling on Vanessa. With the second pregnancy, Dan had predicted a girl with the same confidence.

"Another dream?" Robin had teased.

She intended her second pregnancy to be her last, and she was hoping for a boy.

"Two of us, two of them," she said. "Two females, two males."

"We're not boarding an ark," Dan quipped.

When he was proved right again, Robin began telling her pregnant friends to let Dan predict the gender of their unborn babies. In a spirit of fun, a couple of them did ask, but Dan always begged off.

"It only works if the kid is mine," he'd say.

"Maybe you could teach my husband the trick, then," one woman countered jauntily.

"No trick. Just lucky hunches."

"Don't listen to him," Robin put in. "He was absolutely positive both times. Couldn't be shaken."

"All right, Dan," the friend persisted. "Give it up. What's your secret?"

And what if I told you, Dan had thought, that there was, indeed, a secret? What would you all say if I told you I was sure I was going to get daughters because Fate or God or Chance had already given me a son and I'd lost him? I'd let him get lost.

Dan turned away from the refrigerator and went back out onto the balcony, but he didn't sit down. Instead, he lifted his glass to the night sky. The ice shifted with a small clinking sound.

"To you, son," he said softly. "Sleep well, young Daniel."

17

AT HOME IN Cape May Point, back inside life as it was before she'd gotten Hunt's letter, Janine found her impulse to search ebbing. For one thing, she didn't know where to turn next. But that wasn't the whole reason, nor even the main reason.

The few facts she had unearthed were like the Cape May diamonds tourists combed Sunset Beach for. Those small pieces of polished quartz crystal took thousands of years to tumble the 200 miles from the upper reaches of the Delaware River to the shores of Cape May Point. What Janine had learned about Hunt had traveled from 1966 to 1984. Other facts were out there, buried in the sand, but at the moment, she felt no compulsion to dig. She wanted to hold close the little bits she had — the revived memories and the small details like the baptism. She wanted to cup them tenderly, finger all their edges and curves. They felt immensely private.

Janine's inclination to cordon herself off from the drama of looking for Hunt became clear to her when Dan called a week after their trip to Trenton.

"No luck with the marriage licenses so far," he'd said.

"That's all right. We knew it was a long shot."

"Are you throwing in the towel?" He sounded dismayed.

Am I? Janine thought. She felt as if she'd reached a plateau midway through striving up a mountain, and she welcomed the respite. She was in no rush to seek another steep, rubble path whose length she didn't know, to knock down another "Do Not Enter" sign. She'd resume the struggle eventually, but she didn't know when or how, and not knowing didn't bother her.

"I just need to be out of harness for a while."

"Oh... Then...I'll call if the marriage license pans out. Or if it doesn't. So we can decide what else to do."

That had been at the beginning of last week, and Dan hadn't called again. Janine had thought two or three times of calling him, but she couldn't summon a specific reason to call, so she didn't. Both Dan and Hunt migrated to the background of her days. She immersed herself in work, preparing to start a new painting and catching up on framing orders. Otherwise, her time was claimed by friends, the boys, and the ocean.

Janine and Clark had chosen their house for its proximity to the ocean. They weren't close enough for a view, but a beach was within walking distance. They'd taken the boys in Snugli packs when they were babies, later in a double stroller. Now, with Tim and Larry walking, the trip took longer, but it was a pleasant route along sidewalk-less streets, passing a pond where turtles could sometimes be spotted.

Cape May Point was a sleepy residential area with a mixture of summer houses and modest year-round homes. It didn't get the tourist traffic that Cape May did, with its shops and restaurants, coastal hotels, and lovingly tended Victorian houses and gardens. The Point only had beaches, both ocean and bay. You had to go into Cape May to food shop, or get your car fixed, or grab a bus to Philadelphia or New York. Janine and Clark had been happy to accept those inconveniences.

The house itself was small, but it had a large, grassy backyard with shade trees, a luxury in a beach area. Even after Clark had built Janine a two-room studio, there was enough space to add a wood deck off the kitchen, to plow a vegetable garden and plant a grape arbor.

At present, a large tent was set up at the far end of the back yard. Tim and Larry hadn't braved sleeping in it yet, but they played in it every day, morphing it from castle to spaceship to pirate ship. Today, they'd dragged pots and pans and cooking utensils out to the tent to make a restaurant. It had been the idea of Dot, the baby-sitter who came afternoons so that Janine could paint for three uninterrupted hours while the light was good. Mornings, the boys went to a day camp in Cape May.

Dot had arrived fifteen minutes ago, and Janine was in her studio preparing to do a third study in oil crayons for a larger picture whose final composition was still taking shape in her mind. She wanted to do a painting of Shadyside Home that represented the fracturing of time. She wanted to represent time like the Cubists had represented form — present beside past beside future. It had been the natural state of the girls during their residencies at Shadyside. It was an ambitious idea, and her pencil sketches and crayon studies so far had fallen short, though of what exactly, she couldn't articulate. They simply weren't working.

Setting out her materials, Janine happened to glance at the wall calendar. Friday, August 3. Two and half weeks ago, she and Dan had made their excursion to Newark and Trenton. And five weeks ago, on June 27, she and the boys had been heading up the Garden State Parkway towards Teaneck for their ritual start to summer and her two fateful meetings, with Mr. Wilson and Belle Martine. She'd been in the lap of the gods on that trip.

"Get to work," she said aloud to herself. "Dot won't be here all day."

In one impulsive movement, she scooped up the crayons and put them away, deciding to take one step back and do some more exploratory sketches. Perhaps she'd moved out of that stage too soon.

She took a large pad and a set of lead pencils to the drafting table beside an open window. As usual, a soft breeze was blowing. Breezes came almost constantly off the sea and kept even the hottest days bearable. She could hear the boys' voices, the clang of metal spoons against pot lids, an occasional admonition from Dot. Despite the creative problems before her, she felt supremely content, as she usually did when she was in the studio and her boys were nearby but not in need of her.

She decided to attempt an abstract drawing of her old room at Shadyside, but not so abstract that a viewer wouldn't know it was a bedroom, particularly a bedroom for teenaged girls. But teenaged girls with something different about them, something somber.

She began by trying to recall exactly how the room had been laid out — the bunk beds, the one dresser, the deep set window with its wide ledge. She could see herself sitting on that ledge with a sketch pad on her lap, drawing the pattern of raindrops on the old, bubbled glass.

She had learned to draw at Shadyside. She'd pursued more rigorous studies in art later, but it had begun at the maternity home. A volunteer came in twice a week to give lessons to interested girls. A wholesome leisure time activity, Janine supposed the staff had thought.

After two hours, Janine had a sheaf of sketches and a more solid idea of where she'd like to go next. She'd get up early tomorrow and work some more. She liked working in the early morning. Sometimes the yard would be made mysterious by fog, and her studio would feel like a small, worthy boat moored in a friendly channel. If the boys got up and didn't find her in the kitchen, they'd run across the yard to the studio, yelping as their bare feet hit the cold, dewy grass.

Besides finding it pleasurable to be in the studio at sunrise, Janine had another reason for planning to get up early on Saturday. Lee and her kids were arriving Sunday afternoon and staying for a few days, and she doubted she'd get out to her studio again until they left. She'd invited them on the spur of the moment on her last day in Teaneck, when Lee had looked so hot and encumbered. Now she regretted it a little because she'd been enjoying so much being back on her own turf, busy in the present, holding the distant past at bay except to mine it for her art. But she would get into the swing of the visit. It'd be fun to take Lee and her brood to favorite beaches, to the clam shack and the frozen custard place, to the lighthouse and the bird sanctuary. As a grand finale on their last night, they'd hit the boardwalk at Wildwood. The twins were delirious at the prospect.

—∞—

On Monday, Lee and Janine were sitting on beach chairs under a blue and white striped umbrella at the beach near the lighthouse. Lulu was

179

stretched out on her stomach on a towel in the sun, her skin glistening with tanning oil. Lee had argued with her about sunscreen but had finally thrown up her hands. The only concession she could wring out of the girl was that she'd cover up in half an hour.

"Fifteen minutes on a side, Mom," Lulu had said, as if speaking to a moron.

"You'll regret this in 20 years."

"Not even!"

"Oh, you will. And don't think I won't remind you."

Sam was boogie-boarding, and Tim, Larry, Max, and Howie were at the edge of the surf digging holes and piling up cones of sand. Janine had brought Dot along to supervise the younger boys. She thought Lulu got stuck often enough in the role of junior mother. The girl had put in plenty of time this morning readying the picnic hamper. She'd assembled stacks of sandwiches, squeezed fresh lemonade, cut up carrot sticks and celery sticks and chunks of watermelon, and made chocolate chip cookies with the dubious assistance of Tim and Howie. Janine had had to snatch a couple of hours in the workshop to finish framing a photograph for a client who'd called unexpectedly and wanted it that day to take to someone as a gift. She'd left the picnic preparations on Lee's shoulders. Lulu had done the lion's share of the work.

"Well, look at us," Lee said, stretching out her legs and digging her toes into the sand. "We're like those spoiled, rich ladies in the Hamptons who spend all week lounging on the beach while their hubbies are toiling away in the hot city to pay for it."

"Sort of."

"Oh, God, Janine, will I never stop making an ass of myself? I forgot...I mean, I didn't forget, I just—"

"It's all right. Really. In a way, it's a good thing."

"A good thing?"

"Not to be defined as a widow. Not to have that be the first thing someone thinks of when they think of me."

Lee nodded, but she didn't look as if she understood.

"I *am* a widow, of course, but lately I haven't been thinking of myself in that way. I feel instead like I'm a...I don't know...an *un-married* person."

"You mean single."

"Not in the usual sense."

"I don't get it," Lee said, frowning.

"When Clark died, we got *un*-married. Death un-married us. At first, that loss, that absence was at the center of who I was. I used to wake up every morning feeling like there was a mound of wet sand lying on my chest. I didn't change the sheets on our bed for two weeks after he died because I wanted to save his smell. Then, when I finally did change them, I woke up the next morning in the middle of the bed. I think I must have migrated in my sleep towards his side searching for that smell."

"I've heard of that," Lee said. "People not washing the person's clothes to keep the smell, or not erasing his voice from the answering machine."

"Oh, I'm sure it's all very typical. Knowing that doesn't make it easier, but it does reassure you you're not crazy."

Lee looked at her watch. "Turn over," she called out to Lulu.

The girl moaned in protest, but she flipped to her back, wiggling her hips to make a nest in the sand for her bottom.

"So things are better now?" Lee asked, turning back to Janine.

"There are still times grief pounces on me out of the blue, but that's happening less and less. I'm past all the firsts."

"The firsts?"

"First Christmas, first birthdays, first anniversary. Now, life's new. I'll never forget Clark. But he's not at the center of my life any more, and his memory isn't the center, and being a widow isn't either."

"So what is?"

Janine smiled.

"Me," she said. "A mother, a painter, a gardener. And whatever else the future brings."

181

"Well, good for you," Lee said. She brushed away a horse fly that had alighted on her knee.

"Janine," she said slowly, "do you think...since it's been a *recent* development...do you think it has anything to do with—"

Janine stood up.

"I'm going in the ocean," she said, interrupting Lee. "And then let's dig into that picnic lunch."

Janine ran to the water's edge. The surf rushed around her ankles. She knew where Lee had been heading: straight for Dan. And Janine didn't want to discuss it. Discuss *him*, she silently corrected herself. There was no it.

"Mommy!" Larry called, running to her side. "Can I go in with you?"

"Let me get wet first. I'll come back for you."

Dot was already on her way to retrieve Larry, who was perfectly capable of following his mother into the ocean.

Janine plunged into the water, striding awkwardly against the incoming waves until she was waist-deep. She stood there watching the waves heave towards her, the sunlight sparkling on their undersides as they rose up to break. Most of them crested and fell a few feet away from her, and she stumbled back a little each time the rushing white foam surged past her. Once, a wave held its peak and slapped her chest as it passed, breaking behind her. Her face was splashed with salty spray, and she laughed out loud — at the energy of the ocean and its cold embrace, at the simple joy of being alive.

Laughing like that felt so good. It was an actual sensation, in her chest, in her throat, in the muscles of her face. She realized she hadn't felt that particular kind of physical release in a long time. Of course she'd laughed since Clark died, but it had never felt so thorough. Then she remembered laughing in the car with Dan on the way home from Trenton, when he wondered if the hugely pregnant girls at Shadyside had played ping pong. That had been some kind of start. Or some kind of ending. She'd felt, then, that something inside her had unlocked.

She moved out into slightly deeper water, jumping up to meet the cresting waves. She was as pleased as a child by the way the passing water lifted her up and gently set her down again. When one rising breaker threatened to fall right on top of her, she dived under it, exulting in the tingle of cold water over her scalp and the tug of the shoreward-rushing water on her feet. She came up into the air just in time to see another wave looming. Again she dived. Again she felt the drag on her feet, the envelopment of the sea. When she bobbed up from that dive, she found herself immediately below the falling crest of a very large wave with no time to react. It crashed down upon her. She was tumbled over and over, until she felt the scrape of sand beneath her and sat up.

Larry, Tim, Max, and Howie were dancing around her laughing and screaming, like four Rumpelstiltskins around a campfire. She'd washed up right in the midst of their construction zone. Her suit and her hair were full of sand, and one elbow was stinging, but the children's glee was so infectious, Janine, too, started laughing. It was a rollicking laughter, more consuming than her joy alone in the waves, bigger than her amusement at Dan in the car. As she slowly got to her feet, she remembered again the strange sense of unlocking she'd had on the way home from Trenton. Whatever had opened up then, apparently it hadn't snapped shut again. Somehow she knew it wasn't going to.

EARLY THURSDAY MORNING, Lee and Janine sat on the deck watching robins patrol the yard for grubs and enjoying a lazy breakfast of fresh pineapple, bagels and lox, espresso, and, for Lee, mint tea. The children were all still soundly asleep. They'd gotten home from Wildwood at one a.m., after hours of amusement park rides, infusions of cotton candy, caramel apples, and ice cream with hot waffles, and general euphoric pandemonium. Janine was finishing up her coffee when the phone rang.

"Hmm," she said, getting up. "Kind of early for anyone to call."

"Probably Red wondering what time we're taking off today. He misses us if he has to eat supper alone, and here we've been gone four whole days."

Janine carried her empty cup into the kitchen, intending to re-fill it after she'd answered the phone. She set the cup down beside the espresso machine, and took the receiver from the wall unit.

"Hello, Mrs. Linden? This is Father O'Hanlon. From St. Bartholomew's in Trenton."

Janine was immediately jittery.

"Good morning, Father," she said, forcing her voice to sound casual.

She walked into the living room, extending the coiled phone cord as far as it would go. Lee might not go out of her way to eavesdrop, but she was bound to listen to an easily overheard conversation if it came to her on its own through the screen door.

"I hope this isn't too early to be calling. I thought you'd like as much notice as possible."

"Notice?"

"I took it upon myself — I hope you don't mind — but I got to thinking after your visit, and I prayed over it..."

"Yes?"

"I took it upon myself to contact the pastor of the parish we talked about. The family is still there."

Suddenly weak-kneed, Janine leaned against the wall.

"Father Nonas has talked to the mother," the priest went on, "and the family has agreed to meet you, with Father Nonas present. Not an unreasonable condition, under the circumstances. They can be at the church Saturday at 2:00."

Janine's jitters amped up to the vicinity of panic.

"Mrs. Linden?"

"Yes, I'm here. Sorry, Father. Is it the *whole* family?"

"That's my understanding. I didn't ask Father specifically who."

"And where's the church?"

"In Malaga. Same area code as yours, so I assume it won't be a long drive."

"I...I don't know, Father. This is so sudden."

This is so sudden? Janine thought. What am I, in a bad play? And isn't that what's supposed to be said in response to a hasty proposal of marriage? This is neither a suitor nor make-believe. This is my son. The day after tomorrow.

"Well, yes and no," the priest said gently. "If you consider the whole 18 years."

Considering the whole 18 years was exactly what Janine feared. Finding out how Hunt's life had been. Telling him what her life had been. Explaining to him why she hadn't kept him. Making herself understood. Making herself known.

"Would you like to check with Mr. Gannon first? To see if he's available? The impression I got is that the family is not only willing to meet you, but anxious to. They would probably agree to a postponement, but I think they'd rather it happen as soon as possible."

I have to call Dan, Janine thought. I don't want to call Dan.

"I'll try to reach him today."

"All right, then. I'll wait to hear."

"Good-bye, Father. Oh, and thank you."

Janine walked slowly back into the kitchen and hung up the phone. She started to fix herself another cup of espresso, but she knocked over the can of coffee, and the aromatic powder spilled across the kitchen floor in a wide swath. She took a dustpan and brush from beneath the sink, but her hands were shaking as she swept. Dark smears of ground coffee colonized the grout lines between the stone tiles of the floor. She left them. She poured herself a glass of water and carried it out to the deck.

Janine sat down. She picked up her partially eaten bagel and put it down again without taking a bite. The thought of putting anything into her mouth nauseated her.

"Are you okay?" Lee asked.

"It was that priest I told you about."

"What did he want?"

"He's found Hunt. I can meet him on Saturday if I want to."

"Oh, my God! Wait — if you *want* to? I'm amazed you're not breaking open the champagne!"

Janine stood up and walked to the railing of the deck. She looked out over her yard — the studio under the old maple tree; the lush flower and vegetable gardens; the grape arbor, heavy with fruit; the tent in the far corner, two Big Wheels parked in front of the door flap. She felt pride of possession and something more subtle, a sense of security. That had been sorely tested by Clark's death, but it was back in place at last. As much a sense of security as she ever let herself feel, at any rate. And now? Was her life about to be turned upside down again?

"This is what you wanted, right?" Lee said to her back. "To meet him?"

"That's what I thought," Janine replied, turning around. "But do I really? This all started because *he* tried to find *me*. It seemed like the right thing to look for him, so he wouldn't think I'd refused to answer his letter. Then I told myself I wanted to know if he was all right, if his life had turned out all right."

"Well, don't you want to know that?"

"Yes..."

"So what's the problem?" Lee speared a piece of pineapple with a fork and popped it into her mouth.

"The problem is that's not all of it. Yes, I want to reassure him, and yes, I want to know he's all right, but if I'm honest, I'm hoping for something *from* him, too. I want *his* reassurance. I want his acceptance. Maybe even his forgiveness."

"Look," Lee said breezily, spearing another pineapple chunk and waving it expressively. "It's like a blind date. You're uptight now, but as soon as you get there, you'll cool out and handle it, whatever it turns out to be."

"A blind date?" Janine exploded. "That's a birdbrained thing to say! You have no idea what you're talking about."

186

"Well, pardon me for breathing!" Lee retorted. "Up to now, all you looked for was encouragement in making this search — rah, rah, rah — so I gave it, even though I thought you could be heading for heartbreak. And now that you've accomplished the impossible, I'm supposed to agree that turning your back on it is absolutely, hands-down the way to go? I'm trying to be supportive here, Janine. So which is it, hot or cold? Do you want this kid or not?"

The trembling Janine had had in the kitchen returned, and now it wasn't only in her hands. Her entire body was seized by tremors. She felt as if she might throw up.

Alarmed, Lee came over to her. She put her hands on Janine's wrists.

"You're shaking. Come sit down."

Janine let herself be led back to her chair. Lee stood next to the chair, as if afraid Janine might fall out of it. Janine could see the profile of her friend's body through her thin summer nightgown, the slight droop of her breasts, the pouch of early pregnancy.

"I can be a birdbrain, I know that," Lee said meekly. "But it's hard to know which way is up with you on this."

Janine couldn't think how to explain herself, how to put into words the quiet, closeted pain she'd lived with since the day she'd handed over her first-born, and how the imminent exposure of that pain to him frightened her. She'd lived with his ghost for so long. She knew how to do that. To exchange that ghost baby for a real 18-year-old man was a terrifying gamble. She could lose them both and be left with nothing. She was about to step off a crumbling ledge in pitch darkness, not knowing if she'd land on a pile of goose down pillows or on briars and gravel, nor how long the fall would last.

"Finding him has really knocked you for a loop, hasn't it?"

Janine nodded.

"It's all happening so fast. There are so many things swirling around inside me — feelings and discoveries and memories. I need more time to let the dust settle."

"But what about Hunt? Can you ask him to wait?" The kindness in Lee's voice kept the questions from being accusatory. "And what about Dan?"

"Oh, God, Dan," Janine said. "That's another kettle of fish."

Rubbing the small of her back, Lee returned to her chair.

"He likes you, doesn't he?" she said when she'd sat down. "I mean, he really likes you."

Janine looked at Lee. Don't ask me that, she wanted to say. I'm not asking myself, so don't you ask me.

"Life doesn't give second chances like that," she said instead.

Lee raised her eyebrows.

"No? And what is all this detective work you two have been running around doing if it isn't a grab at a second chance?"

"That's different."

"Is it?"

Janine contemplated her yard again and all it signified — her young sons, her work, her sense of home and belonging. Where in all that was there room for Hunt? Or Dan? But she was jumping the gun. Neither of them had yet asked her to make room. But she knew that in both cases, the possibility of such a request was there. Well before it appeared, she needed to decide where each of them fit in her heart and in her sense of herself. Even if a request never came, she needed to decide those things.

"It's not just the speed of what's happening," she said, "or even all the questions it stirs up. It's that it's happening at all. I never expected it."

"I can see that Dan having feelings for you might have come as a surprise. But what? You went looking for Hunt without expecting to find him?"

"I knew it could go either way. I could find him sooner or later, or I could never find him. But now that I have... I can't count on good coming out of it."

"Why the heck are you thinking like that? Did the priest put a flea in your ear?"

"No. In fact, he said the whole family is anxious to meet us."

"Well, then?"

"It's me, Lee. It's just how I am. I don't trust good luck. I don't ever think it can last. I always expect the sky to fall."

"And you'll always be right. The sky *does* fall, eventually, on all of us. But in the meantime, there can be a lot of very good stuff. That's where we've got to live, Janine. In that good meantime."

Janine understood what Lee was saying, but at her core, she continued to feel that she didn't rate a good meantime. She'd known contentment, joy, fulfillment — with Clark, with the twins, through her art — but she hadn't felt worthy of any of it. The feeling made her prize her "undeserved" good fortune, but it also made her suspicious of it. This attitude used to drive Clark up the wall. *You're always waiting for the other shoe to drop*, he'd say, exasperated. *Probably mud-caked and with broken laces, too.*

"Listen," Lee said. "You do what you want about this. Go, postpone, cancel — whatever you want."

First, Janine knew, she'd have to figure out what she wanted. And how far past her distrust of happy endings she could push herself.

18

Two hours later, after much scrambling to provide breakfasts, locate shoes and boardwalk souvenirs, and retrieve damp, sandy swimsuits from the clothesline and the floor of the shower, Lee and her children were gone, and the twins had been delivered to day camp. Janine returned to a house that was slightly topsy-turvy but blessedly empty.

She wandered out to the vegetable garden, carefully keeping her mind unfocused. It was how she always solved a knotty problem — letting her sub-conscious work on it, waiting for signs in her body as to whether the ideas that floated up were promising or unwise, appropriate or risky, integral to who she was or imposed from outside. What floated up now, as she pulled weeds between the bean rows, were thoughts of plunging ahead despite misgivings, thoughts of delaying the inevitable, and thoughts of abolishing inevitability with an unequivocal no. Whatever she decided, Hunt would no longer be an abstract notion, nor a frail memory. He'd be, from now on, an actual person separated from her by mere miles and, possibly, by her own will, or his. Whatever she decided, he'd-be there, and she'd be here, and they'd both know it.

Getting up from the bean rows, she searched under the broad leaves of the zucchini vines for ripe squash. She picked five fat zucchini. Thank goodness she'd told her neighbor to harvest whatever he wanted while they were away. Otherwise, she'd be faced now with zucchini the size of the boys' Tonka trucks.

"Like the poor, the zucchini are always with us," she remembered Rose saying once when her garden had been overrun with them.

Cradling the zucchini in her shirt tails, Janine carried them to the kitchen and dumped them onto the counter. One rolled into the sink with a thud. This afternoon, she and the boys would make zucchini bread. They'd get several loaves. She'd bring a couple to the neighbors. Maybe Dan would like one.

"Gotcha!" she whispered to herself. Thinking of giving Dan a loaf of zucchini bread meant that she'd decided to go ahead with the Saturday meeting. Her nerves weren't completely steady, but she could feel a relaxation of tension in her body, so she knew that whatever ultimately happened, going was the right choice, the one she wanted, and that Dan must go, too.

"*This* Saturday?" Dan said when she called with the news.

"Father O'Hanlon said we could re-schedule, but he was pushing for Saturday."

"The thing is, this is my weekend to have the girls."

"Oh. Well, I guess I could go on my own. But—"

"No. I don't want you there alone. Besides, I want to go."

They were both quiet, contemplating the impasse.

"Where is 'there,' by the way?" Dan said.

"Malaga. It's between here and Philadelphia. I could be there in an hour probably. Dan, he's been an hour away from me for years."

"We should probably plan on staying there two days. Maybe even three."

"Why?"

Janine was beginning to wonder about her own child care needs.

"Meeting Hunt with his whole family, we won't get to talk much. If we stick around extra days, we'd be available to meet him privately. At least we should allow for that. We can always go home if the one meeting turns out to be enough."

"I suppose it makes sense to stay over at least one night. But I don't like leaving the boys that long."

"Not even with your folks?"

"Taking them to Teaneck would be out of my way. Malaga is close enough that I could drive back and forth each day. If you wouldn't mind hanging around a motel room on your own waiting for Hunt to call."

"I could do that," Dan replied slowly. "But what if he called and wanted to come to the motel right then, because it was his only opportunity? I wouldn't feel right talking to him without you. Or what if we get to see him alone one afternoon and the meeting runs on but you feel like you have to leave, or you end up driving home late at night tired and maybe upset?"

So many if's, so many scenarios, so many possible pitfalls.

"If you drop the boys in Teaneck," Dan went on, "we can drive together. I think it'd be a good idea."

As soon as he said it, Janine realized she'd been hoping he'd suggest that. She didn't want to put off Hunt, she didn't want to go alone, and she didn't want to commute between Cape May Point and Malaga.

"What about Vanessa and Sally?" she asked.

"I'll make it work."

After Janine hung up from Dan, she retrieved an old auto club guidebook from the back of a desk drawer and looked up accommodations in the vicinity of Malaga. There were listings for the usual chain motels, but a small ad for a bed and breakfast in Pitman set her on a different track. A bed and breakfast might provide them with use of a living room or some similar space to meet with Hunt. That would be much nicer than sitting in a restaurant or a dreary motel lobby. It would be more comfortable for her and Dan, too. They might have to cool their heels for any number of hours waiting for Hunt to contact them.

She found the Wisteria Inn after only two calls. It had not only a living room available to guests, but also a large garden gazebo furnished with wicker chairs. Janine reserved two rooms for Saturday night. Then she called Father O'Hanlon and told him he could let Father Nonas know that both she and Dan would be coming.

Janine spent the next hour packing for the weekend. She spread several outfits on her bed and vacillated among them, shifting around tops and skirts and slacks in various combinations. She finally stuffed everything into a suitcase, along with too many pairs of shoes and two purses. She'd get her mother to help her choose. Rose wasn't what anyone would call a fashion plate, but she was never without an opinion, and she herself was always well turned-out on formal occasions like anniversary parties and wakes, favoring simple classic lines and good jewelry, a kind of workingman's Coco Chanel.

When Janine picked up the boys from day camp and told them they'd be going yet again to their grandparents' house the following day, they were amenable. They were still at an age where they didn't question the adult motivations that shaped their daily lives any more than Janine would question rain or snow. Nevertheless, they did want to know where she was going overnight without them.

"I have to go see somebody I used to know a long time ago," she said, deciding to keep the explanation as simple and as close to the truth as possible.

They were sitting in the car parked in front of the day camp, the boys in the back seat, Janine looking at them from between the two front seats. The boys were eating potato chips out of little bags. They were always ravenous when Janine picked them up, so she was in the habit of bringing food — something small if they were heading directly home, something more substantial if they had to do errands or were off to the beach.

"A boy or a girl?" Tim wanted to know.

"A young man. Like Dot."

"Dot's not a man!" Larry squealed.

"I mean the same age as Dot. A teen-ager."

Larry was shaking his head, still smiling over his mother's outrageous error, but Tim was eyeing her suspiciously.

"Why can't we come?" he said.

Larry, who'd been digging in the bottom of his bag for the last crumbs of chips, looked up with interest.

"I'm going with Dr. Gannon. It's a grown-ups only thing."

They knew about grown-up parties and grown-up dinner dates without kids, but Janine hadn't been out to many of those since Clark's death.

"We weren't invited, Tim," Larry said matter-of-factly, crumpling up his empty bag. "Can you share some chips?"

Tim gave his brother a single chip and then transferred his bag to the hand away from Larry. Larry wouldn't grab, but it was a signal to him not to ask for more.

Janine waited a moment for more questions, and when none came, she turned around and started the car.

That night at dinner, more questions did arise, but the details the boys asked for concerned what they'd be doing rather than what Janine's plans were.

"Will Howie and Max and Sam be at Gram's?" Larry wanted to know. "Can we go to Nessie and Sally's pool?"

"No, you'll just be at Gram and Grandpa's. It's only for two days."

"And a night," Tim added.

"Two nights," Janine corrected him. "Friday and Saturday. I'll be there tomorrow night — that's Friday — but not on Saturday. *Maybe* we'll all have to stay Sunday night, too, if I get back too late to drive home."

She'd already explained this to them, but it bore repeating. She knew they were worried about the overnight without her, though Larry would never admit it.

"We can stay alone because we're bigger boys now," Larry said, through a mouthful of spaghetti.

"Swallow before you talk," Janine told him.

Tim was poking at his iceberg lettuce salad with a crust of garlic bread.

"Who's gonna give us our bath?" he said.

"Gram," Janine said.

"I don't need Gram," Larry declared. "I can take a bath by myself."

"You can't wash your hair," Tim said. "You cry from the soap."

"I don't have to wash my hair."

Tim looked at Janine expectantly.

"I'll talk to Gram," she said soothingly to both of them. "You can skip the shampoo."

"Can we skip the whole bath?" Tim asked.

"It's nice to be clean for bed," Janine said.

"If you're dirty, it means you were having fun," Tim countered. "That's what Daddy said."

Janine felt a pang at the mention of Clark. She was past anguishing over his absence in her life, but it pained her to be reminded of his absence in Larry's and Tim's lives. For them, their father's absence would take on different meanings at different junctures. He wouldn't be there to coach youth baseball at the park rec center or to teach them to ride a bicycle. He wouldn't see them graduate or marry or become fathers themselves. They'd never be men together.

"Daddy was right," she said, "but Daddy took a shower every morning."

Larry had been laboriously twirling strands of spaghetti onto his fork, but now he put the loaded fork down, his face lit with the excitement of discovery.

"Daddy was dirty in bed!"

Janine burst out laughing. The boys laughed, too, as delighted by their mother's unbridled amusement as by Larry's bold remark. When they all resumed eating, there was no more talk about baths or nights apart or Daddy, only speculations about whether Grandpa might take them to fly kites, and the concoction of a plan to stop, on the ride north tomorrow, at a favorite pizza joint near Tom's River.

AT TEN O'CLOCK on Saturday morning, Dan arrived at the Pettorinis' to pick up Janine. He was dressed with casual elegance in lightweight cocoa brown slacks and a pale blue linen shirt.

"You look nice," Janine said when she opened the door to him.

She hadn't meant to say it. It had flitted across her mind as she approached the door and saw him through the screen. Then the thought had just jumped out of her mouth.

"So do you," Dan said.

"Oh, dear, we're not too Ken and Barbie, are we?"

Quite by coincidence, Janine was well-coordinated with Dan. She wore a blousy cotton dress in a floral print of blues and greens, with a tracery of brown to represent branches. Rose had wanted to lend her a pearl bracelet, but Janine had opted instead for several silver bangles of her own and a wide Navajo cuff bracelet studded with irregular beads of turquoise.

Rose appeared behind Janine and frowned at Dan.

"Good morning, Mrs. Pettorini."

"I hope so," Rose answered ominously.

"We all hope that," Dan replied, entering the house.

Janine was grateful he'd found something to say that neither challenged her mother nor kowtowed to her. Rose was troubled about Janine meeting Hunt. She was afraid she was going to get hurt. She'd been mollified to learn that a priest would be present, but what she really wanted was to be there herself. Janine had said no, and Dan's inclusion in the trip took away Rose's strongest argument, which was that Janine shouldn't go alone.

"You'd be like a mother bear," Janine had told her last night.

"And what's wrong with that?" Rose had said.

"For one thing, I'm not a cub any more. And for another, I think there's going to be enough mother energy stirred up in that room as it is."

"Well, that Dan Gannon better keep his wits about him for a change," had been Rose's final words on the matter.

Now, Dan pointed to a small suitcase sitting next to the door.

"Shall I take that to the car?" he asked Janine.

"Hold on while I say good-bye to the boys."

She called up the stairs, and Tim and Larry ran down, still in their pajamas, wildly imprinted with Masters of the Universe characters.

"Hi, Dr. Gannon," both boys called out.

Rose gave Dan a sharp look.

"They know you," she said.

"Of course, Ma," Janine quickly put in. "From the barbecue."

"My Mom's going to see somebody from a long time ago," Larry informed Dan.

"I know."

"We're not invited," Tim added.

Janine squatted down, and the boys encircled her in tight hugs. She breathed in the endearing puppy dog scent of their sweaty, crew-cut heads.

"Now you be good," she said. "I'll call tonight, and I'll see you tomorrow."

"When tomorrow?" Larry said.

"Before dark probably. We'll go to Bischoff's for ice cream sodas."

"Yay!"

"Grandpa's making pancakes, and he needs some help flipping," Rose told her grandsons.

They galloped off to the kitchen.

Janine stood up and walked to the door, where Dan was waiting, her suitcase in hand.

"Now, Ma," she said. "you've got the number at the church and the number at the bed-and-breakfast, right?"

"Yes, yes."

"Let me give you my pager number, too," Dan said. "It might be the quickest way to reach us."

He put down the suitcase, took his wallet out of his back pocket, and handed Rose a business card. Rose took it but she was shaking her head.

"And you think all these numbers are gonna keep me from worrying?"

"No," Dan said. "I expect there's nothing could do that."

"You keep your wits about you today, Dan Gannon."

———

TEN MINUTES LATER, Dan and Janine were on the Turnpike heading south toward Malaga.

"You know, I almost went to Glassboro State College," Janine said. "Malaga's practically next door."

"Where *did* you go to college?"

"University of Pennsylvania. But not right away."

Janine thought about her two hurly-burly years in a commune in Philadelphia, but she didn't want to talk about any of that now. One chunk of the past rising up from its ashes was enough for one day.

"I've got what Larry calls dentist stomach," she said to forestall Dan asking about her college days.

"I know exactly what you mean. But I call it butterflies. As a professional courtesy."

Janine laughed softly. He really was easy to be with, even under these stressful circumstances.

"So," Dan said, "I gathered your mother doesn't know about you and the boys coming to our pool."

"It just seemed easier..."

"Believe me, I get it. I wouldn't have told my mother, either, except the kids spilled the beans."

"What did she say?"

Dan let out a sigh. He sliced a glance at Janine, and his face was full of apology.

"I know she's no fan of mine, Dan. C'mon, what did she say?"

"She thinks you're after me."

Janine laughed again.

"What's so funny?"

"That's exactly what my mother thinks about you. Because of this overnight."

"No wonder she was giving me the evil eye."

As they came abreast of New Brunswick, the sky clouded over. A few miles farther on, a light rain began to fall. Dan turned on the intermittent mode of the windshield wipers. Janine thought again of the raindrops on the windows at Shadyside, which led her to contemplate her planned painting. Her butterflies eased as she became absorbed in thought.

"Would it be so inconceivable, Janine?"

"What?" she said, thinking she must have missed some remark preliminary to his question.

"You and me."

"Oh, Dan, do you really think this is the right time for—"

"We could have been happy together. I know we could have."

She didn't answer him. It had crossed her mind. What might have been. She had even wondered about what it would be like to be in his arms again. She'd been so long without a man, and this wasn't just any man, not just any pair of available, attractive arms. But there was so much against them. Geography. Their kids, so young and all of them still getting used to a family life that wasn't made up of Mommy-and-Daddy-forever. The unknown impact Hunt was going to have. The simple but potent danger of mistaking the present for the past, let alone daring to imagine it could ever lead to a future. She wouldn't let herself do that. She wouldn't let him do it.

"Even Robin thinks you and I are going to get back together. Though Lord knows that she, of all people, shouldn't think I'm such a great catch."

"I'm sure she did think you were a great catch. And that you were. Are. Would be. Oh, never mind. How come she has an opinion about us at all?"

"We got into a royal battle when I had to beg off taking the kids this weekend. She was furious I'd never told her about you and the baby before. Hurt, too. Though she managed to gloat that it proved something against me. Cold, buttoned-down bastard were her exact words. I felt like a heel. Besides wanting to strangle her."

"Dan, I don't think we should—"

"Forget it. I'm being clumsy. Forget I said anything, okay?"

The rain let up, though the sky was still overcast. Dan switched off the wipers.

"Do we need a game plan for this meeting?" he said.

"Hopefully, Father Nonas will moderate. Make introductions, at least. Otherwise, I think we should let Hunt take the lead."

"Now *I'm* getting dentist stomach."

Janine looked at the dashboard clock. They'd wanted to give themselves plenty of time for the drive, but at this rate, they were going to arrive in Malaga way too early. They could check into the B and B, maybe drive around a bit, get a feel for Hunt's home town. They could get lunch somewhere, though Janine had absolutely no appetite and probably wouldn't.

"Let's stop," she said. She'd just spotted a sign for an upcoming services plaza.

The last thing she needed was an infusion of caffeine, but she longed to wrap her hands around a hot cup and to pause their headlong rush south. She wanted to sit still for a while with Dan across the table from her also sitting still, looking into her face and not asking anything more of her than to be there then.

"Just what I was thinking," he said, and he moved into the exit lane.

19

St. Mary's was a little red brick church with a charming rosary garden. Arriving fifteen minutes before their appointment, Janine and Dan wandered around it, looking at the plantings, the statuary and the stations of the cross. Father Nonas, a large man with a friendly, pockmarked face and slicked black hair, found them seated on the concrete benches whose backs were carved in the shape of angels' wings. He escorted them inside, informing them that the Dombrowskis were waiting in the church basement.

Janine's heart was thumping as she descended the stairs behind the portly priest. His bulk necessitated him going slowly, leaving her too much time to think. Two impulses were warring within her — to push past the lumbering man and burst into the meeting room ahead of him, or to turn around and flee before he could reach the door and open it. She did neither, following obediently, step by step by measured step, like a bride.

When they finally arrived at the door, Father Nonas stood aside to let Janine enter first. Three people were seated on folding chairs at a long table, their faces turned toward her — a man and woman who looked about ten years older than Janine, and a girl of 14 or 15. The man stood up. Janine scouted the room for Hunt and quickly ascertained he wasn't there. There were no places in the open room in which he could have been lurking out of sight. Was he in the sanctuary upstairs, waiting to be called for? Praying for courage or guidance? Or had he changed his mind? She felt a gentle pressure at the small of her back and realized Dan was urging her forward. The priest had already eased past them and was now standing across from the seated woman, who was clutching a flat handbag on the table as if she thought someone might wrest it away from her.

"Mrs. Linden?" Father Nonas said, pulling a chair out from the table and indicating with his hand that he meant it for her.

Janine went forward. What else was there to do? Dan stood beside her while the priest made introductions. Pete Dombrowski and Dan shook hands. Everyone else acknowledged one another with nods. Then the three men sat down, Dan on one side of Janine and Father Nonas on the other, Pete and Margaret Dombrowski across the table from them, and their daughter, Paula, incongruously at the head of the table.

The girl was propped on her forearms, regarding Janine and Dan with frank curiosity. She was pretty, with milky skin, blue eyes, and wavy, dark hair cut in a mullet. Her prettiness contrasted sharply with her parents' workaday looks, the mother with limp, light brown hair and velvety brown eyes like a doe's, the father with darker hair and eyes as brown and hard as river stones. He was wearing a starched dark gray mechanic's uniform with Pete embroidered in red above his shirt pocket. So much for Hunt's having been adopted by a "professional man." Janine wondered if all the girls who gave up their babies were told that. Another lie fed to keep them docile. There couldn't have been enough childless doctors and lawyers to go around.

"Don't stare, Paula," her mother said. "It's not polite."

The girl shot her mother a peeved look, but she straightened up and redirected her gaze to the priest. Let's get this show on the road, her posture said.

"I expect," Father Nonas said warmly, "that everyone has questions. Who would like to begin?"

We said we'd let Hunt take the lead, Janine thought. So now what? Margaret Dombrowski looked at her husband, but he kept his eyes on Janine.

"He looks some like you," he said.

202

"Yeah, Dad, he does," Paula agreed. "And like him," she added, pointing to Dan, "in the eyebrows."

Margaret Dombrowski pulled her purse closer to her, holding it so tightly, the tips of her fingers were white. Janine examined the woman's face, which was awash with emotion. Nervousness was there, of course, and indecision. And something else. Terror? The description leapt up in Janine's mind, but she dismissed it as a product of her own wrought-up state. She herself wasn't afraid, at least not in the sense of alarm. She was afraid of leaving this room as ill-informed as when she'd entered. She was afraid of making a bad impression. She was afraid of not having whatever patience might be required before Hunt arrived. But Margaret Dombrowski seemed truly fearful.

"Mrs. Dombrowski—" Janine began.

The woman looked a little startled to be directly addressed. Trying to defuse the situation, Janine smiled at her, and she reciprocated with a wan smile of her own, but she still looked apprehensive.

Janine went on anyway. "I know it must have been a shock when Father Nonas called you. It was certainly a shock to me to hear from Hunt, and I—"

"Where is he?" Mrs. Dombrowski said in anguish.

"Where is he?" Dan echoed. "What do you mean?"

The woman didn't look at him.

"Father said you got a letter," she said to Janine.

"Yes, I did," Janine said, confused. "I received it near the end of June, but it had been written in May."

"Hunt took off in the middle of May," Pete Dumbrowski said. "After...after a family disagreement."

"*I* didn't have any disagreement with him," Paula declared.

Her father frowned but he didn't rebuke her.

"We thought he'd cool down and come back quick enough," Margaret said. "He liked going off on his own sometimes to Atlantic City or Philadelphia. Malaga's a small town. The young people get bored. But before, he'd only be gone for a Saturday."

203

"He's kept in touch, hasn't he?" Father Nonas asked her.

"Yes, Father. He called every Sunday. But he didn't ever say where he was."

"He called on my birthday, too," Paula said. "July twelfth. And he told me I could take some money from a drawer in his room and buy myself a present. I got a wallet that looks like real alligator."

"Never mind about that, Paula," her father said.

"That was his last call," Margaret said. "Thursday, July the twelfth. When he didn't call that Sunday, I didn't think too much of it. But he didn't call the next Sunday neither."

Janine's head was spinning. She'd come prepared to talk to Hunt, to open up to him and to encourage him to open to her. She hadn't anticipated questions from his parents, especially not questions on his whereabouts. They knew so much about him that she didn't. She had to reorient her brain so that she could figure out what to ask them.

"What about the police?" Dan said.

"There's been no crime, they said," Pete replied. "Hunt's of age, and he can go where he pleases."

"They did ask around," Margaret added. "But nobody knew anything."

"Do you mind telling us, sir," Dan said, addressing Pete, "what the disagreement was?"

The man's face darkened, and he inched his chair away from the table. Wait, Janine wanted to say to Dan, don't scare him off. I want to know what Hunt was like as a boy, what made him laugh, what made him cry, if he had a favorite toy, a favorite book. We haven't asked any-thing like that yet. But in another part of her mind, she knew Dan was right to explore Hunt's more recent history. That's where clues to where he was would lie. If there were any.

"It was because of what you said," Paula accused her father. "That's why Hunt booked."

"Hush, girl," Margaret said. "Hunt knows Dad didn't mean it. It'll be all right when he comes back. They'll get it all figured out."

"I love my son, Mr. Gannon," Pete said. "It was just a misunderstanding. And it was private."

Dan nodded. Clearly, he wasn't going to press further for details of the argument. Janine saw the propriety in that, but she also knew that they might never have an opportunity to speak to these people again.

"Please, Mr. Dombrowski," she said. "We all want to know where Hunt is, don't we? To make sure he's all right? What happened in the family right before he left could be—"

"Mrs. Linden," Pete said. "I know my son. I know what happened. There's nothing in it to tell where he went."

"You said you *didn't* know him," Paula burst out. "You said 'you're no son of mine.'"

"Hunt pushed him to that, Paula," Margaret said. "Hunt pushed him too hard."

Dumbrowski's face twisted with an effort at self-control, but it wasn't anger he was suppressing. It was grief and shame. He stood up, and his wife reached out and laid her hand on his arm.

"I've got to get to work," he said, pulling away from her. "Thank you, Father, for trying to help. I told Margaret it wouldn't do any good. They're looking for him, too, I said. And you think if they find him, they'll bring him home to us?"

He turned to Dan and Janine.

"You seem decent enough people," he said, "and I know you were only kids yourselves back then, but you walked away from Hunt when he was a baby, and I think it's better if you stay away."

"Now, Pete," Father Nonas said. "We can all respect—"

"Better for who, Mr. Dumbrowski?" Dan said tensely.

"Please, Mr. Gannon..." the priest said.

"I'll be in the car," Dombrowski told his wife.

When the door shut behind him, Margaret rose from her chair.

"It's all right, Father," she said. "I always knew this day would come."

"What day is that, Margaret?"

"The day my children's mothers would come and want them back."

Janine sat back in her chair, aghast. It was as if the woman had struck her. Suddenly, it was six years ago. She was in the car with Clark, on the way home from the hospital, their two newborn sons asleep in infant seats in the back. Clark was being inordinately cautious, lingering at stop signs, refusing to pass slow-moving vehicles, giving everyone and their cousins the right of way, even when it was clearly his. When Janine snapped at him about driving like an old man, he looked at her in surprise, but he didn't speed up or change the way he was driving.

No doubt he put her irritability down to postpartum hormones. In reality, it was something almost as primitive. From the moment they'd left the maternity ward with the twins, Janine had been expecting someone to come up to them and say, sorry, there's been a mistake, these aren't your babies, give them to us. The unreasonable fear persisted for the entire ride home. Hurry, hurry, she wanted to say to Clark. Hurry before they discover I'm not a fit mother and take my babies away. Again. But she didn't say it. She endured the terrible ride, constantly checking on the boys in the rear view mirror, and watching, too, for the flashing lights of some official car in pursuit behind them. The fear waned when they got home, and it never reasserted itself as strongly again. But she knew what Margaret Dumbrowski was feeling. She knew the grip it could exert. And today Janine was the cause of it.

"Mrs. Dombrowski," she said, "I wouldn't do that."

The woman regarded her with sad eyes.

"Maybe not. But it could happen anyway." She turned to her daughter. "C'mon, Paula. Dad's got to get to work."

Paula stood up.

Margaret said to Janine, "I do understand, I think, Mrs. Linden, why you'd be curious about Hunt, but I just can't talk about him with you."

Paula walked to her mother's side.

"I want to stay a little, Mom," she said. "I brought Hunt's yearbook to show them. I can walk home."

Margaret stared at her, unsure. Then she looked at the priest.

"You'll stay, too, Father?"

"Certainly."

"All right, then," she said flatly.

Paula gave her mother a hug.

"It's okay, Mom."

Margaret turned and walked out. There was a moment of awkward silence in the little group. Paula had not sat down again. Janine glanced at Father Nonas, but it appeared he was comfortable waiting to see what would unfold. Perhaps it was a habit from the confessional box.

"You said you had your brother's yearbook?" Janine prompted Paula.

The girl gave her a fugitive smile that showed a flash of braces on her upper teeth. She picked up her satchel handbag from the floor beside her chair and pulled out a hardcover book with 1984 emblazoned on its cover in red. She paged through the book to where the individual senior photos were and spread it on the table open to a page of D names.

"That's him," she said, tapping a black and white photo with her finger.

Hunt was wearing a tie and sports jacket, as were all the boys. But his jacket was suede, while theirs were wool, either solids or quiet plaids. Pete Dombrowski was right. Hunt did look like Janine. He had her chin, and he seemed to have her coloring. And, as Paula had said, the eyebrows were Dan's, strong and expressively arched, giving Hunt, as they did Dan, an air of expectancy and receptiveness. It was a handsome face, but soft, the kind of face that would change with time and experience more than most. But there was the promise in it, too, that he'd always be attractive. He wasn't smiling, but Janine noticed that neither were several of the other boys on the two pages in front of her. Some adolescent pose of sophistication or machismo, she supposed. But there was something wistful in his eyes that the other students didn't show. Or was she reading too much into a neutral studio portrait that had been taken at a single moment on one day in his life?

Paula reached across the table and started flipping the pages. Janine wanted to study Hunt's face longer, but she didn't protest. The girl stopped at a section labeled Clubs and Organizations.

"He was in the Art Club," she said, turning pages more slowly now, reading the captions under a series of group photos.

When she found the picture she was looking for, she pointed out Hunt, but he was in a back row, his face partially obscured by a tall girl in the row in front of him. Janine could gather no impression at all from the small image. Indeed, she wouldn't have recognized him if she'd been looking through the book on her own.

"When I was little, he used to draw pictures of princesses and horses and stuff for my room," Paula said.

"He did a fine rendering of our proposed renovations for the Building Fund donation envelope last year," Father Nonas put in. "Margaret got him to do it. He hasn't been very active at church in recent years."

Paula slid the yearbook away from Janine and Dan and started leafing through it again. Perhaps she was hoping to find another photo of Hunt, but she seemed aimless, almost lethargic.

"He was gone when the books came out," she said as she slowly turned pages, "but he already paid, so I picked it up for him."

"Paula," Dan said quietly, "what did your brother and your father argue about?"

She looked at Father Nonas.

"Mr. Gannon," he said, "Pete Dombrowski made it clear, I think, that that is a private matter."

Dan ignored the priest. "From what you said earlier, Paula, it seems like you have an idea why Hunt left."

Again she looked at Father Nonas. This time he didn't say anything, but he didn't need to. His previous statement and his presence were inhibiting enough. The girl shook her head. She started turning pages again, keeping her eyes cast down.

"I see you wear braces," Dan said in a more conversational tone. "Did Hunt have braces, too?"

"No. He was lucky."

"I'm an orthodontist."

"Oh," Paula replied without interest. She closed the yearbook.

"Hey," she said, suddenly brightening, "maybe that's why Hunt's teeth were so straight!"

Dan smiled. "I doubt it."

"We have different teeth genes. I'm adopted, too."

Janine said, "Did you and Hunt ever talk about looking for your birthparents?"

"A little, I guess," the girl answered with a shrug.

"Paula," Father O'Hanlon said, "you don't have to talk about this if you don't want to."

"I don't mind."

She began slowly tracing her fingertip over the lettering on the yearbook cover.

"We knew our mom wouldn't understand, that she'd think we didn't love her and Dad and wig out, so we thought we'd wait, you know, maybe until after they died, and look then. They told us a long time ago about being adopted, but they said they didn't know anything about the people who...well, about you."

Janine wondered how true it was that the Dombrowskis knew nothing about their children's birthparents. Presumably, they'd been given at least a few demographic facts. Had they ever known her name or Dan's? Hunt's birth certificate had been amended and so had the baptismal certificate. Had they known about Shadyside or the hospital? Had they talked to anyone in either place? She was sure of one thing. They had finalization papers. They knew the name of the law firm they'd hired. How had Hunt found his way to the lawyers? Had Margaret or Pete worn down under pressure from him? Teenagers could be persistent. Is that what the fight had been about?

"Do you know how Hunt managed to find me?" Janine said to Paula.

"No."

Paula dragged her purse in front of her and put the yearbook inside it. She was shutting down.

"I'd like to give you my phone number," Janine said, "in case you hear from Hunt, or remember anything else you think we might like to know."

Paula waited while Janine tore a slip of paper from a small notepad and wrote on it. The girl took the paper without looking at the number and stuffed it into her bag.

They all walked upstairs together, pausing at the door of the church to peer up at the sky, which had filled with black thunderheads while they'd been in the basement room. It was windy. An eddy of dry leaves and dust spiraled across the walkway. The air was yellow-green, and it smelled of rain and ozone.

"Do you have far to go?" Dan asked Paula. "We could give you a lift."

"No, thanks."

"Let me get you an umbrella," said Father Nonas, turning back inside. "You can return it at mass tomorrow."

The priest's exit left a gap between where Dan and Janine were standing and where Paula was standing. None of them moved to close it.

Abruptly, Paula started speaking, keeping her gaze fixed on the gathering weather outside.

"When me and Hunt did talk about maybe meeting our natural parents some day, it wasn't 'cause we wanted a new mother or father. We *have* a mother and father. We just wanted a few answers."

She paused, shifted her big bag from one shoulder to the other. She stepped outside the doorway and lifted her face, as if she were an animal searching for a scent.

"Like, who do we look like?" she continued, her back to Janine and Dan. "How come Hunt likes opera and I'm a good athlete, when nobody else in our family is into that stuff? What country are our people from? What kind of person was our real mom and dad? There's things missing inside us. Holes. It's like we don't really know who we are."

Father Nonas appeared with a large black umbrella. Paula took it and thanked him. Then she skittered down the steps and out into the wind without saying good-bye.

Father Nonas wagged his big, square head.

"I hope you didn't take offense at anything today," he said.

"No," Janine said.

There was no room in her mind for offense. She was too full of disappointment, frustration, defeat, and fatigue.

"We knew it was going to be touchy," Dan said.

"And I hope you can forgive my subterfuge in not telling you ahead of time that Hunt had gone missing. I was afraid if you knew that, you wouldn't come, and the family's been so worried. We all hoped you might shed some light..."

"It was an unnecessary blow," Dan said tersely. "We would have come anyway."

"My sincere apologies," the priest said, looking genuinely contrite.

"Can we rely on you, Father, to pass on any news?" Dan said.

"If I have the family's permission."

"You seem to think we have no standing at all here," Dan protested, "while in fact we—"

"Dan," Janine said, "leave it."

She didn't want to witness any more anger or sorrow or contrition or yearning. She was done for today. She was done, maybe, for good. Dan looked perplexed, but he didn't go on with his objections. Father Nonas wasn't as cooperative.

"The two of you have understandable needs and desires, certainly," he said. "Some would say rights. But try to put yourself in Pete and Margaret Dombrowski's shoes. First, they had to suffer the grief of infertility. Then they had to endure being scrutinized and evaluated as prospective adoptive parents. Finally, they got a baby — your baby. They were told they'd rescued him, that he didn't need you and that he didn't ever need to know anything about you, that he was completely theirs. They may even have been told that if he did ask questions, it meant they had failed. But the Dombrowskis know you are out there somewhere. What if you appear? What if Hunt finds you more exciting, more interesting, more lovable than they? And then, you *do* appear."

A gust of wind lifted the hem of the priest's cassock.

"Oh, dear, I have a lot of windows to close before the rain starts," he said.

"We're quite ready to go," Janine said. "Thank you, Father, for your help and advice."

Did she mean that? She was too tired to know.

"To answer your earlier question more fully, Mr. Gannon," Father Nonas said. "I must abide by the family's wishes, but I will do everything in my power to convince them that you should be notified immediately when Hunt returns or gets in touch."

"We would appreciate that, Father."

"In exchange, I want to ask both of you to recognize that as difficult as your search may be, you, at least, have the hope that at its end, you will meet your son, and that together you and he will resolve any pain your separation has caused. I feel emboldened to believe that even today's imperfect meeting has given you some relief. But there is no search available to the Dombrowskis. The unborn children they still grieve do not exist. I hope remembering that will help you be patient with them."

They each shook the priest's hand and descended the church steps. By the time they reached the car, fat raindrops were falling, and as soon as they'd gotten into the car, the drops rapidly multiplied until rain was coming down in wind-driven sheets.

"That girl's going to get drenched," Dan said.

"Let's not talk about them yet."

Dan started the car, turned on the headlights and the windshield wipers.

"I know it's August," he said, backing out of the parking space, "but I hope they've built a fire in the living room at the B and B. Do you think they could scare up some brandy? A hot toddy wouldn't be amiss."

"I don't want to go there."

"You don't? Where do you want to go?"

"Home."

"To Teaneck?"

"Yes."

Dan stopped the car at the parking lot exit and let out a long exhalation.

"Dan, I just can't feature sitting around the B and B making small talk with a bunch of strangers and then going through the same charade at the breakfast table tomorrow. And I don't want to exile myself to my room either."

"Okay. We'll go get our stuff and hit the road. Let's just hope we drive out from under this storm."

When they reached Wisteria Inn, they ran inside holding newspapers over their heads. Janine felt a twinge of remorse when she passed the living room and saw that someone had, in fact, started a fire, but the feeling — which was all on Dan's behalf — evaporated when she also saw that there were two jovial couples in there opening a bottle of wine. It was the precise scene she'd known she couldn't stomach.

Not only was it still pouring as they pulled away from the inn, it had begun to thunder and lightning, too. Dan drove slowly, leaning forward at times to squint through the rain-whipped windshield.

"I think we've been on Route 40 too long," he said after a while.

Janine took a map out of her purse and opened it up.

"What was the last main road we passed?" she said after studying the map a minute.

"Route 54."

"Damn, we're going the wrong way."

"I'll turn around when I get a chance."

"No, wait, keep going. In this direction, 40 will take us to the Atlantic City Expressway."

"Atlantic City?"

"Then we can catch the Parkway."

They reached the Expressway in 18 miles. Dan concentrated on his driving, and Janine kept checking signs to reassure herself they were on the right track. They didn't have to go far on the Expressway before it met the Garden State Parkway.

As they approached the on-ramp, Janine suddenly said, "Go south."

"What?"

"Take the Parkway south."

Dan swung the car into the correct lane.

Once they'd merged into the traffic flow, he said, "Mind telling me why we're going south?"

"It's two and a half hours from here to Teaneck, longer in this rain. And after you drop me off, you still have to get to Alpine. But from here to Cape May Point is barely an hour. I don't have a fireplace, but I do have brandy. And I'm exhausted. I'll go bonkers cooped up in this car longer than I have to be."

A bolt of stick lightning brightened the interior of the car with a flash of white light. A few seconds later, thunder cracked and rumbled loudly overhead.

"Well, the sooner we're out of this weather, the better," Dan said. "And I'm holding you to that brandy."

20

THE STORM MUST have been heading north, because by the time they were passing Ocean City, the rain had stopped, and the heavy sky had thinned enough that Janine could locate the early evening sun by its glow behind the clouds. Fifty minutes after getting on the Parkway, Dan's car was crunching onto Janine's crushed shell driveway.

It had rained there, too. Janine took a deep breath of the cool, fresh air.

"I feel like an escaped convict," she said.

"Okay," Dan said, amused.

"Let me call the boys and change my clothes, and we can go for a walk on the beach. I need to move."

Rose was in the middle of preparing dinner. "How did it go?" she asked.

"He wasn't there."

"What?"

Dan had wandered out to the backyard to give Janine privacy. Looking out the sliding door to the deck, she saw him peeking into the windows of her studio.

"I'll tell you all about it tomorrow, Ma. Let me talk to the boys."

"But, Janine, what are you going to——?"

"Please, Ma. Tomorrow."

A loud, resigned sigh.

Tim and Larry got on the phone together, one on the kitchen line and one on the extension in the bedroom. They tumbled over each other telling Janine about their day, which had included a trip to a pet store to look at puppies and kittens and parakeets, and the purchase of waterproof cushions for Al's boat. Now they were looking forward to a dinner of Rose's justly famous ziti and meatballs.

"We got a video," Larry informed her. "*Star Wars*. And we're gonna make popcorn."

"I think I'm sick, Mommy," Tim said. "I think my stomach hurts."

"Maybe you should have some chamomile tea and go to bed early, like Peter Rabbit."

"You can't go to bed early," Larry insisted. "You need to watch *Star Wars*."

"And eat popcorn," Tim added.

"Only if your stomach feels better," Janine said.

"I think it will. Not even with any chamomile tea."

"I think it will, too."

"And I have a loose tooth," Tim suddenly recalled.

"All right, boys. Have a good evening. I love you."

Janine shouted to Dan after she'd hung up, and he trotted back to the house to make his own check-in call. She enjoyed watching his graceful, loose-limbed approach.

While he was on the phone, she went to her room and changed into a long-sleeved Oxford shirt, sweatpants, and sneakers, and wrapped a cotton sweater around her shoulders.

"Everything okay back at the ranch?" she asked when she found him drinking a glass of water in the kitchen.

"Well, Vanessa hid Sally's Cabbage Patch doll, so Sally put Vanessa's My Little Pony in the toilet, though Sally claims it fell when she was giving it a bath in the sink."

"How did you resolve that long-distance?"

"I didn't have to. Robin got them involved in washing all their dolls in plastic tubs in the back yard, and in the process, the missing Cabbage Patch kid turned up, her face was duly scrubbed, and she was laid on the lawn in the sun with everybody else."

"Did Robin ask about Hunt?"

"Not a word. It's a matter of pride, I think. How about your folks?"

"My mother's consumed with curiosity, but I managed to put her off."

Dan rinsed his glass and set it in the dish drainer next to the sink. He stared a moment at Janine.

"I didn't say where I was," he said. "It seemed simpler."

"I didn't say, either."

She couldn't hold his gaze any longer. She looked out the window.

"Might be cool on the beach," she said. "I've got a flannel shirt my father left here, if you want it."

The beach closest to Janine's house was never crowded, and today, because of the iffy weather, there was hardly anyone on it. Janine strode along the hard-packed wet sand at the water's edge, enjoying the stretch in her legs, the rise of her heartbeat. Dan kept up easily, hands jammed into his pockets, Al's shirttails flapping behind him like flags. Janine felt the distress of the day drifting to a deeper level of consciousness, like when the twins finished splashing in a pond with sticks and the stirred-up silt drifted back to the muddy bottom.

After twenty minutes of walking, Janine stopped and stood regarding the heaving sea. Dan meandered on, stooping to pick up several large white Atlantic clam shells.

"For the girls," he said, showing Janine the shells. "They love to beach-comb, but we rarely get to the ocean."

"You should bring them down here some time."

Dan looked at her with an unnamed question in his eyes.

"Really?"

"Sure," she replied, in a tone she intended to relay a casual *why not*, as opposed to the closer-to-the-truth *I hope you will.*

She took one of the shells out of his hand. It was thick and heavy, scored with concentric grooves on its convex outer side, smooth on its concave inside, with an indentation like a thumbprint at the point where it used to be joined to its other half. A crude, homely shell, but appealing in its simplicity and sturdiness. She'd once done a still life of a pile of Atlantic clam shells. It was surprising how many shades of white and ochre could be found on them if one only looked carefully enough.

"It's beautiful in its way, isn't it?" Dan said, watching her turn the shell in her hand.

"Yes, it is."

She gave the shell back to him.

"Do you believe in fate, Janine?"

"Do you?"

"I want to. I'd like to believe there are paths that are better than others for a person to go down, and that if things happen to turn someone aside, there will be a fork in the road later on where he gets a chance to choose again."

"But he won't be the same person by then. For that matter, the path probably wouldn't be quite the same, either."

"They might be enough the same."

Janine started walking back in the direction from which they'd come.

"I think you're ready for your brandy," she said.

On the walk back, Janine talked about the various features of Cape May and Cape May Point she enjoyed most, and Dan played along, asking questions about the area and, in turn, telling her about his hikes along the Palisades. Neither of them mentioned Hunt or the Dombrowskis, nor how they felt about what had happened, what they feared or wished for the future of their search. They would get to all that, Janine thought. An entire evening stretched out before them. Plus the long drive tomorrow. Now there was the storm-tossed ocean, the cold, damp sand between her toes, the waiting brandy, the luxury of hours in the company of an old friend, an old love.

⊗∞⊗

WHEN JANINE FOUND a bottle of good red wine in the back of a cabinet, Dan decided to eschew the brandy. She set out two of her prettiest wine glasses next to a platter of the stub ends of five different cheeses, a bowl of humus, and some crackers and toast. They sat at the kitchen table with this unlikely feast and watched fireflies emerge among the tangle of tiger lilies back by the boys' tent. Once it was dark enough that the mosquitoes had abated, they moved out onto the deck with their wine. The sky had cleared sufficiently that the light of a full moon was silvering the gray weathered wood of Janine's studio and rendering the greens of the yard almost blue.

"I'd like to see more of your paintings," Dan said.

Janine had already shown him the four she had hanging in the house, but none of them was recent.

"I always feel on the spot when I let someone new into my studio."

He slouched down in his deck chair.

"I'm not new."

"You know what I mean." She poured a small amount of wine into her empty glass. "You can see the paintings in the morning. I prefer to show them in natural light."

Janine sipped her wine carefully, deciding this would be her final glass. She was pleasantly tipsy, feeling soft around the edges, with all her senses heightened, and she didn't want to go beyond that into dizziness or silliness or melancholy.

"How did you get into painting? You said there were art classes at Shadyside, but how did you actually get to *be* an artist?"

"I try not to think of myself in such lofty terms."

"But I am not so constrained, madam. I can think of you in lofty terms. And I do."

"When you're in your cups."

"*In vino veritas.* C'mon, spill."

Okay, Janine thought, which version do I give him? The straightforward I went to college and studied art and got a job teaching art in a high school in Philadelphia and met Clark and married him and he encouraged me and built me a studio when we moved here and took the babies so I could have protected hours for painting? That version, while all true, would skip over the dark months after Hunt was born and the head-down months getting her high school diploma, and the wild commune years. All that was part of her becoming serious about art, in a subterranean sort of way, but it felt at this wine-soaked, moonlit moment, like a long, boring tale.

"Remember when we were driving to Trenton and I mentioned a turning point?" she said.

"You were very mysterious about it."

"Well, I think that's really the crux of things. I think if I tell you about that, it'll answer your question better than if I just go on and on about college and jobs and hours at the easel, blah, blah, blah."

"Okay," he said, picking up the wine bottle and topping off his glass.

He tilted the bottle towards her, but she shook her head no, so he set it down on the deck again.

"I had some rocky times after Hunt was born," Janine began. "I had to go back and finish high school. The less said about that the better. Then I ended up in a commune in Philadelphia, enrolled in one course at Penn, so I was nominally a student, but really I was just working as a waitress, hanging out, getting stoned, drawing and painting but not in any disciplined way, sitting around smoky rooms hour after hour after hour waiting for someone to arrive or someone to leave or just waiting for something, anything, to happen."

Dan leaned forward, elbows on his knees. They'd lit a couple of citronella candles, and she could just make out his features in the yellow glow.

"How'd you get out of that life?"

Not *what were you thinking, living like that?* Not *how did you sink so low?* Not *I don't want to hear this story after all.* Janine was grateful for all the things Dan didn't say. She was confident he wasn't even having to suppress them. He just wasn't thinking them.

"It was the strangest thing. I woke up one morning next to a guy — a perfectly okay guy, Andrew was his name, typical hippie, all the trappings, long hair, silky and blond in Andrew's case, low-slung bell-bottoms, no underwear, skinny, always high to one degree or another, minor dealer, mostly marijuana, sometimes LSD or mescaline, nothing hard—"

"Your boyfriend?"

"No. Andrew was affectionate in a detached sort of way, but he made no pretense of being boyfriend material. And I had just enough sense not to expect him to be."

"Okay, I get the picture." Dan swatted a mosquito off his arm.

"So, I woke up next to him one morning, which was a little unusual in that we rarely spent the whole night together, and I sat up, and the strangest thought popped into my head, which was that I didn't want to die. I looked out the window. It was a gray morning in late winter. I looked around my room. It was messy, clothes flung over chairs, some on the floor, a smelly ashtray full of cigarette butts and roaches—"

"Roaches?"

"The ends of joints, not the insects."

"Oh."

"Anyway, there was nothing in view — not Andrew asleep, not my room and my meager belongings, not the natural world outside — nothing to inspire me to feel so strongly that I did not want to die. And it wasn't that I'd decided that the way I was living was dangerous, either, though it did have its dangers and I didn't respect them the way I should have. What I'm saying is, there was no stimulus that I could point to and say, *that's why I don't want to die.* I just knew it with every fiber of my being, knew it so deeply that I almost started to cry with the longing to live, to live a long, long time. It's the kind of thing people feel on mountaintops, I guess, or after they've had some near-death experience. But I felt it on an ordinary morning — ordinary, at least, for how I was living then — for no good reason, for no reason at all. Somehow, it just came to me that whether you're happy or not, life is pretty interesting, every inch of it — the litter in the gutter as much as the flowers in the fields — and I wanted to stick around and see more of it."

"What did you do?"

"I woke up Andrew and sent him home."

"What did he think was going on?"

"I don't know. He didn't complain and he didn't ask questions. Going with the flow was like a religion with him."

"What else did you do?"

"I cleaned my room. I signed up for a degree track at Penn. Eventually, I finished and got a teaching job and met Clark."

"So, basically, you decided to live and then you *did*."

"You make it sound a lot more impressive than it was."

Janine stood up. She felt a mild spinning sensation. She was glad she'd stopped drinking. Dan stood up, too, and reached out and grasped her elbow. Had she staggered a bit?

"I'm glad you told me all that."

"You know what? I'm glad you asked."

He let go of her and looked up at the high, white moon.

"What time do you think it is?" he said.

"It feels like three a.m., but it's probably about 9:30."

"That's all? God, why am I so beat?"

"It may be only 9:30, but it's been a long, long day."

Dan picked up the wine bottle and his glass and went to the edge of the deck, where he poured the dregs of wine in his glass onto the grass.

"Would it be awfully rude of me," he said, "to call it a night?"

"Not at all. If you pull out the sofa bed, I'll get you sheets and pillows."

They moved together through the small domestic tasks — making up Dan's bed, putting away the left-over food, rinsing dishes and glasses. Janine told Dan where to find a clean towel, and he went to the bathroom to brush his teeth.

She stood indecisively in the middle of the living room. Like Dan, she was weary enough to go to bed, but she feared that she'd fall asleep only to wake in an hour or two with her mind buzzing. Really, should they let this day close without a word about Hunt? The silt had settled, yes, but it was still there. She sat down on the end of the sofa bed.

Dan emerged from the bathroom carrying a glass of water and wearing a sun-faded red tee shirt and blue and green plaid cotton pajama bottoms. The attire gave him a boyish appearance. Or perhaps, Janine thought, it was just that anyone barefoot and in pajamas looked candid and vulnerable.

"What's up?" he said.

"The time has come, the walrus said, to talk of many things: of shoes and ships and sealing wax, of cabbages and kings."

"Huh?"

"Lewis Carroll. *Alice Through the Looking-glass.*"

Dan set his glass on the end table and rounded the bed, climbing into it on the side opposite where Janine was sitting. He dug his feet under the sheet and propped the two pillows at his back.

"Is that your way of saying it's time to talk about the Dombrowskis?"

Janine felt a trembling twinge in her chest.

"It's over, isn't it?" she said. "He's hiding from them and he's hiding from us. We've gone as far as we can, haven't we?"

"Well, I haven't got any brilliant ideas on what else to do, but that doesn't mean there isn't some avenue we haven't gone down yet."

"I know more about Hunt now than I ever thought I would. Yet there's so much I don't know. I don't even know what I don't know."

"But Janine, do you think you'll ever know Tim and Larry completely? Especially when they're grown? That's one thing divorce has taught me, that your children are constantly moving away from you. From day one."

"That's a heartbreaking thought."

"I think heartbreak is part of the landscape when you're a parent."

Janine watched as Dan took a long drink of water and turned to plump the pillows at his back. She assumed the heartbreak he'd experienced so far was due to his divorce and the resultant regular separations from his daughters. But what about before that? He'd been less of a parent to Hunt than she had in practical terms, but what had he felt in his heart about him? Father Nonas had talked about the grief of the Dombrowskis for the children they never had. What about Dan, a father in name only to a child he'd never seen, his firstborn, his only son?

All those years ago, everyone had drummed into Janine that she should forget and move on, for her own good. She'd resented the advice, but at least it was advice. It was evidence, however meager, that she'd participated in something significant. Had anyone given Dan the respect of offering advice, even unwanted or misguided advice? His mother had demanded he quit Janine. Had she bothered to recommend he not give the child a second thought? Or did she think that, as a man, he wouldn't concern himself anyway?

Erasure. They'd all been erased in some form — Janine, Dan, Hunt. But in Dan's case, it dawned on Janine, the erasure had been more like the slash of a sword than the swipe of a wet cloth. She herself had helped erase him. She'd written his name on some official forms, and she'd whispered a little about him to her newborn baby, but she'd stopped answering his loving, aching letters without explanation. Rose had called Dan's mother to inform her of the birth, but Janine hadn't followed up to make sure that Dan was told. Of course, she'd been in a welter of emotions at the time, but she should have found the grit to do it.

"Dan," she said softly when he'd leaned back against the pillows again, "before this all started, did you know Hunt's birth date?"

He looked flustered.

"You didn't, did you?"

Dan raised his hands in the air as if he were being arrested.

"Guilty!" he said sourly. "Nobody told me — that's my alibi. And I didn't press the issue — that's my sin. But I knew it would be in spring. I may have been an irresponsible louse, but I could count to nine. I called your father in April. April Fool's Day, to be exact. He told me you'd had a boy. End of information."

"Oh, Dan," Janine said, putting her hand on his knee. "You *weren't* an irresponsible louse. *I'm* the louse for not getting in touch with you myself."

"You did have a few other things on your mind." His voice was still bitter, but he was calmer.

"And one of them should have been you."

He looked over her head at the far wall of the room.

"One of them *was* you. But to get your number or your address out of your mother, to pick up the phone, to write — it was all beyond me. I could barely get out of bed some days. The only reason I did was because getting out of high school meant I could get out of town."

Dan looked at her again. Her hand was still on his knee, and he put his hand on top of hers.

"I feel like I deserted him," he said. "I feel like I deserted my son. That's why I never told anyone. I knew what would come next. The looks, the questions. *How could you be so cold? Why didn't you step up to the plate? Wasn't there something you could have done?*"

"I'm sorry I closed you out."

"The deck was stacked against us from the start. We both did the best we could."

She knew he meant it, but he sounded miserable.

"You can say that now, but I know you were hurt."

He took away his hand, and, feeling embarrassed to continue touching him, she took her hand off his knee.

"I really did care, Janine."

"I know. I've always known it."

She had the urge to reassure him further by patting his hand or his shoulder. Then she saw suddenly that she wanted to touch him again for her own sake, that when her hand had been on his knee, she'd felt in equilibrium despite the painful memories they'd been discussing. Flummoxed, she stood up.

"Is it okay if I go to bed? Are we okay here?"

He nodded. "Sure."

"I'll bring you a quilt from my closet. It can get chilly in the early morning."

He moved the pillows and lay down.

"Or you could get in here with me to keep me warm."

It was said lightly, but he wasn't smiling.

"Dan..."

"No funny business. I promise. I just... After this whole insane, sort of wonderful day, I want you next to me. It just feels like the right thing."

She knew what he meant. There was something absurd about them being together in the little house asleep in separate rooms. At the back of her mind, she realized she wouldn't object if he didn't keep his promise about no funny business. And if he were true to his word, that would be all right, too. Better, probably. But she did want his nearness. She wanted his heavy warmth, the sound of his breathing. She wanted his stirring beside her to be her first knowledge of the new morning.

"Move over."

She got under the sheet with him. He was lying on his back, and he lifted his arm so that she could nestle against him. She felt the rasp of his unshaven cheek against her forehead. She breathed in the scent of his body mingled with the delicate fragrance of the aired cotton sheets.

"Now doesn't this feel right?" he said.

She hooked her ankle over his.

"Do you think we're ever going to meet him?" she said.

"I intend to call that priest every week so he doesn't forget us."

"Will you be disappointed if this is as close to him as we get?"

"Of course. But I think I'd be okay if I knew that he was back home and that he had our information if he ever wanted to contact us. How about you?"

"If this is really the end, I guess I can handle it. I'll have to, won't I?"

"Look, let's not say this is the end. Let's say it's a rest."

"That's what's called magical thinking."

"Hey, I'm beginning to believe in magic. Look where I am tonight."

He squeezed her shoulder, then took his arm out from under her head and rolled onto his side, scooting backwards so that his body was pressed against hers and the two of them were curled together like quotation marks. Janine put her face close to the nape of his neck and wrapped her arm over his waist. It did feel right. For this one particular night at least.

21

WHEN DAN AWOKE, he knew it was early by the pearl color of the daylight behind the sheer curtains at the bay window. He'd wakened several times during the night, partly because the sofa bed wasn't very comfortable and partly because of the novelty of having someone beside him. Each time, he'd lain for several minutes watching Janine sleep before he closed his eyes again.

He wanted her, of course, but he also felt something more profound than desire. He wouldn't call it love because it seemed mad to do that, though all the reasons he'd loved Janine in high school were still present. Back then, he'd felt completely safe exposing his dearest hopes and his deepest insecurities to her. And she was still easy to confide in. It was still easy to laugh with her, to share both crises and mundane experiences with her. He actually felt more connected to her now than he had when they were young. Though he hadn't known it before, he'd left something of himself in her keeping, and now he'd recovered it. He'd reclaimed himself. Making love to her would be one way to express that, but not making love wouldn't cancel it.

Janine opened her eyes and frowned sleepily at him.

"Coffee?" she said.

"Is that a request or an offer?"

She rolled onto her back with a small grunt and stretched her arms over her head, pushing her sleeves up above her elbows.

"Tell me where everything is," he said. He didn't want to get up, but even more, he didn't want her to get up.

"Coffee and cream in the fridge, coffee-maker on the counter, mugs in the cabinet next to the sink."

From the kitchen, he had a partial view of the sofa bed. He saw her get up and head towards the bathroom. Then she returned to bed. He was preposterously glad. When he carried the mugs of coffee into the living room, she sat up and accepted her mug with both hands. She took a swallow of coffee and sighed contentedly.

"Not too strong?" he asked, sitting down on the edge of the bed.

"Perfect."

Outside, the ocean haze was burning off. Through an open window came the sound of someone's power lawnmower in the distance and a screech of gulls closer by. Dan could have sat like that for hours. But in only a few minutes, Janine had finished her coffee and set her mug down on an end table next to the sofa.

"More?" he said.

"Not yet."

She was looking at him with such soft sweetness in her eyes, it jerked his heart.

"You know," he said, "last night was the most romantic night of my life."

Her face betrayed no response. Then, miraculously, she got up on her hands and knees and slowly leaned forward and kissed him. When she sat back on her heels, there were tears on her cheeks.

"You're crying. Why are you crying?"

"I don't know." She managed a small smile.

"Don't cry, don't cry," he said, kneeling on the bed and circling her head with his hands.

He drew his thumbs across her eyebrows and traced the hollows of her temples. Then he passed his thumbs slowly along her jawbone to her chin, and with tender pressure, turned her face up to his mouth. When he felt the shape of his kiss begin to lose its form in the melting answer of hers, he moved his hands down, fitting his thumbs into all the natural shelters of her body — her throat, the soft valleys of breast and armpit, the curves at her waist and under her buttocks. Here was no courting, only confirmation. No petition, only mutual possession.

She raised her hands and flattened her palms against his ears. Her tongue moved eloquently in his mouth. He was rendered deaf, dumb and blind to the world around him, all his sensibilities open to her alone.

She canted herself against him, and he tottered a bit on his knees. Then their arms were around each other, and he was pulling her down onto the mattress. She turned her face away from him, breathing hard. His conscience flickered.

"Janine," he mumbled into her neck.

She turned her head to face him again.

"This is a bad idea."

"Really?" he said, stroking her shoulder.

"I don't...I'm not on any birth control," she said, sliding her shoulder out from under his hand. "Do you have any...?"

"Nothing," he said. Then he had to laugh. "It's *deja vu* all over again!"

He propped himself up on one elbow.

"Look," he said seriously, "I can go buy some condoms. I will. But not right now. I don't want to leave you now."

He gave her a quick kiss and smiled at her. He kissed her again and again, quick, nibbling pecks, until she was smiling, too.

"Take off your clothes," he whispered.

He felt her body stiffen.

"Please," he said. "We won't go all the way."

She hesitated a moment longer, and then she sat up and began undressing, fumbling ineptly with the buttons of her shirt, as if she were a child learning the puzzle of clothing. Dan's body responded to her awkwardness as though it were a deliberate provocation. When she sat there, at last, naked and almost shy, his desire quickened almost unbearably. Before him was the young Janine just as he remembered her, beautiful and ripe, and today's Janine was there, too, even more beautiful because he'd regained her. He felt incredibly young himself, vigorous and intense.

He pulled off his t-shirt and pajama pants, and she lay down beside him and laid her lips tremulously against his. He kissed her firmly, wishing he could climb inside her mouth. He had never wanted anyone so strongly before.

He caressed her breasts, gently pinched the nipples. Reaching between her legs, he was so happy to find her slippery and open, he wanted to shout.

"Look at me," he ordered, and she opened her eyes and watched him watching her face as he slid his fingers slowly back and forth. She moaned and lifted herself towards him, but then she pushed his hands away.

She began stroking him, coaxing him to rock rhythmically against her cupped hand. He felt stretched tight, exquisitely held in thrall.

"Oh, God, your touch. The way you touch me..."

He resumed petting her, and she didn't stop him. At the peak of coming, she cried out loudly, and he, seconds behind her, let out his own cry, a strange, animalistic burst that convened every inch of him into one long, smooth, rushing sensation, as if he were a divining rod straining down to the sweet promise of water.

Afterwards, they lay beside each other, enjoying the refreshment of a salty breeze from the open window as it trailed across their sweaty bodies. Dan regarded her, cataloging the signs on her of what they'd just done — her disheveled hair, the flush on her cheeks, a damp sheen on her collarbone. She was lying still, but she exuded vitality and some-thing close to triumph.

Unbidden, Robin came to mind, pale, serene Robin, as complacent and obvious as the full moon. Janine was like a forest. He could get lost in her. He felt that he could go to her again and again and never know what he'd find, but that it'd always be good.

"Janine," he began, but she put her fingertips on his mouth.

"Don't say anything."

"I was just going to say I'm hungry."

She laughed, and it was such free-wheeling laughter, he had to join in.

"I've got bread," she said. "Oranges, yogurt, Cocoa Puffs—"

"Eggs?"

"Probably a few."

"I'm an expert omelet maker. Omelets are the bachelor's fall-back position, you know. I bet if I dig around in your kitchen, I could come up with some interesting ingredients."

"Like a scavenger hunt?"

"Right. A scavenged omelet. My specialty."

She kissed his bare shoulder.

"Not your only specialty, sir, I'd say."

The omelet was a success, though Dan thought Janine would probably have praised even plain scrambled eggs. They were both so brim with contentment they were practically purring. He used the left-over Cheddar from the previous evening, a few scallions and sliced avocado, and topped the finished omelet with dollops of sour cream from a half-empty container. Janine brought tomatoes and lettuce in from the garden and made a simple salad. Toasted challah and fresh coffee rounded out the meal.

It was early enough that the deck was still shaded, so they ate outdoors. Even out of the sun, however, it was hot and muggy. There wasn't a cloud in the sky, and the air had retained some of the moisture from yesterday's rain.

"It's going to be a scorcher," Dan remarked.

"We should have time for a swim before we leave."

"I didn't bring my trunks."

Janine smiled.

"I know a bay beach where we can skinny-dip."

He smiled back.

"When in Rome... But I'm not forgetting you promised to show me your paintings. And I still have that trip to the drugstore to make. Or do I?"

She actually blushed. It was charming.

"Yes," she said with a mock frown, "but try not to look so much like the cat who swallowed the canary."

"Paintings first?"

"All right, come on."

The long grape arbor was situated between the house and the studio. Janine could have walked around it, but instead she entered the vine tunnel, and Dan went in after her. The air was thick with the rich aroma of ripe grapes. Dan's head bumped against a low-hanging cluster.

"I've got a good crop this year," Janine said. "These grapes make delicious jelly. Here, try."

She picked a large grape and pressed it to his lips. It was warm and a little dusty. His teeth burst the tough, slightly bitter skin. He rolled the juicy, meaty flesh of the sweet fruit around with his tongue.

A simple plank bench had been pushed up against the trellis wall. Unexpectedly, Janine sat down on it. The wood creaked. She bent her head back so that she was peering up into the canopy of grape-laden vines. Shadows dappled her face.

"I get the feeling," Dan said, sitting down beside her, "that it's my turn to sound the warning about not saying anything."

She looked at him.

"Can we really trust our emotions here, Dan? Do we even know what they are?"

"Yes, definitely warning time."

"There are warnings, and there are warnings."

"I'm not going to ask what that means," he said, dropping his air of casualness. "And as far as knowing about emotions, I knew within minutes of meeting you again that I wanted to be with you. And I don't only mean like this morning, as fantastic as that was. I can wait. I can take it slow. What I won't do, unless you definitely insist on it, is walk away again from the most authentic relationship of my life just because it seems messy or confusing."

"You're really that sure?"

"I really am."

"People will say we're living in the past, that we're in for a rude awakening, that we're moving too fast or—"

"Those people can go to Hell."

"Dan..."

"Do you believe any of those things yourself, Janine?"

As soon as it was out of his mouth, he wanted to snatch it back. He was taking a big risk. If she said yes, the skids would be on. They'd have to be. There was still the unfinished business of Hunt, but it would be excruciating if that became their only connection. And it could be years before they'd need to see each other again related to that. Well, it was out on the table now.

"I can't be as sure as you are," she said at last, and his heart dared to lift a little. "I've had inklings in that direction, yet there are times I lean pretty far the other way. But I vowed to ignore nay-sayers a long time ago. So I can guarantee you this: whenever I make a decision, it will be mine and nobody else's."

Dan thought his face would crack, he was grinning so broadly. He must look like a fool, but he didn't care a bit.

"I'm so relieved, I could kiss you," he said.

"Well, why don't you?"

They did kiss, and then they stood up, and holding hands, they continued on to the studio.

Janine opened a padlock on the door of the little building and stepped inside.

"This is where I do my framing."

They were in a small room that smelled of sawdust and linseed oil. There was a sturdy workbench with a table saw and a stool, a wall of hand tools, another wall of L-shaped frame samples, and partitioned shelves stocked with mat boards of various colors. An open doorway led to another room.

"My painting studio is in here."

Janine led him into the back room. Large windows took up most of the three outside walls. An empty easel was set up close to one window. Canvases leaned against the wall that adjoined the frame workshop. There was a shabby easy chair in a corner. The only art on display were several children's crayon drawings tacked on one wall. The bare wood floor was well-swept but spattered with paint. A long, narrow table under one of the windows held jars of brushes and pencils, tubes of paints, clean rags, palette knives, a small boom box. A white drafting table sat under another window. Spotting several drawings, Dan went over and picked them up.

They were sketches of rooms, but there was something awry about them, as if they were rooms in a fun house where the floors were uneven, the furniture distorted and almost sentient.

"Those are studies for a painting I want to do of Shadyside," Janine said. "They're pretty rough. Sort of thinking out loud with a pencil. I'll probably do some oil crayon drawings, too, before I start the final canvas."

"That's a lot of steps."

"I don't always do so much prep. But I've set myself a challenge with this painting."

Janine took one of the sketches from him and studied it as if she were looking at someone else's work.

"I want to paint the place in a such a way that the human stories that played out there are depicted, too. The welter of feelings and expe-riences. Like you'd do in a portrait of a person — show the physical appearance, but with undertones of emotion and personality."

"Stories from when you were there?"

"There are years of stories in that old house," she said, looking up from the sketch. Her face was lit with animation. "Our story, with countless variations."

"How will you show that?"

He couldn't fathom how Janine, or anyone, could accomplish what she was describing. He admired her for even having the notion, to say nothing of attempting to bring such a painting into being.

"One thought I had was to portray it like a dollhouse or a stage set, with one wall missing to show the furnishings and people inside."

"That would work."

"Except that I don't want to be so literal. My most recent thought is that there won't be any people at all."

"But the people are the stories, not the place."

"Both are, really. I'm thinking that maybe by distorting shapes and being bold with color, I can infuse the stones and stairs and rooms of the house with strong enough hints at the lives it encased that I won't need human figures."

"It's an exciting idea."

"It definitely has potential. Whether I can actually succeed at it is another thing altogether."

Dan wanted to encourage her and to communicate his admiration without sounding trite. But before he could formulate what to say, the phone in the frame workshop rang. Janine handed him the sketch she'd been holding and turned to leave.

"Ignore it," he said.

He felt that if Janine answered that phone, everything would change. It wasn't just that the call was invading the lovely mood of their morning. That cocoon couldn't last longer than a few more hours in any case. But he'd caught the look in her eyes at the sound of the ring, a look of guilt and fear. She'd tamped it down immediately, but it had definitely been there. She could say she wouldn't listen to nay-sayers, but was she really immune? Could anyone be? He'd have his own critics to face: Robin, his mother, maybe other relatives and friends, maybe even his girls. Janine was undecided. She'd said so herself. There were chinks in her armor. It was too soon to test it. Oh, Lord, why did they have to think about armor?

"It could be my mother. Something about the boys..." Janine said, continuing out of the room.

"But Janine," he said, following, "if your mother couldn't get you at the B & B, she would have called my pager. It was next to the bed all night."

"If it's an emergency, she'd call here whether she expected to find me or not," she said as she lifted the receiver.

"Hello?" she said anxiously.

Dan focused on her face, ready to read trouble, hoping to find the relief of a call from a neighbor or friend or salesman.

235

"Hello? Could you speak up, please?"

She threw Dan an excited look.

"Yes, this is Mrs. Linden."

So it wasn't Rose Pettorini. He made a questioning gesture with his hands. Janine put up one finger, cautioning him to be patient.

"I promise you, Paula," she said, emphasizing the name, "that whatever you tell me will be held in confidence."

Paula Dombrowski. Dan was amazed. He pulled out the stool and sat down.

"That means I won't tell anyone else what you said without your permission. Not anyone."

Janine picked up a flat carpenter's pencil that was lying on the workbench and flipped over a scrap of maroon mat board to its white side. Dan watched her write down a phone number with a New York City area code. Beneath it she wrote *Something Youth Center.*

"Thank you, Paula. I'll let you know if I find out anything. How can I get in touch with you?"

She wrote down another phone number, this time with a South Jersey area code.

"And your friend's name?"

Janine wrote *Vera* beside the New Jersey number.

"All right. Again, thank you so much."

Dan waved his hands in front of Janine's face, and mouthed, "Wait!" He pointed to himself.

"Oh, Paula," Janine said quickly, "is it all right if I share this information with Mr. Gannon?"

Janine nodded at Dan.

"Yes, we will," Janine said into the phone. "Good-bye."

She hung up. "Whew," she said, exhaling loudly.

"What?"

"She's got a phone number. It's a center of some kind. I remember the lawyer saying that the number they had for Hunt was a place to leave messages. Hunt gave Paula the number two weeks after he'd left home — reached her through a friend of hers, this Vera." She tapped the name on the cardboard scrap. "He made her swear not to tell their parents. He just wanted her to have a way to get hold of him if anything important came up."

"Seems kind of tough on the Dombrowskis."

"Paula said that in the beginning it felt all right because Hunt was calling home regularly. The parents didn't like not knowing where he was or what his plans were, but at least they were assured he was okay. Her mother counted on his Sunday afternoon call, Paula said."

"Not the father?" Dan was still convinced that the argument between Pete and Hunt held vital clues to where the boy had gone.

"He probably counted on the calls, too," Janine surmised, "but Paula said Hunt would speak only to her and their mother. But he'd been softening towards his father."

"How so?"

"In his last call, Hunt said that he'd been thinking a lot about what had happened and that he wanted to talk to his father about it, but that he wasn't quite ready. Paula thinks he might have spoken to him on the next Sunday, but he never called again."

"And that was when? July?" Dan said, his temper rising.

"July 12. Paula's birthday, remember?"

Dan paced the small room.

"He missed calling for four Sundays! And it never occurred to her to give her parents that number?"

"She promised her brother she wouldn't."

"You saw those people. They were at the end of their rope."

"Paula called the number herself a few times and left messages for Hunt. She's just a kid. She probably kept hoping he'd call or come home any day, that it would all work out."

"And now *we're* in on this secret. I don't like it, Janine."

She came over to him and put her hands on his waist.

"Dan, you know what it's like, don't you, to want answers and to be afraid of them at the same time, to have actions available to you and to be unsure whether to take them?"

He wrapped his arms around her and folded her close. Yes, he knew about answers both longed for and dreaded. He knew about the postponement of decisions and about blind faith.

"What do you want to do?" he said.

"I want to locate an address for that phone number and go there and find out everything we possibly can about where Hunt is, or..."

"Or?"

"Or...what happened to him."

Keeping his arms around her, he pulled back and looked into her face.

"All right," he said. "But we do it without delay, and we tell the Dombrowskis the results immediately, even if the only thing we have to pass on to them is the phone number."

"What about Paula? She'll feel like she broke her promise to Hunt."

"We'll be the ones breaking a promise, not her. We can't be party to hiding things from the Dombrowskis."

Janine sighed.

"You're absolutely right, of course. I should've thought faster when I was on the phone."

"So, who's going to call that number, you or me?"

"Now? It's Sunday."

"If it's some kind of social services place or rec center, it might be open Sundays. Or there could be a recorded message with the address."

Dan cocked his head at a clock on the wall.

"And if they *are* open," he said, "and we skip our swim and — I hate to say it — the drugstore, we can be in New York in three and a half hours. I'm not expected home until tonight. You?"

"Dinner. And I'd rather not be late."

"Do-able, I think."

He drew her close and kissed her, and then made a joke of stiffening his arms out straight and pushing her away. "If we get going right now."

22

BY 2:00 THAT afternoon, Dan was parking his car on a street of tall brick apartment buildings and converted brownstones in Brooklyn. He and Janine walked three blocks to the Youth Enrichment Programs Center, or YEP, as the person who'd answered the number Paula had provided called it. The place was an old elementary school. As Dan and Janine walked down a wide hallway, following signs to the office, they passed rooms in which children of various ages were busy at different pursuits — ceramics, singing, calisthenics. The noise of shouting and a referee's whistle told them there must be a gymnasium at the far end of the hall.

When they entered the office, they found a young man behind a counter, and to the left of the door, two middle-aged women, one Black, one blond, standing at a table on which were spread large calendars for September and October and an array of papers and file folders. The women were engrossed in poring over these materials. They didn't look up when Dan and Janine entered.

"May I help you?" the young man chirped, adjusting the rolled sleeves of his over-sized white blazer, which he was wearing over a pale turquoise t-shirt. Very *Miami Vice*, thought Dan.

"I hope so," Janine said. "We need some information."

The young man pointed to three neatly stacked piles of brightly colored flyers on the counter. They advertised a pre-school program, teen talent show try-outs, and a back-to-school study skills class.

"These have registration deadlines coming right up," he said. "Our full fall calendar will be out next week. There'll be some new classes.

On-going programs will meet at the same times, but you should double check that the room assignment hasn't changed. Sometimes it does."

He said the last in a stage whisper, as if it were insider information he didn't want the women to know he'd given out.

"Actually," Janine said, "we're looking for information about someone who may have been here recently."

"You mean to take a class or join a group?"

"Maybe," Dan said. "He gave the number of your center as a place to leave messages."

The Black woman turned around. She was holding a clipboard, and as she turned, she tucked a pencil behind her ear.

"We don't do that," she said to Dan. "We're an activities center and a support center. We don't take messages or accept mail for our kids, and they can't use our phones unless it's a bona fide emergency."

"What about the networking board, Mrs. Washington?" the young man put in.

He hadn't been addressing the blond woman, but she straightened up from the table, where she'd been writing something on the September calendar.

"The networking board?" she said. "That's supposed to be for when people want to sell or trade something or are looking for an after-school job or need a ride somewhere, things like that. Not for phone messages."

"But I've put phone messages there," the young man said. "Like if someone's mom is going to be late picking them up, or a teacher calls to cancel a class."

"Well, you shouldn't, Horace," Mrs. Washington said. "The kids don't look at the board for that. And if you've got enough time on your hands to be taking down messages, I'd like to know about it, because there's plenty other work needs doing around here."

"I only did it two or three times maybe," Horace said defensively.

"And I bet every time, those kids came in here asking where was their mom or where was their teacher, right?"

"Yes," Horace admitted.

"But that's not what you folks meant, was it?" Mrs. Washington said to Dan and Janine. "I'm Ellen Washington, by the way, center director."

She held out her hand first to Janine, then to Dan. When they shook, Dan could feel calluses. His surprise must have shown on his face because the woman smiled at him.

"We have a community garden," she said. "And I'm the resident Little Red Hen."

"God blessed Mrs. Washington with a green thumb," the blond woman said.

Mrs. Washington introduced the blond as Dale Claxon, associate director, and then introduced Horace Jones, administrative assistant. Dan and Janine gave their names in turn, but without identifying labels.

"We're trying to locate someone," Dan said, "and all we have to go on is your phone number."

"I don't believe he would have expected messages on a regular basis," Janine said. "He just told his sister this was a place she could reach him if she had to."

"You know," said Miss Claxon reflectively, "some of our teens might use the board for messages. They might have set up little networks of their own. We do encourage them to make connections, after all, especially in the support groups."

"Horace," Mrs. Washington said, "have you noticed anything like that when you check the board to clear away out-dated postings?"

"Maybe once in a while," he replied cautiously, obviously unsure whether or not he was laying himself open to rebuke.

"Who are you looking for?" Mrs. Washington asked Dan.

He deferred to Janine.

"Our son," she said.

"Runaway?"

"Not exactly."

Mrs. Washington gave her clipboard to Miss Claxon.

"You folks had better come into my office."

She led them behind the counter, Horace watching with open curiosity, and into a small office whose walls were plastered floor to ceiling with children's drawings, certificates of appreciation from various city government departments and civic groups, candid snapshots of young people in casual kinetic groupings, including a few of children picking vegetables in the vexatious garden. There were formal photographs of the casts of plays and the members of basketball teams, and high up on the wall, framed pictures of President Reagan, Mayor Koch, and Jesse Jackson.

"First off," Mrs. Washington began after they'd all sat down, she behind a cluttered desk, Janine and Dan on mismatched chairs that appeared to have been retired from some institutional waiting room, "we don't have any services specifically for runaways. We get addresses when kids register for classes, but we're also a drop-in center, so we don't always know if someone's a runaway. At least not right away. My staff have pretty good antennae, though, and kids do come to trust us."

"What do you do if you find out someone is a runaway?" Dan asked.

"It depends." Mrs. Washington folded her arms over her substantial chest. "We'd probably refer them for services. We might try to convince them to contact their families. We might even call in the police, especially in the case of the younger ones. How old is your boy?"

"Eighteen," Dan said.

Mrs. Washington shook her head. "That's the upper limit of our client population. And at that age, he has privacy rights. Who are we talking about, anyway?"

"Hunt Dombrowski," Janine said, "and I should explain our situation."

Mrs. Washington gave an encouraging nod, and Janine succinctly presented the history of the three of them from 1966 to the present day.

"I'm familiar to some extent with every child we serve," Mrs. Washington said, "but I can't always match names with faces, especially if the child only takes one class or is an infrequent drop-in."

She got up and went to the door. Opening it, she leaned out and asked Horace to pull the rosters for all the groups and classes an 18-year-old might attend and to look for the name Hunt Dombrowski.

"I remember him," came Horace's voice from the outer office, "and I know what group he came for."

Dan felt a prickle down his back that was part anxiety, part thrill. He was afraid to move, afraid even to breathe too hard for fear he'd disrupt the revelation taking shape before them. It was as if he were balancing a raw egg on the tip of one finger. He looked at Janine. Her face had paled, and her eyes danced with apprehension.

"Nevertheless, Horace," Mrs. Washington was saying, "check all the possibilities."

She returned to her desk.

"We'll see what Horace turns up."

They had to wait about five minutes. During that time, Mrs. Washington accepted two phone calls. Dan and Janine had no opportunity to speak to each other.

At last, there was a rap on the door. Horace came in, handed Mrs. Washington a piece of paper, and left. She read it and laid it face down on her desk.

"He was a member of one of our on-going peer support groups," she told them, "but he last attended on July 30th."

"A support group for what?" Dan asked.

"I'm sorry, Mr. Gannon, but that's confidential."

"I'm not asking what he said in the group, just what it was for," Dan said, suppressing his irritation with difficulty.

Why did everyone have to be so obstructionist? The kid had written to Janine. He'd given Paula the center's phone number. He'd called his mother every Sunday for weeks. And then he'd dropped off the radar. Was it so unreasonable to be worried? Or was it just that no one thought he and Janine had any right to worry, let alone to receive information?

"Confidentiality is the foundation of our support groups," Mrs. Washington said patiently but dogmatically. "Our clients rely on it. They know we never break confidentiality unless someone's physical safety is threatened."

"But that could well be the case here," Dan protested.

"You don't know that for a fact. Nor do I. All we know is that the boy stopped coming. There could be any number of reasons for that, most quite benign."

"Isn't there anything you can tell us?" Janine said to the woman. "Anywhere you could refer us?"

"I'm sorry, no."

You're not sorry, Dan wanted to shout at her. You're sitting there smugly with your little piece of information that might not even be valuable, and you are not sorry. But underneath his ire, he didn't really believe that. The woman was acting dutifully. She was serving her client, who was Hunt, not Dan or Janine.

They all stood up simultaneously, knowing without it having to be said that the interview was over.

"If you like," Mrs. Washington said, "you may leave a notice on the networking board. Hunt's not participating in group any longer, but he may still come to check for messages. No one has to sign in to enter the building."

She walked them to the door and opened it for them.

"Horace," she said from the doorway. "Please show Mrs. Linden and Mr. Gannon where the networking board is. And Dale, bring the Wednesday activities list into my office, and let's see if we can't resolve that scheduling conflict."

Dan and Janine exchanged subdued good-byes with Mrs. Washington and Miss Claxon, and then they followed Horace out of the office, down the hall to a broad staircase.

"It's on the second floor," Horace explained, starting up the steps.

They had to move to one side when a dozen or so children raced past them down the steps, two of the boys with volleyballs under their arms.

"Walk!" Horace yelled, but they ignored him.

"I'm in the wrong line of work," he said to Dan and Janine. "I'm not that crazy about kids. I do enjoy the teenagers, though. A lot of them have attitude, you know, but they're kind of sweet, too, trying to act all grown and cool. They like to hang around the office when Mrs. Washington and Miss Claxon aren't there. It's air-conditioned."

They'd reached the second floor and were walking down another wide hallway with large classrooms on either side, identical to the hall downstairs, except that these rooms were empty of people.

"You said you remember Hunt," Dan said to Horace.

"Yeah, he was nice. Kind of sad sometimes, but nice. Lucky for him the GALA group met late. He was working somewhere as a busboy, and he couldn't get here before 4:00."

"GALA?" Janine said.

"Gay and Lesbian Answers. Mostly about coming out. Lawd, I wish there'd been something like that when I was in high school. But what can you expect in a podunk town in the middle of Ohio, right? That's why I'm here. Noo-oo Yawk City, baby. Land of the free. Here's the board."

Horace stopped in front of a large bulletin board crowded with handwritten and typed notes on index cards, as well as copies of the three flyers that had been on the counter in the office.

"You have to date your notice," Horace instructed them, "but I supervise the board, so I'll make sure your note stays up."

He handed Janine a blue index card, pivoted, and walked away.

"Best of luck," he called back to them.

"Gay and Lesbian..." Janine said to Dan.

"I guess we know now what the family disagreement was about."

Janine stared at the blank blue card. Then she took a pencil out of her purse and hastily wrote a few lines.

"How's that?" she said, handing the card to Dan.

August 12, 1984

To Hunt Dombrowski: I received your letter on June 28 & have been trying to locate you since. You can reach me at 609-842-1231.

Janine Linden

"How about adding that he could also contact you through Father Nonas? He might feel safer doing that, plus then Father Nonas would be able to let the family know he's heard from him or maybe even get Hunt to get in touch with them himself."

"Good idea."

Janine added *or through Father Nonas* after her phone number. She tacked her note up on the board between a card offering free puppies, German shepherd and Doberman mix, and another card advertising baby-sitting services, unlimited on weekends, until ten p.m. on school nights.

"It looks so small," Janine said, stepping back and taking in the whole board with its scores of cards.

"It is and it isn't," said Dan. "You could say it's lost there in the middle of all those other signs, but you've got to remember that if Hunt comes to look at this board, he's going to be searching for something with his name on it."

"It feels like I stuffed a note in a bottle and tossed it into the ocean. All of it feels like that. I left my phone number at the lawyer's office, at A Future for Families, with Father O'Hanlon, with Father Nonas, with Paula Dombrowski, and now here."

"That's lots of bottles," Dan said, trying to impart an optimism he didn't really feel.

"This place..." Janine said, looking around. "He must have felt safe here, or he wouldn't have given Paula their number."

"Probably he did. And maybe the group he was in was helping him get ready to talk to Pete."

"Then why did he stop coming?"

The same question was eating at Dan, but he hated hearing Janine so cut up. And he hated being powerless to do anything about it.

A loud electric bell sounded through the building.

"I guess they're closing," Janine said.

She looked up and down the hall, as if a classroom door might open, and Hunt might step out of it, materializing like a genie in a fairy tale. Indeed, despite Dan's encouraging words to Janine, he was beginning to feel as if nothing short of supernatural forces would produce the boy.

"Come with me," he said decisively.

"Where?"

"Outside. We're going to waylay our talkative friend from downstairs. He knows more than he's telling, and I'm going to get it out of him."

"Is that wise?"

"I'm sick of being wise. Aren't you?"

"Yes, but—"

"Don't worry. I doubt we'll have to press Horace too hard. He rather likes the sound of his own voice."

Dan and Janine stationed themselves at a window table in a coffee shop across the street from the YEP Center. During the next fifteen minutes, they watched children exit the building in rowdy clutches. Then a few adults left, teachers or coaches, presumably. Finally, the office staff exited. Mrs. Washington locked the heavy doors, and Horace helped her pull a thick chain through the door handles. Miss Claxon secured the chain with a large padlock. This little ritual completed, they descended the cement steps together.

"Luck is with us," Dan said, as the women headed down the street towards a subway entrance and Horace strode off in the opposite direction.

They'd already paid for their coffees, so they jumped up and left the shop, hurrying to reach Horace before he got on a bus or disappeared around a corner. They caught up with him at the end of the next block, where he was waiting to cross the street.

"Horace," Dan said, a little out of breath.

"Oh, hello. Lost?"

"No. We've been waiting for you."

"For me?"

"We want to ask you about Hunt Dumbrowski," Janine said.

Horace shook his head. "You need to see Mrs. Washington about that."

He started briskly across the intersection. Dan and Janine crossed, too, keeping pace with him, one on either side.

"I'm not much more than a glorified errand boy," he said, trying to brush them off. "I don't know anything."

"You knew he was in GALA," Dan said.

"Yes, well, I probably shouldn't have mentioned that. People say I talk too much, and I'm afraid they're right."

They'd reached the sidewalk. Horace continued his quick pace. Dan and Janine kept abreast of him, though it was less easy now because there were more pedestrians on this block.

"Please, Horace," Janine said. "We're his parents."

He stopped suddenly and looked from one to the other.

"His parents? In that case, I *really* have nothing to say to you."

He took off, leaving Dan and Janine momentarily mystified.

"He thinks we're the Dombrowskis!" Dan declared and ran after him.

When he was close behind the young man, he grabbed his arm and halted him.

"Hey!" Horace said, wriggling in Dan's grip. Adrenaline flowing, Dan held tight.

Some passers-by stared as they skirted the two men in the middle of the sidewalk. A woman with a stroller turned and went the other way.

"Keep your shirt on," Dan clipped. "We're not his parents."

Dan felt Horace stop struggling, so he let go. Janine came up to them.

"Well, which is it?" Horace said. He was pouting and making a big show of rubbing his arm, as if Dan had injured him.

"Are you all right?" Janine said solicitously.

Good cop, bad cop, Dan thought, and I'm the heavy. He was a bit shaken by the realization.

"Hunt said he was in New York because of a beef with his parents," Horace said. "Especially *you*," he added, glaring at Dan.

"We can explain," Janine said. "But not here."

"I'm not going anywhere with him that there aren't witnesses," Horace said theatrically.

Dan suspected Horace was having fun a little. He didn't think the young man was really afraid of him. This would make a good story for Horace to tell later. That could work to their advantage. He was already curious about the parents-not parents bit.

"You pick the place," Janine offered.

"There's a little park up the block with benches. But I haven't got a lot of time."

Janine nodded agreement, and they walked to the park. Horace positioned himself at one end of a bench, and Janine sat next to him, ostensibly as a cushion between him and Dan. She repeated the historical summary she'd given Mrs. Washington, with the addition of the argument she imagined Hunt had had with Pete Dombrowski.

"Typical dad in denial," Horace said, rolling his eyes. "So you guys have never met Hunt? That's insane."

"Do you have any idea why Hunt stopped coming to the Center?" Janine said. "Where he lived? Where he worked?"

"No to all that. Honestly."

"But he talked to you about his family?" Dan said. He found it difficult to believe that Hunt would have made such confidences and yet been secretive about the details of his living arrangements.

"We only had a couple of deep conversations like that," Horace said. "The GALA meetings let out just when I was leaving work, so we walked together sometimes. I guess he had stuff on his mind from the meetings, and he knew I could relate, so..."

"He never mentioned where he lived or worked? Not even in a general way, like a neighborhood?" Dan pressed.

"I told you," Horace said petulantly. "What I thought when he stopped coming around was that he went home. He'd been talking about it. He realized he'd completely freaked his parents and that now that they'd had a chance to get used to the idea a little, maybe they could all be okay again together. And he was too smart a kid to stay in a dead-end job like bus boy. Look, I really have got to go."

He stood up.

"But he didn't go home, Horace," Janine said.

It was an entreaty, and Dan saw that the young man recognized it as such.

"There is one thing," he said hesitantly. "But it could be nothing. Lead nowhere. Truly."

"What?" Janine said.

"Another reason I thought he might have gone home was that I thought he might have gotten fired. He had this cold that he couldn't kick, coughing all the time, like those old movies about people with consumption. Well, not that bad. I exaggerate. It's, like, a handicap I have."

"So you think he was sick enough to lose his job?" Dan said.

"I wouldn't want him around any food *I* was eating. I even told him so once. And I told him there was a free clinic at Bellevue if he didn't have money for a doctor. So maybe if you went there...?"

"Thank you," Janine said. "We'll do that."

Dan stood up and offered Horace his hand. After a second's pause, the young man shook it.

"No hard feelings," he said. "And if you find Hunt, tell him I said hi. And tell him to hang in. There *is* life after parents. I'm living proof."

23

THE FREE CLINIC at Bellevue was closed. A notice on the door advised patients to return at eight a. m. Monday, or to go to the Emergency Room. The clerk there was a young woman, skinny, maybe Puerto Rican, with large, gold door-knocker earrings and bangs teased to an impressive height.

"We don't have those records here," she told Dan and Janine when they asked if Hunt was a clinic patient. "The only records we got is if somebody came to Emergency."

"If we call the clinic tomorrow, would they give the information over the phone?" Dan said.

The clerk shrugged.

"You could try Admitting, in case your friend could maybe be in-patient. But it's just skeleton staff on Sundays. They maybe don't have time to look stuff up."

"What if *you* called over there?" Janine said. "Would they look up something for you?"

"Sure, of course," the girl said with self-importance. "But I don't think my supervisor would be big on that."

"We live in New Jersey," Dan said. "It'll be a hassle for us to come back tomorrow just to get one little question answered."

"Hey, I got it," the girl said with a big aren't-I-clever smile. "There's pay phones in the main entrance lobby. You could call the hospital switchboard and ask what room your friend is in, like you want to send him a get well card, and if they tell you a room number, you know he's here. Or, they'll say he's not."

Dan thanked her, though her idea had only the slimmest chance of yielding anything. Hunt had a cough, Horace had said. Setting aside old movies about consumptives, a cough was probably not cause for hospitalization. They might find an address for him through the free clinic tomorrow, but that, too, was chancy, and dependent, as ever, on the cooperation of petty bureaucrats.

Getting an address would require a series of felicitous circumstances. Hunt had to have gone to the clinic in the first place, *and* he had to have given an address, *and* whoever guarded patient addresses would have to be feeling merciful. Nevertheless, Dan thought, here they were at Bellevue with an hour to spare before they ought to be on the road to Teaneck, and making one phone call was easy enough. Besides, there was as much value in eliminating possibilities as in receiving confirmations.

Janine must have gone through a similar train of thought, because she asked the girl for directions to the main lobby without asking Dan if he thought that's what they should do.

Dan leaned against the wall next to the phone while Janine made the call. He was terribly tired. The day, the entire weekend, had been so eventful. It was as if he and Janine had been navigating a wild river in a narrow canoe, shooting rapids, tensely alert even during placid stretches, always aware that the next bend might face them with even more turbulent waters. And apart from all that was the bewitching, luxurious island of their passion this morning. He felt overwhelmed by the mere fact that it had occurred. He wished he and Janine could go from here to a hotel overnight. He wanted her in his arms again, without restraints. He wanted to talk to her about all that had happened, to hear her thoughts. He wanted to dream a little and to invite her into his dreams.

The thought of going into work tomorrow, of calling Robin's house tonight to talk to the girls, of visiting his mother one evening this week, of rejoining the whole usual routine of his life seemed incomprehensible. How could anything ever be usual again? He knew even as he felt it that it was hyperbole. But he also knew that whatever eventually transpired — with Janine, with Hunt — it was no exaggeration to say that he had changed and that his life, however outwardly the same, would be different from now on.

He was roused from his reverie by Janine's voice. She'd been on hold, but now she was saying "thank you" into the phone, and "ICU, 5th floor."

"ICU?" he said, and before the last syllable was out of his mouth, he knew the significance of the utterance.

"He's here, Dan. We found him."

She reached out and took his hand, and they walked to a nearby sofa.

"What's wrong with him?"

"I only spoke to an operator."

"Oh, right. It's so incredible... Are you okay?"

"Not quite."

He put his hand on the back of her neck and kissed her. It was a chaste kiss, yet he felt desire welling up in him, and also love. He'd been afraid to think it this morning, but he couldn't deny it. He was falling in love. He already loved her, and now he was falling in love again.

Janine pulled away from him gently.

"Do you think they'll let us in?" she said. "Aren't there special rules for ICU?"

"Hospitals differ. Doctors, too. Some are very protective of their ICU patients, while others encourage visitors. It depends, too, on what exactly Hunt has."

"Maybe he's too sick for this. For us. Maybe someone should prepare him."

"Who?"

"Father Nonas? Margaret Dombrowski?"

"I wouldn't count on a free pass from those quarters."

"We found him, Dan. That ought to earn us *something*."

He was glad to see her inflamed and righteous. She must still be powerfully anxious underneath — he certainly was — but her determination to demand fair treatment from the Dombrowskis would help her through that.

"Why don't we go upstairs, since we're here?" Dan said. "We won't try to see him. I think having someone prepare him is a good idea. But maybe we can get some information on his condition. At the very least, we'll find out the ICU rules. Then we'll call the Dombrowskis. Whatever happened before Hunt left home, they should be here."

"But we don't have their number."

"I'll get it."

He meant to sound confident for Janine's sake, but as soon as he'd spoken, he actually felt confident. They hadn't come this far to be derailed by lack of a phone number.

"I'll weasel the number out of Father Nonas or Paula's friend, Vera," he went on. "Christ, for all we know, they're in the phone book."

When they stepped off the elevator on the fifth floor, they found the Intensive Care Unit rules listed on a placard on the wall in a small waiting area furnished with a couch, two molded plastic chairs, and a rack of well-thumbed magazines. Only immediate family was allowed to visit, the rules stated, unless the patient requested otherwise and the doctor agreed. Only two people at a time were allowed at a patient's bedside. Visits could be made at any hour, but they were to last no longer than thirty minutes for family and fifteen minutes for others. Nurses were authorized to deny entry to any visitor.

There was a phone mounted on the wall next to a set of swinging double doors. A typed sign instructed visitors to use the phone to contact the nurse's station in order to be buzzed in. Dan picked up the receiver, heard three humming tones, and then a woman's voice saying, "ICU 5."

"We're here for Hunt Dombrowski."

A buzzer sounded, and the double doors automatically swung open. Janine went in, Dan right behind her. They walked down a short hallway to a large, brightly lit open area. Eight small glass-walled cubicles were fanned out in a U-shaped configuration, with a nurse's station in the center of the curve. In two of the cubicles, visitors were standing beside hospital beds. Not a lot of conversation seemed to be going on. There were nurses performing tasks on patients in three other cubicles, and in the remaining three, bodies lay motionless on their backs. High-pitched machines beeped constantly, some slowly, some rapidly. The air was humid and stale, and too warm, at least for healthy people.

Dan began to scan the six beds without visitors. No one in Hunt's family knew the boy was here. He wouldn't have visitors. Dan had passed over two beds, one holding an old man and the other an old woman, when Janine grabbed his arm. She was staring at the bed in the part of the U farthest from the entry hall. The patient's face wasn't fully visible — he was wearing a plastic oxygen cup over his mouth and nose — but it was clearly a young man. His arms in the short-sleeved hospital gown were smooth and muscular. His hair was the color of Janine's, and even from this distance, you could see that he had thick, arched eyebrows.

"You're here for Mr. Dombrowski?" came a woman's voice from the desk at the nurse's station.

Dan stepped over to the desk, and after a momentary hesitation, so did Janine.

"Yes," Dan said to the nurse. "We don't want to see him today, but we'd like to know his condition. We only just learned he was here."

"And you are...?"

"Relatives," Janine said.

"Let me get his chart."

The nurse got up and went to the bed Janine and Dan had been observing. She took a metal folder from the foot of the bed and brought it back.

"Hmm," she said, flipping through the pages inside the folder. "There's no next of kin here. An address in Brooklyn, but no phone. Apparently that's all the hospital social worker could get out of him. You're family, you say?"

Janine had been staring at Hunt's cubicle, but she turned around at the nurse's question.

"I'm his mother," she said. "But he was adopted as a baby. We're in touch with the adoptive parents. They don't know he's here, either. What's his condition? It's the first thing they're going to ask when we call them."

"You'd have to speak to the doctor about that." The nurse flipped to the chart's cover sheet. "Dr. Wang. He'll be here tomorrow."

"We'll want to speak to the doctor, of course," Janine said, managing to sound as if she were both acquiescing and squaring off for a fight, "but if we could have, now, at least a diagnosis..."

"A diagnosis without discussion of the particulars really wouldn't help you."

"Being kept in the dark isn't helpful either, even if it's just until tomorrow. You must have seen that over and over, working here."

The nurse looked hard at Janine, but Dan couldn't tell if the woman were deciding whether or not Janine could handle hearing bad news, or if she were wondering if Janine would make a scene if she didn't get what she wanted.

"He has aspergillosis, a fungal infection of the lungs. He's being treated with antibiotics and steroids, but it tends to be a very resistant disease, particularly if there are underlying conditions. If I were you, I wouldn't delay getting those parents in here. At the very least, it could help his morale. And working here, as you pointed out, I do see things over and over. The power of mind over body being one of them. Sometimes."

The nurse had kept her eyes fixed on Janine's face throughout her declaration, like a toreador watching a bull. But Janine hadn't lunged and she hadn't flinched. The nurse seemed oddly pleased by that, as if she'd been rooting for her.

"Are you sure you don't want to see Mr. Dombrowski?" she said, standing up with the chart in the crook of her arm. "He's asleep quite soundly, and I doubt he'll wake up if you're quiet."

Janine looked questioningly at Dan.

"I'd like to," he said. "Wouldn't you?"

She nodded yes. The nurse came around from behind the desk, and they followed her to Hunt's cubicle. Janine stepped to the left side of the bed, Dan to the right. The nurse re-hung the chart at the foot of the bed and left.

Dan looked down at the still figure in the bed. His son. The boy was too thin, maybe because of his illness, but his skin was almost golden. He must like going to the beach. Or hiking. Maybe tennis. Dan wondered if he'd ever get to learn what his son liked, if he'd ever have an opportunity to share an experience with him. He felt a hot tightness in his chest.

He looked over at Janine. She was staring at Hunt's expressionless face. His dark hair was on the long side, and a hank of it lay across his forehead and over one eyelid. Janine put out her hand, as if to brush the hair aside. Her fingertips hovered over Hunt's forehead. But she turned abruptly and left the cubicle without having touched him. Dan stayed a few seconds longer watching him breathe, wishing he'd wake up, greedily wanting to be alone with the boy when their eyes first met. Hunt didn't move at all.

DAN STOOD AT Robin's front door at 10:00 that night suddenly hesitant to knock. He'd driven over without calling ahead. He hadn't wanted to chance Robin telling him that it was too late, that he was being impractical and sentimental, that he wasn't welcome.

He'd dropped Janine at the Pettorinis' at 5:30, then instead of going straight home, he'd driven to the Alpine Boat Basin and hiked the Shore Path to Peanut Leap Cascade, a pretty waterfall that ribboned its way down a jagged face of dark gray stone. It was the most difficult of the hiking choices open to him. The rough section known as the Giant Stairs, a huge rockfall beside the river, required fifteen or twenty minutes of scrambling over large, sharp rocks and boulders, watching every step in order to avoid turning an ankle. Normally, he would have continued on to the top of the cliff, looping back to the boat basin by an easier path, but there wasn't enough daylight left for that. Besides, by going in to the waterfall and out again, he could traverse the Giant Stairs twice. He needed the distraction.

After leaving Janine, Dan's mind had been a whirlwind of speculations and far-flung emotions. There were snakes uncoiling in his belly and frightened birds beating inside his chest. He couldn't tame the chaos. But on the demanding Giant Stairs and in empty-headed contemplation of the lovely waterfall, his attention would be drawn away from the whirlwind. It would become background noise. The snakes and the birds inside him would settle. That had been his hope, and it had worked.

By the time he returned to his car, it was almost dark. Calmed, he'd been able to go home, call the girls, shower, eat a ham sandwich. But later, he got restless again. As tired as he was, he was too keyed up to go to bed. His apartment felt confining and lonesome, as if he'd been quarantined from the comforts of a home and family. He'd felt an aching need to see his daughters, if only to look in on them while they slept and witness their solid reality. But now, standing at Robin's door, he felt foolish and pathetic.

The light over the front door came on, startling him. The curtain at the narrow window next to the door was pulled aside an inch, and Robin peeked out. The door opened.

"Dan! You frightened me. I thought I heard something, and—"

"I'm sorry. I should have called. Did I wake you?"

She was barefoot and wearing a knee-length nightgown of limp, pale green satin. He didn't remember it.

"No. I was reading." She stepped back from the door. "Come in."

It was dim in the hallway, which was lit only by an amber night light plugged into a wall socket next to the staircase.

"I'll be right down," Robin said, heading up the stairs.

Dan went into the living room. There were no lamps on. If Robin was telling the truth about reading, she must have been doing it in bed.

He sat down on the couch, avoiding the wide, immensely comfortable upholstered chair that had been "his" chair in the days of their marriage. He had wanted to take the chair for his apartment, as well as a few other pieces of furniture, but Robin had objected.

"Taking those things will leave gaps in the house," she'd said.

"You can shift things around."

"It'll be disruptive for the girls." Her ace in the hole.

"What about me, Robin? Don't you think the gap *I* leave is going to be disruptive for them?"

She'd given him a chilly stare. "That can't be helped. We've got to manage the things that can."

He had sat in the chair only once after moving out, while waiting for the girls to finish their breakfasts one Monday morning. He'd been swept with melancholy as soon as he leaned back into the ample cushions, and he'd never sat there again.

Now he glanced around the tidy room, mildly illuminated by the yellow light from a street lamp at the curb out front. There was a new vase on the mantle, different slipcovers on the couch and his old chair, dating from about six months ago, but otherwise it was the same room he'd known for years. Except that he didn't belong here any more. As familiar as the place was, it felt foreign. This is what it's like to be an orphan, he thought.

"Why are you sitting in the dark?" Robin said, entering the room.

She switched on a floor lamp. Dan saw she'd put a cotton robe on over her nightgown. He found her modesty both silly and strangely sweet. Sitting down in a wing chair near his end of the couch, she folded her legs up under her and looked at him expectantly. He knew she was inhibiting her natural inclination to pepper him with questions, and he appreciated her self-control.

"I've seen my son," he said. Please don't ask me how I feel, he thought. "In New York. In a hospital."

He rubbed his hands on his knees. His body was waking up to agitation again. The snakes began to uncoil; the birds spread their wings.

"What's wrong with him?"

"Some kind of lung infection."

Robin nodded at him solicitously, as she might have done to Vanessa or Sally to keep them talking when they were struggling to explain a problem.

She was being so tender. He hadn't seen this side of her in a long time. Maybe she was gratified at being taken into his confidence about Hunt. Maybe she considered it a peace offering. She'd been indignant and wounded when he broke the secret to her on Thursday. Maybe she regretted that outburst. He did want a modicum of peace between them.

"He was asleep. We didn't talk." Another nod from Robin. "He looks like me." He smiled faintly. "The eyebrows."

"They *are* pretty distinctive."

"Hopefully, when I see him tomorrow, he'll be awake."

"Tomorrow?"

"Yes, sorry, I have to beg off on my day again. I should have told you when I called the girls earlier. My brain is just...I'm not thinking too straight."

He saw her grow taller in her chair as her spine stiffened. Her mouth cinched up. Clearly, she wasn't happy at this news, delivered at this hour. But, surprisingly, she made no complaint. She wants to keep the wheels greased, he thought.

"How'd he end up in New York? How did you, for that matter? I thought he lived in South Jersey."

"It's a long story."

Robin waited. But it seemed to Dan beside the point to tell his long story. Hunt was the story that mattered now, and he was still a story with more questions than answers to it.

"So," Robin said with a tinge of exasperation, but still trying to elicit information, "if he couldn't talk, I guess you didn't find out what he's like, what kind of person he is."

Dan thought of the few things the Dombrowskis and the priest had said about Hunt. He thought about Horace Jones calling Hunt nice and sort of sad. He thought about Paula's reckoning that Hunt was almost ready to come home and about Horace's corroboration of that, and how it spoke of a maturity and generosity of spirit on Hunt's part. And he thought about GALA. It had been a major topic of his and Janine's ride from Manhattan to Teaneck.

"How do you feel about Hunt being gay?" he had asked her bluntly.

"I almost can't have any reactions yet. He's like an unassembled jigsaw puzzle. Everything about him is new and second-hand and out of context."

"But you have to admit that his being gay is a pretty big fact."

"Is it a problem for you?" she'd said.

"It's not something I expected. And it scares me. The whole AIDS thing. Finding him in an ICU isn't exactly reassuring."

"The nurse didn't say anything about AIDS."

"It's not the kind of thing she'd tell just anybody. Remember, she knew we aren't his legal parents."

They were on Route 4, passing the exit for Jones Road, their old parking spot from high school days, and Dan's mind flitted to those long-ago nights of adolescent fever. He'd glanced at Janine to see if she'd noticed the exit sign, but if she had, she gave no indication of it.

"What if it were Tim or Larry?" he'd said, continuing their discussion. "How would you feel if one day one of them told you he was gay?"

"Honestly? I'd worry he wouldn't have a happy life. I'd worry he'd suffer prejudice and intolerance. Maybe even that he'd feel shame."

"Well, it seems like Hunt isn't ashamed. If he told his family and he joined that group, he must feel pretty clear about who he is, and he must be basically okay with it."

"Then I guess we'd better be, too."

Dan knew Robin was still waiting for him to elaborate on the meeting with the Dombrowskis, and how it had led to a New York hospital, and how he was feeling about all of it. But truly, it *was* a long story, and there were important parts he'd have to omit. Making love to Janine, for obvious reasons. And Hunt's homosexuality, because the information had come to Dan indirectly and he didn't know if Hunt was ready to have it broadcasted. Yet Dan would feel dishonest telling the story without those parts. It would be a nebulous but very real betrayal. Better to tell none of it.

"He's still a mystery," he responded to Robin's comment about his not having learned anything about Hunt as a person.

He hoped she would let her inquiries drop now. He'd tried to discourage her politely. She wasn't really out of line in trying to draw him out. In the fullness of his emotions when he first arrived, he had led her to believe that he was not only open to making intimate revelations, but that he was seeking to.

"Was she there, too?" Robin threw the question at him like a dart.

"Janine? Yeah, she was there."

"The holy family."

Her voice had a definite edge, but what was it precisely? Jealousy? Mockery? Where was she heading with a remark like that? Well, if it was bait, he wouldn't take it.

"I want to see the girls," he said, standing up.

Robin was taken aback at the turn in conversation. "They're asleep."

"I won't wake them," he said, leaving the room.

He didn't think she'd make any further protest, but he didn't want to hear her permission either. These children, at least, he could get to without anyone else's by-your-leave.

The girls had twin beds, but they often slept together, jumbled like kittens. Tonight they were in Sally's bed. Sally was on her back in the center of the bed, her mouth agape, her arms flung out, one of them across her sister's shoulder. Vanessa was curled on her side, precariously close to the edge of the bed. Dan lifted Sally closer to the wall and Vanessa closer to Sally, rescuing Vanessa from the brink. She opened her eyes and turned her head towards him.

"Daddy," she murmured, seeming not at all surprised to find him there.

"Go back to sleep, pumpkin," he said, pulling the sheet up over both girls.

"Sally wants waffles for breakfast," she mumbled.

"I'll tell Mommy."

Satisfied, Vanessa closed her eyes and snuggled against her sister.

The window unit air conditioner was humming loudly, set on high. It had been a perennial point of contention between him and Robin. Her notions about filtered air and allergies and summer colds versus his about fresh air and pacifying night sounds and natural body rhythms. He thought about Hunt in the fetid air of the ICU. There weren't even any windows to open. There was no way to tell if it were day or night. He'd like to try to get him moved. He wondered if the doctor would allow it. But who was he kidding? Neither the doctor nor the Dombrowskis nor maybe even Hunt himself was going to listen to his opinions. He'd be tolerated at best.

Dan went to the window and turned off the air conditioner. Then he opened the other window wide. Warm air floated into the room and with it, the faintest odor of a distant skunk. He could hear crickets, and staring out into the darkness, he made out the stealthy silhouette of the neighbor's cat padding across the lawn.

As he descended the stairs, he smelled the aroma of freshly made coffee. He went into the kitchen and found Robin at the toaster.

"I'm making myself a Pop Tart," she said.

"I'm gonna head out."

"Sit," she said in a practiced mother-knows-best tone.

He didn't sit, but he didn't leave, either. It might be better, he thought, not to let the holy family crack be their final exchange.

"You look terrible," she said. "If you don't mind me saying so."

"And if I do mind?"

"You still look terrible, but I won't belabor the point."

He shammed a smile. She poured out two cups of coffee and set one in front of him on the butcher block island. She drank hers leaning against the sink regarding him.

"Your mother called," she said.

"Really? What for?"

263

"She does once in a while."

"I'll go see her Tuesday. Oh, before I forget, Sally wants waffles for breakfast."

Robin frowned. "You said you wouldn't wake them."

"I didn't."

Robin continued to frown, but he saw it was only for show. He might have been a reserved, taciturn husband, as she'd claimed, but he wasn't oblivious. He could read his wife. Most of the time, anyway.

"Your mother's fretting about you and Janine."

He made a dismissive motion with one hand. "She should let go of that old bone."

"Don't be evasive, Dan."

"I'm sorry," he said sarcastically. "Were you asking me a question?"

Staying for a cup of coffee was beginning to look like a bad idea. He should have quit while he was ahead. If he could have identified when that was.

"If you're going to be introducing new people into our children's lives, I think you owe me—"

"I *owe* you?"

"You know perfectly well what I mean."

"It's too soon to be having this conversation, Robin. That's the most I can say right now."

"And that's supposed to be reassuring?"

She put down her cup and stood away from the counter where she'd been leaning, planting her feet more widely, as if bracing herself against an expected shove.

"It's not *supposed* to be anything but a statement of where things stand right now, which is in limbo. If you find that reassuring, more power to you. If not, that's your problem, not mine. I can't worry about your state of mind."

"As if you ever did," she hissed.

"Okay, I'm going now," he said, adding sourly, "Thanks for the warm shoulder."

He left the bright kitchen, passed through the shadowy dining room and living room, and out the front door. He would have liked to slam it, but he didn't want to wake the girls or give the neighbors fodder for gossip or give Robin the satisfaction of knowing she'd gotten to him. But as he slid into his car, sadness bubbled up through his irritation. She really had offered him a warm shoulder for a few minutes there, and it had eased him, but she hadn't been able to do it cleanly, and he hadn't been able to show his appreciation cleanly. He didn't intend to do anything to rectify that. It might only lead to more resentment and misunderstandings. And that was sad, too.

24

JANINE AND THE twins didn't go back to Cape May Point on Sunday evening as she'd planned. Nor were they leaving today, Monday, which had been her secondary plan. All plans were on hold.

It had turned out that the Dombrowskis' phone number was listed. Dan got it from the Information operator yesterday. Janine thought he'd been a little disappointed that he hadn't had to work harder for it. Margaret Dombrowski answered the phone, and as soon as she learned it was Dan, she got her husband on the line, too. Standing in the niche off the hospital lobby where the pay phones were located, Dan had tilted the receiver away from his ear, and Janine had put her head close to his so that she could listen in.

"I'm glad you're both there," Dan had begun. "We have some news about Hunt."

There was a sharp intake of breath, probably Margaret's.

"News?" Pete said. "What kind of news?"

"Well, for one thing, where he is."

"Is he all right? Is he with you? Put him on," Margaret said in a rush.

"Where you calling from?" Pete said before Dan could react to Margaret.

"New York. Bellevue Hospital."

"What's happened?" Margaret wailed.

"He's ill, in Intensive Care. We don't know the details. They said you can see his doctor in the morning."

"We'll come right away. Tonight," Margaret said. "Right, Petey? Tonight."

Pete Dombrowski cleared his throat loudly.

"Did you see him?" he asked Dan.

"The doctor?"

"No. My boy. Did you see Hunt?"

"Yes, but he was asleep."

"Did he say anything?"

"He didn't even know we were there. We wouldn't have gone in to see him if the nurse hadn't assured us he was soundly asleep."

There was silence on the line. Dan and Janine exchanged questioning looks.

"Will you be coming to New York tonight?" Dan asked.

"Yes," came Margaret's quick reply.

"Yes, we will," Pete confirmed.

"Hunt's on the fifth floor. You can go in to see him any time. A nurse told us he has a lung infection. His doctor's name is Wang."

"I'm getting off now," Margaret said. "To get some things together. Pete, I'll need you to bring the big suitcase down from the attic."

"All right."

"Thank you, Mr. Gannon," Margaret said, faltering a little, "for finding Hunt."

There was a click as she hung up.

"Mr. Dombrowski?" Dan said.

"I'm still here."

"We'll come to the hospital in the morning. We'd like to be there when you talk to the doctor. And we want to see Hunt. Awake."

These statements took Janine by surprise. She and Dan hadn't yet talked over what they should do next. But she had no quibbles with what he was saying. As soon as he'd said they would be at Bellevue in the morning, her gut told her it was the right thing to do.

"I don't know about that," Pete responded in a slow drawl. "If he's not strong..."

"I think it's for the doctor to say whether or not Hunt's well enough to meet us. If you and your wife want to talk to Hunt first, we'll certainly wait for that. But when I say we'll wait, Mr. Dombrowski, I'm talking about hours, not weeks, or even days."

"Now you just hold on. You got no right—"

"Actually, I think I do have some rights here," Dan interrupted. "But that doesn't mean we have to be enemies. I'm not trying to take over your place with Hunt. I hope you can believe that. And in the end, it's going to be Hunt, not you and not I, who gets to say how far all this is going to go."

Janine marveled at how calm Dan had managed to keep his voice. She could see by his face that he was experiencing deep emotions. Another stretch of silence followed. This time Dan waited it out.

"It's not that I'm not grateful," Pete finally said, sounding leaden. "You've got to understand. It's all the worry, the not knowing..."

Janine's jaws had clenched. Why was it that she and Dan were always the ones expected to understand? To see reason, make accommodations, shut up, disappear? As for not knowing, she'd endured years of it.

"All this time with no word," Pete was saying. "Then you and Mrs. Linden showing up. And now, Hunt in a hospital..."

"We'll be there by 9:30 tomorrow."

"9:30," Pete repeated. It hadn't quite been a concession, but it hadn't been a prohibition either.

Now it was dawn. Janine was alone in her mother's kitchen drinking coffee. Dan was due at 8:30. That seemed like eons away, but really it was the blink of an eye. A blink, anyway, of God's eye.

Against so many odds, Janine had moved from whether she'd ever meet Hunt to when. Dan's calm insistence on the phone with Pete Dombrowski had worn down the final obstacle, at least for the time being. Dan hadn't exactly used honey, but he hadn't been heavy-handed with the vinegar either. She wasn't sure she'd have been able to strike the right balance. She'd have found another way in eventually, but it would have meant more delays, a longer season of being at the mercy of the Dombrowskis.

She wanted, suddenly, to hear Dan's voice. She felt that, as early as it was, he'd be awake, for the simple reason that she was awake. It was the way she'd thought about him when they were in high school, that there was a mystical bond between them beyond the ordinary ties of the other steady couples among their friends. She was amused at herself now to find that a strand of belief in that bond still lingered. She took the cordless phone out into the back yard and called Dan at his apartment. He answered on the second ring.

"You're up," she said to his hello.

"Yes. I saw the sun rise."

"Are you nervous about today?"

"I'd be lying if I said no, but I'm trying not to think about it too much."

"How do you manage that?"

There was only a swallow or two of coffee left in Janine's cup, and it had gone cold. She poured it out on the grass.

"By arming myself with facts."

"Oh?"

"Last night I talked to a friend of mine who's an internist about aspergillosis."

Janine had wandered across the yard while they were talking. She was feeling chilled in the early morning air, so she lay down in the hammock and pulled its canvas sides around her shoulders.

"What did he say?"

"Well, like the nurse told us, it's caused by a fungus. A pretty common fungus, apparently. It's all over — bread mold, mildew, on potatoes, on cotton and bedding, on plants and trees, in the soil. It can cause superficial infections like athlete's foot, or it can cause systemic illness. Certain people are more susceptible to serious reactions when they breathe in the spores — people with asthma, people with scarred lung tissue. And people with AIDS."

"You think that's the problem with Hunt, don't you? But he's so young."

"I admit it's hard to believe. But my friend said they just identified a virus in April — wait, I wrote it down." He was silent for a few

269

seconds, presumably retrieving his notes. "HTLV-3. Seems it's linked to AIDS, precedes it. He thought just having been infected by that virus might make it more likely Hunt would develop the more serious type of aspergillosis."

Janine thought of the list she'd brainstormed in July on the possible outcomes of a search for Hunt. One of them had been finding out he'd died. Was that going to come true?

"People with AIDS die," she said. "If they live a year, it's a long time. If they live half a year."

"I know."

Of course he knew. She had just had to say it out loud, like a child whistling in the dark to keep fear and wild imaginings at bay.

"We don't *know* that Hunt has AIDS, or that virus," she insisted. "We shouldn't jump to conclusions. We don't even know how serious the aspergillosis is. Your friend isn't Hunt's doctor. He doesn't know the case. He's guessing."

"Educated guesswork."

"Yes, yes, all right."

Janine noticed a fat blue jay hopping from branch to branch in the tree over her head. He cocked his crested head at her, as if he were trying to ascertain whether she posed a threat or if she offered any promise of food scraps.

"Janine? Are you there?"

"I'm watching a blue jay."

"I wasn't trying to be the voice of doom."

"I know."

"It's all generalities. Just my way of taking my mind off the rest of it."

"You mean the reunion with Hunt?"

"Yeah, that small matter."

The blue jay flew away, and Janine sat up, swinging her feet out of the hammock and resting them on a patch of dirt scuffed free of grass by the twins' shoes.

"You were great with Pete Dombrowski," she said. "Did I tell you that?"

"I just winged it, really."

"I keep composing little speeches in my mind for Hunt, but they all come out stilted or too convoluted. Even a perfect speech could fall right out of my head as soon as I'm face to face with him."

"I'll have your back," Dan said.

Janine smiled. "Ditto."

When Dan and Janine got off the elevator at Bellevue's fifth floor, they found Paula Dombrowski slumped on the couch in the ICU waiting area. When she saw them, she sat up and glared at Janine. Even the rhinestones on her jeans jacket seemed to be glittering with grievance.

"Hello, Paula," Janine said.

The girl didn't answer. Dan and Janine sat down on the plastic chairs facing the couch.

"Are your folks in with Hunt?" Dan asked.

Paula nodded.

"Have you seen him yet?"

"For a minute last night and once today. I could tell he wanted to know why I ratted on him, only he couldn't ask right out 'cause my mom was there."

"He was feeling well enough to talk, then?" Janine said, feeling encouraged.

"You told," Paula said angrily. "You promised you wouldn't, and then you did."

"That's not exactly true, Paula," Janine said, knowing it wasn't exactly false either. "We never mentioned your name to anyone, or that you had a number for Hunt. We haven't explained how we found him at all."

"But you will."

"We'll keep you out of it. Just as I said."

Paula's glare wavered.

"My brother thinks I'm a fat mouth," she said, her voice breaking. "He thinks I'm a fat mouth, and I can't see him alone to break it down for him, and he could die and never even know that I—"

"Who said he's going to die?" Janine demanded.

"Nobody," Paula admitted. "But they never tell me things. They act like I'm an airhead or something."

"Have your parents talked to the doctor?" Dan asked.

"I don't think so."

"Well, let's wait and see what he has to say, all right?"

Paula gave a grudging nod. She picked up her over-sized purse from the floor, dug out a used tissue, and blew her nose.

"Do you think Hunt was sorry or angry to see you and your parents here?" Dan said gently.

"No," Paula muttered.

"Was he glad, maybe? Relieved?"

"I guess so."

"Then I don't think he'll fault you for giving us the number of the youth center. And you can be the one to tell about it. When you're ready."

"You did the right thing giving us that number, Paula," Janine assured her. "Otherwise Hunt would still be here all alone."

The swinging doors opened, and Margaret and Pete Dombrowski appeared. Dan and Janine stood up.

"Mr. Gannon, Mrs. Linden," Pete said, dipping his head to each of them.

"Please, it's Dan and Janine," Janine said, and Dan nodded agreement.

"Margaret and Pete," Margaret said unenthusiastically, after giving her husband a sidelong glance.

Pete didn't object, but he looked as if he were feeling boxed in.

Paula slid over to make room on the couch for her mother, and Janine sat down on her chair again. The men remained standing.

"Can I go in and see Hunt?" Paula asked.

"Not right now. His breakfast is coming," Margaret said.

"So?"

"He can eat, then?" Janine asked Margaret. It seemed another hopeful sign.

"He can, but they said he doesn't eat much. The treatments take away his appetite."

"What *are* the treatments?" Dan said.

"A medicine, in an IV. What was it called, Pete?"

Pete took a scrap of paper out of his shirt pocket and unfolded it.

"Amphoterracin," he read out. "It's an anti-biotic."

"Right," Margaret said. "The nurses call it Ampho-terrible because it makes you feel so bad. Like cancer drugs, they said. They give it at night, dripping for a few hours. And he gets something for nausea at the same time and something to help him sleep. Sometimes morphine, too."

"Sounds pretty powerful," Dan said.

"He's been having it a week already," Pete said glumly. "And he's still sick."

The elevator doors slid open, and an orderly pushing a wheeled metal cart of covered food trays exited the elevator. He went to the swinging doors and was buzzed into the ICU.

"Maybe I should go see if I can get Hunt to eat more," Margaret said, starting to get up.

Pete motioned her to stay put. "Let me," he said.

She gave him a searching look, then nodded acquiescence. Janine wondered if this would be the first time father and son would be alone together. If so, maybe Pete had in mind to do some fence-mending. If Hunt was up to that, shouldn't he also be able to see her and Dan? They were going to wait for the doctor's okay, and for the Dombrowskis to prepare the boy, but it looked as if Pete might already think Hunt was fit enough for serious interactions.

After Pete disappeared through the swinging doors, Dan turned to Margaret.

"Is there a specific time you expect Dr. Wang?"

"He's supposed to see Hunt at eleven."

"In that case, I think I'll go call my office to check that all my appointments got cancelled, and then I'll hit the cafeteria. Care to come along, Paula?"

The girl looked at the closed doors to the ICU.

"Dad's gonna be a while, I think," Margaret said. "And afterwards, Hunt might need to rest."

"Okay," Paula said, answering both Dan and her mother. She slung her bulging purse over her shoulder and went to push the elevator button.

"Can we bring you anything?" Dan asked the women.

"No, thank you," Margaret said.

"Something sweet," Janine said.

The elevator bell rang. Paula held the doors open for Dan, and he hurried over. Janine, sitting opposite Margaret, could think of nothing to say. Margaret was avoiding looking at her, her gaze roving from magazine rack to vinyl floor tiles to elevators to ICU entryway. It lingered there.

She looks like a mother, Janine thought suddenly. In the way that my own mother looks like a mother — settled, non-sexual, queenly. And fierce. Yes, for all Margaret Dombrowski's politeness, for all her deference to her husband and her priest, and despite her Sears wardrobe and her pleasant but not-quite-pretty face, she had a fierceness to her, and Janine sensed that the ferocity was tied to her motherhood. She'd die for her kids. She'd kill to protect them. As Janine would do for Tim or Larry. Such primitive instincts were latent most of the time, but now Margaret's were roused. She had a sick child, and she had rivals for his attention and loyalty.

Margaret finally glanced her way, and Janine thought she caught a flash of judgment in the woman's eyes. All the old charges rose up in Janine's memory: wild; irresponsible; delinquent; tramp; failure. Janine's pulse thumped with the heat of impotent anger. Well, Mrs. I've-got-your-number-missy, failure's one place we're the same. I failed to hold on to my baby, but you failed to have one. I made you a mother. You couldn't do it for yourself. Pete couldn't do it. God couldn't. Your happiness with Hunt, the fierceness in which you are bathed this very minute, are only possible because of my loss.

Janine took a deep breath. She had to get a grip on these turbulent thoughts and emotions. All she really needed from Margaret was for her to get out of the way. She didn't need friendship. She didn't need her to drop the stereotypes about frivolous, wicked unwed mothers and understand the confused, frightened, sad teenager Janine had been when Hunt was born. It would satisfy Janine in a profound way if Margaret acknowledged that her gain had come from Janine's loss. Such an acknowledgment would penetrate the old wounds and loosen the scabs, and a small, tight spot in Janine's heart might finally unclench, but it probably wasn't going to happen. She wasn't going to try to make it happen. And she wasn't going to let herself hope for it. As much of a balm as it could be, she would not let herself need it.

Margaret was staring at the rack of magazines as if she might be deciding which one to get up and take, but there wasn't a flicker of true interest on her face.

"What did you tell Hunt about me?" Janine said, aware only a split second before she said it that she was going to.

"When?"

Margaret made a minute shift to move herself a tiny bit farther back against the couch, as if she were a snail drawing in its antennae in response to a touch.

"When he was a child. I assume he asked."

Margaret nodded, lacing her fingers together in her lap and looking down at them pensively.

"I told him what we knew. That his biological parents were high schoolers, that they were from Catholic families, one Irish and one Italian." She looked up at Janine. "I used to think about you myself some times..."

"Did you?"

275

"I used to worry that there'd be a knock on the door one day and there'd you'd be, a princess with a beautiful basket all lined in blue satin to take my baby away in. They told us you didn't want him, but I thought maybe you might change your mind. They said you were from a good family, clean and healthy, and I thought maybe a girl like that might change her ways and change her mind."

"Change my ways?" Janine said, bristling.

"Well...you know."

Margaret looked embarrassed. With difficulty, Janine smothered further protest.

"That's all you told him? He didn't want to know more? When he was older?"

"He did. He even asked to see the papers, so I showed him. Pete said it was okay because they didn't have any names on them except ours and the lawyers. I don't know if it was a name Hunt wanted, anyway. I think what he wanted was to know why."

"How did you deal with that?" Janine said, though she was afraid to hear the reply.

"I told him that you were too poor to keep him. I told him you wanted him to come to us because you knew we would love him so much. Nobody ever said any of that, but I thought it would make him feel better."

"And did it?"

"I don't know."

"Did it make *you* feel better?"

There was a bitter taste at the back of Janine's mouth. Her words had to burrow through it.

"Me?"

"Did it make you feel more like his real mother? Like Hunt came to you with no history, no other family? Like he would have if he was born to you?"

Margaret sat bolt upright, as if she were a marionette whose strings had been twitched.

"I *am* his real mother! He was a little innocent baby who needed to be wanted, and I was full of want. I took care of him. He wasn't just a mistake of two horny kids who were too selfish to be bothered with the work and trouble of a child, who didn't want to—"

Janine leapt to her feet.

"You have no idea of what I wanted! You have no idea of what it's like to hold a baby in your arms that you've sheltered inside your body for nine months, and then to let him go and have your arms feel empty ever after, even when you're holding your other babies later on."

"Why do you want Hunt now?" Margaret accused her. "Is it to get your hooks into your old boyfriend again? He looks pretty hooked already to me."

"Hunt wants *me*," Janine said, slapping the flat of her hand against her chest. "I'm his mother. I didn't feed him or house him or teach him. But he came from my body. That counts. I count. He and I will always be a part of each other. You can't deny that. No one can. The ache in my empty arms — that's what makes me his mother."

Janine stopped. If she went on, the sobs would begin, so she walked urgently to the elevators and back, to the elevators and back, again and again. Margaret's back was to her. She saw her reach for her purse on the seat beside her, take out a white handkerchief, and press it to her face.

Selfish, selfish, Janine's footfalls seemed to drum. Margaret had resurrected that old bugaboo. Was it selfish to want a shot at Hunt's acceptance? Was it selfish to pray for his survival in part because she didn't want to lose him again so soon? Was it ever okay to be selfish?

Don't be selfish, they used to say at the Home whenever a girl talked about keeping her baby. Such an ugly accusation. It always stings. A very effective persuasion tool, too. Well, she wasn't going to let the Dombrowskis wield it against her. She had warts. So what? Hunt started this. Let Hunt finish it. Let Hunt assess if she and Dan were worth bothering with or not. Let him decide if their sin against him was too great to forgive. He's the only one with the right.

Slowing her pace, Janine ducked around the corner from the elevators and took a long drink of icy water from a stainless steel fountain mounted on the wall, and then she went and sat again in her chair opposite Margaret. She was relieved to see that the handkerchief had been put away.

"I knew you took care of him for a week," Margaret said quietly after a few moments. "After I had him a week, I could never have let him go."

"Well," Janine said tartly, the bitterness lingering despite her attempt to walk it out of her system. "Now you are being asked to let him go. And if you love him, you will. Just like I did."

Margaret gaped at her with animal terror.

"What do you mean?" It was almost a moan.

"Let us see him. Today. Before he's doped up for his treatment."

Margaret slowly shook her head no. She raised one hand in a blocking gesture, and then she rested it on her chest, fiddling with the pearl buttons of her flowered rayon dress.

"What are you afraid of, Margaret?"

Margaret lowered her fidgeting hand to her lap. "Afraid?" she echoed.

Janine thought she knew the answer. Margaret was afraid of losing Hunt. She could understand that. She was afraid of losing him, too, and she didn't even "have" him yet. And there were so many ways in which Margaret might imagine losing Hunt. He could prefer Janine and Dan to her and Pete. He could disappear into a lifestyle that Margaret couldn't figure out how to join. He could die. All, all beyond her control. The only place for a finger in the dike was at the threshold Janine and Dan were asking to cross. Yes, Janine knew what Margaret was afraid of, but she wanted to hear her say it. It would be the first step in disarming the woman's fears, at least the part about Janine and Dan pushing her and Pete out of their primary place in Hunt's life. But when Margaret finally spoke, what she said was an utter surprise.

"God. I'm afraid of God."

"God? Why?"

Margaret closed her eyes a moment, marshaling her thoughts.

"When I was younger," she said, opening her eyes, "we used to call having your period the curse..."

"So did we. Other things, too. My cousin from Red Bank. Flying the flag."

"Well, for me, it really felt like a curse. I mean, it did when me and Pete started trying to have a family. Father Nonas used to tell me that children would come in God's time. Then he stopped saying that and only talked about God's will and Gods' plan, but I couldn't figure out how me not getting pregnant could be any use to God. I tried to believe, later, that His plan was for us to be able to save Hunt and Paula from being orphans. And I'm grateful for them. I truly am. But it's always been a kind of gratefulness that just goes out into the air, like a toy balloon floating higher and higher, but not really aiming at God. Not...well, not feeling like He deserved it."

"You think Hunt being sick, or Dan and I showing up are some kind of punishments from God?"

Margaret gave her a steely gaze.

"I deserved children," she said passionately. "The only thing I ever wanted without stop since I was a girl was to be a mother. God did give me Hunt and Paula, but not in the natural way, and He teased me a long time first. He still keeps reminding me, every month like clockwork."

"Reminding you of what?"

"That all I can 'bring forth,' like the Bible says, is useless scraps of my own flesh. Why do I have to have it if it's no good for anything?"

Margaret had gradually leaned forward as she spoke so that her upper body was canted out into the space between the couch and Janine's chair, her elbows pressing into her knees, her face lifted to look up into Janine's. Now she flopped against the couch back. Janine guessed such an outpouring wasn't typical of her.

"I'm going down to the chapel after we see the doctor," Margaret continued more calmly. "But I've already apologized."

"Apologized?"

"To God. For blaming Him, even after I got my babies. 'Cause maybe He finally decided to take me to task for that. Maybe He sent you to turn Hunt's head and sent the sickness to show me what being deprived can really be like. But I'll earn Hunt all over again, like I earned him in the beginning. With all that wasted blood. I'm offering it up. All my times of the month from the past, and all the ones I got left coming."

"I don't know what to say."

"There's not anything to say. I don't even know why I told you." Margaret crossed her legs at the ankles and smoothed her skirt. "I don't usually..."

"I didn't think so."

The orderly with the food cart came out of the ICU. Margaret watched him go to the elevator. She watched him push the button and wait, then enter the elevator when it arrived.

"Pete's been in a long time," she remarked.

"I'm sure the nurses wouldn't let him stay if it was too much for Hunt."

"Last night, Hunt was groggy and feeling sick because he was having his treatment, but when Pete took his hand, he squeezed it and he said 'Dad' so sweet and easy, like he was a little boy again." She looked dreamily towards the ICU. "He was real good-natured as a boy."

"Was he?"

Janine felt her throat constrict with grief for all the years of Hunt's life she'd missed out on.

"Were you ever sorry?" Margaret said, pulling herself back from whatever daydream of Hunt's childhood she'd been in.

"Sorry?"

"About Hunt."

Janine had been lulled into relaxing her guard during Margaret's speech about God, but now she became alert again.

"Sorry's not the right word," she said.

"What is, then?"

Janine studied her. Was this some kind of trap? Were they going to end up clawing at each other again? Finally, she decided to gamble that Margaret's interest was genuine.

"I never regretted having him." Janine was choosing her words carefully. "I knew I was supposed to feel guilty and ashamed, but I didn't. Not about him, or even about being pregnant, except that I did feel awful about upsetting my parents. But giving him away? I've never felt right about that. That's where my guilt lives."

Janine paused to get a grip on her self-control, then she continued.

"I handed my baby over without knowing where he was going, who was taking him in, or when. What kind of mother does that? I get weepy seeing kittens and puppies without their mothers in pet stores, and I gave away my own baby."

"But you said you did it for him."

"It still felt wrong."

Janine lifted her hands in a helpless gesture. There was no way out of the guilt. She'd built a good life for herself. Clark and the twins had been part of making her feel better about herself. Her art, at times, served as a purge. The guilt didn't obsess her, as it had in the first year after Hunt's birth. It didn't define her. But she knew it would never leave her completely. Even reuniting with Hunt wouldn't banish it.

If Janine got past the Dombrowskis, it would be Hunt's grown personality she'd gain access to, not his baby self, captured in her memory like a leaf in ice, and it would be up to her to win a place with that Hunt, and up to them both to build a relationship that was its own living entity, not a version of what Hunt had with Margaret, nor an adaptation of what Janine had with Tim and Larry, but something that was uniquely theirs, forged out of the pain of the past and the joy of a second chance.

"Did you ever—?" Margaret began, but just then the automatic doors of the ICU swished open, and both women turned to see Pete Dombrowski come out into the hall.

His wife got up and went to him. They talked together in hushed tones for a few minutes, and then they came to the waiting area. Janine thought Margaret looked relieved.

"Pete got him to take most of his breakfast. More than the nurses ever could, one of them said."

"That's good," Janine said.

Both elevators arrived. Dan and Paula exited from one, Dan carrying a cardboard tray with four drink cups, and Paula a lidded styrofoam box and a tall cup with a straw protruding from it. A slender Asian man in a white coat, with a stethoscope slung around his neck, came out of the other elevator. He walked briskly to the little waiting area.

"Mr. Dombrowski?" he said to Pete.

"Yes."

"I'm Dr. Wang." He held out his hand. "I've been overseeing your son's care."

Pete shook his hand.

"This is my wife," Pete said, indicating Margaret.

"Hunt's mother," she said, with a tiny tic of anxiety playing at the corners of her mouth.

"Janine Linden, a friend," Janine said quickly when the doctor glanced at her.

She wanted to spare Pete and Margaret the awkwardness of trying to figure out how to describe her. And she wanted to sidestep the worse possibility that Pete might not introduce her at all.

Dan and Paula had reached the little group by the time Janine was speaking, and Dan followed her lead, also calling himself a friend.

"Hunt's my brother," Paula announced, neglecting to give her name. "Is he gonna be all right?"

The doctor smiled at her. "That's what we're here for."

He looked at Pete and Margaret.

"There's a family meeting room over there," he said, pointing down the hallway leading away from the ICU entry. "If you'll wait there, I'll go check on Hunt, and then I'll come and review his condition with you."

Without waiting for their agreement, Dr. Wang turned away from them and went to be buzzed into the ICU. Paula started towards the meeting room, but before she went around the corner that would have put her out of sight of the waiting area, she stopped and looked back over her shoulder at the four adults still milling around.

"Come on, Mom," she said insistently.

"Guess we better go wait for the doctor," Pete said, taking Margaret's hand in his.

They reminded Janine of Hansel and Gretel facing the unknown forest with no trail of bread crumbs to show them the way through. Pete looked pointedly at Dan and her.

"All of us," he said.

25

THE WINDOWLESS FAMILY meeting room smelled of reheated coffee. A full pot was sitting in a coffee maker flanked by Styrofoam cups and packets of sugar and powdered creamer on a small white table in a corner. The center of the room was taken up by a Formica top table and eight metal chairs with padded seats. The walls were bare except for a clock and a poster of a cat dangling from a tree branch by its claws, with the caption *Hang In There* splayed across the tree trunk in calligraphic script.

Everyone sat down, the Dombrowski family on one side of the rectangular table, Dan and Janine across from them. Dan took two Cokes and two coffees out of the cardboard tray he'd been carrying and set them in the middle of the table. Janine took a soda, and so did Pete. Paula already had her own giant cup of 7-Up. She opened the lid to the styrofoam box, revealing an assortment of rolls and pastries. After grabbing a stack of white paper napkins from the little corner table and tossing them down beside the box, she extracted a jelly doughnut and bit into it. No one else took anything. Janine felt strangely disinclined to eat in front of Pete and Margaret, as if by doing so she'd be exposing a damning vulnerability.

"How did Hunt seem today?" Dan asked Pete.

"All right. Weakish."

"I talked to a friend of mine — a doctor. He told me there are some conditions people have, like asthma, that can make aspergillosis worse."

"Hunt doesn't have asthma," Margaret said.

"That's good," Dan said. "But there are other risk factors..."

Janine knew where he was headed. She wanted to stop him, but she also wanted him to keep going. Her stomach felt full of jellyfish.

"Like what?" Paula wanted to know around another mouthful of doughnut.

Dan looked at her uneasily, then looked back at her parents.

"We tracked Hunt down through a youth center in Brooklyn," he said. "He went there regularly to attend a support group for young men and women who are gay."

"A what?" Pete exclaimed.

"Is that what the family disagreement was about, Pete?" Dan said quietly. "Hunt's homosexuality?"

"You got it, mister," Paula said.

"Paula!" Margaret admonished her.

"What? They already know."

"I don't see," Pete said to Dan, "that it's any business of yours. Like I said before, at the church."

There was menace in Pete's expression and in his voice. Janine seriously doubted he would get violent, especially in this setting, but she felt fearful anyway.

"I'm not going to debate that now," Dan said, his voice as taut as Pete's.

It was as if the two men were faced off in a corral holding back teams of stomping, skittish horses. Janine could almost visualize clouds of dust rising up between them.

"I only brought it up," Dan continued, "because I think it's information the doctor should have."

"It's none of his business, either," Pete growled.

"It could influence how he manages Hunt's case. If Hunt has... If Hunt's aspergillosis is complicated by AIDS..."

"AIDS?" Margaret said, looking frightened.

"You mean that gay disease?" Paula said. All bravado had left her, and she looked as frightened as her mother.

"Hunt doesn't have AIDS," Pete intoned with angry authority.

"You don't *know* that, Dombrowski," Dan insisted. "We've got to tell the doctor. It could be vital information."

"We?"

Dan let out a sigh of frustration.

"All right. *You*. You tell him."

"What do you mean, vital information?" Margaret put in. "Do you mean like life and death?"

"I don't know. What I *do* know is that the fuller a picture the doctor has, the better equipped he'll be to treat Hunt."

Pete's forearms were resting on the table. Margaret placed both her hands on his right arm.

"Petey?"

He didn't move or speak. Margaret withdrew her hands, seemingly satisfied. Janine realized the pair had come to an agreement, but she wasn't sure what their decision was. Which impulse was stronger — hiding Hunt's homosexuality or offering the doctor a possibly important medical clue? Had one parent won out over the other, or did they share the same leaning?

Dan removed the lid from one of the coffees and took a sip. Apparently, he wasn't going to press the matter further. Janine wondered if he'd speak up to the doctor if the Dombrowskis kept quiet. She decided she'd play the villain if he didn't.

They sat in silence for some minutes. Paula got up and walked over to look at the cat poster, then returned to her seat.

"Mrs. Linden—" Margaret began timidly.

"Janine."

"Yes. Janine." Margaret cleared her throat. "Do you...?" She looked at Dan and then back at Janine. "Do either of you...in your families...is there anyone like Hunt?"

"You mean gay?" Janine said.

She thought immediately of her mother's older brother, Dominic. He had been Janine's favorite uncle. He'd held that place with all the cousins. Uncle Dom was a reliable source of treats and outings that parents couldn't afford or didn't think of: expensive dolls and remote control cars and planes; the Rockettes' Christmas show at Radio City Music Hall; rides to Bear Mountain and Lake Hopatcong in his big yellow convertible; tortoni and spumoni at a little Italian place in Greenwich Village.

Dominic was dead now, done in years ago by lung cancer. Janine still remembered his long ivory cigarette holder, in almost constant use. She'd thought it elegant. Rose called it silly. Once, when the family was going out to dinner together, Al had stopped Dominic at the restaurant door and told him to put it away. "You're asking for trouble," he'd said, and Dominic had slipped the cigarette holder into his pocket without protest.

Janine knew Margaret was looking for someone to blame for Hunt's homosexuality. Should she serve up Uncle Dom? To do so smacked of circus side show.

"It doesn't work like that," she said to Margaret. "It's not something you inherit."

"Well, it's not Pete's fault," Margaret said in a huff. "He always gave Hunt the right picture of how to be a man."

"We're not gonna talk about it here, Margaret," Pete said sternly.

"No one is to blame," Janine said. "Blame shouldn't be a part of it at all. It's just who Hunt is."

"You act like it was a shock," Paula said to her parents. "But I coulda told you."

"But it is a shock, isn't it?" Margaret said to no one in particular, her head turned slightly towards Pete. "When you've tried to do everything right. And then your child turns up a stranger to you."

"A stranger?" Dan said.

Margaret looked at him, as if surprised to find he'd been listening.

"Well, different. Different than you thought."

"But does that really make him a stranger?" Janine asked delicately. "I mean, sexuality is only one part of a person."

"I won't ever be a grandmother," Margaret said. "Not to any child of Hunt's, anyway."

"Don't go making a flap ahead of yourself, Margaret," Pete said. "Stick to what's in front of us now."

"I'm gonna have kids some day, Mom," Paula said soothingly. Margaret smiled weakly at her.

There was a quick rap on the door, and Dr. Wang entered. He stood at the head of the table like a teacher in front of a class, his body angled towards Pete and Margaret.

"Your son has a serious fungal infection in his right lung," he began. "He came to our clinic a week ago complaining of sharp pains in his back when he breathed in. When Radiology found a mass, we admitted him for a bronchoscopy and isolated him. After we'd grown a culture for a few days, we knew it was acute invasive pulmonary aspergillosis, which isn't infectious, so we removed him from isolation and commenced treatment with antibiotics. The nurses told you all this already, no?"

"Some," Pete replied.

"Why does he have to be in ICU?" Margaret asked.

"Your son wasn't responding to our original line of antibiotics," the doctor said. "The fungus was continuing to grow. He developed a fever and shortness of breath. ICU seemed warranted. And we started him on Amphoterracin B, which carries its own threats."

"Side effects?" Dan asked.

"Yes. I'm afraid it's a rather toxic drug. But we're up against a systemic infection that can race through the body like a wildfire, causing organ damage and even organ failure. The potential benefits of the drug outweigh the side effects."

"What are the side effects?" Margaret asked.

"Electrolyte imbalance. Seizures. Progressive renal failure."

"Oh, sweet Lord," Margaret said, reaching out and grasping Pete's hand.

"So far we've avoided them," Dr. Wang said. "We're taking every precaution. We pause the Amphoterracin every fifth day to monitor Hunt's kidney function."

"How long will he need this drug?" Janine said.

"That's difficult to say. We're trying to disintegrate the fungal membrane, but it can be very resistant."

Paula leaned towards her mother.

"When can he come home, Mom?" she asked in a stage whisper.

"When he's all better, love."

"When will that be?" Paula blurted out, addressing the doctor directly.

"We don't know, but it appears today that the fungal growth has stalled."

"That's good, right?" Paula said.

"We'll need to observe him further."

"But if it stopped growing, that's good, right?"

Paula was pushing for what they all wanted, a concrete indication that everything was going to turn out all right eventually.

Dr. Wang looked away from the girl and focused on her parents.

"This disease carries a 64 to 90% mortality rate even with treatment," he said soberly. "But your son is getting the best care available. Plus, he's young and otherwise healthy, so—"

"Doctor," Pete interrupted him, "was he tested for that...for AIDS?"

Dr. Wang showed no reaction, not even a blink.

"Should he be?"

Pete hesitated.

"AIDS would present a complication," the doctor said flatly. "I'll order the test." He turned to go.

"One other thing, Doctor," Pete said, getting up.

Wang turned back. His sparse eyebrows were lifted inquisitively.

"Other visitors. Is that okay?"

"Yes. But use good judgment. If he seems tired or under a strain, best leave. Visiting in the evenings while he's receiving the Amphoterracin is probably not advisable. But tonight will be his evening off the medication."

Wang swept his glance over the group, bestowing a small, neutral smile on Paula. Janine thought that if he'd had a hat, he would have tipped it. Then, without another word, he left. Pete stood staring at the closed door, his back to the table.

"Tomorrow morning," he said. "You can see Hunt tomorrow morning."

"No," Janine said, ignoring a warning look from Dan. "Tomorrow, you'll just put us off again. I want Hunt to know that we're here and that we care."

Pete turned around.

"You're not the only one," he said to Janine, anguish in his voice.

Was he asking for more time to make peace with his son?

"We *will* tell him," Margaret said, speaking to Janine as if they were the only ones in the room. "I guess he's done with secrets in his life. I guess he made that crystal clear."

"They will," Paula assured Janine. "They keep their promises." She looked at her father. "You're promising, right, Dad?"

Pete nodded, looking at Dan and Janine.

"We wouldn't be here now if you didn't call," he said to them. "We know that."

"HUNGRY?" DAN ASKED Janine.

They were on the street in front of the hospital. People hurried by them, medical workers in scrubs or white coats and ordinary people, some heading into the hospital with tense faces, others bustling along the street to less worrisome destinations. Janine felt disconnected from them all. Her stomach still quivered with jellyfish, and she felt shot through with itchy apprehension.

"I know a place in midtown," Dan continued. "It's quiet, and the food is excellent."

"Okay."

She supposed she should eat. And she was in no rush to return to New Jersey, back to her parents' questions, back to an evening of putting on a normal face for the boys, and then a night of tossing and turning on her narrow bed in the sewing room.

But once she was seated in a comfortable chair at a table spread with an immaculate white cloth, with a glass of good Cabernet and a silver basket of warm breads in front of her, Janine recognized not only that she was, indeed, quite hungry, but also that food wasn't all she needed. She needed to be taken care of. She appreciated Dan's having known that and having devised such an agreeable way to provide it. She peered over her menu at him and smiled. He looked up from reading his menu and caught her.

"What?"

"Nothing. What are you having?"

"The steak, I think. I feel like I need fortifying. You?"

"The gnocchi maybe. Or the sole."

"The gnocchi here are like little clouds."

"That's it, then. Want to share a salad?"

"Sure. And some clams casino, too."

After they'd ordered, they sat quietly sipping their wine. Janine glanced around at the other diners, mostly parties of two and three. She thought of the Dombrowskis stuck in the dreary waiting room or standing anxiously at Hunt's bedside, and her heart began to feel heavy again.

"I feel a little guilty being here," she said.

"I know what you mean. But who does this hurt? I'm not trying to forget what's happening across town. I'm not even trying to pretend it's not busily gnawing at the back of my mind. But there's nothing more we can do today. Not for Hunt, anyway."

"So we should just indulge ourselves instead?"

"Something like that," Dan said, looking dissatisfied with the portrayal.

He broke open a round brown roll and put the two pieces down on his bread plate.

"I've got to take one thing at a time," he said. "Put as much of my attention into each thing as I can: argue with Pete Dombrowski, talk with the doctor, tomorrow meet Hunt, and now..."

Janine felt a catch in her throat. His face was alive with emotion. She had a ridiculous urge to get up and move her chair smack up next to his, but she sensed that even that wouldn't get her close enough to him.

"Now you're here," she finished for him.

"Now I'm here. With you. I intend to pay very close attention to that. And to enjoy it."

The waiter arrived with the appetizers. Both dishes were beautiful. The salad was a tangle of various shades of green, from pale, whitish endive to dark, curly young spinach leaves, and the clams were a study in browns set off by bright yellow lemon wedges. At another time, they would've delighted Janine's artist's eye, but now, though she noticed the visual appeal, she couldn't summon any real interest in it.

"Do you think the Dombrowskis will really come through tomorrow?" she said while Dan was placing a couple of clams on his plate.

"I think they believe it's the right thing, plus I think they're worried that if they keep us away from Hunt and he finds out later, it'll create a wall between them. I'm counting on their being more afraid of that than of us."

"I may have blown it."

"What do you mean?"

"Margaret and I had a bit of a set-to while you were downstairs with Paula."

"What happened?"

"We started talking... I thought I should try to connect somehow with her, show her I wasn't some kind of ogre coming to snatch her baby away from her. Anyway, before I knew it we were both really wound up and saying all kinds of things. It was pretty out of control."

"She seemed okay to me."

"We sort of got to a place of mutual understanding. After we each got a quick glimpse into the other's dark corners."

"Well," Dan said, not sounding totally convinced, "could be that was a good thing."

"I guess." Janine stabbed a piece of Bibb lettuce with her fork, but then she put it down and looked earnestly at him. "But you know what, Dan? I *am* kind of an ogre. Part of me *would* like to snatch her baby. The only trouble is, there's no baby to snatch."

"Sorry, I won't ever buy you as an ogre."

Janine smiled. "Thanks."

She took a swallow of iced water from the tall glass the busboy had filled when they'd sat down. It left a trail of coolness down her esophagus.

"Dan, if we do see Hunt tomorrow—"

"*When* we see him tomorrow."

"*When* we see him...would you mind if...? Could I go in first, alone?"

He gave her a pained look.

"I guess so."

"Oh, I shouldn't have asked. I'm not even sure why I want to. We'll go in together."

"No, it's all right. He came looking for you, not me. Besides, you went through more than I did...back at the beginning. You earned the first turn."

"You're sure?"

"It's settled."

She nodded, deeply touched by his consideration.

"Margaret talked about feeling like she earned Hunt," Janine said. "By all the years she tried to get pregnant and couldn't."

"I can understand that."

"So can I. Even though I don't want to."

"Oh, that's just the ogre in you talking."

"Hey!" Janine said, laughing.

The waiter came and cleared their empty plates while a busboy topped off their water glasses. Throughout, Dan stared steadily across the table at Janine. His gaze was intimate and interrogatory. Flustered, Janine looked down at the table and straightened her silverware.

"A penny for your thoughts."

"I take the Fifth," she answered, looking up.

"Want mine, then?"

"Okay."

"I was thinking about yesterday morning, at your house."

"I thought we weren't going to analyze that."

"I wasn't analyzing. I was reveling in the memory."

Janine blushed. Had he seen it? The lighting in the room was low, and their table was some distance from the windows where the afternoon sun was slanting in obliquely. She rested her hands on her silverware, but she managed to keep from fiddling with it again. He reached across the table and laid his hands over hers.

"Let's not go home," he said. "Let's stay in the City tonight."

Janine's heart hiccoughed, stirred by surprise and trepidation. But also, she noticed, by a tingle of anticipation.

"I want to hold you again, Janine. I want to make love to you. Even with all that's going on."

"Maybe *because* of all that's going on?"

What am I doing? Janine thought even as she was speaking. Does he have to pass a test?

"Only in the sense that what's going on is part of you and part of us," Dan answered. "The old, long-ago us and the us now, whatever that is."

"Whatever that is."

He removed his hands from hers and sat back in his chair. It's up to you, his face said.

"You said yesterday that you'd be patient."

"Is that what you really want right now? Today I'm asking for today, Janine. I won't lie: I want more. But today I'm asking only for today."

She knew it was his final appeal. If she didn't give him a positive sign in the next few seconds, he'd drop the idea and he'd do his best to act as if he'd never raised it. They'd finish their nice lunch. They'd drive to New Jersey, make arrangements to meet in the morning. Then they'd separate, and she'd enter a gulf of time without him. He was right to challenge her hesitation. She didn't want him to be patient. She herself didn't want to be patient or practical or prudent. She wanted his arms around her. She wanted her mind, for a while at least, to be filled only with him.

"All right."

There was a shadow of disbelief in his eyes.

"Yes," she said more firmly. "Let's stay over."

To her amazement, he suddenly stood up.

"Let's go."

"But our lunch..." she objected feebly.

"We'll get something later. If that's okay?"

In answer, she stood up, too, and lifted her purse from the back of her chair. Not wanting to look Dan in the eye, she put on her sunglasses, looking up only after he'd turned away and started for the cashier.

She waited near the front door while Dan settled the bill and made a phone call. She felt embarrassed, as if everyone there knew why they were leaving, and she was glad when Dan returned from the phone booth and they stepped outside.

"There's a hotel eight blocks from here where I attended a conference once," Dan said, pointing down the crowded sidewalk. "I just reserved a room."

As they walked, Janine didn't look in the shop windows they passed, nor at the people around them, as she normally would have done on a Manhattan street. Her hand was tucked under Dan's bent elbow, and she held tightly to his arm as they walked, acutely aware of the physical fact of his body in motion beside her and of her body in sync with his. Her embarrassment had cooked to lust. She wanted this man. She wanted him now.

After Dan checked them in, he handed her the key.

"Go on up. I'm going to stop in there." He indicated a small convenience store in the lobby.

The hotel was stately and gracious but not extravagantly luxurious. Just right, as far as Janine was concerned. There were two white terry cloth robes laid out on the bed. Impulsively, Janine undressed and wrapped herself in one. She was standing at the window looking out at a thicket of skyscrapers and the stabs of blue sky between them, when she heard the door being unlocked.

Dan paused just inside the room, looking surprised. He probably hadn't expected to find her in a bath robe.

"I got us toothbrushes," he said, holding up a small paper bag.

The room seemed a wide expanse between them, but Dan wasn't venturing any farther in. Slowly, Janine walked towards him, enjoying him watch her approach, relishing the upwelling of desire in her body as she drew nearer and nearer to him. She stopped two feet in front of him. They stood motionless for a few exquisite seconds. Then Dan took a step, and they were embracing, his mouth on hers, then traveling rapidly over her face and neck, returning again and again to her mouth, each time more hungrily. He threw the paper bag onto the bed.

Janine untied her belt and let the robe drop to the floor. Dan's hands began a slow, sweeping orbit of her body. She wanted to feel him naked against her and inside her, yet at the same time, she didn't want his caresses to stop. Finally, however, she backed up towards the bed, stopping when she felt the side of it behind her knees. He stumbled along with her. They broke contact when she flopped down on the bed. He tore at his clothing, his gaze roaming her body greedily.

"Oh, baby, you don't know, you don't know..." he mumbled.

Undressed, he stood looking down at her and slowly stroking himself. Janine's arousal quieted, but she still longed for him to take her. She handed him the paper bag, and he readied himself.

"Come on," she said, lifting her arms in invitation.

But instead of getting on the bed with her, he took her hands and pulled her to her feet on the floor. Lowering his head, he kissed each breast in turn, running his tongue slowly around the nipples until they stiffened in response. Janine let out a low moan of pleasure. He passed one hand down over her belly and glided two fingers just inside her, rocking them in and out, exploring, stroking firmly then lightly, languorously then more rapidly, until it seemed to Janine as if twenty expert fingers were playing over her. Eyes closed, tipsy with sensations, she grabbed the headboard for support.

Then, just when she thought she couldn't stand another second of attention, he nudged her on to the bed and entered her. She bucked to meet his every move, wishing she could swallow all of him whole.

26

JANINE FELL ASLEEP nestled against Dan, and when she awoke, the blue sky visible between the buildings was paling, on its way to evening. She rose on one elbow to look at the bedside clock, but before she could read it, Dan reached over and turned it face down.

"I've got to call home," she said.

"After."

"After what?" she said, laughing as he rolled onto his back and pulled her on top of him.

They kissed a while, then she slid down his chest and tantalized him with her mouth. They made love again. It was different from the first time, which had been almost frenzied. She stayed on top, controlling the pace, keeping it slow until she didn't want it that way any more. Afterwards, they lay catching their breath, both of them staring at the ceiling.

"I feel happy," Dan said.

"Me, too." She sat up. "However..."

She picked up the telephone and dialed her parents' number. Al answered, and Janine gave Dan a thumbs up. Her father would have questions, but unlike her mother, he wouldn't pry.

"Pop, I just wanted to let you know I'm staying over in the City tonight."

"You are?"

"Let me give you the number." She recited the number to him.

"How'd it go today?"

"Kind of uneventful." Janine slapped away Dan's hand as he tried to cup her breast. "We talked to the doctor, but we didn't get to see Hunt. That should happen first thing tomorrow."

"What did the doctor say?"

"I'll give you the details when I get home, but basically, he's got a really bad infection, and they're treating it with a really strong drug that's making him feel even worse."

Dan got up and put on one of the terry cloth robes. He draped the other one over Janine's shoulders.

"Well, you take care, Janine."

"I will, Pop."

"And you'll be back tomorrow?"

"Probably some time in the afternoon."

"Hold on. Your mother wants to speak to you."

"No, wait, Pop, I—"

"Janine?" came Rose's voice. "You're at a hotel?" She always spoke loudly at the start of phone conversations, as if she feared she couldn't be heard, but now her raised voice felt like an accusation.

"Yes. Pop has the number."

"Why couldn't Dan drive you home? Is he there, too?"

"Yes, Ma, he is."

Silence. Janine was beginning to feel like a squirming teenager.

"I know you're a grown woman—"

"Do you, Ma? I hope so."

"What about the boys?"

"What about them?"

"Well," Rose stalled. "They're gonna want to know where you are."

"Tell them I'm staying over in New York and I'll see them tomorrow. Put them on. I'll tell them myself."

"They're at the park."

"By themselves?"

"With Veronica from across the street. She baby-sits around the neighborhood. She's saving up for a car, so we thought—"

"All right, Ma. Do you want me to call back later?"

"No, we'll explain. It's only that... Just keep them in mind, Janine. That's all I'm saying."

"It's *not* all you're saying. Don't do this, Ma. I don't need this now."

"I only want you to be all right," Rose said, aggrieved.

Janine forced herself to calm down.

"I *am* all right. I really am. I'm sitting in the middle of the biggest tangle of my life, and I am all right."

"Okay, then," Rose said, sounding unpersuaded.

After Janine hung up, she sat with her hand on the phone for a moment.

"Are you really all right?"

"Not exactly."

"Let's shut it all out, Janine. For this one night. Let's shut everybody and everything out."

"We're not kids any more, Dan."

"I know that." He bestowed light kisses on her forehead and her mouth. "Though you do make me feel 18 again."

"And you make me feel like a beautiful girl."

"You *are* beautiful. Even more than when you were a girl."

"Flatterer!"

"The gift of the Irish," he said jauntily. "But you, my dear, are a truly beautiful woman by anyone's reckoning."

Janine stood up.

"We're going out," she said, "and I'm going to show you that I'm more than just a pretty face."

"I never doubted it. But lead on."

They showered and dressed and went out into one of those rare New York summer evenings when the heat of the day was departing with the setting sun, and an improbably fresh breeze scented by distant rain was slipping down the streets and avenues so playfully it seemed alive. Or maybe, Janine thought, it's that we feel so alive and so lucky. The shape of tomorrow, in its specifics and in its broader meanings and repercussions, was a huge unknown. They had no "right" to feel happy and lucky, and yet they did.

Once they hit the street, they were both seized with hunger, so they went to Grimaldi's in Brooklyn and feasted on pizza and beer, finishing up with an elegant dessert at the River Cafe down the block, tucked under the Manhattan Bridge. By then, night had fallen. They sat at a window table, where they could watch tugboats and other craft pass, churning up the black water in which reflections from the lights of lower Manhattan danced.

Then Janine took Dan to the Big Apple Gallery, where he was suitably impressed to learn she'd soon be showing. It was closed, so they pressed their faces up against the plate glass like two penniless children at an expensive bakery and scanned the room, picking out pieces they liked and didn't like, debating the best spot on the walls for Janine's work.

The night was so lovely, they didn't want to go into the subway again, so they set out to walk at least part way back to the hotel and ended up going twenty blocks before hailing a cab.

In bed, Dan rubbed Janine's back until she drifted into sleep.

◦◦◦

WHEN DAN AND Janine arrived at the ICU waiting area the next morning, Pete and Margaret were already there. Janine thought Margaret gave them a funny look. Was it because they were wearing the same clothes as yesterday? Janine reminded herself there were more serious reasons Margaret might be eyeing them suspiciously. She enjoyed a moment of private amusement when she recalled how carefully she'd chosen her outfit when they'd gone to Malaga expecting to meet Hunt. Now here she was, knocking at his door, so to speak, and she wasn't even wearing fresh underwear.

"Paula's sleeping in," Margaret said after they'd exchanged awkward good mornings, though neither Dan nor Janine had asked about the girl.

"Good for her," Dan said.

The Dombrowskis had gotten up from the couch when Dan and Janine came out of the elevator, and now all four of them were standing indecisively in the little waiting area.

"How was Hunt's night?" Janine asked.

"He was glad not to have the medicine," Margaret said. "I told him he's just got to be brave about it."

"He's managing," Pete said crossly, as if Margaret had insulted Hunt.

"And how is he this morning?" Dan said.

"We haven't seen him yet this morning," Margaret said. "We thought we'd wait until..."

"He's expecting you," Pete said.

"What did you tell him?" Janine asked.

She could hardly believe that in a matter of minutes she was actually going to get to talk to Hunt, that he was only yards away, waiting for her.

"We said we knew he went to the lawyer, and that the lawyer found you," Margaret said, "and that then you found us from Father Nonas, and that then you came to New York and found him, and that now we're all here praying for him to get well."

"Did he ask any questions?" Dan said.

"Just when you would come," Pete answered.

Dan let out a long, audible breath. "Ready?" he said to Janine.

Janine nodded and turned to go to the ICU entry doors. She felt she had to head that way immediately because a small, frightened part of her wanted to take off in the opposite direction as fast as her feet would carry her, and she didn't want that part to get any stronger, even in imagination. Dan turned to follow her.

"Gannon," Pete said, and both Dan and Janine stopped. "You should know about that test. Since it was your idea."

"Yes?"

Janine's heart was thumping. Did she want to know this now?

"It's like I told you. Hunt doesn't have AIDS."

301

"Thank God."

Pete sat down on the couch, and Margaret joined him there, the whole time keeping her eyes on Janine as she went to the button on the wall and pushed it.

As soon as they were inside the swinging doors, Dan put his hand on Janine's arm.

"I'll wait here," he said. "I only came in because I didn't want to be stuck out there with them. Come get me when it feels right."

"You're sure it's okay?"

"Just don't take too long."

She moved close to him and he held her tightly for a moment, then she stepped away and walked down the short hall to the semi-circle of glassed-in beds.

She stopped at the nurses' station to sign the visitors' log, purposely avoiding looking towards the far end of the semi-circle, where Hunt's room was located. When she did look over, she was shocked to find herself confronted with Hunt's direct gaze. He was sitting up, staring straight at her through the plate glass. She felt pinioned by the intensity of his regard. Without thinking about it, she'd been expecting to find him as she had yesterday, lying down, perhaps even asleep. She'd anticipated a gradualness to their meeting as he slowly opened his eyes. She realized now that even if it had played out that way, the first time they looked at each other would have to be a jolt. For both of them. Janine's awareness that Hunt, too, must feel scared and unsure helped her break the paralyzing spell of his stare. She walked forward.

His expression was serious as he watched her advance. No smile. His eyes were dark brown, like her father's. An unwavering vigor was beaming out of them, as if he were on fire inside. Janine was amazed to see it in someone so sick. What force there must be to him when he was well.

She opened the door to the little room, entered and went to the head of the bed. He was so close, she could hear him breathing. She noticed again what she'd noticed on Sunday — the long lashes, the muscular but slender arms and bony face, the full mouth turned slightly down at the corners as if he were sulking. Dan's mouth did that sometimes, when he was deep in thought.

When Hunt leaned forward in order to sit up higher, a pillow behind his head slipped to the side, and instinctively, Janine reached out and pushed it back in place. Her hand brushed his shoulder. He twisted his body towards her, and simultaneously, they opened their arms to each other and hugged. It all happened in a matter of seconds — her arrival at the bed, his movement, her push on the dislodged pillow, their embrace. Yet in those seconds, Janine flew to the last time she'd held Hunt, tiny and milk-scented, his little body warm against her chest. Now she was holding a man in her arms, a stranger who was somehow not a stranger, literally a dream come true. She could have held on to him for hours, but when she felt his embrace loosen, she released him.

"Oh, my," she said, putting her hand over her heart. "I didn't expect that."

"Me neither."

Their first exchange of words, Janine thought. So banal. So simple. But better, she realized, than some fancy speech or shy, self-conscious introductions. A good start, she decided. A human start. But now what? She was the grown-up. He'd initiated the search, but she had finished it. It was up to her to set them on the path to their future. He'd participate in where the path led and how far, but it was up to her to cue their first step.

What she wanted to do was ask questions. Big questions. Did the Dombrowskis love you enough? Are you happy? Do you know I never forgot you? Did you miss me? But she knew all that had to wait. Maybe she'd never get to ask such things. Maybe she'd have to guess at them or get to them indirectly. Or learn to be resigned to not knowing.

"I understand you just graduated from high school," she said, deciding instantly that it was a stupid opening. Stupid.

Hunt didn't reply. Janine's mind foraged madly to find another avenue, but she came up empty.

"What are your plans now?" Stupidity compounded.

"Dunno," Hunt said, shrugging. "Guess I better get out of here first."

"Of course."

Janine looked down the curved line of the other glass-enclosed rooms, each housing a hospital bed and attendant IV poles, monitors, and arcane medical machines, as if an answer to when Hunt might be released were hiding somewhere amid the tubes and wires and gleaming stainless steel. There was an IV pole next to Hunt's bed, with a bag of golden liquid hanging from it. The Amphoterrible, Janine assumed.

"Has the doctor said anything about when that might be?"

Hunt shook his head no.

"Are you feeling any better?"

"Not much."

Okay. School, health. Any other clichés you want to hit? Janine chided herself.

"I did get into Rutgers," Hunt mumbled.

"Congratulations!"

He shrugged again, but his cheeks pinked up and the corners of his mouth lifted briefly in a tentative almost-smile. He was pleased by her compliment. Janine realized he must want her to approve of and like him as much as she wanted him to form a favorable impression of her.

"I wish we'd been able to meet somewhere else," she said. "Somewhere beautiful and open. We could have walked. We could have taken our time."

"How long do we have?"

"There's a fifteen minute limit if you're not family. We might get more if the nurses are too busy to notice."

Hunt leaned forward, his expression ardent. One hand gripped the edge of the mattress.

"You *are* family," he said. He coughed raggedly. "I'll tell them. You *are* family."

Janine's eyes abruptly filled with tears. There'd been no warning ache, no slow build-up of sadness, just a swift spasm of feelings — grief, gratitude, relief. And the bursting open of the hard, constricted kernel of love and longing for this boy that had been lodged deep inside her for 18 years. The tears fell. She didn't sob or wail, though sobs and wails would have come if she let them. She put her hand on top of Hunt's, unclenching his fingers.

"Sit back. It's all right. I'll stay."

Obediently, he lay back against the propped pillows. There were tears in his eyes, too, but he managed to draw them in. He coughed again, a deep racking shudder, then concentrated for a few seconds on his breathing until it became even.

"Tell me," he said quietly.

"Tell you what?"

"Everything."

Janine let out a small, mirthless laugh.

"I don't know where to start."

"I'm a knot," Hunt said. "Untie me."

The beginning, then, Janine thought. Not who I am now. Not how I kept him alive in my heart all these years. The very beginning. Me and Dan. The newborn in the blue blanket.

"I think you know the basic outline. I was 17 when I got pregnant, just about to start my senior year in high school."

"My mother told me that."

Janine winced. His mother. Margaret.

"My boyfriend and I talked about getting married, but our families were dead set against it. They did everything they could to keep us apart. We could have run away, I suppose, but neither of us was that kind of kid. And we weren't equipped financially to make a home and raise a baby."

Janine paused, her mind flailing about, trying to design a different way of telling the story. What she'd said was the truth, but it sounded like she was making excuses. And she was leaving out the despair and loneliness. But did she have the right to inflict that on Hunt? Maybe sticking to the facts was best after all.

"I went to a home for unwed mothers in Trenton. That's where you were born. Everyone said the best thing I could do for you was give you up. So I did. But... It wasn't...it wasn't because I didn't want you."

Janine tried to gauge his reactions. He had the entranced look that Tim and Larry wore when they were listening to a particularly absorbing fairy tale. And this must seem like a fantastic tale to him, Janine thought. Fantastic yet true. His story at last.

"I used to talk to you," she continued. "Whenever I had a private moment, I used to bend over and whisper to my big belly."

"What did you say?"

Janine felt the threat of tears again, but this time she held them down.

"Oh, bits and pieces of what my day had been. Asking how you were, especially when you kicked. But mostly...most of all...I used to tell you that I loved you."

Hunt turned his face away from her, as if he didn't want her to witness what this meant to him. Did he believe her? Young and untried in the world, could he understand that she could love him and also abandon him? Was he capable of looking at the woman in front of him, marked with signs of competence and confidence, and imagining the trapped, frightened girl who had given birth to him?

"Hunt?"

He turned to her. His expression was guarded, but she thought she detected a wish to believe her, if not complete belief.

"You know, your father is here, too."

"Is he your husband?"

"No. I'm a widow."

"What's he like?"

"I happen to think he's a very nice man. Would you like to meet him?"

"Does he want to see me?"

"That's why he's here. He helped me find you."

Janine wondered if it was too much for the boy to take on all at once. She wondered how she herself would feel when the three of them were in the same room together.

306

"Okay."

Janine turned to go.

"Wait."

She stopped at the foot of the bed.

"Did he ever see me? When I was I baby?"

"I...I wasn't... No, he didn't."

Janine felt a surge of sadness at the fact. It was exacerbated by the stricken look on Hunt's face.

"I named you Daniel after him."

Hunt's eyes grew wide.

"I always wondered if I had a real name — I mean, a name that came from you. My mom didn't know."

Maybe that was true, but, Janine reflected, if Margaret had known Hunt's original name, she wouldn't have told him. It would have destroyed the careful illusion that he was as thoroughly a Dombrowski as a child of their blood.

Pete and Margaret are your family, Janine wanted to say to Hunt, but their ancestors aren't your ancestors, your story isn't fully contained inside their story. You have other people. Pete and Margaret shared theirs with you, but you have people and a history all your own, too. But she would say none of it. Even if this were to be her only chance to talk to him. On some level, he must already know it, anyway. It must have been one reason he searched for her.

"I'll go get him?" she said. Hunt nodded permission.

Dan was leaning against the wall just inside the entry doors. He pushed away from the wall and stood waiting alertly as Janine walked briskly down the short hallway towards him.

"How's it going?"

"Pretty good so far. We're both... We're being careful, but it's still so... It's an emotional wallop."

"What's he like?"

Janine smiled. "He asked the same thing about you. Come see for yourself."

Janine led the way back into the ICU, but she dropped back as they neared Hunt's room so that Dan could move in front of her. He went to the head end of the bed, and she stayed at the foot.

Dan put out his right hand, and Hunt took it immediately. It was more of a clutch than a handshake, a grip that might be used to pull a drowning person out of the sea onto a boat deck, only in this case, they were both rescuers. Their eyes were locked on each other.

It was mind-boggling to see the two side by side. Their thick eyebrows were the most obvious physical similarity, as Paula had noticed at the church. But Janine picked out other, more subtle duplications. The line of the jaw, square and masculine. The width of the mouth. And in Hunt's lithe physique, she saw the athletic lifeguard's body that had so called to her as a girl. Hunt wore male physical beauty as Dan had at his age, with a disinterested, nonchalant ease that served to heighten the beauty. Janine wondered if Hunt's walk was like Dan's, or the way he threw a ball, or curled up to sleep. It seemed to her, studying them, that they might be jointed in the same way.

"I'm Dan Gannon," Dan said, letting go of Hunt's hand. "I guess you know that."

"She said I had your name," Hunt said, pointing to Janine. "In the beginning."

"Yes. I just found that out myself recently. I was glad to hear it. I sure as hell wasn't able to give you anything else."

"That's all right," Hunt said, looking down at his lap.

"No, it's not. It was the way things had to be, but it's not all right. And it wasn't fair."

Hunt looked up quickly.

"I used to think that," he said. "That it wasn't fair I was adopted, when nobody else I knew was. Except for Paula. I mean, what was wrong with me?"

"Nothing was wrong with you!" Janine said. "Nothing at all."

"Yeah, well, I suppose I'm no worse than any other kid. But I didn't always *feel* it, you know? I still don't."

Janine felt a plunge of guilt. It was inevitable, she saw, that Hunt would feel "wrong." His mother had rejected him. No matter how it was explained, the bald fact was that his mother had given him away. Would they ever be able to get past that?

"Did you ever have more kids?" Hunt asked.

"Yes. Twin boys, six years old."

"And I've got two little girls."

Hunt looked glum. Was it because, unlike him, those children had been kept?

"How come?" the boy said urgently, looking back and forth between Dan and Janine.

"How come what?" Dan asked.

"How come it was the way things *had* to be?"

Dan and Janine glanced at each other unsurely.

"There was a girl in my class who got pregnant and didn't marry the guy," Hunt said, speaking rapidly. "She stayed in school and lived at home, and her mom helped her, and her dad even put up a tire swing in the yard for when the kid would get bigger. And her boyfriend still came around — I saw them once at the mall with the baby. How come you guys couldn't do something like that?"

It was the accusation Janine had feared most, the accusation she'd turned on herself again and again in the early years, the one that had reared its ugly head anew when she started searching for Hunt. Why didn't I fight harder to keep my baby? She knew Dan had his own version of the same self-reproach. Now, at long last, the accusation had to be answered.

"It was different in those days," she said. "If an unmarried girl got pregnant, everyone looked down on her. Her entire family was shamed. You weren't allowed to stay in school. I was sick a couple of mornings in homeroom, and the school nurse told the principal, and I was required to drop out immediately."

Hunt looked bewildered. Janine knew the world she was describing was completely foreign to him. She herself would have faced a different world if she'd gotten pregnant only a few years later, during the much-touted era of sex and drugs and rock-and-roll. She and Dan wouldn't have had to conceal their relationship. Her pregnancy would still have upset her parents, but they wouldn't have insisted on her disappearing in order to protect her reputation. Relinquishing her baby would have been presented as an option, not a necessity. After 1973, a legal, safe abortion would have been available, too. Janine's Catholic upbringing would have made that an extremely difficult choice at any time, but in 1965, she would also have had to risk serious injury and death at the hands of an illegal abortionist, if one could even be found.

"Did you read *The Scarlet Letter* in school?" Janine said, grasping at straws.

Hunt nodded. At least he was listening.

"It was something like that."

"But that was back in colonial days," Hunt argued. "How could it be that bad? I know lots of kids that live with just their moms because they're divorced or something, and nobody says anything."

"But people *would* have said things about me," Janine said dismally. "And about you, too. Cruel, ugly things. I'm sure that people who guessed why I disappeared *did* say things. I had to *hide*, Hunt. I had to leave my home and hide."

Hunt shook his head in disbelief.

"Every time period and every community has its ideas about sex," Dan said, "about what's okay and what's not. Sometimes, you can break the rules and people will look the other way or pretend they don't know what you're up to. When we were your age, it was pretty much assumed that kids going steady were probably having sex. At least, other kids assumed it, not the parents. But if it came out in the open, like through a pregnancy, everyone was shocked and horrified. Even the other kids. Or they had to act like they were, so nobody would think they thought it was okay. The hard truth, Hunt, is that there are always rules about sex, and even if they're mostly for show, they can only be broken in private. Most people don't want to have to face it out in the open."

Hunt studied Dan keenly for several long moments, then he nodded.

"I get that," he said softly.

Janine relaxed a little. He hadn't written them off yet.

"Tell me some more about you," Hunt said to both of them, his tone more conversational. "Where do you live? What did you do after you...after I was born? I like to draw, and I fish with my Dad. What do you like to do?"

"I'm not a fisherman," Dan said after Janine had nodded that he should go first, "but I enjoy the outdoors, hiking mostly. I live in Alpine, so there's good hiking nearby, along the Palisades and up around Bear Mountain. I'm an orthodontist..."

Dan's voice trailed off and his face grew heavy. Something was going on beneath the breezy biographical sketch. He was staring at Hunt, misery sharp in his eyes, and the corners of his mouth were turned down. Janine waited a moment for him to pick up his narrative again, then decided she'd better step in.

"I'm an artist," she said to Hunt. "Acrylics and oils."

"Are you good?"

Janine chuckled. "Sometimes. You like to draw, you said?"

"Yeah. Pen and ink mostly. Stuff out of my head — you know, science fiction type stuff — and real faces, my friends or people I see on the street or somewhere."

"Drawing from life is—"

"I felt lousy after you were born," Dan interrupted hoarsely. He'd continued to stare at Hunt during the brief exchange about art, but now Janine realized he hadn't really been hearing it.

"I hung around home for a few months, put off leaving for college," Dan went on slowly. He had Hunt's rapt attention, and hers. "I had a part-time job pumping gas. Nights, I drank too much beer, I drove too fast. Weekends, I went up into the Ramapo Mountains and walked and walked and walked. I had no one to talk to about you. None of my friends knew. My brothers and sisters didn't know. My mother refused to hear a word about it, and my father had died when I was 11. Janine's parents wanted nothing to do with me, and Janine...well, Janine was gone."

"It...it was better that way," Janine said quickly to Hunt, her gut writhing in protest: no, no, it wasn't, and yet it was, wasn't it? "We weren't going to keep you, so why should we...how could we still be..."

Janine took a deep breath. This was no good. Hunt was never going to understand the people she and Dan had been at the time of his birth, the stew they swam in, the pressures and pulls. They'd be lucky if he came to take hold of it with his intellect, but they'd be foolish to hope his heart could ever accept it without reservation. It wasn't explanations Hunt needed. It wasn't only explanations.

"Hunt," she said shakily. "Hunt, I'm so sorry."

The boy's rigid posture slackened almost imperceptibly, but his handsome face was dark with anger.

"Yeah, right," he said scornfully.

"I *am* sorry," Janine said, refusing to come to her own defense. "I apologize for every...I apologize for giving you up...and for every...for every moment of doubt or unhappiness or insecurity or resentment that ever caused you."

"I apologize, too," Dan said. "It wasn't right, and it wasn't fair."

Hunt closed his eyes and laid his head back against the pillows. His face yielded no clues to what he was thinking or feeling. When he finally opened his eyes, the boy slowly looked first at Dan and then at Janine. His expression was wooden.

"So," he said with a fleck of challenge in his voice, "are you two back together?"

Janine hesitated to answer. Were their apologies not going to be acknowledged in any way? Really, she thought, did it matter? They'd been spoken. Let Hunt change the subject if that was what he needed to do. But what a subject!

"Are you?" he repeated.

Dan said, "Yes," and at the same time, Janine said, "No."

Hunt nodded knowingly, impish glee in his eyes. Dan shot Janine a quick, imploring look.

"You could say we're a work in progress," he said to Hunt.

"I was the reason you broke up," Hunt said, folding his arms across his chest, "and now, I'm the reason you're together again. Pretty neat, I guess."

He sounded hurt and embittered.

"There's nothing neat about it," Janine replied quickly. "There's nothing neat about any of this. It's messy and disruptive and thrilling and scary, and it's all up for grabs."

"That's not the kind of neat I meant," Hunt said with adolescent disgust.

"I know that."

Janine was dismayed to find she was annoyed with the boy. But in the next instant, she was glad to feel annoyance because it meant she was responding to him not as a fantasy made into perfect flesh, but as a real person.

"I don't know why you wanted to meet me," she continued, "but I wanted to meet you because I wanted you to know that I have loved you since the day you were born. Even before then. And I will always love you and remember you, even if I never see you again."

Janine stopped, afraid to say that she hoped she would see Hunt again. They'd been daydreams to each other. There'd be nothing tidy about finding out who they each really were. What right did she have to ask him to take that on?

"When you're adopted," Hunt said, malice and petulance gone from his voice, "you're always supposed to be thankful you've got a home. But I couldn't. Not all the time, anyway. Don't get me wrong — my folks are good people, and I'm glad they raised me. We've had some troubles lately, but we're gonna sort things out. We already started to."

He was interrupted by a bout of coughing.

"Maybe you shouldn't be talking so much," Dan said.

Hunt shook his head vigorously. Dan handed him a glass of water that was on his bedside table, and the boy took a long drink.

"I guess every kid some time thinks things would be better if only they were in a different family," he went on, "but when you're adopted, it could really be true, you *could* have been in a different family. I went looking for you to see if maybe I'd fit in more with you and because I wanted to see where I came from, *who* I came from — not just the two of you, but to hear about your folks and maybe theirs, and to have the chance, some day, to be in a room and look around and see people who look like me and to be able to say stuff like our grandfather did such and such, or our cousin used to say this and that."

A nurse tapped on the door and entered.

"Time for you to lie down, young man," she said. "And about time for your visitors to go," she added as she cranked down the bed. "You know it's not good for you to get too worked up."

"But we're not done," Hunt protested.

"It's been enough, don't you think?" Dan said gently.

"But am I gonna see you again?" Hunt said, lifting his head from the slowly reclining mattress.

Janine's spirits soared. She didn't trust herself to speak.

"We'd like very much to keep on seeing you," Dan said to Hunt, "but we're putting you in the driver's seat." It was the stance he and Janine had agreed on.

"Paula has my phone number," Janine said.

"All this was a lot to take in," Dan continued. "Give yourself a breather. Concentrate on getting well."

"Okay," Hunt replied, sounding tired.

The nurse left the room, and Janine went to the head of the bed to say good-bye. She longed to kiss Hunt's cheek, to draw up the crisp, white sheet and smooth it over him, as she did for the twins every night. She wanted, for one unzipped instant, to sit on the edge of the bed and pull him into her lap and rock him, as she had done with baby Daniel for seven days all those years ago. But Daniel was gone. Now there was Hunt. Janine had found her son, and in doing so, she had lost her first-born child, but she would never let that disappointment touch him.

She dared to lay her hand lightly on Hunt's shoulder. To her immense elation, he bent his head and kissed her hand.

27

WHEN THEY EXITED the ICU, they spotted Dr. Wang just turning away from the Dombrowskis in the waiting area. As he passed Dan and Janine on his way to the ICU entrance, he inclined his head in polite greeting.

"Doctor—" Dan said, trying to buttonhole him.

But the doctor kept going.

"I'll let the parents tell you the good news," he said, hurrying through the automatic doors.

Dan felt frustrated by the doctor's elusiveness, but there was no real oomph to the feeling. Dan was too full of turbulent emotions from the visit with Hunt. And that had come on top of the bewitching night with Janine. My cup runneth over, he thought as he followed Janine to where Pete and Margaret were standing. Paula was behind them, in a chair.

"They're moving Hunt out of ICU today!" she piped up before any of the adults could speak.

"Hunt didn't mention that," Janine said.

"The doctor's telling him now," Paula said. "It'll be a few days before he feels like he's better."

"*Is* he better?" Janine asked, turning to Pete and Margaret.

Margaret nodded excitedly.

"You remember the doctor said it looked like the fungus stopped growing? Well, early this morning, they saw that it was covering a smaller area of his lung than yesterday, so it seems like the tide turned, the doctor said. And the tests showed Hunt is tolerating the medicine, so they're going to give him another week's worth."

"Five nights, starting tonight," Pete corrected her. "Five nights before he needs another day off."

"But by then, the doctor said, maybe it'll be licked, and he won't need any more treatments at all."

"That *is* good news," Dan said. "Very good news." My cup runneth over and over.

"It's the answer to our prayers," Margaret said. "The whole Novena Society at home has been praying for him."

"I even said a rosary last night in the hotel," Paula informed Janine seriously. "Plus..." She slid a sideways look at her mother. "I prayed for you guys, too. You know...for today and stuff."

Margaret glowered at her daughter, but she didn't rebuke her. How could she scold the girl for praying? She was probably after her all the time to do so. Dan guessed that from now on she might also suggest appropriate subject matter for prayer. In any case, Margaret seemed more interested in Janine at the moment. She'd retracted her attention from Paula and was studying Janine's face intently.

"Can I ask what you and Hunt talked about?" she said.

"Of course you can ask, Margaret," Pete said with a frown, but his crossness didn't seem directed at any one of them.

It's the situation that has him off-kilter, Dan thought. He doesn't know where he stands. He doesn't know what's going to happen next. He doesn't know what his role is supposed to be, or who expects what from him. He's probably got feelings that he can't name twisting his insides like saltwater taffy. Welcome to the club, Pete.

"I think we should let Hunt give you the details," Janine said.

Dan saw one corner of Margaret's mouth twitch to the side. Clearly, she was dissatisfied. Janine must have seen it, too, because she added, "He told me he got into Rutgers."

"Oh, I hope that means he's planning to go," Margaret said, unbending a little. "We made the deposit, but we can't put down the whole tuition if he's not going to go."

"He'll go," Pete said. "Hunt's no dummy. He knows college is important."

"Me and Pete, we never went. But, of course, we want the kids to. We've always encouraged them in their schoolwork."

"When does the semester start at Rutgers?" Dan asked.

Margaret had a blank look.

"I don't know. Some time in September? Oh dear, I wonder if he'll be well enough by then."

"We'll ask the doctor what he thinks when he comes out," Pete said, staring fixedly at the automatic doors, as if the utmost vigilance were required to catch the doctor. Dan thought he wasn't half-wrong there.

"I was going down to the chapel for a little while..." Margaret said to Dan and Janine.

She sounded irresolute, as if she were hosting them in her home and felt it rude to leave.

"We've got to be getting back to Jersey," Dan said.

"So you're done with Hunt, then."

How, Dan wondered, did the woman manage to imbue those simple words with so much import? The sentence wavered between statement and question, and it was just caustic enough to be heard as criticism. At the same time, it was a hopeful plea and also an expression of relief.

"I want you to promise not to see him again," she added belligerently.

"We can't do that," Janine said.

Dan could tell that she was at the end of her social energy and that it was costing her extreme effort to speak at all, let alone to remain civil.

"It's Hunt's choice, all the way," Dan told Margaret, trying to deflect her from Janine. "We're not going to push it."

"You say that, but you haven't—"

"Maggie," Pete said softly, turning away from his watch of the door, "they're right."

"And just whose side are you on, Peter Dombrowski?" Margaret fumed.

"Hunt's side. Same as you. But it's got to be his choice. We got to let him decide without any pushing from us either."

Pete put his arm around Margaret's shoulder.

"Now we had real good news today, didn't we? And when you went to the chapel, weren't you going to call Father Nonas and let him know?"

Margaret nodded. Her whole body seemed to melt as she leaned into Pete. It was such a tender moment, Dan was almost embarrassed to be witnessing it. It made him want to put his arm around Janine in a similar fashion. It made him want to have the legitimate right to do that in public. He wanted people to see that they belonged to each other.

"It's going to be all right, Mags," Pete continued. "We've been tested pretty hard lately, but it's going to be all right. I feel it in my bones."

"Dad's bones usually are right," Paula said encouragingly to her mother.

Margaret gave the girl a grudging smile.

"We'll be going now," Dan said, holding his hand out to Pete.

Pete took his arm from around Margaret and shook Dan's hand. There was reserve in his grip, but no hostility.

"It's been an emotional few days for all of us," Dan said. "Thank you for your patience."

Margaret raised her eyebrows slightly and looked askance at Janine.

"There's no turning back now, I guess," she said frostily.

It was probably the closest they'd get to being accepted by her, Dan thought. You two are a fact of my life now, her clouded look said, like mildew on a shower curtain.

"You'll let us know if there's any change in Hunt's condition?" Dan said, handing his business card to Pete. Pete took it and nodded yes.

"And thanks for the prayers," Dan said to Paula.

"No problem," the girl said, ducking her head shyly.

In the elevator, Janine kept her eyes fixed on the floor numbers lighting up one by one above the door. The elevator made two stops between the fifth floor and the ground floor. People got on and off. Dan touched Janine only once, laying his fingertips lightly on her elbow when they had to move to the rear of the elevator to accommodate an orderly pushing a wheelchair.

They maintained their silence as they walked through the parking garage and while Dan unlocked the car doors and they both got in.

As he maneuvered his way north on the FDR Drive, Dan was glad to have his attention absorbed by the task of driving. Janine mostly kept her face turned to the side, peering out her window at the passing scenes. At one point, she reached down and unbuckled her sandals. They were in the middle of the George Washington Bridge when she finally spoke.

"What did you think?"

"I think it was good," Dan said, hoping the promptness of his reply didn't discredit it. "I think we made an honest start."

"It was a roller coaster for me."

"For me, too. And for him, I'd bet."

"Do you think he'll want to see us again? Once everything from today really sinks in?"

"I do."

Dan was being truthful, but he wasn't as locked on to optimism as he sounded. It was going to take months, if not years, to clear the air with Hunt.

"I should have told him about the week I took care of him when he was a newborn. How could I have left that out? And why did I blather on about how hard it was 'back in the olden days', like a self-pitying toad? 'Poor me.' Why should he give a damn about poor me or about how hard it was for us?"

"Janine, stop. We're going to make mistakes. Hell, so is he. It's a relationship. There'll be time to set things right."

Janine returned to looking out the side window, this time at the river. Was she paying attention at all to what she was seeing? Dan reached over and put his hand on her thigh.

When he drew up to the toll booth, he took his hand away in order to pay the attendant, and then he had to negotiate a couple of lane changes to aim towards Route 4. Traffic was light. They were soon through Fort Lee and Englewood and entering Teaneck. With each passing mile, Dan found it harder and harder not to interrupt Janine's distracted silence. His mind was plagued by questions, and they all stemmed from one pressing concern. When would he see her next?

They left Route 4 at Queen Anne Road. The River Road exit, a bit farther on, would have been more efficient, but Dan had the impulse to go down Cedar Lane.

As a boy, Dan hadn't gone more than two or three days at a stretch without hitting Cedar Lane for one reason or another. Getting groceries for his mother or taking his brothers to browse at Davis Toy Store or buy comic books and black-and-white ice cream sodas at Woolworth's. To J & J for aspirin and band-aids or, when his father was still alive, for razor blades and shaving soap. Once, when he was 14, he stood at the back of the Teaneck Theater watching a preview for *Splendor in the Grass*, though he knew he shouldn't. Even if the Church hadn't put the movie on its forbidden list, the lovely, lonely ache in his loins during the preview told him it was sinful. The following Saturday in confession, he tacked the transgression on to his recital of sins, and the priest added an extra Hail Mary to his penance. That was when he was still going to confession. He stopped three years later, when the priest instructed him to quit necking and petting with Janine.

"I miss you already," he said to her now as they passed the Theater.

Her only response was to turn her head towards him momentarily. Then she resumed looking straight ahead.

"I've read," she said, "that the biggest fear of an adoptee searching for his birthmother is that she'll reject him — maybe she won't want to see him or talk to him, or after meeting him once, maybe she'll refuse to have anything more to do with him. Some adoptees don't search, no matter how much they want to, because of that fear."

"But Hunt did search."

"And then he dropped it."

"You don't know why. There could be a dozen reasons."

"Maybe he was afraid."

"All right, say he was. He got up his courage to meet us anyway. And we certainly didn't reject him."

"He could still be extra sensitive in that area. He doesn't remember the actual act of me giving him away, but the experience must be *in* him. Like Pete said, a feeling in his bones. I don't want Hunt to think that our looking for him was just a way for us to reconnect."

Dan wanted to reassure her, but of course, he couldn't. He wanted to tell her that she was being unreasonable, and that if Hunt was that thin-skinned, he was being unreasonable, too. But Dan knew reason had nothing to do with it, which, he supposed, was Janine's point. And what about me? he wanted to say. What about my unreasonable need for you?

He turned left onto Larch Avenue. In seven blocks, they'd be at Terhune Street. Four blocks. Three. They were passing Kipp Street.

"I have my girls weekend after next. How about I take you up on your offer?"

"My offer?"

"To bring them to the beach."

"I don't know..."

Dan turned onto Terhune and pulled up in front of the Pettorini house. He parked and left the motor running. Janine bent to buckle her sandals.

Straightening up, she said, "Right now, I feel like crawling into a cave and going to sleep for a long, long time. I can't make plans. I can't handle another roller coaster."

He took her face in his hands and kissed her. She didn't resist, but she was passive. He knew he wasn't home-free.

"My roller coaster ride started the day you walked into my office. Before then, I thought I had all my ducks in a row. The end of my marriage shook me up and forced me to make big adjustments, but mostly on the surface. Basically, I went on like I'd been going on since...well, since you and I broke up back in 1965. Not to get too head-trippy, but I straighten crooked teeth for a living, I impose order on disorder, and I lived the same way. Safely, rationally, inside the rules. The picture of normality. Seeing you again upended all that. I lost control — in a good way. At last, I knew what was missing."

"I'm not that girl, Dan."

"I know." He manufactured a smile. "You're better."

She opened the car door, but she didn't get out. Sighing, she slid her hands over her face and up through her hair.

"I don't want Hunt to think that he's not my priority. I want to prove to him that I'm not going away again."

"By keeping me at arm's length?"

"Maybe we need to accept that what we had is all we get. What we had when we were kids, and this...this brief re-capture. It's more than a lot of people have, ever."

Experiencing a wave of vertigo, Dan gripped the steering wheel tightly. What could he say to stop this runaway train? How could he turn it around?

"I can't believe you mean that."

"I can't think about us now, Dan. It's too much. Today at the hospital, last night..."

"You were happy last night."

She nodded, and her strange, beautiful eyes began to fill with tears. He thought he'd never tire of looking into her eyes.

"Last night was easy, almost uncomplicated," she said. "Nothing else about us is."

"That doesn't change my feelings."

"How about your kids, then? And mine?" she snapped. "How about the miles and the things that hold us in place? Robin, your practice, my studio... And now Hunt to try to fold in, and—"

"Do we really have to think about practicalities now?"

"I feel like I'm tiptoeing on a skinny, wobbly plank over quicksand, and you're asking me to look up and admire a pretty sky."

"If you and I are that sky, you bet I am."

She picked up her purse and started to leave. He grabbed her wrist, more roughly than he'd meant to, but there was something very satisfying in the roughness.

"You're my happiness, Janine, and I want to be yours. It's as simple as that."

She jerked her wrist away.

"No, it's not. It never was, and it never will be."

She was angry, and he realized with a jolt that underneath his desperation, he was angry, too. Angry enough and desperate enough to throw down a gauntlet.

"I want you in my life, Janine. I won't say it again."

She got out of the car without saying good-bye and without closing the car door. But he knew there was nothing even remotely open-ended about her exit. The topic was finished, and so were they.

BEFORE LEAVING THE hospital, Dan had called Robin to say he wanted to take the girls out to dinner that night. He'd pick them up at 5:00. He promised it'd be for only a couple of hours. To MacDonald's or Gino's Pizzeria and then maybe a stop at the park while the daylight held. He didn't want to wait a whole week to see them. It had been a week already since he'd spent time with them, not counting the brief, sleepy conversation with Vanessa Sunday night. Yes, yes, he assented, he'd been the one to cancel both his assigned weekend and his usual Monday, but it couldn't be helped. No, he wasn't expecting any more such short notice occasions.

When he got out of his car in Robin's driveway, Dan heard the girls' voices in the back yard. They caught sight of him as soon as he rounded the side of the house. Hollering "Daddy, Daddy, Daddy," they jumped off the swing set and ran to him. They collided against him, tugging at his arms and legs like Calcutta street urchins.

Squatting, he put an arm around each of them and pulled them close. They smelled of baby shampoo and ironed cotton. They were wearing matching pink sun dresses, and their hair was wet and combed off their faces, Vanessa's in a ponytail, Sally's held back with barrettes. Robin had spruced them up for the little outing. Dan was touched. He sometimes thought Robin did such things to show him up or to emphasize her maternal attentiveness, but today he wanted to believe she'd readied the girls for his sake and not her own, in his honor, so to speak. His ego could use the boost. Maybe friendlier motives were always lurking underneath such actions by Robin. Way underneath. Maybe she herself didn't know they were there.

"You two go swing a little more," he said, standing up. "I'm going inside to tell Mommy we're leaving."

He found Robin in the kitchen unloading the dishwasher.

"Hi," he said. "I just wanted to let you know I was here."

"I heard the girls. Hail, the conquering hero."

Her remark was sarcastic in and of itself, but she hadn't put much spin on it. It was almost pro forma: Thou shalt not give thy ex-husband the glad hand.

"I guess absence actually can make the heart grow fonder," he said, forcing himself to smile.

Self-deprecating humor. It had often worked in the past to defang Robin, and it, too, was pro forma: Thou shalt not dignify thy wife's cuts with serious attention. The little exchange discouraged him. Not the content of it, which was relatively mild, but the fact that they had ever developed such a pattern and that even at this late and altered date they were still using it.

"You should know," she said, holding fast to her scorn, however mild. She was still bent over the dishwasher.

The kindly feelings for her that had welled up in Dan outside were in danger of evaporating. He didn't want that to happen. During the past six weeks, he had felt himself expanding, as if a fist inside him were opening, a fist that had been clenched so long and so tightly he'd forgotten it was there. Dan had grown accustomed to the fist inside him long before he met Robin. Had she seen it and taken him on anyway, confident she could induce him to uncurl? Or had she only come up against that closed, defended part of him after living with him for years? Either way, he wanted to be different with her now. She was the mother of his children. He had loved her once, if incompletely. It hadn't felt incomplete at the time. Not to him, at any rate.

"I finally met him," he said abruptly. "I met my son today."

Robin straightened up with a meat platter in her hand. She put the platter down on the counter and turned to face him, digging her hands into the pockets of her shorts as if she felt a need to do something with them and couldn't think what. He was offering her a gift, and she knew it. The gift of self-exposure.

"How was it?"

"Amazing. I felt high as a kite and guilty as the devil. Full of hope and joy one minute, and horribly sad the next."

"What now?"

"More of the same, I guess. More ups and downs, I mean, more pieces of our stories coming out. We have a lot of lost time to make up for."

Robin frowned a little, thinking.

"You can't, Dan," she said softly.

"Can't what?"

"Make up for lost time. Erase the past. Don't break your heart trying."

He started to protest I can, I can, but he quelled his knee-jerk resistance to her. When you open a fist, you reveal the palm of your hand, and sometimes people are going to put unexpected things into it. She was right. His task was to get to know Hunt and to let the boy know him in the here and now, and to move on from there. The past could be defused — and that might take years — but it couldn't be erased.

"Daaddeeee!" came Vanessa's outraged voice from the back door. "We're waiting and waiting! What's taking you?"

Dan and Robin smiled at each other.

"Back by 7, 7:30?" Robin said.

"Yes." He turned to leave, then turned back. "The girls look very nice, by the way."

"Thanks."

"Thank *you*."

28

WHEN JANINE ENTERED her parents' home after Dan dropped her off, the house was hushed, silence and stillness boxed up inside it like treasures. She stopped in the middle of the familiar, quiet living room. She was, just then, only herself. She didn't need to sort through the conflicting pulls exerted by the various parts of that self. But she couldn't maintain the state of suspension. She called out to her parents and her sons.

"Down here!" came her mother's muffled response from the cellar.

Janine was struck by a nostalgic pang. When she used to come home from elementary school, she'd call out to her mother as soon as she opened the front door, and if Rose didn't answer or if she called out as she'd just done, Janine would head for the cellar. Finding her mother at the washer or dryer, she'd sit down on the cellar steps and talk to Rose's back, telling her about her day — anecdotes about friends, interesting scraps from lessons, complaints about teachers. Sometimes she'd help fold the clean clothes. Her mother didn't say much. But she laughed at amusing stories and clucked her tongue over tales of trouble, so Janine always felt she was listening attentively, despite her turned back and busy hands.

In Janine's memory, these *tête-a-têtes* were a daily occurrence, but she knew it couldn't have been as often as that. A family of three didn't generate that much laundry, and Rose wasn't given to rigid routines, so laundry wasn't always done in the late afternoon. Maybe the homecoming chats on the cellar steps felt more frequent than they had been in reality because the memory of them was so pleasant. The cellar was warm in winter because the coke furnace was near the laundry area, and cool in summer because it was underground, and that corner of it, lit by a bare light bulb or by a bar of sunlight from a small, high window, smelled of soap and starch and heated fabric. It was a private place that belonged only to them.

The little cellar visits began to peter out during junior high. By sophomore year in high school, Janine was spending nearly every afternoon with Dan, arriving home just before dinner. If Rose missed the visits, she never said so.

"Has Pop got the boys out somewhere?" Janine said as she descended the steps.

Rose was moving wet towels from the washer to the dryer.

"Pop's golfing," she said without turning around. "The boys are at Lee's. They spent the night."

"They did? How did that happen?"

"Pop and the kids bumped into Lee at the video store yesterday, and she invited them. He's going to pick them up after his game."

Janine had hardly given Tim and Larry a thought since yesterday, but in their unexpected absence, she suddenly missed them.

"I'll go get them now," she said.

"Not so fast. You have to tell me about Hunt first."

Rose leaned back against the washer, folding her arms over her chest. Janine sat down on the cellar steps.

Janine had described Hunt's physical appearance after she'd come home from New York on Sunday, so Rose didn't need that information. Janine started, instead, with the doctor's encouraging report. Rose nodded her head approvingly, as if Janine were a student answering a tough question correctly. Rose tended to take good news that way, as if she'd expected it all along and the only iffy thing was when, precisely, it might arrive. It was part of a convoluted theory of hers that though you should always be humbly grateful for good news, to express surprise at receiving it was a form of bad manners and could result in a dearth of good news coming your way in the future.

"Was he awake this time?"

"Yes. Sitting up and waiting for us. His eyes, Ma...he's got Pop's eyes...he was looking at me like he wanted to eat me."

Rose nodded again, although this time she didn't look completely sure whether this was good news or not. Certainly, her expression seemed to say, it couldn't be classed as bad news.

"What did he say?"

"Oh, lots of things. But first...first we hugged. Before either of us said a single word. I hadn't planned to. It just happened, like...like a flash of lightning."

"Did he hug Dan, too?" Rose said, awed.

"Dan wasn't there right then. You know, when I saw Hunt the other day, I had wanted so much to touch him. It was such a strong, strong urge. So to actually have my arms around him and to have him hugging me back...it was...it was..."

Janine paused to collect herself.

"I had my baby in my arms again," she finished in a whisper.

"Oh, Janine."

Rose lifted one hand and rested it at her throat. She was staring straight into Janine's eyes, with almost as much longing as Hunt's stare had held.

"I'm going to the hospital," she declared.

Janine was thrown into confusion. Her mother had spoken as if it were the most natural thing in the world that she should go to Bellevue, as if it were something they'd already discussed and agreed upon.

"That's not a good idea. You'll meet Hunt some day, I hope. If he decides to keep up a relationship with me. But we have to go slowly. I don't want to overwhelm him."

"That's my grandson, Janine. I want him to know the truth."

"The truth?"

"How you wanted to keep him and I talked you out of it."

The raw pain in her mother's voice and face alarmed Janine, yet she didn't get up and go to her. There was something about Rose that warned her off, something that said *not yet*. And something in herself that said *I need to hear all of this.* Still, she wanted to assuage her mother's obvious suffering.

"You weren't the only one who encouraged me to surrender Hunt."

"You don't have to let me off the hook. I know what I did. I thought it was for the best, but it hurt you, and maybe it hurt him, and I don't mind him knowing my part in it. I *want* him to know, for your sake. And I want him to know, too, that it wasn't because I didn't care about him. I don't want him to think I didn't ever care."

"He'll know, Ma. I've already told him some of it. And we can *show* him. By how we treat him now."

Rose stepped forward and took both Janine's hands in hers.

"I am so, so sorry."

Janine felt flooded with love. Love was pouring out of her mother towards her, and love was pouring out of Janine towards her mother. With one sincere sentence, Rose had completed the healing that had begun when she gave Janine the medical record with Hunt's footprint on it. Janine stood up and embraced her. Their heights were uneven because she was on the stairs, so she ended up resting her cheek against her mother's forehead, as if the positions of child and parent were reversed.

Rose broke away and wiped her eyes with her hands.

"Well!" she said. "Come upstairs and tell me all about him."

———

LULU ANSWERED JANINE's knock at Lee's front door. She had an open bottle of bright pink nail polish in her hand and pencils sticking up between her toes to keep them separated. Her parachute pants were rolled up to mid-calf. She backed away from the door on her heels to let Janine enter.

"Everybody's out back," she said.

Janine went to the kitchen and out the back door. Lee was seated on an aluminum lawn chair in a triangle of shade cast by the house. She had a foam pillow at her back, and a magazine lay open on her lap. Her feet were propped up on another pillow on top of an overturned plastic bucket.

"Thank God, another grown-up," she said. "Take a load off." She pointed to a folded chair leaning against the house.

Janine heard boyish shouts and looked across the yard. A large play-house had been built around a big maple at the back of the yard. The voices were emanating from there.

"They'll come out when they're hungry," Lee said.

Janine opened the chair and sat down.

"You know, I specifically didn't tell you I was coming to town because I didn't want you offering to take my kids."

"It just happened. Story of my life. But they've been great. Kept my three guys out of my hair and off each other's backs. Their being so busy together cut Lulu a break, too. I'm not supposed to be on my feet too much."

She plucked at the hem of her cotton skirt to show Janine that she was wearing thick support hose.

"Those must be hot," Janine said sympathetically.

"They are, but they help with the achiness. Varicose veins. Get worse with every pregnancy, and act up sooner each time, too."

"Well, thanks for inviting the boys over. I'm sure it wasn't as easy having them around as you're making it out to be."

"Forget it."

The playhouse door burst open, and five boys ran out, led by Lee's oldest son, Sam. His brothers were close behind him, Tim and Larry behind them. Janine called out to her sons. They ran to her, flung their arms briefly around her neck in greeting, then stood hopping in front of her like caged crickets, obviously torn between hanging out with her a bit longer and returning to their game.

"I see you've had fun," Janine said, smiling as she wiped her fingers across a large smudge of dirt on Tim's cheek.

The boys' bare arms and legs were downright grimy.

"We don't make guests bathe," Lee said.

"Do we have to go right now?" Larry asked.

"You've been here since yesterday!"

"But we're not finished."

"Sam's the captain," Tim said.

"Ten minutes more. We're driving home today, and I'd like to get there before dark."

"We're coming, Sam!" Larry yelled, taking off across the grass with his brother.

"Ten more minutes, Captain!" Tim shouted.

"So," Lee said, "I'm all ears. What happened?"

Janine hesitated. She felt as if she'd been swept up in a tidal wave which had just now set her down, where exactly, she couldn't yet say. She wasn't even sure where the wave had picked her up. At the church in Malaga on Saturday? In her sofa bed with Dan Sunday morning? When she gazed down at the sleeping face of her long-lost son? At the hotel last night? Tidal waves. Roller coasters. Handy metaphors, but woefully inadequate.

"Quite a lot happened."

"Your dad said Hunt was in the hospital. I didn't press him for more information. It seemed like he thought maybe he'd already said too much. Is the kid okay?"

"It looks like he will be."

"So? What's he like?"

Janine wished she didn't have to answer that question again so soon, but Lee's curiosity was understandable. Besides, talking with her about Hunt would be different from talking to Rose, and Lee had a way of showing Janine her own mind. Sometimes it could be like plunging into a cold pool, but as with that experience, Janine always felt invigorated afterwards.

"It's hard to say. I mean, he's sick, plus meeting us was very emotional for him. For all of us."

Lee picked up her magazine and used it to fan herself.

"You must have gotten an impression of him anyway."

"Well," Janine said, sorting adjectives in her mind, "he's definitely not shy, though he is a little unsure of himself. He seems like a sensitive kid. He's artistic, it turns out. He's good-looking — he looks a lot like Dan, actually."

"How did he treat you?"

Janine spread her hands flat on her knees and looked down at them. She'd put away her wedding ring on the one-year anniversary of Clark's death, but there was still a very faint white stripe on her finger. She was well into her second summer without the ring, and the sun still hadn't tanned out the line. She'd wept as she wiggled the ring off and slipped it into a small velvet bag that was now in the box of Clark's belongings she'd put aside for the boys, but within a few weeks, her hand had gotten used to the odd sensation of no ring. Her thumb stopped reaching to touch and turn the wide gold band, as it used to do habitually. What a simple declaration the ring had been. I am someone's wife. There were no easy symbols for the roles that were staking claims to her now.

"Was he glad to meet you?" Lee said when Janine didn't answer.

"Glad? Yes...but... More relieved, I guess. Released somehow... Plus, he's angry with us. But he wants to know everything about us, and, really, he was surprisingly accepting."

Janine looked away from Lee's eager, listening face and out over the yard. The boys were sitting cross-legged on the grass in front of the playhouse. Ten-year-old Sam was holding forth, but from time to time one of the other boys would lean forward and gesticulate. A scheme was being hatched. They could have been on a desert island without a grown-up in sight for all the notice they gave Janine and Lee. Yet without grown-ups, they wouldn't have the marvelous playhouse or the spacious yard or the sheltered time in which to scheme and plot. Janine hoped Hunt had had such protected, magical moments during his childhood.

"You know, Lee, I think he wants us to love him."

"Can you?"

"Of course," Janine shot back at once. "I already do."

Lee studied her for a moment.

"Stop me if I'm crossing a line here, but isn't who you love the little baby from 18 years ago? You've got a full-blown teenager on your hands now. Somebody you didn't raise. Plus, there's Tim and Larry. Loving Hunt, whether it's instinct or whether it grows gradually — how can it be 'of course'?"

Janine stood up. She folded her chair and leaned it against the wall of the house again.

"Ten minutes aren't up yet," Lee said.

"I don't want to sit any more."

"Or talk?"

Janine looked down at Lee, who was still fanning herself. Lee's forehead was shiny with sweat, and Janine suspected she was sweaty beneath her breasts, too, and under the curve of her swollen belly. She *had* crossed a line, venturing into territory that Janine had held back from entering fully. Lee had taken a few steps into the darkness and was beckoning to her.

"I did love that little baby. Blindly, like you do with babies — with your own babies, at any rate. It's the bedrock of what I feel for Hunt now."

Janine looked out into the yard again, but this time she wasn't seeing what was there. She was remembering. She was feeling her way forward.

"I thought of him over the years. Now he's five, I'd say to myself, now he's nine, and so on. I'd think about what kids did at those ages, what they learned, what toys he might like, things like that. So I'm ready to find out who he is now. And even if I discover parts of him I don't like, I know I'll love him because I have already *been* loving him."

"But it's so different from the usual parent–child thing."

"Oh, it's a totally mysterious land! I'm his mother, but I'm not his mom. So who am I? A friend? A ghost? Auntie Mame? This is going to be unlike any other relationship I've ever experienced."

"You need a Sacajawea."

Janine gave a short laugh. "Know anyone?"

"What about the support group the librarian told you about?"

"Not my cup of tea."

Janine called to Tim and Larry, who came trudging across the yard as slowly as if they were wading through foot-deep snow.

"Can I get you anything from inside before I go?" she said to Lee.

"No, I'm fine."

"I don't expect to be up again any time soon, but I'll give you a call if I am."

"Call me anyway."

"Okay."

When the boys reached her, Janine told them to go get their pajamas and anything else they'd brought with them. Still dragging their feet, they went into the house.

"I've got one more 64-dollar question," Lee said.

"What?"

"Dan."

"That's not a question."

"It isn't?"

Janine pulled her car key out of a side pocket of her purse.

"I'm not thinking about that now. I can't."

"That doesn't sound very juicy."

Janine couldn't think of a safe way to respond, so she turned and called to the boys through the screen door. Turning back, she tried to present a let's-drop-it-now expression.

"Don't let it happen again," Lee said quietly.

"What?"

"Don't let Hunt be the reason you turn your back on Dan."

Janine's whole body flushed with heat. If she opened her mouth now, what would come out? A torrent of outrage? A wail of grief? A scream of frustration?

"Hunt's got a family, Janine. I hope he wants to stay connected to you, but he doesn't *need* you."

"You don't know what you're talking about! As usual."

"So, what's the deal? Giving Hunt away was some kind of original sin you have to pay for the rest of your life? Because baptism erases original sin. And if your reunion wasn't a baptism, I don't know what is. To say nothing of whatever you and the good doctor have been up to."

"I am *not* having this discussion with you! You have absolutely no idea—"

"All I'm trying to say," Lee interrupted, "is that you can do right by your kids — *all* your kids — *and* have a romance. Especially *this* romance."

Janine was visited again by the overwhelming desire to slink away somewhere and drop into a long, dreamless sleep.

"It's too crazy," she said wearily.

"'Crazy doesn't have to be bad. Crazy is just...crazy. It helps to have a buddy. You know, like deep sea divers do. Except I mean the kind of buddy who keeps your feet warm at night."

Janine's insides quivered as she recalled Dan's hands and mouth on her body, his breath on her face, the salty taste of his skin.

"He wants to," she admitted.

"I'll bet he does. And what do you want? That's the real 64-dollar question."

Janine flashed on Dan in the swimming pool with Tim on his shoulders, Dan standing beside her peering through the gallery window, Dan grasping Hunt's hand as if he would never let go. She thought about her studio and how she was yearning to get back to it. She thought about her little home near the sea.

"Everything," she said to Lee. "I want everything."

"Nothing wrong with that."

"Except that on top of it's being complicated beyond belief, I don't deserve it."

"That's crap."

Lee held up her hand to prevent Janine from saying anything.

"I'm not going to sit here and argue about how deserving or undeserving you are. Everyone gets things they deserve and things they don't deserve, so why bother to consider it?"

"Force of habit, I guess."

"Habits are for breaking. You want everything, you go for it," Lee said emphatically. "Crazy, bumpy, wildly romantic, dark night of the soul — whatever. You just go for it. Like that song Lulu is forever playing: go ahead and jump."

I can't, Janine thought. I want to, but I can't. But she was tired of arguing and explaining, and she didn't want to hear any more advice, so she didn't say anything.

What was it Dan had said? *It's as simple as that.* As simple as not looking a gift horse in the mouth. As simple as defining happiness as something attainable. Not a fluke. Not a loan. Not a will-o-the-wisp. Something that she had as much right to as anyone else. But she still didn't believe it. Wanting everything was something she hadn't felt in decades. She supposed that was some kind of step forward. But wanting everything was far different from reaching out for it.

29

THE NEXT DAY, at home in Cape May Point, Janine called Bellevue to verify that Hunt had, indeed, been moved to a regular room. The operator informed her there was a phone. Despite a hammerlock of stage fright, Janine let the operator put her through to him.

After awkward hellos and a ridiculous inquiry about the quality of the hospital food, she spilled out information haphazardly — her week with him at Shadyside, descriptions of the twins, her acceptance at the gallery. He had a question or two, nothing deep. Afterwards, she paced the living room, her mind skittering around second-guessing itself. Had she been friendly enough without being overbearing? Had he sounded pleased to hear from her, or was he simply surprised? Was she failing or succeeding? Was that even the right framework for thinking about it?

Too restless to buckle down in her studio, she biked into Cape May and back instead, choosing a route that made it a round trip of five miles. In Cape May, she purchased a box of wooden matches and rubber flip-flops for the boys, neither of which was an urgent necessity, nor something that couldn't be found in Cape May Point. The urgency had lain in an overpowering need to exert her body, to spin out the turmoil in her mind.

Hunt called two days later, on Friday, with the news he was scheduled for discharge the following Monday, August 20.

"That's wonderful!"

"Yeah, well, I'm keeping my fingers crossed."

He was more talkative than during their first phone conversation, full of queries about the Pettorini family and the Gannon family. No detail was too small for him. Janine extemporized biographies for her extended family, but the only facts she supplied about the Gannons were the names of Dan's siblings. She told Hunt he'd have to ask Dan about Gannon history.

"He called once when the doctor was here and I couldn't talk," Hunt said. "He didn't call back."

"He's probably waiting for you. He's trying to respect your privacy."

"I didn't think of that."

There was a beat of silence.

"Did you tell your kids?" Hunt said abruptly.

"Not yet," she answered, feeling contrite. "I thought I'd tell them when it was definite that they were going to meet you. Having a big brother they've never seen is a little abstract."

"A big brother?"

"That's what you are," she said warmly.

After hanging up, Janine went straight from the phone to the garage for her bike. Within five minutes of setting out, however, she noticed a difference. This time, her mind was free of doubts, and her heart was singing. It helped that Hunt had called her, rather than the other way around. And it had been a real conversation, a give-and-take as might have occurred between any two people getting to know each other. Her mind hadn't raced to come up with the next topic, even during the few gaps of dead air. It hadn't all been easy, but it hadn't felt forced or stiff. I feel good, she realized, as she pumped her legs going up a small grade. I feel good.

Her next thought was to call Dan and tell him. The idea sprang into her mind too suddenly to be censored, but she dismissed it at once. Dan hadn't called her. Their last exchange had been in the car outside her parents' house. She had pulled away from him then, literally and figuratively, and he'd given her the solitude she'd asked for. But she missed him. So many details of daily life formed themselves as anecdotes she'd like to share with him — the rainbow over the salt marshes, a certain aspect of a painting, a quirky framing customer, an interesting magazine article. Well, she'd just have to get a handle on that. She hadn't refused one kind of craziness only to succumb to another.

HUNT'S DISCHARGE DATE arrived. Janine didn't want to call him at home because she didn't want the awkwardness of Margaret or Pete answering. Besides, she felt the next move had to be Hunt's. Days passed. No call.

Janine put it out of her mind as well as she could. She had a long phone conversation with a woman from Concerned United Birthparents who told her such lapses were quite common. Adoptees had to begin to splice together their two worlds. They had to re-think who they were, a big enough job for an adult, even more so for an adolescent.

Hunt's first week at home in Malaga was also the final week of day camp for the twins. Summer was waning, and with it, the indolence of the season, which, in June and July, always seemed to be a luxuriously low-gear state that would never end. Tim and Larry would be around full-time next week, until school started after Labor Day. Janine figured she'd have to let most things drop during that interim week, so she was jamming as much as she could into the few child-free summer days left. She had a spate of framing orders, and her Muse was in overdrive. She'd been working steadily on the painting of Shadyside. Not only was it coming along very satisfactorily, it, along with all the recent commotions, had spawned a raft of ideas for other paintings, a series she'd given the working title *Biographies*.

Janine's mind and energies were so well-occupied that when Hunt finally did call, on Thursday, she was caught off-guard. The purpose of his call was a request to come on Saturday to meet the boys. She agreed immediately, hoping her voice connoted pure pleasure and held no hint of the trepidation she also felt. The latter increased significantly when Hunt said he'd like Dan and his girls to come, too.

"I asked him, but he said I had to check with you first. He works Saturday mornings, so he couldn't come until late in the afternoon."

"You've been talking to him?"

"Yeah. I decided you were right that I shouldn't wait for him in case he was maybe waiting for me. So, is it okay?"

"Yes, of course," Janine said, praying she sounded natural. "We can all have dinner together. But come earlier, if you can. Spend the day."

⸺∞⸺

"Do you remember Dr. Gannon and his little girls?" Janine asked the boys at dinner that night.

"Vanessa and Sally," Tim said.

"They're all coming for dinner on Saturday. And we're going to have another visitor — a very special visitor — who's coming Saturday morning."

"Who?" Larry said around a mouthful of hamburger.

"Remember when I went with Dr. Gannon to see someone, and you stayed with Gram and Grandpa, and—?"

"Who special is coming?" Larry asked again.

"A long time ago, before you were born, and before I knew Daddy—"

"Is this a story from your mouth?" Tim said.

Larry made an impatient grimace. The boys liked hearing stories about their mother's childhood, which they called "stories from your mouth," as opposed to stories from books, but Larry was clearly dubious that such a story could shed light on the mysterious visitor.

"Is who's special from a long time ago?" he demanded.

"Just listen, please, both of you. This is important."

Tim scooped a handful of French fries from a bowl in the center of the table and dropped them on his plate. He picked one up, and nibbling at it, looked expectantly at Janine. Larry also served himself a handful

340

of fries, even though he still had quite a few left from his first portion, perhaps fearing that his mother's serious tone meant that loading up his plate while she was telling her story would not be appreciated. He slid the ketchup bottle closer, and then he, too, looked at Janine. Their trusting, undivided attention sharpened the anxiety that had been gnawing at her like a cankerworm since Hunt's call that afternoon.

"A long time ago," she began again, "I had a baby."

She stopped to judge their reaction. They both sat watching her impassively, waiting for the punch line. Tim had started on another French fry. Apparently, their mother with a baby long ago made as much sense to them as anything else that had happened outside their lifetimes. The baby had never impinged on them. The identity, or maybe even the existence, of the baby's father didn't seem to have entered their minds yet, nor where this baby had been in the meanwhile. She knew from experience in dealing with other tricky issues with the boys that it was best to give only basic information and wait for questions.

"Now that baby is a teenager, and—"

"Boy or girl?" Larry said.

"Boy."

He nodded approvingly.

"What's his name?" said Tim.

"Hunt."

Janine's face flushed with heat. She'd spoken the name of her lost son to her other sons. She'd never dreamed it could happen. She'd known adoptees did search sometimes, but she'd never believed it would happen to her. The cankerworm was still busily chewing, but a softening sense of wonder was edging up beside it.

"Hunt?" Larry hooted. "Like an Easter egg hunt?"

"No. It's just a name. The most important thing is that Hunt is your brother."

Both boys appeared stunned, and as they often did when perplexed, they looked at each other. Under other circumstances, Janine would have laughed because their exchanged looks so clearly said *what should we do?, she's lost her mind.*

"When children have the same mother," she continued, "they are brothers, or if they're girls, they're sisters, even if they never lived together and they have different last names."

"Where does Hunt live?" Tim said.

"In a town not too far from here."

"How come?"

"How come?"

"How come he doesn't live with us?"

Bingo. What was she going to do with that?

"Well, Hunt grew up in another family, with another mother and another father. And he has a sister."

Tim sat stock still. A tiny knitting of his eyebrows and a blankness in his stare told Janine he was rolling all she'd said around in his mind. In contrast, Larry was wiggling, which wasn't unusual behavior for him.

"Is the sister your baby, too?" he said.

"No, she's not. I had Hunt a long time ago, and I had the two of you, and that's all."

She was tempted to put on a sunny face and prattle about what fun it was going to be to have a big brother, but it wouldn't be honest. It might come true, but she didn't know that it would. She wanted, now, to tell them only what she knew for certain.

"Why did he grow up in another family?" Larry said, his voice tremulous.

Tim looked sympathetically at his brother and then at Janine. His expression held an appeal for help. It wasn't farfetched, Janine thought, to interpret it as an appeal for mercy. Larry was Tim's bulwark, and if Larry was upset, there was cause for worry.

"I...he went to live there because...because there was a Mommy and a Daddy there, and I was...I was just a Mommy alone."

Larry's face darkened, and his lower lip began to quiver. Tim put his hands on the edge of the table and pushed his chair back, as if intending to get up, but he stayed seated, still gripping the table edge.

"You said we're still a family," Larry accused Janine angrily. "When Daddy died, you said..."

Janine jumped up and went around to their side of the table. She pulled them off their chairs, hugging them tightly and kissing them repeatedly. Both boys were crying now, and she could taste the salt of their tears.

"It's all right," she said, fighting back her own tears. "We *are* a family. And we're staying together. Nothing will ever change that. Nothing. Ever."

She was aghast at her own clumsiness. Of course they'd translate the news of Hunt as they did all news, into what it highlighted about themselves. And in their childish logic, if their mother could send away one child to a "better" family, what was to stop her from sending them away as well? Who cared about the gain of a brother if you lost your mother? Especially after you'd already lost your father. She couldn't have flubbed it any worse if she'd tried. Not only had she frightened Tim and Larry, she'd laid a minefield for Hunt. Because in spite of the twins' fears and misconceptions, they were still going to have to meet this threatening interloper.

When the boys had calmed down, Janine took each of them by the hand and led them into the living room, where the three of them snuggled together on the couch.

"Now, I'm putting you two in charge of the plans for Saturday. You decide what food we should have. And think about if we should take Hunt anywhere, or if you just want to stay home."

"He could come into our tent," Tim said generously.

"We could have macaroni and cheese for lunch," Larry mumbled, sounding as if he begrudged Hunt any sustenance at all.

"And Coke," Tim ventured.

"All right. Mac and cheese and Coke."

"And banana splits for dessert?" Larry dared.

"Banana splits: check."

The boys traded amazed, gleeful looks.

"And let's go to the horseshoe crab beach," Larry said.

"That's a good idea," Janine said. "Could be Hunt's never seen horseshoe crabs before."

"Really? Never?"

"Maybe only in books. Lots of people haven't ever seen real ones."

"If he finds a shell, he can take it home," Tim said. "One that's all dried out and not stinky."

"We'll help him find one that's not cracked," Larry said with the air of an experienced explorer.

They all rested back against the couch cushions, lost in private thought. Janine supposed that with a guarantee of treats and a desig- nated outing under their belts, the boys felt braced up.

"Mom?" Tim said.

"Yes?"

"Are you gonna have another baby?"

"No, Timmy, no more babies."

"Is Hunt a big brother like Sam?" Larry asked.

"Bigger."

"Cool," Larry said, trying to whistle but managing only a soft whooshing sound.

"But it's our house," Tim pointed out, "so we get to be the captains."

"Right. You are the captains in this house."

<hr />

THEY LAID IN their provisions Friday evening. The boys had decided on a Saturday dinner menu of hot dogs, baked beans, grilled pineapple slices, and a salad from the garden, with apple pie and chocolate ice cream for dessert, *a la mud,* as Tim called it. Janine picked up steaks for herself and Dan and Hunt.

At home, they discovered they'd forgotten maraschino cherries, so the boys dug out their flashlights, and they all walked to the little gen- eral store on the traffic circle. The clerk wasn't sure they carried mara- schino cherries, but he sent them to a back corner to search, and Tim, methodically running one finger along the edge of every shelf in that area, discovered one dusty, pot-bellied jar of the neon red cherries partially hidden behind a Betty Crocker cake mix. Janine considered it a good omen.

Saturday was warm but overcast, the sun a white smudge behind a gauze of low-hanging, opal-gray clouds. As a counterpoint to the monotony of the day's light, Janine dressed in a bright orange shirt and a paler orange skirt, and tied a purple and green sash around her waist.

Hunt arrived at 10:00. Janine, hearing the crunch of tires on the crushed shell driveway, went to the window for a peek before going out to greet him. A black Volkswagen bug sat in the middle of the driveway, looking, indeed, like a huge, shiny beetle against the bright white shell fragments surrounding it. She could just make out Hunt in the driver's seat. Following the line of his sight, she spotted Tim and Larry standing next to the large hydrangea bush beside the outdoor shower. They were staring straight into the windshield of the VW.

When the car door finally opened, Tim took a step backward. Larry, not turning his gaze away from the car, reached his hand behind him, and Tim took hold of it. Hunt got out of the car and stood beside the open door looking at the twins. Then he smiled at them. Janine realized with a start that it was the first time she'd seen him smile. It was dazzling, transforming his handsome face into one of outright, absolute beauty. It must have impressed the boys, too, because they drew nearer, stopping at the front fender of the car.

"Are you Tim and Larry?" Janine heard Hunt say.

Larry nodded.

"Which is which?"

"I'm Larry, he's Tim."

"I've got the cowlick," Tim said, pointing to an unruly hank of hair springing from a whorl above his right eyebrow. It was the standard aid the boys offered to people trying to tell them apart.

"I'm Hunt. No cowlick."

This earned him a small smile from Tim.

345

"You were a baby a long time ago," Larry said as if it were an indictment.

Hunt's smile broadened. "Yes, I was."

He leaned inside the car and emerged with a long cardboard tube.

"I brought you something. But we have to put it together."

"What?" Larry said, stepping forward.

"A kite."

Larry looked back over his shoulder at Tim.

"We like kites," Tim said to Hunt.

"This one's a bat kite. You know, in the shape of a bat, with those wings they have?"

"Do you like horseshoe crabs?" Larry said.

"I don't know. I've never thought about that before."

"We're going to see some today, but maybe only dead ones, you can't ever tell until you get there. And we could take the kite, 'cause there's good wind at the bay and not so many people laying around that you might maybe step on if you're looking up and not watching where you're going."

"Sounds good."

"We made the plans ourselves," Tim said importantly.

"Do you like maraschino cherries?" Larry said. "Tim found the last ones, and we're going to have them on our banana splits and maybe on the *a la mud*, too."

At this point, Janine opened the front door and came out. The three boys looked over at her, and her heart capered like a dragonfly over a sparkling brook, because all of them were so obviously pleased to see her.

THE KITE WASN'T easy to assemble, especially with the assistance of two competing six-year-olds, but an hour later it was done. Janine thought it a stroke of genius for Hunt to have brought a project. The hour had been filled with homey interactions, as she and Hunt puzzled over the terse directions and Tim and Larry made endless suggestions based on their scrutiny of the diagrams and their own idiosyncratic ideas of kite construction. A wooden stick was broken and repaired with duct tape. Rags were sought and torn up for the tail. The black nylon was turned this way and that, stretched, and turned again, and finally attached to the mostly rigid frame.

"Do you think this is how the Wright brothers got started?" Hunt said, holding up the finished product.

"Let's go test it!" Tim said.

Happily, the kite did fly, thanks to a steady offshore breeze at Higbee Beach. Janine ran with it to get it to lift because she didn't think Hunt should be running so soon after his illness. Once it was up, she passed him the string reel, and he showed the twins how to pull on the string to make the kite dip and glide and rise again. Clark had taught them the same tricks, but they were polite enough to let Hunt think he was showing them something new. When Hunt gave Tim the reel, he ran off with it, Larry leaping beside him. They passed the reel back and forth as they ran, stopping now and then to make the kite cavort.

"They're pretty cute," Hunt said, watching them.

"You've made a good first impression."

"Two down, two to go."

"Vanessa and Sally? I don't know them well — I've only met them once. But don't worry. You seem to have a way with children."

"Only once? I thought you guys were together. You seemed, like, so in sync."

"No... We're just..." She smiled at Hunt. "We're old friends. I guess that's where the in sync comes from."

"But didn't you used to be in love? Way back when?"

"Yes... Way back when."

Hunt stared out over the bay.

"I'm glad," he said. "I'm glad I came from two people who loved each other."

Euphoria clutched Janine. She had the impulse to put her arms around Hunt, except they hadn't reached that level of easiness yet. But what he'd just said about her and Dan made her believe that ultimately they would be easy with each other.

"Hunt?"

"Yeah?"

"Why didn't you keep in touch with the lawyer after you left the letter?"

He shrugged and kicked at the sand. They'd all left their shoes in the car. Janine noticed the arches of his feet were unusually high. Like Dan's.

"Did you not get his messages?"

"I got them." More sand-kicking. "But I wasn't so sure any more." He looked at her. "Sometimes, you know, it can seem better to stick with what you have than to take a chance."

"Mom! Mom!" came Larry's shouts from down the beach.

Both he and Tim were racing towards the bay and pointing up at the sky. The kite, high above, was sailing steadily west, its reel bouncing across the ground, the hummocks in the sand providing enough traction to keep the string taut and the kite aloft.

"The kite'll drop when the reel hits the water," Hunt said as he and Janine headed towards the boys.

They didn't bother to run because there was no way they'd make it in time to grab the reel. It looked like Tim and Larry wouldn't catch it, either, though they continued to run.

Hunt's prediction proved wrong. When the reel hit the water, it continued to skip along the surface just as it had on the sand. The string stayed taut. The kite whizzed on, out over the bay now.

"It's getting away!" Tim said breathlessly, standing knee-deep in the water.

"It's going to China!" Larry said.

"Or Delaware," Janine said.

The kite was getting smaller and smaller as they watched. It gave no sign of dropping.

"It must have just the right combination of wind strength in the air and surface tension on the water," Hunt said. "Like some kind of gnarly physics experiment."

"Yeah, gnarly," Larry said, patently pleased with the word.

Tim waded out a little deeper, as if reluctant to give up the retrieval effort, even though it was clearly a lost cause.

"Ouch!" he shouted. "I stepped on something sharp!"

He moved a couple of steps to the right.

"Ouch! Ouch!"

He raised his foot out of the water. A large blue crab had one of its pincers clamped on to Tim's big toe. The boy shook his foot, but the crab held on. Squealing, Tim shook harder, lost his balance and fell over. Hunt was already wading into the water. He scooped Tim up, knocked the crab off his foot, and carried him to shore.

"You got your pants wet!" Larry said, impressed.

"I don't care," Hunt said, rolling up his soggy cuffs.

Janine squatted to examine Tim's toe.

"It didn't break the skin," she said.

"It still hurts."

Hunt picked up a stone.

"See this?" he said to Tim. "This is that toe-pinching crab."

He heaved the stone out over the water.

"Good-bye, crab, and good-bye, hurt," he said when the stone splashed down.

He looked around and picked up another stone, which he also threw into the bay.

"Good-bye, aspergillosis." He looked at the boys. "Got anything you're glad to be rid of?"

Larry picked up a stone and threw it. "Good-bye, poison ivy."

"You had that in June!" Janine said.

"That doesn't matter," Hunt said. "It's for anything you want to forget about."

"Good-bye, Jimmy Parker," Tim shouted as he threw a stone.

"Who's Jimmy Parker?" Janine asked.

"He's at camp."

"He called Tim a jerk-head," Larry explained.

"Worms in your apple!" Tim shouted on his next stone.

"Worms in Jimmy Parker's apple!" Larry shouted.

"No, that would be good."

"Oh, right."

"Okay, my turn," Janine said, stooping to pick up a stone. "Aspergillosis!"

"Hunt already said that," Larry pointed out.

"I know. I'm glad it's gone, too."

"What is it?" Tim wanted to know.

"It's like a pinching crab that's *inside* you," Hunt said.

Tim's eyes grew large. Larry knelt and dug his hands deep into the sand.

"Good-bye to all the inside crabs!" he yelled as he splashed into the bay.

He tossed both fistfuls of sand high into the air. It dimpled the water with an effervescent hiss.

30

J ANINE WAS IN front watering the zinnias, and Hunt was in the backyard tent with the boys when Dan and his girls arrived. Janine turned off the spigot, coiled up the hose, and went to the curb. Dan was lifting a large paper bag and a watermelon out of the trunk. Sally and Vanessa were close beside him, like seedlings at the base of a tree.

"Corn," Dan said, indicating the bag. "We passed a farm stand on the way in."

Janine took the bag from him. It was a good excuse for not offering a physical greeting. A hug would have been inappropriate, and a hand-shake would have seemed silly.

"Tim and Larry are in back," she said to the girls. "They have a tent."

The girls didn't move.

"Shall I show you?"

Janine held out her free hand. Vanessa shook her head no and started up the driveway on her own, pulling Sally with her. Janine walked across the grass to the front door, Dan following with the watermelon.

"Would you like something cold to drink?" she said when they'd deposited their burdens on the kitchen counter.

"No, thanks." He gazed into the back yard. "I'm going to go say hello to Hunt. Introduce the girls."

"Sure, of course."

"I LOVE CORN on the cob!" declared Vanessa as Janine set the steaming platter on the dinner table.

"Me and Tim picked all the other food," Larry said.

"Except the steaks," Tim corrected him.

"That's not for everybody, that doesn't count."

"I can count to 20!" Sally announced. "One, two, three, four..."

"All right," Dan said. "Let's save the counting for later."

"Why, Daddy?"

"Because at the dinner table, conversation is more interesting than counting."

"Remember, Sally?" her sister said grandly, "Mommy said no *singing* at dinner, either. And no burping."

"No burping!" Tim said, giggling.

Vanessa and Larry giggled, too, and after a quick evaluation to determine that she wasn't the butt of the joke, Sally joined in.

A flurry of activity ensued. Janine used tongs to put an ear of corn on each plate. Dan helped his daughters push corn-holders into each end of the cobs. Butter, salt, and pepper made the rounds. Hot dogs were nestled into buns after being inspected for burns — Larry wanted a blackened one, the other children didn't. Condiments circulated, and baked beans and salad were distributed, entailing many repetitions of "please pass" and "thank you" and ardently expressed opinions on the relative merits of relish, ketchup, sauerkraut, and mustard.

"This feels like a party," Hunt said. "A good-bye to summer party."

"We didn't throw a rock for good-bye to summer," Tim said.

"Oh, I'm never glad to see summer go," Hunt replied.

"Where does it go?" Sally asked, her cheek full of hot dog and bun.

"Up into the sky somewhere, I guess, with all the other summers and winters and springs and falls."

"Like our kite," Larry said.

"Hunt brought us a bat kite," Tim told the girls, "but it escaped."

"Yeah, he brought us a kite because he's our brother."

Vanessa set down her ear of corn and turned to Larry with her hands on her hips.

"He's *our* brother."

"Did he bring you a kite?" Larry asked with the flair of a prosecutor.

"I made him a Valentine!"

"It's not Valentine's Day!"

"Nessie is good for cutting out hearts," Sally said. "Hey, my bun is falling apart!"

"Hay is for horses," Vanessa said, swiveling towards her sister.

"Too much relish," Dan said. "Here's a new bun."

Vanessa turned back to Larry.

"My Daddy said Hunt is *our* brother," she insisted again.

"Mom!" Larry cried in his best we-need-a-referee-to-say-I'm-right voice.

"You're both right," Hunt said. "I'm everybody's big brother."

"Everybody?" Vanessa seemed unsure whether to be impressed or skeptical.

"Well, the four of you, and my sister Paula."

"Our mom said you're our brother because she had you for a baby a long time ago," Tim said.

"That's right, Tim," Janine put in. "Hunt is your brother and Larry's brother because you all have the same mother, me. And Hunt is Vanessa and Sally's brother, too, because they..." She glanced at Dan, and he nodded. "Because they all have the same father."

"Me," said Dan.

The children were silent. They looked back and forth among Janine, Dan, and Hunt. Janine was hesitant to say anything further without knowing what Dan had told his daughters.

"Do you guys know about mules?" Hunt said, looking at each of the children in turn.

The girls shook their heads no. Larry just stared at him.

"They're stubborn," Tim said. "That means they don't like to cooperate."

353

"That's what they say. But do you know about the mothers and fathers of mules?"

"They're stubborn, too?" Larry guessed.

"Maybe. But here's the thing. A mule has a donkey for a father and a horse for a mother. So, if we pretend that I'm a mule, then he..." He pointed at Dan. "He is my donkey father, and she is my horse mother. And Vanessa and Sally, you are donkeys, too, because of your dad, and Tim and Larry, you're horses, because of your mom. So we're all connected, but we're different, too."

The children sat immobilized. The older ones looked like they were trying to understand Hunt's analogy, but Sally looked as if she might cry. Dan made a welcoming gesture to her, and she went and climbed onto his lap. Laying her head against his shoulder, she began sucking her thumb.

"Do you all understand what Hunt—" Dan began.

"Hee-haw!" Vanessa burst out. "Sal, we're donkeys!"

"Hee-haw," Sally mumbled around her thumb.

Vanessa closed her eyes and threw her head back.

"*Sweetly sings the donkey at the break of day,*" she sang loudly. "*If you do not feed him, this is what he'll say. Hee-haw, hee-haw, hee-haw, hee-haw, hee-haw.*"

Tim joined in on the last three hee-haws.

"Wait, Tim," Larry said. "We're horses!" And he began to neigh and whinny, tossing his head like a wild stallion.

Vanessa started her song again, with Sally accompanying her, thumb extracted from her mouth. Tim quit singing to neigh. The four voices reached a crescendo during the hee-haw chorus. When the song and the competing neighs threatened to begin yet again, Janine stood up. Startled, all the children were abruptly quiet.

"Okay," she said. "O-kay."

Then Hunt stood up and applauded, bowing to the children.

"You guys were great! All you needed to make it perfect was someone pulling a cat's tail."

"We don't have a cat," Larry said.

"Pulling tails isn't nice," Vanessa added.

"No singing at the dinner table," Sally said, pleased to be one up on her sister for a change. She got down from Dan's lap and returned to her seat.

The children tucked into their food again. Janine and Hunt glanced at each other with raised eyebrows and sat down. Head bent over his plate, Dan hee-hawed softly. His girls grinned, and Hunt and Janine laughed. The twins started laughing, too, and Janine could hear that it was liable to escalate into mania.

"Fellas..." she said gently, and they stopped.

After dessert, equipped with glass jars lidded with aluminum foil, the children went outside to catch fireflies. Hunt and Dan cleared the table while Janine rinsed dishes and put them into the dishwasher. Then the three of them sat down at the kitchen table with cups of coffee.

"I hope you didn't mind about the mule thing," Hunt said. "It just popped into my head."

"I doubt I could've done better," Dan said.

"They're not going to be satisfied with that explanation forever," Janine said, "but it seems to be enough for now."

"I guess it's kind of embarrassing for you to have to tell them about me."

"No, no," Janine said quickly. "It's just a little challenging. Because they're so young."

"You were a big help tonight," Dan said to Hunt, "but don't feel you have to take on the responsibility of explaining things. That's our job."

"Okay."

Stories, Janine thought. Families are stories. We three have backpacks stuffed with stories from the families we grew up in and the families before them, and Dan and I carry the stories, too, of the families we made. Including this beautiful boy seated at my astonished kitchen table. Slowly, all the stories will get told. Slowly, new ones will accumulate.

"How are things at home?" Dan said.

Letting the question hang, Hunt seemed to be assessing how detailed he wanted to be in his answer. He'd never revealed to Janine why he'd left home, never acknowledged what she and Dan had learned at the youth center, and he hadn't mentioned how his parents were feeling about his visit today. She wondered if he'd told Dan anything.

"Better," he finally said.

So, Janine thought, those dogs are still sleeping, and he wants us to let them lie undisturbed a while longer.

Hunt began cracking his knuckles, methodically pushing and tugging on each finger until it snapped. It was a habit Janine heartily disliked.

"So, um, what should I call you guys?"

Janine and Dan looked at each other.

"I mean, like, I *have* parents. My mom might freak if she heard me call you Mother or something. But you *are...*"

"You can call me Janine."

Dan furrowed his brow. "Do we have to pin each other down?"

"What do you mean?" Hunt blazed. "I thought we were gonna keep going. On the phone, you made it sound like you wouldn't skip out on—"

"Whoa! I'm not talking about skipping out. It just feels weird to choose names before we've come to anchor in each other's lives."

"So, I should just say *hey, you*? Or are you mad 'cause I'm not automatically calling you Daddy like your real kids?"

"My *real* kids?"

"Hunt, you're not being fair," Janine said.

The boy scowled at her.

"I shoulda known you'd take his side."

"Hardly," Dan said bitterly.

"This isn't a case of sides," Janine said, irritated at both of them.

Dan leaned forward over the table towards Hunt.

"What I was trying to say is that labels like Mom and Dad, or real mother, real kids are all loaded. And we have plenty to untangle without them. But, as you rightly point out, we can't go around saying 'hey, you.' So, using first names seems like the best idea. If it's all right with you."

Hunt nodded reluctantly and began cracking his knuckles again.

"You've been drawing?" Janine said, pointing to ink stains on his fingers. She wanted to steer him away from the tiff and away from the knuckle-cracking.

"A little. Not much else to do."

"I'd like to see your work some time. Although I find, myself, that pieces have to get to a certain point before I'm ready to let them be seen."

"I like that self-portrait you have in the little space off the living room," Hunt said.

"A lot of people don't. It's been said I look too fierce."

"But it's a true angle," Dan said. "That's in you."

Janine looked at him appraisingly. He really did know her. But was his comment negative, positive, or neutral? Dan returned her look with equanimity. She saw that he would be faithful to what he'd said in the car. He wouldn't declare himself to her again. But he wasn't tiptoeing around her, either. She was the one tiptoeing. Around herself.

"I like the twitchy flowers in the background," Hunt said, continuing his assessment of the self-portrait. "They're like the sky in 'Starry Night.' You know, almost alive. The flower stems look like snakes."

"It's an old piece," Janine said, beginning to feel self-conscious. "I wouldn't have framed it except that my husband wanted me to. That alcove used to be his study."

"Why don't you take Hunt out to the studio? I'll keep an eye on the crew."

Janine was incensed. How could Dan make such a blunder? Did he not understand that she didn't let just anyone into her studio just any old time? She tried to recall what paintings and sketches were in plain view in the studio at the moment. The Shadyside painting was on the easel. Was she ready for Hunt to see that?

But life didn't always wait until you were ready to spring things on you. Dan hadn't blundered. He was pushing her. Hunt's here, he was saying. You say you want to let him in. On your mark, get set, go.

⎯⎯⎯⎯⎯⎯

"WAS IT REALLY like this?" Hunt said, staring at the Shadyside painting.

"Like what?"

"Dark. You've got these splashes of red and pink and light blue, and the white sky at the top, but if I closed my eyes and tried to picture it, I'd come up with dark."

"It was an old house. They kept the shades drawn a lot, and there were big trees all around it. The furniture was donated, mostly large, heavy pieces of dark wood... Lord, I'm making it sound horribly ugly, aren't I? It wasn't, really. But it did have a gloom about it."

"What about the crooked stairs and the wavy floors and these chairs that look like they're melting?"

"Oh, *we* were the crooked ones. We girls."

Hunt looked at her with compassion.

"You don't still feel like that, do you?"

How amazing, Janine thought, to be asked about the shackles of my past by the one person best equipped to free me from them. She felt as if she and Hunt were traveling together in two directions at once, down a twisting path into the past and out onto a freshly paved road unrolling through mist into the future. Yet she didn't feel fractured or divided.

"I'm letting it go. Not keeping the secret any more helps. Secrets are for shame and for staying invisible. Meeting you helped, too. A lot."

She went to a shelf and slid out a portfolio. Opening it on the table, she spread out several small, impressionistic seascapes.

"I've been playing with watercolors lately. It's a new medium for me."

Hunt moved the paintings around on the table to see them all.

"I heard watercolors are hard."

"They can be tricky. Boundaries are softer, forms bleed into each other. You lose some compositional tension."

"So...is that good or bad?"

"I don't know yet. It seems like it might work well for a series I'm planning called *Biographies*. Life as a tapestry, not a house built of blocks."

Janine started gathering up the paintings.

"I'm making it sound way too highfalutin. It's just a different way of expressing what you see."

Hunt picked up the last watercolor from the table and looked at it.

"Or a different way of seeing."

He handed her the painting, and she slipped it into the portfolio.

"I'll bring some of my drawings next time. I mean, if..."

"Next time. Music to my ears."

Hunt flashed a quick smile.

"But I don't know when, exactly. I've got orientation at Rutgers next week, then I've got to move in, and classes begin—"

"Call whenever. We could drive up there some time."

"Okay. I will."

WHEN HUNT AND Janine returned to the house, they found Dan on the deck and the children watching a video in the living room.

"I should be hitting the road," Hunt said. "I'll go say good night to the kids."

After Hunt had gone inside, Janine asked Dan in a low voice, "So, everything went pretty well, don't you think?"

"Yes...though it did feel like we all jumped into a vat of plastic balls like they have at Chuck E. Cheese."

"What an image!"

Hunt returned to the deck, and they walked him to his car. He offered his right hand to Dan. When Dan grasped it with both his hands, the boy wrapped his free arm around Dan's shoulders. Janine's heart swelled to see them together like that. The men separated, and Hunt turned to her. They embraced.

"Oh, I almost forgot." Hunt leaned into the car and picked up a manila envelope from the passenger seat.

"I thought maybe you'd want to see some pictures of me as a kid," he said. "My mom helped me pick them out. You can keep 'em, she said. They're extras."

Janine pressed the envelope to her chest while they watched Hunt back out of the driveway and take off down the street.

"It's so sad watching him go. Almost like the first time."

"Hey." Dan moved to stand in front of her so she'd have to look at him. "You can feel sad without feeling guilty."

They walked slowly around the side of the house to the back. They could hear the musical soundtrack from the video as they passed the open living room windows.

A lamp in the kitchen was shining a rectangle of light on the deck. Janine went to this bright spot and opened the envelope. Dan stood beside her. Four photographs slid out into her hand. There was Hunt as a young baby, looking as Janine remembered him, only plumper; Hunt at three or four in a cowboy suit; Hunt smiling in a formal school photo from second grade, a wide gap in his upper front teeth; and another school photo from eighth grade, his mouth a serious line, with a hint of mustache.

"Oh, my God, Dan, look at him."

Dan took the baby picture. Janine couldn't stop staring at the other photographs, though they were lacerating her heart. Here was what she'd given up. Here was what was irretrievable. Here was the Hunt she'd never have.

Dan emitted a deep, guttural sound. His face was twisted in grief.

"This baby is so... I've just been thinking of him now, you know? How to be with him, what to say... But to see these..."

Dan thrust the baby picture at her.

"Put them away."

Janine did as he asked without objection. She set the envelope down on the picnic table.

"Whew!" Dan said, flopping down on a deck chair, "I didn't see that coming. It was like somebody yanked out a plug somewhere inside me."

Janine leaned against the deck railing near Dan's chair.

"I know what you mean."

"Do you?" he said sharply.

"Of course I do. Those pictures are in-your-face, undeniable evidence of what I gave away, what I missed out on."

"What *we* missed out on."

"We. Sorry. I wasn't trying to exclude you."

He gave her a skewed, joyless smile.

"All I meant," he said, staring out into the dark yard, "was that you and I had different experiences 18 years ago. We both lost Hunt. We both lost our...what? Our innocence? Our optimism? You had the pregnancy to endure, too, and the birth, and the actual, physical act of giving him away, while I had...emptiness. Emptiness and defeat. When I put out my hand, all I found was thin air. I was nobody. Somehow, those photographs resurrected that feeling. That's what I thought you wouldn't get."

"You were never nobody to me," she said quietly. "Never."

He turned his face towards her, and though his chair was deep in shadow, she saw his eyes lock on hers.

"God, what an expense we were to each other," he said in an anguished voice.

It was true, the sad legacy of their young love. Janine had sensed it slumbering beneath all their recent times together, but she wasn't sure Dan had. Yet he wasn't wearing rose-colored glasses after all. When he'd said he wanted her back in his life, he'd known that the toll their past had taken on each of them was going to be part of the package. The awareness wasn't hers alone. She wasn't alone.

As Dan continued to stare at her, Janine was reminded of Hunt's fixed gaze across the ICU at their first meeting. She read the same thirst and the same guardedness, and she felt in herself the same desire to find a satisfactory reply.

"Hunt asked me today if you and I had been in love."

"What did you say?"

"I said yes."

Dan nodded slowly.

"He said he was glad to know he'd come from two people who loved each other."

"I'm glad, too. That we had that. Even with the expense."

"So am I."

Dan bent his head and looked down at the deck, and when he looked up again, he was different. The reserve he'd arrived with was back in place, but disencumbered of stiffness and grievance. They had openly affirmed the strength of what they'd lived through, in all its ramifications, and now, paradoxically, they could let each other go with easier hearts.

"Memory lane!" Dan said jocularly. "Not exactly paved with gold, is it?"

"Not entirely."

"And there are probably bumps ahead, too. Places we won't be sure how to navigate through. With Hunt, I mean."

"There are bound to be," Janine agreed, gamely carrying the shift in their conversation forward. "All the firsts, for one thing. The first time he meets our parents, the first Mother's Day and Father's Day, the first argument—"

"Didn't we already have that?"

"Actually, I think we're honeymooning right now. My point is it could be rough the first time we come up against problems or disappointments, or harsh reminders like those photos."

"Well, you can cross one 'first' off the list because my mother has categorically refused to meet Hunt. She thinks he's after my money." Dan shook his head. "She has a highly inflated idea of my net worth."

"Maybe she'll change her mind."

"Don't hold your breath."

It was thoroughly dark now. There were fewer fireflies than earlier, and Janine could tell from the size and whiteness of their lights that they were the big ones the boys disliked, feeling squeamish about the insects' fat, soft abdomens and large, dark heads.

"Does Hunt feel like a stranger to you?" Dan said.

"No. Does he to you?"

"No. He didn't even that day in the hospital. He is a stranger, of course, but he's so familiar somehow, too. Maybe because he looks like me, or...I don't know..."

"I tried to explain it to Lee. That there's this bond. He has a whole life we know hardly anything about, but—"

"We know that he likes kites, and ketchup on steak, and that he cracks his knuckles when he's nervous..."

"Drops in the information bucket."

"...and that he's an artist, like you."

Janine felt a small leap inside her, like a tiny fish breaking the surface of a twilit lake.

"It's so great having that in common," she said. "It gives us something we can understand about each other. But it's more than a conversation-starter. It's like proof that we're related, that we...well, that we belong together."

Dan looked as if he were holding himself back from saying something. Don't hold back, Janine thought suddenly. Tell me again that you want me. Complicate my life. Crowd it. It was like Lee said, we get what we deserve and we get what we don't deserve. It was lopsided and vaguely sacrilegious to accept difficulties as one's due and to doubt good fortune.

Vanessa appeared at the sliding screen door.

"Video's over, Daddy."

Dan stood up.

"We'll be going, too," he said to Janine. "Thanks for everything."

363

Janine stepped away from the railing.

"Would you like to bring the girls to our beach tomorrow?"

"No need. We're at the Windward Inn in Cape May, right by a beach."

"Sally's asleep, Daddy. You have to come carry her."

"I'll be right there," Dan replied, but he was looking at Janine, not at his daughter.

Say it, Janine willed him. Whatever it is, say it. But he didn't.

———∞∞∞———

TWO HOURS LATER, the Gannons were gone, and Tim and Larry were in bed. The house was locked up for the night. Janine was in the living room alcove staring at her self-portrait.

Hunt was right. The flower stems did look like snakes. Snakes poised to strike. She'd had jungle vines in mind, which is why she'd made the stems writhe and curl. It was, yet again, the duality Belle Martine had noticed — an ordinary scene or object, in this case, the artist's face, paired or backed with something hinting of imminent disruption, if not outright threat. She'd certainly strived for that effect at times. But not in this picture. Not consciously.

What would a self-portrait look like if she started one tonight? She supposed the fierceness would still be there, but more in the nature of zest. There'd probably be some marks of weariness, but not as much of that as there would have been had she tried to depict herself during the first year after Clark's death. Now, it would be a memory of weariness rather than weariness itself that she'd need to show.

She'd use warm hues, if she started on a self-portrait tonight. She'd paint herself in a sunny location. And behind her? Nothing definite. A wash of colors, all the colors, like a molten rainbow. Definitely not snakes, nor anything else waiting in the wings to take happiness away. Because she'd have to show that she was trying to learn to trust happiness again. She was no Pollyanna. She knew happiness could be snatched away, but she no longer believed it could permanently disappear. She no longer expected it to disappear. Now she felt capable of happiness. She could go after it. She could take hold of it and not look over her shoulder. She'd started to do so with Hunt. Thankfully, he was responsive. He didn't seem concerned about whether they deserved the chance or not. They had it. It was theirs for the taking.

She went into the kitchen and looked at the clock on the stove. Ten after eleven. Not the best time to call someone, but not totally outrageous. She picked up the phone and punched in a number.

"Dot? It's Janine Linden. I hope I didn't wake you, or anyone else."

"No. We're watching t-v."

"I wonder if you could come over for an hour or two?"

"Now?"

"Yes. I...it's sort of an emergency. I have to go into Cape May. The boys are asleep."

"I guess so. Sure. I'll be right over."

———— ∞ ————

WHEN DAN OPENED the door, he was in the same plaid pajama pants that he'd worn two weeks ago, but with a different t-shirt. His hair was rumpled.

"Is something wrong?" he said.

"Not exactly."

He motioned her inside. She followed him past two double beds, in one of which his girls were sound asleep. He led her out onto a small balcony. They were close enough to the ocean that Janine could hear the rhythmic, sibilant thwack of the surf. Dan drew the drapes, blocking the girls' view of the balcony, but he left the glass door open so that he could hear them if they woke.

How should she start? What she wanted to do was put her arms around him and squeeze tightly. What she wanted was his mouth on hers. That's how a man would start. Skip the words. Or wedge them between caresses, if the woman insisted. But, she thought, Dan probably wouldn't do it that way. Not in this situation. Words were needed first. Words that covered all the bases. Because what she really wanted, as she'd told Lee, was everything. He was waiting. Janine got the impression he'd stand there silently until sunrise if he had to.

"Lee says we're having a romance," she finally blurted out, feeling immediately foolish.

Dan snickered. But at least she'd started.

"What do *you* say?" he asked.

"I think you and I are...that we could have something...more complex than a romance. More complex even than a rekindled romance."

"As I recall, complexity was the reason you gave for squelching our rekindled romance."

"Complications. Not complexity."

He stared at her a few seconds across the length of the balcony. She tried to read his face, but she couldn't.

"You weren't wrong about the complications, Janine. And they're all still there."

"So, you don't believe in fate after all."

"Oh, but I do."

He took one step towards her. Desire seeped through her like juice through the split skin of an over-ripe peach.

"And I also believe in giving fate a helping hand or a kick in the pants if I have to."

He took another step. They were very close now.

"I'm not going to move," she said.

"I hope not."

"No, I mean I'm staying in Cape—"

He leaned forward and kissed her, his lips lingering on hers until she felt as if she were made of pure light. She moved to close the small space between them, and as soon as her breasts grazed his chest, he pulled her in tightly, his mouth pressing harder and harder against hers. Just at the edge of real pain, he stopped and loosened his embrace, while still keeping his arms around her.

"If the room next door were empty..." he said, a piquant break in his voice.

366

"I love you," she whispered.

"You'd better. Because I sure as hell love you."

He ran his hands slowly down her back and over her buttocks, pushing his pelvis against her.

"Dan," she said, sighing, "don't make me the policeman."

"Is it my fault you look so delicious?"

She moved his hands to the more neutral area of her waist.

"All right," he conceded. "But I'm going to dream about you. You can't deny me that."

"I have more to say."

He let go of her and crossed his arms loosely over his chest. He was waiting again.

"I want to keep what we have, Dan. What we've begun to have. But I want to keep my life as it is, too. I know there'll be shake-ups, and I'm willing for there to be, but the basics — my home and my kids' roots there, my painting — those I won't disrupt."

Dan let out a sigh. He put his hands on the railing of the balcony and peered out over the parking lot of the motel, his face turned in the direction of the sea. Janine moved to stand beside him.

"Can't we make...an island in our lives?" she went on, speaking to his profile. "To get to when we can. For making love, for sharing talks and walks and meals and games of Chicken..."

"Do you hear the surf?"

Janine looked towards the ocean, though it couldn't be seen from where they were.

"Like breaths," she said. "A giant's breathing."

"Nothing stops it. Not storms. Not breakwaters. Not sandbars. It's turbulent, or it's calm, but it's always seeking the warm shore."

He turned to her.

"Do you think, Janine, we could be as steady as that?"

"I'm ready to try. If an island would be enough for you. Do you think you could be happy with just that?"

"For now," he said, reaching out and caressing the side of her face. "Possibly for a very long time."

"I can't promise, Dan, that I'll ever—"

"No promises. Except to love each other. And stay honest."

He took hold of her hand.

"Earlier tonight, you said we were in a honeymoon phase with Hunt," he said. "You and I are probably going to have a honeymoon phase, too."

"I know. And I know that honeymoons don't last."

"But romances can. True friendships do. I was your lover and your friend before I learned how to hide, Janine. It was real, what we had. And it's real now."

She gave him two quick kisses.

"I know that, too."

He led her back through the motel room and opened the door for her. They stood looking at each other. The dim sconces on the exterior wall of the motel were almost like candlelight.

"Beach tomorrow?" she said.

"Beach tomorrow," he replied.

Out in her car, Janine buckled her seat belt and put the key in the ignition, but then she hesitated. She undid the seat belt, opened the car door, and leaned back against the head-rest. Sounds from the timeless ocean softly invaded the quiet car. Smiling, Janine closed her eyes and listened.

ACKNOWLEDGEMENTS

Although *Out of Love* is a work of fiction, the emotional reactions of its characters were based on extensive research into the experiences of real-life birthmothers, birthfathers, adoptees, and adoptive parents, through scholarly works and oral histories. *The Girls Who Went Away* by Ann Fessler was a particularly helpful resource. I am especially grateful to Veronica Pastel for sharing her personal story and for answering my questions with unflinching honesty.

I wish to express my gratitude, too, to Jacqueline de Angelis and Julia Gibson, who have been such good friends to both me and my novel, acting, as needed, as buoys, spurs, constructive critics, and cheerleaders, and to my other generous early readers, Victor Parra, Jeffery McGraw, Cricket Freeman, and Allison Sampson.

PRAISE FOR THE HISTORICAL NOVELS OF NOËLLE SICKELS

Walking West

**heart-rending...stirring and soulful...
a tribute to pioneer women**

"Sickels has garbed her first novel in such authenticity that she may as well have been there herself. ... Sickels' approach is homespun, with patches of poetry..."
—*Los Angeles Times*

"A gentle and compassionate tale that is very well written...with almost lyrical precision."
—*Ocala Star-Banner* (Florida)

"...a thoroughly researched tribute to pioneer women..."
—*Kirkus Reviews*

"The westward expansion is expertly chronicled in Sickels's heartrending first novel. Historically accurate in its scope and detail, this is a stirring and soulful tale of triumph over despair."
—*Publishers Weekly*

"...a woman's perspective on a historical period more often portrayed through the male icons of cowboys, outlaws and goldseekers..."
—*The River Journal* (Wyoming)

The Shopkeeper's Wife

a quiet thriller

"*The Shopkeeper's Wife* is a strong and finely crafted psychological novel about friendship, gender, and murder. You might call it a quiet thriller."
—Ursula LeGuin, author of *The Earthsea Cycle*

"A well-paced and provocative novel, with a cinematic wealth of minutely observed period detail."
—*19th Century Magazine*

"*The Shopkeeper's Wife* captures the essence of suspense."
—*The Times at the Jersey Shore*

"Sickels uses...friendships as a foundation for exploring an array of social issues."
—*Book List*

"...succeeds with a blend of period detail and psychological acuity. ... Sickels builds her plot slowly and layers her characters' relationships with subtlety."
—*Publishers Weekly*

The Medium

exhilarating...fascinating...heartwarming

"*The Medium* contains enough mystery, suspense, romance, and paranormal premonitions to keep the reader fascinated, intrigued and breathtakingly waiting to turn the next page."
—Viviane Crystal, *Crystal Book Reviews*

"This is an exhilarating historical paranormal thriller starring a fascinating lead character. A strong, unique 20th century tale."
—Harriet Klausner, *BookReview.com*

"Sickels' in-depth portrayal of a young woman with an unusual gift sheds light on psychics, a little-understood group, and offers a vivid view of the home front."
—Patty Englemann, *Booklist Review*

"A compelling paranormal love story with deft historical detail and timeless characters."
—*Publishers Weekly*

"No matter what beliefs one holds about an afterlife, Helen's story and America's are realistically done and sure to fascinate. *The Medium* is a highly unusual tale set during important moments in our history; it's also a heartwarming love story."
—Jane Bowers, *Romance Reviews Today*

"A highly enjoyable, meticulously researched coming-of-age tale with an intriguing twist."
—Barbara Samuel, *BookPage.com*